A PERFECT SHOT

ALSO BY ROBIN YOCUM

A Welcome Murder

A Brilliant Death

A
PERFECT
SHOT

A NOVEL

ROBIN YOCUM

SEVENTH STREET BOOKS®
AN IMPRINT OF PROMETHEUS BOOKS
59 JOHN GLENN DRIVE • AMHERST, NY 14228
www.seventhstreetbooks.com

Published 2018 by Seventh Street Books®, an imprint of Prometheus Books

This is a work of fiction. Characters, organizations, products, locales, and events portrayed in this novel are either products of the author's imagination or used fictitiously.

Cover photo © Rick Gershon / Getty Images
Cover design by Nicole Sommer-Lecht
Cover design © Prometheus Books

Inquiries should be addressed to
Seventh Street Books
59 John Glenn Drive
Amherst, New York 14228
VOICE: 716–691–0133 • FAX: 716–691–0137
WWW.SEVENTHSTREETBOOKS.COM

22 21 20 19 18 • 5 4 3 2 1

Library of Congress Cataloging-in-Publication Data

Names: Yocum, Robin, author.
Title: A perfect shot / by Robin Yocum.
Description: Amherst, New York : Seventh Street Books, an imprint of Prometheus
    Books, 2018.
Identifiers: LCCN 2017048140 (print) | LCCN 2017052139 (ebook) |
    ISBN 9781633884182 (ebook) | ISBN 9781633884175 (paperback)
Subjects: | BISAC: FICTION / Mystery & Detective / Historical. | FICTION /
    Suspense. | GSAFD: Suspense fiction.
Classification: LCC PS3625.O29 (ebook) | LCC PS3625.O29 P47 2018 (print) |
    DDC 813/.6—dc23
LC record available at https://lccn.loc.gov/2017048140

Printed in the United States of America

To Frances Kennedy
The Irish Rose

PROLOGUE

On May 24, 1994, a warm, clear Tuesday in which the Ohio River Valley was finally shaking off the gray doldrums of a cold and damp spring, the most popular man in the history of Mingo Junction, Ohio, dropped off the face of the earth.

Not a single person in that gritty little steel town could explain his disappearance. There were no signs of foul play. No notes or clues were left behind. It was as though the earth had opened up and swallowed Duke Ducheski alive, classic Buick and all. In the months and years that were to follow, there was never one credible reported sighting. His credit cards were never again used; his bank account remained untouched.

Simply, he had vanished, and all that remained were unanswered questions.

The people in Mingo Junction were heartbroken at their loss. For weeks, that's all they talked about at Wheeling-Pitt, the VFW, Isaly's, Carmine's Lounge, and, of course, Duke's Place, each taking a turn to tell about the last time they saw him. They offered theory after theory, but not one mother's son of them had a substantial clue as to his whereabouts. Everybody had an opinion, but nobody had an answer. The last man known to have seen him alive was the overnight employee at the crematorium. While he enjoyed a brief period of local celebrity, interviewing for the newspapers and the lone television station in Steubenville, he could offer nothing beyond wild speculation.

No one wanted to believe what they all were thinking and feared, that the great Nicholas "Duke" Ducheski was dead. How else could it be explained? His prized automobile was gone. He might have left his troubled wife, but he certainly wouldn't have just walked away from his thriving, namesake business. Then came the rumors, ugly and whispered. He had angered the mob that controlled the vice in the Upper Ohio River Valley. There was talk of missing gambling receipts—tens of thousands of dollars. It was the only logical explanation, most agreed. The Buick had been fed into a shredder, probably with Duke still behind the wheel.

Nothing made sense.

As a journalist, I was fascinated by the story.

As a blood relative, I was devastated.

Duke and I had practically grown up together, and I had long treated him more like my hero than my cousin. Although I was older by just twenty-three days, he was always bigger, stronger, faster, and a better athlete; and he seemed infinitely more mature. People were drawn to Duke Ducheski. When you were in a room with him, he made you feel like you were the most important person there. He was the kind of guy you wanted to be around. His good friend, Moonie Collier, often called him "Bo-Peep," because, he said, everyone followed him around like a flock of lambs.

His personality had nothing to do with his popularity, though. My cousin was known throughout the Ohio Valley for "the shot." On March 20, 1971, Duke Ducheski made the most memorable shot in the storied history of the Ohio High School Basketball Tournament. Capping a miracle come-from-behind flurry, Duke launched a shot from the corner that gave the Mingo Indians a victory in the state championship game in Columbus.

If he had never done another thing in his life, that would have been enough for the people of Mingo Junction. On the streets of that eastern Ohio community, Duke Ducheski could do no wrong. He was a living, breathing legend.

And then, he was gone.

I found out that Duke had disappeared in the most embarrassing way a journalist can learn of a big story: I read about it in a competing newspaper, the Steubenville *Herald-Star.*

On the morning of Sunday, May 29, 1994, two days after he was reported missing by his wife, the *Herald-Star* ran a terse, four-paragraph story on page five of the local news section under the headline:

MINGO JUNCTION MAN LISTED AS MISSING

A Mingo Junction man has been reported missing by his wife.

According to a report filed Friday with the Mingo Junction Police Department, the missing man is Nicholas Ducheski, 41, of Frank Avenue.

Ducheski is 6-foot-3, approximately 210 pounds, with brown hair and green eyes.

According to the report, Ducheski's wife, Nina, said she last saw her husband late Monday afternoon. Anyone with information on the missing man is asked to contact the Mingo Junction Police Department.

Whoever had written the story clearly did not understand the significance of this man's disappearance.

When I asked the slob of a police chief in Mingo Junction about Duke, he shrugged and said, "Maybe he went on vacation." I had inside information that I could not, and would not, share with the police. However, I knew, without question, that Duke Ducheski was *not* on vacation.

Years passed.

Still, nothing.

And then, out of the blue, a gift dropped into my lap.

Finally, I controlled the narrative.

This is the final chapter.

They had a fort—Angel, Moonie, and Duke. I guess that's where this story really begins.

It was as fine a fort as ever had been built in Mingo Junction, Ohio, by three boys who had just graduated from the fifth grade. Pressed hard against the base of the sandstone cliffs north of town, and overlooking the Ohio River beyond the soaking pits at Wheeling-Pittsburgh Steel, Fort Logan was made of honey-locust posts that were cut from the hillside with dull axes and determination.

It was 1964 and the best summer of their youth.

They drank orange Nehis, played baseball, fished in the old stone quarry, swam naked in Goulds Creek—an action that would have earned them the beatings of their young lives—and built a most magnificent fort.

They cemented their friendship that summer, the bonds of which were stronger than any I-beam rolling out of the mill below. This is a story about that friendship, loyalty, and doing what is right.

CHAPTER ONE

September 18, 1988—Tony DeMarco made a handsome living selling drugs, breaking bones, and, when the opportunity presented itself, sending a .22-caliber bullet ricocheting off the inside of a mark's skull. As an overlord for the Antonelli crime family, Tony was proficient at dispatching those who displeased his boss.

The fact that he thoroughly enjoyed his work was simply a bonus.

Thus, under a darkened Ohio Valley sky, it was with great and perverse pleasure that he held Pinky Carey by the ankles and dangled him over the side of the Pennsylvania Railroad trestle just north of downtown Steubenville, sixty feet above the northbound lanes of Ohio Route 7. Pinky's jacket and shirt had fallen down over his head; his arms, one of which was wrapped in a dirty plaster cast, swung in the wild panic of a poor swimmer fighting the current. The inverted view of the asphalt below had so terrified him that he had pissed himself, and urine was streaming down over his chest, dribbling in pellets onto the creases of his terrified face.

Tony DeMarco had killed ten men on behalf of Salvatore Antonelli. Six of those had been rivals who had encroached on Antonelli's turf. One had been an Antonelli capo whom the boss suspected of spying for a rival family. Another, a Weirton, West Virginia, produce distributor, made the mistake of disrespecting Tony when he was in a foul mood. The other two he had killed for repeatedly failing to pay their gambling debts.

Pinky Carey was perilously close to becoming number three.

Two weeks earlier, Tony had grabbed a handful of Pinky's collar and yanked him off a barstool at Hollywood Lanes. Pinky was crying and pleading for mercy as Tony pushed him through the swinging doors to the kitchen and into the darkened parking lot behind the building. Pinky was long overdue on a $1,500 gambling debt and knew what was coming. The meeting was brief. Tony took his powerful right hand and interlocked his fingers with Pinky's left. The grip was crocodilian, and the prey was helpless to escape. Tony snatched Pinky's index finger and snapped it sideways, popping a jagged bone through the skin. He twisted and pulled the middle finger, yanking it out of the socket. Pinky screamed and cried and begged for mercy. All the while, Tony chided his victim in a calm voice.

"Pinky, I don't understand why you insist on ignoring your financial obligations to Mr. Salvatore Antonelli."

The ring finger snapped backward. "This is not a good thing, Pinky. Your account is badly in arrears." The little finger went south with a snap, leaving the hand in a grotesque gnarl—four dirty birthday candles dying in the noonday sun. When Tony released his grip, the pain dropped Pinky to his knees. He cradled his left hand and sobbed.

"You have seventy-two hours to get me the money, Pinky," Tony said, sliding behind the wheel of his still-running car. "Seventy-two hours. Don't be late, and don't make me come looking for you again."

A rational human being couldn't possibly forget such an encounter or dismiss the threat as idle. But Pinky Carey was such a pitiful drunk that soon after leaving the emergency room, his hand stitched and wrapped in a cast that covered his fingers, his overriding concern was to get another drink. Rather than beg and borrow from family and friends to repay his debt, Pinky elected to hide from Tony, a tactic that worked until thirty minutes before he found himself dangling over the side of the railroad trestle.

Tony caught Pinky slipping out the back door of the Elks Club. As soon as he saw Tony, Pinky started crying.

"Get in the car, Pinky. For God's sake, be a man." Tony reached around Pinky, clamped hold of his neck, and shoved him into the back seat.

"Go," Tony said to the driver.

They drove in silence to the north end of Steubenville and parked behind the abandoned Ohio Valley Tire warehouse.

"You boys wait here," Tony told his two lieutenants in the front seat. "Me and Pinky, we're going to go have a little talk."

Tony was dressed in his usual attire of all black: loose-fitting slacks, a knit shirt that fit tight around his muscular chest and revealed a gleaming gold crucifix atop tufts of black chest hair, and boots that had been buffed to a high sheen. He led Pinky down a narrow path where foxtails and thistles leaned over and scraped at their pants. Pinky followed, dutifully, like a sullen third-grader trailing a teacher to the principal's office. There was no escape. Why attempt it? Tony was a beast, thick through the arms and chest, and a full two heads taller than Pinky, who was a shuffling, puny, seventy-year-old with rheumy eyes and an alcoholic's nose—bulbous, cratered, and lined with dark-blue veins.

"Please don't hurt me, Mr. DeMarco. I'm sorry I haven't gotten you the money," Pinky said.

There was no response. Tony just kept walking, stepping off the path and onto the siding of the railroad trestle. The grating rattled under his feet; the diesel exhaust of the semis passing beneath on Route 7 hung in the air.

"Mr. DeMarco, please . . ."

"Just keep up, Pinky."

Pinky knew he was in deep trouble. He knew how the Antonellis operated. Fingers were broken in a public display, but worse things happened in private. Pinky assumed there was a fierce beating coming, and he would have no choice but to take it. "I'll get you your money, Mr. DeMarco. I promise, I will. Please, just don't hurt me no more."

"What do you know about respect, Pinky?" Tony asked, continuing to walk.

"I respect you, Mr. DeMarco."

"You do?"

"Oh, yes, sir."

They crossed to the middle of the trestle. The clouds and billowing smoke from the Wheeling-Pittsburgh Steel plant to the south melded over the West Virginia hills, blocking the light from the rising moon. The lights and fire of the Weirton Steel plant to the north reflected off the water of the Ohio River. The grind of the valley echoed through the hills, and the air burned with the tang of sulfur and fly ash. When Tony stopped walking, the two men were virtually invisible in the darkness. "You say you respect me, Pinky, but I don't think that is so. Otherwise, we wouldn't be out here, would we? You see, in my line of business, my reputation is very important. Do you understand that, Pinky?"

The old man kept his head lowered and nodded.

"Answer me, goddammit."

"Yes, sir. I understand."

"I gave you a break, and you repay me by hiding? Do you know how that makes me look? I'll tell you, Pinky, it makes me look weak. And, when people think you're weak, they take advantage of you."

"I'm sorry about that, Mr. DeMarco. I really am. I didn't want to cause you no problems, but I didn't have the money."

There is, within the brain of every predator, a neurological switch. The hair trigger for that switch could be hunger, fear, or anger. Regardless of the genesis, the switch also removes emotion from the situation, leaving the predator both cold and fearless. There is no sense of conscience, no empathy for the prey. Like the summer wind dies, the eyes of Tony DeMarco narrowed and the skin stretched taut over his chin and jaws. In that instant, a rage swelled in his chest, and he lashed out with a vicious right hook, splitting Pinky's nose like a ripe melon. The skin tore nearly to his eye sockets, and blood and bits of cartilage splattered over his face. Pinky dropped on his back to the grated walkway, his ample nose an amorphous blob.

The predator was upon his prey.

Tony snatched the little man by the ankles and jerked him upward, lifting him over the walkway railing. He looked down to see two holes, each the size of a silver dollar, in the soles of Pinky's shoes. "Christ, Pinky, why don't you buy yourself a decent pair of shoes?"

He didn't answer. He was barely conscious, his world a swirl of gray, his own heartbeat thumping in his ears. When his feeble, alcohol-saturated brain regained its focus, Pinky was staring at the asphalt. "Oh, God, please, Mr. DeMarco. Bring me back, bring me back."

"I asked you, why don't you buy yourself a decent pair of shoes?"

"I can't, Mr. DeMarco, I ain't got no money," he wailed, loose change falling from his pockets and bouncing on the blacktop as his bladder released. "That's why I ain't paid you yet. I don't have no money. Oh, please let me up."

"Pinky, you should always wear nice shoes. Shoes help make the man. You know who taught me that?" Again, Pinky didn't answer. He could hardly hear Tony over the passing semis and his own wailing. This angered Tony, who shook the little man's legs. "Pinky, goddammit, I asked you a question. Do you know who taught me to always wear nice shoes and keep them polished?"

"No."

"Mr. Salvatore Antonelli. 'Always,' he said, 'always buy good shoes and keep them nice. People respect that.'"

"Please let me up. I'll buy some nice shoes after I get you paid, but I don't have no money right now."

"Pinky, there's booze on your breath. You've got money for booze, but no money to repay your debt to Mr. Antonelli?" He adjusted his grip on Pinky's ankles. "Goddammit, quit squirming or I'm gonna drop your ass," he yelled. "Do you know what you're doing to my reputation by not paying your bills?"

Pinky was bawling. "I'm sorry, I'm so sorry."

"Are you trying to insult me, Pinky? Is that what you're trying to do—insult me and Mr. Salvatore Antonelli?"

"No, God, no. I'll pay. I'll pay tonight. I swear."

"You'll pay me tonight?"

"Yes, oh sweet Jesus, yes. Just let me up."

"Where are you going to find the money?"

"I'll find it somewhere. I'll ask my sister. She's got money. I promise."

"Do you swear, Pinky? Tonight? You promise you'll pay? You swear to God?"

Pinky's tears mixed with urine and the blood from his nose and ran down his inverted forehead, dripping off his bald pate. "Yes. I swear to God. Tonight! I'll pay you tonight!"

"Promise me on your mother's grave."

"I promise. I promise on the grave of my dear mother."

"I don't know, Pinky. I just got this really bad feeling that you're lying to me again."

"No, Mr. DeMarco, I'm not. I swear to Jesus."

"I'm really sorry, Pinky, but I think you're lyin'."

Tony released his grip, and Pinky Carey screamed and flailed his arms and legs until the timely drop sent him through the passenger-side windshield of a north-bound Peterbilt. Pinky never saw the truck. The windshield exploded and his neck snapped. He was dead before he bounced off the seat on the passenger side and fell to the floor, his legs and now shoeless feet draped across the arms of the stricken driver, who screamed and stood on his brakes, bringing a load of canned dog food to a stop in an ear-piercing squeal and a plume of white smoke as rubber burned against asphalt.

Tony calmly walked back to the car and climbed into the back seat. "Did you boys hear about Pinky Carey? Committed suicide tonight. The poor little guy jumped off the bridge onto Route 7."

"I don't think he's going to be able to pay up, now," one of the lieutenants said.

"Consider it an investment, of sorts," Tony said. "Sometimes, you've got to put a little blood on the floor to make people know you mean business. The cops will rule it a suicide, but word will get out how he really died, and why. And, when it does, everyone else will be a little more conscientious about making good on their debts."

This was the kind of efficiency that had so ingratiated Tony to Salvatore "Il Tigre" Antonelli, crime lord and don of the most powerful la Cosa Nostra family between New York and Chicago. Il Tigre controlled organized crime in the tristate area of Eastern Ohio, Western Pennsylvania, and the panhandle of Northern West Virginia. Tony was his most trusted capo, an enforcer without peer and of unquestioned loyalty.

Tony and Salvatore had met in the parking lot of the Oasis, a dive bar and front for one of Antonelli's gambling operations in the shadows of the Wheeling-Pittsburgh Steel plant in Mingo Junction. Antonelli had business inside. Sitting on one of the dried-out railroad ties that rimmed the gravel parking lot, Tony DeMarco was busy waiting for trouble to find him. It was early afternoon when Antonelli pulled into the parking lot and stepped out of his Cadillac. He took a moment to adjust the cuffs of a gray suit with thin, safflower pinstripes. His black Italian loafers were buffed to a high gloss, and the drab strip of Commercial Street reflected in his aviator sunglasses. His salt-and-pepper hair was slicked back with not a strand out of place. He pulled a wad of cash out of his pocket, peeled off a twenty-dollar bill, and pushed it into Tony's palm. "Hey, kid, how 'bout makin' sure no one messes with my ride?"

When Antonelli returned fifteen minutes later, two men with tin lunch pails and yellow hardhats were sprawled on the gravel—one on all fours, throwing up, the other unconscious, with blood streaming from his smashed nose and mouth. Antonelli took a minute to survey the carnage, then said, "Christ almighty, kid, all I wanted you to do was watch the Caddy."

Tony nodded. "Yeah, but some guys . . . you know, they just don't want to listen."

"How old are you, kid?"

"Seventeen."

"What's your name?"

"DeMarco. Tony DeMarco."

Antonelli smiled. "Italian. Nice."

Tony was physically mature beyond his years, with thick pads of muscle covering his neck, shoulders, and chest, an outline of a full beard on his olive face. Antonelli took the kid's hands and studied them. They were huge, with white scars and a thin smear of steelworker blood racing across the knuckles. "You pretty good with these?" Antonelli asked, still examining the hands.

Tony nodded toward the two steelworkers. "Ask them," he said.

A slight smile pursed the lips of the old man. "You want a job, Tony?"

"Maybe. What kind of a job?"

Antonelli lit the cigar he had been carrying between his fingers and used it to point to the front door of the sedan. "Step into my office, son. Let's talk." Tony let himself into the passenger seat; Antonelli slid in behind the wheel and asked, "Do you know who I am?"

Tony nodded. "Sure. You're Il Tigre."

The older man nodded. "I like your style, Tony. But, if you want to work for me, you need to remember this: We don't take care of business in a parking lot in the middle of the day. Someone gives you some grief in public, you just smile and let it go. Then, you wait. You wait until you find them alone in an empty room or a dark alley, then you beat them so that their own mothers won't recognize them. Understand?"

"I understand."

"Good. Very good."

School had never been a priority for Tony, and what little interest he'd had totally disappeared after he met Salvatore Antonelli in the parking lot of the Oasis. He never again set foot in Mingo High School. The next morning, he began working at the bar. He started out running errands and bouncing drunks, and eventually he moved up to bagman. Occasionally he paid visits to those who were late in paying their gambling debts or bar tabs. This was his favorite task, as well as the one at which he excelled. "You must respect Mr. Antonelli, but you had better fear me," he was fond of telling debtors before cracking a handful of fingers or dislocating an elbow.

Tony emulated the old man in every way—dress, style, speech. He worked handfuls of pomade into his hair, attempting to adopt the slicked-back look of the boss. His relationship with Antonelli also gave Tony the material trappings he had always craved. He had fine, tailored suits, silk ties, gold jewelry, a new car, and a wad of cash in his pocket. He loved making purchases where he could make a show of peeling off hundred-dollar bills. To complete the look, he bought a Rottweiler and named him The Great Zeus. The dog had a spiked collar, and Tony liked walking him down the sidewalks of downtown Mingo Junction, the beast growling, straining against the leash, and covering the concrete in slobber.

Tony DeMarco was the only son of an uneducated, semiliterate railroader. Until he went to work for Antonelli, Tony was just another Dago living in one of the shabby houses that lined the flood-plain side of the Pennsylvania Railroad tracks that dissected Mingo Junction. Salvatore Antonelli had provided him with a new life and a degree of respect, and for that Tony was outwardly grateful and fiercely loyal.

Antonelli loved the boy. He was, in fact, the very image of the son Antonelli had always wanted. His own boy, Joseph "Joey" Alphonse Antonelli, was the disappointment of his life. Il Tigre had hoped to someday hand over his organization to Joey, but the boy lacked the discipline for such a post. He had been coddled by his mother and was interested only in parties, women, and spending his father's money. The younger Antonelli resented Tony, who basked in Il Tigre's affection and worked hard to please the old man.

With Tony collecting Il Tigre's debts, there were few problems with late payments. And when there were, Tony quickly handled the situation. When broken bones didn't properly encourage a gambler to pay his bills, like with Pinky, Tony made him a sacrificial lamb. When Mafia families from Youngstown or Cleveland or Detroit attempted to muscle into Antonelli's territory, Tony was the one who quietly made the problem disappear.

To show his appreciation for this loyalty, Il Tigre gave Tony oversight of the gambling and prostitution trade for the entire Upper Ohio River Valley. Antonelli understood gambling and prostitution. There was a demand for such vices, and, since they were victimless crimes, the local authorities could be easily bought off. Antonelli had long shied away from the drug trade, as it drew too much attention from law enforcement. However, Tony insisted that by cornering the cocaine and marijuana trade in the region, Antonelli could reap tens of millions of dollars annually. Antonelli concurred, allowing Tony to organize the operation in exchange for 15 percent of the gross, but with a simple operating directive: "Make sure my name never gets mentioned."

Tony DeMarco became a feared man, the despotic drug lord of the Upper Ohio River Valley, an expanse of bottom land and continuous steel mills and factories stretching from East Liverpool, Ohio, to Wheeling, West Virginia. He was arrogant, malevolent, mercurial, and ruthless. While they are not traits that would make a mother proud, they went a long way toward making him a drug dealer and mob enforcer without peer. The drug trade was highly lucrative for Tony, whose hub of operations was the turn-of-the-century limestone manse atop Granite Hill that had been built by the founder of the Mingo Iron Works. Tony had purchased the home with cash and had restored it with expensive granite, imported marble, and hardwoods. For Anthony Dominic DeMarco, it was all about the money. As vices went, he had few. Only a small portion of the cocaine went up his own nose. He drank in moderation and didn't chase women. "Filthy twats. They want too much of my money and not enough of this," he was fond of saying, grabbing at his crotch.

At age thirty-four, Tony was about to become a made member of the Antonelli crime family. He had a fabulous income and power. He was disliked by nearly everyone in the family except Il Tigre, but he didn't care. It wasn't a goddamn popularity contest. As far as he was concerned, the old man was the only one who mattered.

Two weeks after Pinky Carey did a header through the windshield of the Peterbilt, Tony DeMarco was in the back room of the Italian-American Club in Steubenville, meeting with three of his lieutenants, when the bartender knocked and poked his head inside. "Tony, phone."

He had never before received a phone call at the club. "Who is it?"

"I don't know, but he says it's urgent."

Tony followed the bartender behind the bar and grabbed the receiver off the counter. "Yeah."

"Jesus Christ, where in the fuck have you been?"

Tony's eyes widened. He was not accustomed to hearing such a question directed at him. "Who is this?"

"Chachi, goddammit. I've been trying to track you down all night."

"What's up?"

There was a pause on the phone. "It's the old man. He's had a stroke. It's bad, Tony, really bad. We're at Allegheny General. You better get up here, and fast."

He ran straight for his car and was at the hospital in less than an hour. Chachi was waiting for him in the lobby. "Come on. I'll take you up." Chachi was Il Tigre's nephew—his sister's son. He was one of the few members of the family below Il Tigre who liked Tony. No one else would have even called. "He said he wasn't feeling good this afternoon—said he thought it was indigestion, or something. He felt dizzy and went upstairs to take a nap. They found him a couple of hours later."

By the time Tony got to the intensive-care unit, it was too late. The old guard, their eyes red and moist, huddled around Il Tigre's wife. Joey Antonelli, now the heir to the throne, stood to the side. When he saw Tony come out of the elevator, he took a step and used both hands to shake Tony's one. "I'm sorry, Tony, but he's gone," said Joey, his eyes falling. "He loved you very much. I've always felt of you like a brother, because he loved you like his other son."

Tony DeMarco's eyes uncharacteristically filled with tears. He pulled out a handkerchief and dabbed at his eyes, embarrassed at his display of emotion. Joey draped an arm around Tony's thick shoulders and led him back down the hall, the slightest of smirks creasing his lips. When they were clear of the family, Joey whispered to Tony, "Life's a bitch, isn't it? The old man croaks just before you're a made man. That's a ballbuster, huh, motherfucker?"

CHAPTER TWO

September 1993—Duke Ducheski loved walking to the steel mill on damp mornings after a heavy fog had rolled off the Ohio River and covered Mingo Junction in an opaque mist. The solitude was soothing, walking in a world where he could see no more than a few feet ahead, yet one where he was keenly aware of the industrial rhythm and grind of the Ohio Valley—the clacking of rail wheels over a weak joint, the continual din of the steel mill, the window-rattling vibrations of a passing barge, the echo of a Pittsburgh and Lake Erie Railroad diesel, the guttural groan of a loaded coal truck straining up the grade from Deandale on Ohio Route 7. It was not unlike a blind man whose loss of sight enhances his other senses.

This was one of those mornings. He walked into a fog so thick and wet that the air smelled and tasted of sulfur, and the gritty fly ash that floated in the mist collected on his teeth and in the corners of his mouth. An outsider's face would pinch up at the odor. But in the Ohio Valley, people called it the smell of money, a sign that men had good work and all was well in Mingo Junction, Ohio. The pollution was the price they paid for the privilege of making steel and putting bread on the table. A man could wash his car at night and write his name through a patina of fly ash on the hood the next morning. After getting their men off to the mill each day, women—dressed in slippers and housecoats, their hair wrapped tight in pink curlers—could be seen on their front porches, sweeping plumes of grit into the yard. When Duke played football at Mingo High School, summer practices would begin at 7:30 each morning, a time when the fog sometimes covered the field and the dew always covered the grass. When they finished calisthenics and grass drills, their uniforms would be damp and black, covered with acidic fly-ash particles that collected in the dew and were absorbed by the cotton. The fly ash got into cuts and scrapes and burned like iodine. As the sun broke through the fog and the morning heated up, the uniforms dried and the coating of fly ash could be brushed away like dried oatmeal. Little thought was given to what was collecting in their lungs.

On these foggy mornings, Duke always took a minute to stand on the St. Clair Avenue overpass at Ohio Route 7, listening to the coal trucks groan against the grade and watching as their headlights suddenly materialized out of the mist. Occasionally, Virgil Coffman passed beneath, saw the shadowy outline of a solitary figure on the overpass, and ripped the air horn in his twin-axle dump truck; it happened on this particular morning. Duke waved and smiled. The wipers swatted at the fog and grit, and Duke was unable to see inside the cab, but he knew that his high school classmate was behind the wheel.

Duke continued along St. Clair Avenue, which cuts east and west through the center of Mingo Junction, starting high atop Granite Hill and dropping precipitously onto Commercial Street, near the historical marker noting that George Washington surveyed the area in 1770. The hillside is so steep that walking down St. Clair Avenue required a reverse angle of the upper torso. As he passed St. Agnes Elementary, the lights were on and the nuns already at their desks. The buses had yet to arrive; it was eerily quiet except for the hollow ping of the flagpole rope slapping against steel.

Just east of the high school, St. Clair Avenue bends hard to the left and is the bane of drivers unfamiliar with the curve, as the guard rail will attest. It is a palette of auto-body colors. From the curve, it is just a few feet to Commercial Street. Behind Commercial Street to the east, towering over downtown's patchwork of both frame and brick buildings, was the smoldering behemoth—the Mingo Junction plant of the Wheeling-Pittsburgh Steel Corporation. It was the lifeblood of Mingo Junction, the single engine that drove the entire economy. On clear mornings, it was the view of stacks and flames and billowing smoke that unfolded before Duke as he rounded the bend on St. Clair, lunch pail and folded *Ohio Valley Morning Journal* in one hand, yellow hardhat and safety glasses in the other. On this day, however, all that penetrated the dense fog was the incessant din of the mill.

Duke crossed Commercial Street and pushed open the door to a nondescript, one-story brick building known as Carmine's Lounge. As a youngster, Duke had marveled at how Carmine DiBassio made a living selling only cigars, chewing gum, and newspapers. This was long before he understood the intricacies of running an illegal gambling operation. Taking bets on the ponies, sporting events, and a daily number was apparently infinitely more profitable than chewing-gum sales.

The odor of stale cigar smoke greeted Duke at the door. The regular gin rummy foursome was already at its table in the rear, the cloud of blue smoke floating over the table illuminated by the fluorescent light. Carmine leaned on the front counter, blankets of silver hair curling on his forearms, and a steaming cup of coffee and a half-eaten glazed donut on a paper napkin resting on a glass top scratched dull by decades of transactions. On the end of his nose rested a pair of dimestore reading glasses, and he held the daily horse-race handicapping sheet at arm's length, squinting at the fine print.

"I think you need an eye exam, Carmine," Duke said. The door skidded on the linoleum as he pushed it closed. "You're going to have to start tacking that racing sheet on the far wall to read it."

Carmine folded the paper and set it on the counter before reaching into a glass case for a pack of spearmint chewing gum. He slid it across the counter and said, "Maybe if you bought something besides chewing gum, I could afford a new pair of glasses." Duke slid a dime back at him.

"What else could I buy?" Duke asked. "You sell chewing gum, newspapers, and cigars that smell like horse turds. I get the paper delivered at home, and I don't smoke. That leaves chewing gum."

Ignoring the smart remark, Carmine removed his specs, folded them up, and slipped them into his front shirt pocket. "Did you read the sports page, yet?" he asked, pointing at Duke's *Ohio Valley Morning Journal*.

"I scanned it before I left the house."

"Uh-huh. Did you happen to see the score of last night's game?"

"No."

"The Kansas City Chiefs beat the Denver Broncos—fifteen to seven."

Duke's brow furrowed, and he took a long moment to digest the comment. "Okay, Carmine, I'll bite. Why should I care about the Broncos and Chiefs game?"

"Because that loser-head buddy of yours took Denver and spotted the Chiefs twelve and a half points. In case you're not a mathematics wizard, in the gambling world that makes the final score twenty-seven and a half to seven in favor of Kansas City. And, as usual when he owes me money, which is virtually all the time, there's no sign of his sorry ass. You seen him?"

Duke grinned and feigned ignorance. "Which loser-head buddy would that be, Carmine? You've just described about every friend I have."

"You know which one, goddammit—Collier. When that sonofa-bitch wins, which ain't often, he's in here at six o'clock in the morning, bustin' my chops for his money. He loses, and I don't see his ugly puss for a week, sometimes two, sometimes three. I'm getting tired of his shit."

"Carmine, it's only seven fifteen in the morning. He'll show. Moonie's good for his debts."

Carmine waved an empty hand in the air. "That guy is a bum. A *bum*. I swear to Jesus, why you waste your time playing wet nurse to that idiot is beyond me."

Duke tore open the pack of gum and slipped a stick into his mouth. "I know he drives you crazy, Carmine, but Moonie's a good guy at heart. Granted, he's not the sharpest knife in the drawer, but he's loyal to a fault."

"Yeah, see how far that loyalty thing takes him. One of these days, that clown will be sitting in here playing rummy with the rest of the bums," he said, gesturing with his head toward the foursome. Three of the men ignored him, or simply couldn't hear him through the thick crop of hair growing from their ears. The fourth played a run of sevens, looked briefly up from his cards, and said, "You've become a terribly agitated old man, Carmine DiBassio."

Carmine rolled his eyes and shook his head.

"How much does he owe, Carmine?" Duke asked, snatching his lunch box and paper from the counter."

"Two bills."

Duke's eyes widened and his mouth dropped. "Two thousand dollars!"

"Two grand. He's lost the last three weeks. I'm tellin' ya, the sonofabitch is the worst gambler I know. He lost eight hundred the first week and I carried him, four hundred last week and I carried him, then yesterday the dumb ass lost another eight hundred bucks. I can't carry him for another week, Duke. I got people I got to answer to. You know that, and you know they are extremely humorless individuals. Either he pays up, or I gotta make a call."

Duke knew where the call would be going. "He can't work if his fingers are broken, Carmine."

"That ain't my concern; you know that. I got people breathin' down my neck, and they expect me to keep the books balanced, and if I don't, it's *my* fingers that get broken. I ain't no math genius, but I know I can't balance the books if I'm two bills in the hole."

"Okay, okay. Don't call anyone, yet. Let me talk to Moonie first. We'll get it straightened around. All right?"

Again, Carmine swatted at air. "Yeah, all right. You talk to that dunderhead, and tell him I better be hearing from him, and soon."

Carmine was still grumbling as Duke pulled the door shut and stepped onto the sidewalk that runs along Commercial Street. "Moonie," he said aloud, shaking his head. It was 7:20. There was still time to stop by the restaurant before punching in at the mill. He cut across the street and headed north. The morning coffee drinkers were seated at the bar at Isaly's, and the smell of bacon on the griddle seeped out the door. Despite Carmine's outburst, Duke knew Carmine wouldn't give up Moonie. Not for a while, at least. The old man didn't care for Moonie Collier, but he despised Joey Antonelli and Tony DeMarco.

CHAPTER THREE

The city of Mingo Junction is wedged hard between the Ohio River and the Appalachian foothills that encase the valley. It is a rough, dirty, beer-and-a-shot steel town that wears the grime of the mill on the face of its downtown buildings. Steel mills are tough on the flesh and the soul. For the European immigrants that settled the Upper Ohio River Valley, the mills were a grand opportunity. For those who dreamed of a life beyond the valley, they were a prison. The mills lured in young men with promises of good money, benefits, and security. Once a steel mill put its hooks in a man, there was no escape. Soon, there was a car payment, and a wife, a mortgage, kids, and a cough that never quite went away.

The die was cast.

Sports and athletic scholarships were tickets out of town and an escape from the mills. Fathers stood on the sidelines and watched with the fervent hope that their sons' athletic talents would take them far from the heat and the fire and the smoke. But, mostly, they didn't. Sons ended up toiling next to their fathers in the mill.

Duke Ducheski was no different.

He was raised by a single father who worked at the open hearth at Wheeling-Pitt. Del Ducheski chain-smoked Marlboros, drank Iron City Beer from the can, could barely make a tuna-fish sandwich, and never got over the death of his wife, who died of bone cancer as the hyacinths bloomed when Duke was in the first grade. Duke couldn't remember much about that year, except his mother, Rosabelle, rarely left the quiet confines of her bedroom. Occasionally, she would emerge and walk unsteadily across the living room, her bones and skin as dry as sand, moving her hands from chair to chair for balance as she maneuvered her way to the couch. When she did wander out, her only son would curl up beside her and she would tuck him under an arm, or allow him to sleep with his head on her lap. Not long before, she had been a beautiful woman with flowing blond hair and a strong chin, and she had smiled and laughed and smelled like springtime. But she withered and wore a red bandana around her head to hide her baldness, and her ribs felt like the flutes of a washboard. She smelled stale and worn out, and occasionally a tear would run off her sunken cheeks and drop on her young son's head.

After his mother's death, Duke's grandmother Ducheski made sure he got regular meals, had clean clothes, and made it to school on time. Until she died on Christmas Eve of his senior year in high school, Duke spent more nights at her home than he did in his own. For years, his dad was just a shadow, lost without his beloved Rosabelle. He no longer kept after the house; the paint peeled, and the gutters filled with grit from the mill and sprouted maple saplings each spring. He left each morning with a tin lunch pail containing two cans of Iron City, and an apple, or a banana flip, or maybe a can of sardines. At night, he trudged back up the hill, slouching as though the entire weight of the Wheeling-Pittsburgh Steel Corporation rested on his shoulders.

He would sit down in the kitchen and pry off his work boots, sucking for air, the walk up the hill having drained a pair of lungs battered by the mill and his Marlboros. At least once a week, he lifted himself out of his chair and said, "Study hard, boy, and don't sell yourself short. This ain't no life."

Duke grew up tall and lean, topping out a little over 6'3" and a hundred and ninety pounds. He wasn't much of a student—more a lack of effort than a lack of brains—but he was a good athlete, and in the Ohio Valley that was the more treasured and respected trait. He never had a single person pat him on the back for a good grade card, but he received lots of accolades for the things he did on the basketball court.

Growing up, Duke spent untold hours at the playground, shooting baskets. He would wear the pebbles off a basketball in a month. When there was no one to play, he would practice his signature move—the "jigger and trigger." He would feint a move to the hole—the jigger— then dribble once behind his back as he set up for a fade-away jumper— the trigger.

He was christened Nicholas Wayne Ducheski, but most everyone in Mingo Junction had forgotten that long ago. He was anointed the Duke of Mingo Junction for a feat he performed on a Saturday evening in March 1971. It took just sixty-three seconds, a mere blip in his forty-one years on this earth, yet more than two decades later his life was still defined by that seminal event. It was called the Miracle Minute, the last minute and three seconds of the Double-A state championship basketball game between the Mingo Indians and the Dayton St. Andrew Blue Jays. Red Kilpatrick of WSTV-AM in Steubenville sent it back to the Ohio Valley for the handful of people who hadn't made the trip to Columbus. Bootleg recordings of the broadcast were pressed into 45 rpm records, one of which could still be heard by pushing the buttons G-6 on the jukebox at Welch's Bar. Many people in Mingo Junction could recite the broadcast of the Miracle Minute as easily as they could recite the Lord's Prayer or the Pledge of Allegiance.

(For the record, Duke's last name was pronounced "Du-sheski." However, throughout the broadcast Kilpatrick pronounced it "Du-kesky," which spawned the nickname. In retrospect, Duke said this mispronunciation was fortuitous, as otherwise he would have been forever known as the Douche of Mingo Junction.)

> *Foster off the glass, good, 67-55, Dayton St. Andrew. Mingo calls time-out with sixty-three ticks left on the clock, and it appears the Indians' bid for a state title is falling short as the Blue Jays are in command.*
>
> *Back to the action. Jarrod Ferwerda inbounds to Ducheski, who races up the floor—jumper from the top of the key, Ducheski with a clutch shot. Jays up, 67-57. White inbounds to Foster, and Ducheski steals the ball and lays it in, 67-59—forty-two seconds left. White inbounds across court to Duda, and Ducheski steals it again. He drives, shoots—good, and fouled by White. Mingo refuses to quit. Forget what I said a minute ago, we've got a ball game here.*

Ducheski eyes it up, good, 67-62 St. Andrews, and the Jays call time-out. I'm telling you, St. John Arena is rockin'. The Mingo faithful are fired up by the heroics of Nick Ducheski. Duda inbounds to White, who heads down the right side, across half court, tied up by Hornyak, White back to Foster and, backcourt! Backcourt! Indians' ball. J.J. Piatt inbounds to Ferwerda, who kicks it out to Ducheski. Twenty-footer . . . yes! Ducheski cuts the lead to three, 67-64. Castro inbounds to White, and he's fouled by Ducheski. Seventeen seconds left. White goes to the line, shooting one-and-one. If he sinks these, it's just about lights-out for the Tribe. He shoots, misses, loose ball. Ferwerda passes to Ducheski up the left side, behind the back dribble, shoots, got it. He got it. Time-out, Mingo. Nick Ducheski has single-handedly given the Indians a shot at the state title. Ten seconds left, and the Indians trail by one, 67-66.

Duda takes the ball out of bounds for the Jays. White breaks deep. Ducheski fights through a pick, long pass. White and Ducheski go up, it's out of bounds, off White's hand—Indians' ball. White is upset. He thinks he was fouled. Ducheski went into White as the ball arrived, but the referee ruled both players were going for the ball.

Eight seconds left. Piatt inbounds to Ferwerda, to Ducheski breaking for the basket. Five seconds. Across the lane, three seconds, the jigger, behind his back, the trigger, from fifteen feet, the horn, the rim, it's up and, in! It's in! The Mingo Indians have done it. What an incredible finish. Ducheski scores thirteen unanswered points to lead Mingo to the state championship.

That was a miracle minute, something never to be forgotten. If anyone's left back home, turn on the lights and put out the welcome mat. The champions of all Ohio are heading home with young Nick Ducheski—the Duke of Mingo Junction.

Young boys asked for his autograph. He got fan letters delivered to the high school. His number 23 jersey hung in the trophy case. He was named captain of the *Ohio Valley Morning Journal*'s All-Valley team, and first team All-Ohio. In the cocoon that was Mingo Junction in 1971, Duke had little reason to believe that scholarship offers weren't going to pour in. However, when your universe doesn't extend much past the Appalachian foothills, you don't realize how many kids outside of Mingo Junction can play the game of basketball. He didn't know there were kids in Harlem who could jump so high their elbows were above the rim, or that a 6'8" Indiana farm boy was out there running like a gazelle and rippling the nets from twenty-three feet. How was he to know? John Phillips, the sports editor of the Steubenville *Herald-Star*, had written, "Duke Ducheski is one of the finest basketball players I have ever seen, and one of the best to ever grace the hardwoods of the Ohio Valley." Well, hell, didn't that count for something?

Duke believed his own press clippings and assumed that UCLA or North Carolina would be calling with scholarship offers. Ashland, Findlay, West Liberty, and a few other small schools that he had never heard of offered him scholarships, but the big schools never called.

He was crushed.

On a Saturday in late April of his senior year, Duke's father stared at him across the kitchen table, letters from a half a dozen small colleges in his hand. In a voice that resonated like coal running down a tipple, ground down by five thousand days at the open hearth and tens of thousands of Marlboros, Del pleaded for Duke to accept one of the offers. "Son, it doesn't matter that it isn't UCLA. It's a free education. It's a chance to get out of this valley and be more than I ever was. Call one of these coaches and go."

Sometimes, your stars align.

For most of his life, Duke's stars looked like they were tacked across the sky by laser beams, an arc of electricity rolling across the heavens. He didn't know it that Saturday in early May when he arrived at the junior-senior prom in a tuxedo of white crushed velvet, but his stars were about to look like a spilled bowl of Cheerios. That night, Duke and his girlfriend, Nina, were supposed to go back to his house to change for the after-prom at Sunset Lanes. Instead, they slipped into his grandmother Ducheski's house, slipped out of their clothes, and slipped between the sheets in the guest bedroom. So much slippage. They slipped in, out of, and between, but Duke wasn't smart enough to slip *on* a condom.

Six weeks later, just as Duke was grudgingly about to commit to Ashland College, Nina showed up at his house, mascara-tainted tears running down her face and soaking into the collar of her Mingo High cheerleader T-shirt. She didn't have to say a word. Duke knew she was pregnant. A blast furnace of fire erupted in his testicles, rolled up his chest, and consumed his neck and face. Any thoughts he had of a world beyond Mingo Junction ended that instant. All his life, he had been running at ninety miles an hour, top down, the wind in his hair. His motor was running so hard that he didn't hear the lug nuts coming loose and paid no heed to the warning lights, because the rules had never applied to him. He was the Duke of Mingo Junction—eighteen and bulletproof. The world was his oyster and everyone else just a bit player. That's what he had always thought, but by the Fourth of July, he was married and living in his grandmother's old house, and sweating alongside his father at Wheeling-Pitt.

To those whose lives were swaddled in the insular stretch of bottomland on the western banks of the Ohio River, Duke Ducheski was the luckiest man in the world. He rarely bought his own beer, and he was much beloved in his hometown, an iconic hero who had brought glory to the halls of Mingo High School and the gritty streets of the city. But to those fortunate enough, or determined enough, to have escaped the fires and ash of the steel mill, he was a pathetic caricature of the former high school star who never grew beyond his press clippings.

This realization came to Duke late on the evening of his twentieth class reunion at the Knights of Columbus Hall. Angel, Moonie, and Duke—bachelor, divorced, and scorned—attended the reunion together. As a class, they had done pretty well. There were a couple of doctors; some lawyers, teachers, and nurses; and three or four accountants, including Angel.

And there he was—the mill rat. He had watched his dad struggle home from the mill each afternoon and vowed it would never happen to him. But on that night, his hands carried the permanent grime of a Wheeling-Pitt veteran. He was still the hometown hero, and those who had gone to college and left Mingo Junction patted him on the back and made a little small talk. But once the conversation extended beyond the halls of Mingo High School, they had nothing in common. When the conversation became awkward, they would say, "Great to see you, Duke," and move on.

Duke went home that night and sat alone at his kitchen table, the darkness infused with the hazy orange glow from the slag dump at Wheeling-Pittsburgh Steel, and reflected on the two decades past, during which he had accomplished not one damn thing. There was not a single triumph that he could point to and say, "See! I told you I could do more than play basketball." He had not intentionally stayed locked in 1971, but that's where he was, trapped, the seminal moment in his life fading into the era of disco balls and platform shoes.

His life was a cyclonic mess. He was in a dead-end job. His wife loathed him, and his girlfriend was quickly losing her patience. His son was lying in a bed, lost within a shell of a body, most likely unaware that he even had a father. Yet, on the streets of Mingo Junction, Duke was always smiling and projecting an air of royalty. It was an odd dichotomy. His local fame was also his bane. He treasured the memory of that night in Columbus and did not want to lose his identity. He was, after all, the Duke of Mingo Junction. How many people would love to be so idolized, even in a gritty little steel town? *A fair number* is the answer.

By the time the sun peeked over the West Virginia hills the morning after the reunion, Duke had started to formulate a plan. It was in this dawn that he vowed he would not go to his grave having his only earthly accomplishment be something he did on a basketball court when he was eighteen years old.

Duke bought a spiral notebook and began sketching out his plan for a new restaurant and bar in Mingo Junction. It would provide the best of both worlds. He would play on his local celebrity while creating a new business. When he went to the next reunion in five years, he would do so as a successful entrepreneur. His place was to be a first-class operation, not a shot-and-a-beer joint like the Oasis, but a real restaurant with a nice menu and cloth napkins. He carried that notebook with him everywhere, jotting down ideas, formulating and reformulating his plan.

More than a year later, he was still carrying around the notebook, still jotting down ideas, and still formulating and reformulating his plan, but he hadn't taken the first step toward opening a restaurant. It was Moonie Collier who finally goaded him into making the move.

Moonie, Angel, and Duke went to Welch's Bar after work on the Friday before Labor Day, 1992. Moonie was celebrating his divorce from wife number three, or possibly number four. "How can you not know how many times you've been married?" Angel asked.

"There was this weekend in Manila when I was in the army," Moonie said. "I had a three-day pass, but everything was a blur after about six hours. I met this prostitute in a bar—Angeline—and . . . well, there's a possibility that I married her."

"A possibility that you married a Filipino prostitute?" Duke asked.

Moonie shrugged. "Who knows? Either way, I don't really count that one."

Duke snorted into his beer. "Of course you don't. Meanwhile, there's probably some flat-faced, half-white kid running around the streets of Manila with a head the size of a beach ball."

Moonie threw an elbow at Duke but missed.

The most recent former Mrs. Theodore Collier had held the title just under four months. Moonie met her at the bowling alley and was engaged two weeks later, swearing that she was truly, "the one." Angel and Duke took Moonie to breakfast at Paddy's Diner and tried to talk him out of it. "It's a bad move, Moon," Duke said. "You don't even know her."

Moonie leaned his head back, squeezed his eyes shut, and said, "You know, when I close my eyes and think about her, I can hear angels singing."

No amount of logic was going to change his mind, and they were married at the courthouse the following week—the bride in a too-tight scarlet dress that was riding up her hips, and Moonie in his work jeans and steel-toed boots. A week later, as Moonie was pulling back the covers and running a calloused hand up her thigh, his new bride announced that she could channel the Virgin Mary through a ceramic statue of the Blessed Virgin that sat on her dresser.

"This never came up during your whirlwind courtship?" Duke asked.

He shook his head. "Not one damn word. Then, she also informs me that Mary had been watching my every move."

"That certainly couldn't be good."

"It wasn't. Trust me."

This revelation signaled the end of marriage number three, or possibly four, leading to the celebration at Welch's. "I'm done with marriage," Moonie said, hunkering over a Rolling Rock longneck. "Something about me just brings out the worst in women."

"Maybe it's your habitual gambling and beer breath," Duke offered.

"But those are my only vices."

Duke picked up a half-empty pack of Lucky Strikes off the bar and held it at eye level.

Moonie rolled his eyes. "It's a lot to give up for a woman. I'd just as soon stay single."

"Probably a wise decision," Angel said.

A half-dozen beers later, Angel walked over to the jukebox and played G-6. *Foster off the glass, good, 67-55, Dayton St. Andrew.* A cheer went up from a cluster of millwrights at the end of the bar, and they toasted Duke with their beers. He returned the salute. "Sometimes I wish I'd never made that last shot," Duke said.

Angel frowned. "That's got to be the beer talking."

"I'm serious. What have I done since then? Not a damn thing besides work in that godforsaken steel mill and hack up fly ash every night."

"Duke, you're a legend around here. You're the guy all the rest of us want to be."

"Exactly, for something I did when I was shaving once every other week. I want to accomplish more than that."

"You've been talking since the reunion about opening up your own restaurant. What's holding that up?"

Duke shrugged. "I don't know."

They sipped their beers for several minutes, each staring at their reflections in the mirror behind the bar, when Moonie said, "I know."

"You know what?" Duke asked.

"I know why you haven't opened up the restaurant."

Duke folded his arms over his chest and turned toward Moonie. "Oh, really? Well, by all means, please share," Duke said.

"You're afraid of missing the shot, Bo-Peep."

"What are you talking about?"

"You know what I'm talking about. You're worried that you'll jigger and trigger, then clank one off the rim."

"Are you saying I'm afraid to fail?"

"That's exactly what I'm saying. You don't want to tarnish the legend."

"Bullshit."

"You aren't afraid?"

"No, of course not."

Moonie leaned back and examined Duke's backside. "I don't see an anchor tied to your ass. What's holding you back? Just like Angel said, you've been talking about it for over a year." He made a yapping motion with the thumb and fingers of his right hand. "You're all talk, talk, talk, but no action."

The rebuke stung. It was a surprise slap in the face from his old friend. "Kiss my ass, Moonie."

"The building where Belle's Diner used to be is available. I'll bet the kitchen equipment is still there. If you were serious, you could open it there."

"I could."

"Why don't you?"

"Maybe I will."

"Uh-huh. I'll believe it when I see it."

"You'll see it."

"When?"

"Soon."

"How soon?"

"Soon enough."

"Talk, talk, talk."

The heat raced up Duke's neck and burned his ears. He wanted to punch his old friend in the nose, even though he knew Moonie was absolutely right.

Angel said, "I'll help you, Duke. I'll do the books and work out the finances. Do you have any money saved?"

"I've been hiding some cash from Nina for a divorce. I could use that."

"How much?"

"Thirty-five thousand dollars."

Angel's eyes widened. "Thirty-five thousand? Can you get at it?"

"Yeah. It's in the trunk of the Buick."

Angel pinched his temples. "What's the Buick paying in interest these days?"

"I couldn't put it in the bank where Nina could find it."

"Understood. We'll incorporate. We'll take the cash and put it in an account for a holding company—a corporation where she can't get access to it."

Duke felt instantly energized. "Maybe it would work."

"Sure, it would work. We'll need a name. You could call it Duke's Castle?"

"Clever, but a little pretentious," Duke said.

"Duke Ducheski's Bar & Grill," Moonie offered.

"Too long," Duke said.

"The Miracle Minute Sports Bar," Angel said.

"Smacks of desperation," Duke said.

"Duke's Place," Moonie offered.

Duke thought about that for a moment, then nodded. "I like it."

"Me, too," Angel said.

"Make it happen," Moonie said.

Ducheski breaking for the basket. Five seconds. Across the lane, three seconds, the jigger, behind his back, the trigger, from fifteen feet, the horn, the rim, it's up and, in!

Welch's exploded in cheers.

CHAPTER FOUR

As Duke walked up Commercial Street that foggy Tuesday morning in September 1993, he was one month shy of his forty-first birthday and two months from the opening of Duke's Place. He was determined not to fail. It was to be his ticket out of the steel mill. Everyone in Mingo Junction would forever associate him with the Miracle Minute, and that was fine, but he had to prove to himself that he was not a one-trick pony.

Duke's Place was to occupy the bottom floor of the vacant Weiskercher Building, the former home of Belle's Diner. His long-term plan was to refinish the apartments on the top two floors, but just getting the restaurant open was a mammoth task, and he could only tackle one project at a time. The Weiskercher Building was the ideal setting for his restaurant. It was situated just south of the intersection of Commercial Street and McLister Avenue, and kitty-corner from the catwalk that carried steelworkers from the street, over the railroad tracks, to the north entrance of Wheeling-Pittsburgh Steel. The clientele was readily available. Steelworkers drink a lot of beer, and Duke's Place would be ready for them when they spilled off the catwalk after their shifts. Duke vowed to watch over his business and protect it like a young child. He would not let it fail.

The windows had been soaped white on the inside, keeping the gawkers at bay. He slipped a key into the heavy brass lock and entered. This ritual was repeated nearly every morning, since he liked checking on the progress of the contractors, plumbers, painters, and electricians. The plaster walls had been stripped away and replaced with sheet rock, which was patched, taped, buffed smooth, and covered with the first coat of primer. In the corner were cardboard boxes containing oak strips for the floor. They would stay boxed until the walls and the turn-of-the-century ceiling tiles were painted, and the scaffolding broken down. Against the back wall, a spot had been plumbed in for the bar. It would stretch across the entire back of the taproom, a dominating mahogany structure with ornate carvings, a brass foot rail, and four beveled, inlaid mirrors. It would eventually be the centerpiece of Duke's Place, but on that morning it was disassembled and in several pieces.

As he did on most mornings, Duke resisted the overwhelming urge to call off work and begin stripping the old varnish from the bar. He checked his watch—ten before eight. It was time to punch in. He gave the interior of Duke's Place a final glance. The possibilities this presented for his future sent chills shooting up his forearms, and he rubbed his palms together like a five-year-old looking at a cake full of candles. He locked up, crossed back over Commercial Street, and jogged to the steps of the catwalk. The first hint of sunlight was filtering through the fog and smoke. He took the steps two at a time to the grated walkway, under which trains rumbled in and out of the mill. The incoming trains pulled gondolas carrying the lifeblood of the mill: coal and iron ore. The outbound freights were flats and boxcars loaded with the finished products—I-beams and coiled bands of steel. The exhaust of the diesels drifted up through the grate and left a gritty, oily residue on the surface. The time clock was just beyond the walkway; Duke punched in at 7:53 a.m.

He had a few minutes to spare, and knew he would find Moonie in the locker room where he took a shower every morning before reporting to his job. If Moonie Collier was anything, he was neat to a fault. He showered three times a day—before and after work, and once in the evening for good measure. When Duke had asked him about the idiocy of showering before heading into the bowels of the steel mill, Moonie shrugged and said, "I just can't start the day without a shower."

Moonie was seated in front of his locker, work pants on, a roll of flab the color of a fish belly resting atop his unhitched belt, his back dripping wet, and his last few strands of hair—"the survivors," he called them—plastered to his round, shiny pate.

When the boys were building Fort Logan, Moonie stripped off his shirt one steamy afternoon and revealed a thick matte of hair blanketing his entire stomach. Prepubescent Angel and Duke were mesmerized. "Where'd that come from?" Duke asked, pointing at the fur.

Moonie rubbed the rounded patch and smiled. "Beats the hell outta me," he said. "I woke up one day and I had hair growing everywhere. Look at this." He unsnapped his jeans, hooked a thumb in the elastic of his briefs, and pulled it down below his privates, revealing a continuation of the thicket and a member that would have been the envy of most every man in Mingo Junction.

"Oh, my God," Angel said. "That means you're a man."

Moonie squinted and smirked. "That's right. It means I can pop a girl's cherry if I want." He flicked his thumb and the elastic snapped back into place.

Duke was eleven and had only recently come to terms with the fact that men and women took their clothes off—together—and mutually participated in this act. He found it repugnant, especially when it dawned on him that his parents must have been among the participants. Duke and Angel went back to whacking at a locust trunk while Moonie rattled off the names of a dozen or so girls whose cherries he considered ripe for popping.

Moonie was quite proud of his newly discovered manhood. Unfortunately for him, the same hormonal gallop that produced the chest hair when he was eleven years old would also cause the follicles on the top of his head to start leaping overboard in his early twenties.

He had powdered his feet and was pulling on his socks when he spotted Duke in the doorway. "Hey, Bo-Peep," Moonie said, working the thick, wool sock up to half-calf. "How goes it, my man?"

"Not bad, Moon." Duke set his lunch pail, *Ohio Valley Morning Journal*, and hard hat on the bench. "How about you?"

"Just another day in paradise. We're doing some rewiring down at the blast furnace—heat, fire, smoke, and molten steel. Does life get any better than that?"

"I don't see how it possibly could." Duke straddled the bench and sat down. "So, you had a good night?"

"Yeah, it was a good night."

"Really? Good night, huh?"

Moonie's left brow arched. "Yeah. Why?"

"Well, I was wondering... if losing eight hundred dollars on a single football game and owing Antonelli two thousand dollars constitutes a good night, what's a really bad one look like?"

Moonie's jaw went slack and he emitted a small groan. It was, no doubt, similar to the one emitted when he realized that Denver could not cover the spread. "Christ almighty, how'd you find out about that already?"

"How do you think? Carmine jumped my ass first thing this morning. He's pissed—says you're always there early to collect when you win, which apparently isn't often, but he can never find you when it's time to settle up."

Moonie laughed. "Part of the old Collier charm."

"It won't be so charming if Tony DeMarco breaks your fingers, or worse."

"That little prick isn't going to break anything of mine. I'll kick his sorry, Dago ass. Carmine isn't going to sic him on me. I'm good for the money. He knows that. Besides, I've got a sleeper coming in Saturday night in the seventh race at Mountaineer Park. You want in?"

"No, Moonie, I don't want in. The last time I bet on one of your sleepers, he lost by twenty-seven lengths, and I'm not inclined to take gambling tips from a guy who is two grand in the hole."

"I couldn't believe it. The Broncos were supposed to mop up the floor with the Chiefs. Not only did they not cover the spread, they lost the game outright. The Chiefs are so bad they couldn't even score a touchdown. All their points were on field goals, and Denver still couldn't beat them. The Broncos better get a quarterback; that Elway is worthless. If they think that guy is ever going to win a Super Bowl, they're dreaming. And I'll bet on that, too."

"Maybe you should give up betting on football. Try hockey, or something."

Moonie toweled off his thinning locks. "I don't know nothin' about hockey."

"Yeah? Apparently you don't know anything about football, either." Moonie laughed. "I'm serious, Moonie. You've got to get this taken care of."

He hung his towel on a hook in the locker. "You worry too much, Duke. I've been two thousand in hock before, and I've always gotten out of Dutch without gettin' any bones broke." He held his hands up in front of a sly grin and wiggled his fingers. "See, they all still work."

"All right, man. It's your hide." Duke got up, slapped his friend across the shoulder with his *Morning Journal*, and headed to his job at the rolling mill. "I'm going to finish stripping the old stain off the bar tonight. You in?"

Moonie looked at Duke as though he had asked how to divide decimals. "It's Tuesday night, Bo-Peep!"

"Yeah. And . . ."

"I've bowled every Tuesday night for fifteen years. You know that."

"You owe Carmine two thousand dollars, and your answer is to go bowling?"

He shook his head. "I swear to Christ, you're like an old woman, you know that? I'll take care of it. Get your granny panties out of a wad and quit worrying."

When Moonie Collier was your best friend, that was easier said than done.

CHAPTER FIVE

Moonie, Angel, and Duke camped out at Fort Logan at every opportunity that summer of 1964, sleeping under the smoke and in the comforting cast of the grinding sounds and lights of the Ohio Valley. They would build a little fire and sit on the parapet they had constructed to guard their left flank, roast hot dogs, drink Nehis, and eat Snyder of Berlin potato chips. Below them, barges plowed the Ohio, their floodlights skimming the dark waters from bank to bank; freights rumbled along the shore; and they could stare into the fiery maw of Wheeling-Pittsburgh Steel, a cauldron of fire and smoke and molten steel that belched like the bowels of a volcano. When oxygen was pumped into the conversion ladle, sparks erupted, like thousands of white-hot fireflies dancing above the melt, and orange streams arced into the night. It looked as though they were staring into the fiery gates of hell, and Duke made the mistake of saying so one night.

Angel's Adam's apple bobbed and he asked, "D-do you think that's w-what h-hell's really l-like?"

Duke should have known better. Angelo "Angel" Angelli was the jumpiest little guy he had ever known—seventy pounds of twitching nerve endings—and he spent a ridiculous amount of time worrying about burning in hell, the result of his loony mother forever threatening him with eternal damnation for the slightest infractions. If he didn't eat his peas, God would punish him for his wastefulness. If his bedroom wasn't picked up, God hated the slovenly. Angel thought God had painted a bull's-eye on his forehead, and it was only a matter of time until the lightning bolt struck home.

As if that wasn't bad enough, Angel looked like he had been constructed from a patchwork of spare parts. He was sickly thin and had the most enormous nose ever placed on the face of an eleven-year-old. It was wide across the bridge and knotted in the middle before diving nearly to his upper lip, and it made his mouth and eyes appear cartoonishly small. His long ears were pressed flat against his head, and he had a set of bushy eyebrows—actually, just one extended brow—that looked like a thicket of quack grass. Duke and Angel were once walking downtown when Mr. DiOrtelli was out working in the yard. He held up his hedge trimmers, snapped them together twice, and said, "Hey, Angelo, come over here and let me trim up those brows." Angel laughed, but just to fend off the embarrassment.

Mrs. Angelli also made Angel take cello and ballet lessons. He lived in a valley where men worked with molten steel and others climbed miles under the earth to mine coal. It was a place where strength and toughness were revered, and poor Angel had to don a pair of black tights and practice his entrechat for an hour each day before he could leave the house. The boys spent a lot of time in the vacant field across the street from the Angellis', where they played baseball most every day in the summer. It was not unusual for Mrs. Angelli to break up a game by walking onto the front porch and saying, "Angelo, it's time to practice your cello."

When he got nervous or upset, Angel stuttered badly, and the last thing they would hear before he walked into the house was, "B-but M-Mom, I d-don't w-want to."

As Duke and Moonie were walking home after she broke up one of their games, Moonie said, "My dad says if Angel doesn't grow up to be a queer, he's missing a hell of an opportunity."

"Why?"

"Are you kidding? Because his mom's always making him do that sissy shit—going to the symphony, practicing ballet, playing that fiddle thing."

"It's a cello."

"Well, whatever it is, my dad says it isn't doing him any good."

"Can that really happen? Can you get queer by doing ballet and taking music lessons?"

Moonie shrugged. "I don't know. Maybe. I'm just telling you what my dad said."

Duke was reminded of that summer as he unlocked the door to Duke's Place and walked inside, carrying his dinner—a ham-and-cheese sandwich wrapped in waxed paper, and a vanilla milkshake in a paper cup from Isaly's. Beyond the row of buildings on the east side of Commercial Street, thimble rail cars at Wheeling-Pitt were being tipped, dumping molten slag in a volcanic flow that snaked into the pit, its bright-orange flush reflecting off the low clouds. Downtown Mingo Junction was awash in a hazy orange glow that penetrated the white-soaped windows of Duke's Place. It was one of the oddities of the Ohio Valley. The fires of the mill turned night into day, while the exhaust from the stacks snuffed out the sunlight, causing streetlights to burn at noon. A cold, hard rain had come in from the west just after dinner, washing away a patina of grit and giving the brick facades of downtown a much-needed bath. It was nearly nine o'clock. The rain had slowed, but it still danced in crooked rivulets on the glass. Rivers of filthy water continued to run down the gutters and into the storm sewers.

Duke locked the door behind him and turned on the overhead lights. He ate standing up, surveying the work that remained, including stripping the old varnish from the massive bar. It would be a late night.

Tuesday was bingo night at St. Agnes Catholic Church, and the progressive pot was at four thousand dollars, so Nina wouldn't miss him. She and her mother would be there early to get a seat, then light one cigarette off the other and cackle about what an unfit husband he was, condescendingly referring to Duke as "the former basketball star," or, more derisively, "the Polack." While Duke Ducheski was held in great esteem everywhere else in Mingo Junction, he was treated with derision in his own home and looked down upon by the in-laws, who felt he was a poor provider, and not nearly Italian enough for their daughter.

For reasons that continued to baffle him, Nina got upset when he was not home right after work any other day of the week. It wasn't as though she had a hot meal waiting for him, or was lounging around in a negligee, moist for his arrival. She hardly cooked, and they hadn't had sex since early in the first Reagan administration. Duke was perplexed as to why she wanted to stay married to him. The only logical explanation was that she enjoyed his misery more than her own happiness.

"I think she's a lesbian," he told Moonie one Saturday afternoon while they were in his garage, working on the engine of an antique Indian motorcycle.

"Really? What makes you think that?"

"She never wants to have sex."

"So, every woman who doesn't want to have sex with you is a lesbian?"

"I didn't say that."

He looked up from the transmission he was rebuilding. "You didn't have to, Bo-Peep. We've been friends a long time. I know what you're thinking."

"It's been ten years, for God's sake! Even if you didn't like someone, after a decade, wouldn't the urge eventually overtake you?"

Moonie set his wrench on the workbench and looked Duke right in the eye. "You're asking the wrong guy, Bo-Peep. I don't think you want to be getting marriage advice from me."

"Good point." Moonie's lips quivered as he fought in vain to smother a grin. "Go ahead," Duke said. "Out with it."

"Did you remind her that you're the Duke of Mingo Junction?"

Duke laughed. "The novelty of that wore off with her back in 1971."

On their fifteenth anniversary, Duke bought Nina a gold necklace with a single, black pearl charm. He had saved to buy it and thought it was a very nice gift. She looked at it, snapped the box shut, and handed it back. "I give you fifteen years of my life, and that's your idea of an anniversary gift?" she asked.

For a moment, Duke thought his neck and ears had actually combusted into flames. In a calm voice, but between clenched teeth, he said,

"Maybe if I hadn't spent fifty thousand dollars in psychiatry bills and paying off your credit cards, I'd have a little more money for anniversary gifts." She forced air through closed lips, a brief exhalation of disgust, and Duke trembled from the restraint of wanting to punch her face.

Nina said, "If you hadn't gotten me pregnant, I would have gone back to school for my senior year and been homecoming queen and gone to the prom with Zane Caldwell, and we'd be married and living out in a nice house with a swimming pool on Lover's Lane by the country club. Instead, I'm married to a mill rat who gives me a Cracker Jack prize for an anniversary present."

And there it was.

Zane "the Ghost" Caldwell. In high school, he had been a pasty white kid who never came out of the house, had terrible oral hygiene, had whiteheads peppering his nose and the crease of his chin, played the French horn in the marching band, and had the largest comic book collection at Mingo High School. Nina wouldn't have given Zane Caldwell a second glance when he was in school. That, however, was before he finished medical school, got his teeth fixed, and became a successful plastic surgeon. She was married to the Duke, but she was dreaming of the Ghost.

It was at that moment that Duke decided to divorce Nina. He started squirreling away money in the trunk of the Buick. He worked every overtime shift he could get at the mill, bartended Saturday night at the VFW, sold his baseball-card collection, and umpired Little League baseball for twenty dollars a game. He packed his lunch and scrimped for every penny he could find. It took nearly four years to save his goal of twenty-five thousand dollars.

After his initial meeting with a divorce attorney, he walked into the kitchen full of confidence and told Nina that he planned to leave her. She was making an egg sandwich. When Duke turned his head, she whipped the cast-iron skillet like a tennis racket and smacked him in the side of the head. The skillet burned his ear, and his neck blistered where the hot grease landed. He had spent his life playing sports and running with tough sons of steelworkers, but he had never in his life been hit so hard. It felt like an electric charge went off in his brain. His left, upper canine went down his throat, and the nearest incisor broke off at the root.

"Never!" she said. "I will never give you a divorce."

It was a battle he would fight another day.

Duke sat on a kitchen chair, pressing a plastic sandwich bag of ice to the knot on the side of his head. Cara dipped a cotton swab into a jar of amber paste and gently dabbed it on the burn on Duke's neck. Despite her soft touch, he jumped when the cotton swab made contact. "Sorry," she said. "I'm trying to be careful."

"It's not your fault," he said. "It's really tender."

"You'll have that with second-degree burns."

She finished applying the medicated balm; as she dressed the burn with a gauze pad, she said, "So, let me make sure I understand this. You live with a woman with whom you have no physical or emotional relationship. You basically tolerate each other because you're under the same roof. Is that fair?"

"I'd say you've got it down."

She bit off a piece of white tape and applied it to one corner of the gauze. "So, you ask her for a divorce, which any rational human being would agree is a good idea, since there is zero chance this ship is going to get turned around, and her response is to clock you with a skillet full of hot grease."

"That's it."

Cara capped up the jar of antiseptic and set it on the kitchen counter. "You realize this is total insanity, right?"

"I do, thus the reason for seeking the divorce."

"What if you just moved out and dealt with the nastiness later? My grandmother's farmhouse on the other side of Hopedale is empty. Let's just move in there and deal with it from a distance."

"I'll think about it."

"You'll think about it? That's Ducheski code for: *Please quit bothering me about this. If we move to Hopedale, I'll no longer be the legendary Duke of Mingo Junction. I'll have to be the Duke of Hopedale.*"

"You have to admit there's no rhythm to that whatsoever."

"Keep it up, funny man, and see how gentle I am the next time I dress that wound."

Cara Wilbright was the charge nurse at the Heinzmann Convalescent Center. She was a no-nonsense administrator, and their only conversations for the first two years he knew her were strictly about Timmy. Over time, as she saw his dedication to his son, there were conversations of a more personal nature.

They tried to be secretive about their relationship, but such trysts never remain as secret as you think. Duke was passionately in love with Cara and wanted to spend the rest of his life with her. They agreed to proceed slowly, and for the first two or three years, she had no desire to get married. However, they were now closing in on year five of their relationship, and her patience was wearing thin.

Cara put the last piece of tape over the gauze. "Your wife is damaged goods, Nick. She can never be fixed because she doesn't want to be fixed. She doesn't think she's the problem. She thinks *you're* the problem. Today it's a frying pan to the face. What's next, a bullet to the back of the head while you're asleep? And don't tell me she isn't capable of it. There's a bit of a family history, there." She unscrewed the cap on a bottle of clove oil. "Open up." He did, and she brushed the broken tooth with the oil. "You need to see a dentist."

"I will, tomorrow."

"No, tomorrow will be too late. You need to see one tonight. Maybe they can save that tooth. I'm friends with Dr. Brayden, the oral surgeon at the center. I'll give him a call and see if he can meet us at his office."

"Okay. I hurt too much to argue."

She pulled out a chair and sat facing him; she reached out and gently put her fingers to his chin, steadying his head so that their eyes were locked. "Listen to me, Nick. I love you; I love you with all my being, but the clock is ticking. And, in all candor, I'm concerned for myself and my kids. What's to say Nina doesn't show up here with a gun? You need to cut that cord, and you need to do it soon. I'm not waiting forever."

Duke was stripping a piece of the bar that featured a bas-relief of a carved lion head when a rap at the door jerked him upright and the pad of steel wool flew from his hand. It took him a moment to catch his breath, and he was grateful to be alone so no one saw him jump like a frightened schoolgirl. Through a strip of glass where the soap didn't extend to the glazing, he could see Carmine DiBassio standing on the sidewalk with rain bouncing off his Ben Hogan hat and a brown paper bag clutched to his chest. Duke unlocked the door, and Carmine pushed his way in. "Carmine, what brings you out on such a beautiful night?"

"I was closing up and I saw your lights on—thought I'd stop by and see how things were progressing," he said, handing Duke the damp, brown paper bag that was rolled down from the top. It clinked when he pressed it into Duke's hands. Water dripped off Carmine's raincoat, leaving dark spots on the dusty floor. He circled the taproom, inspecting the work, his movements as much side-to-side as forward, his arthritic hips giving him a wobbly gait. His shoes were cracked over the arch and split down the sides at the ball of his foot, the soles worn low on the outside. The damp leather absorbed the drywall dust and left a film of light-gray paste around the soles. He ran his hand along the drywall tape, pushed open the swinging doors to peek into the kitchen, looked into the dining room, then nodded his head—tacit approval of the work. "Did you talk to that bonehead buddy of yours?" he asked.

"I did. He said he'd be in touch."

Carmine said nothing else on the matter and walked over to the section of bar Duke was refinishing. He inspected the mahogany lion head and said, "This is very nice. Where'd you get it?"

"Jimmy Harkins bought the old LaRocka Shoe Hospital in Brilliant. This was in the basement. He said I could have it if I'd haul it out of there."

Carmine's brows arched. "He didn't know what he had."

"He said it came out of a speakeasy and brothel that once sat on the wharf in Brilliant during Prohibition. The story goes that a local carpenter got to drink free and partake of the ladies in exchange for building the bar."

Carmine nodded slowly, running his hand over the features of the mahogany lion. "She must have been quite a gal."

"Who's that?"

"The whore he fell in love with. Look at the detail on this wood. He was trying to drag out the job as long as he could."

"Maybe he was just after the free booze."

"You know better than that, Duke. It's always about a woman."

He pointed to the paper bag Duke had set on a two-by-ten spanning two wooden horses. "Open that up and we'll toast to the success of your restaurant." He pronounced it "res-ta-raunt."

Duke opened the bag and found a half-empty bottle of cabernet and two glass tumblers. Carmine twisted out the cork and poured. "To your success, my friend," he offered, holding up his tumbler. "Salute." Duke clinked his glass to Carmine's, thanked him, and sipped the wine. Carmine took a short drink, set the glass on the two-by-ten, and pulled up a step stool for a seat. "Sit down. I need to talk to you for a minute," Carmine said. Duke grabbed a chair left from Belle's Diner. The orange vinyl seat was ripped diagonally and sponge stuffing was bursting forth. Duke sat on it backward and rested his forearms on the back.

Carmine took another drink, a healthier swallow this time, and looked at Duke while he cleaned his lips with his tongue. After a few moments Carmine said, "He's coming after you. You know that, right?"

"Of course, I know. But I'm not interested."

"You're a smart boy, Duke, but sometimes you don't listen too good. He has gambling operations in nearly every bar and restaurant up and down the river. The minute you open your doors, he's coming after you, too."

For a moment, Duke set the bravado aside. He was as afraid of Tony DeMarco as the next guy. "I'll deal with him, Carmine."

"He's a no-good, rat bastard."

"I'm well aware of that."

"He can be very . . . what's the word I'm lookin' for . . . ?"

"Persuasive?"

Carmine saluted Duke with his glass. "Yes, thank you. *Persuasive.* That's one word. *Vicious* is another. What are you going to do when he puts the squeeze on you?"

"Tell him to get the hell out."

"Good in theory, but sometimes it's not that easy. You think you know how these guys operate, but I'm not sure you understand how ruthless they truly are."

"I've got a pretty good idea."

"I don't think you do. Let me tell you a little story."

"I like stories."

"You won't like this one. It don't have no fairytale ending. I grew up on the south side of Steubenville—dirt poor. My dad left home when I was a baby, and I grew up a wild-ass kid. When I was sixteen, a cop who was screwing my mom got me a job as a towel boy at Jake Hollowood's Gym. He had this stable of boxers, and my job was to hold the spit bucket, wipe 'em down between rounds, stuff like that. After a couple of weeks, I told old man Hollowood I could whip any guy in his gym. Hollowood, he thinks this is hilarious, so he gives me a pair of gloves and shoves me in the ring with Bartolo Stravagi, who was a middleweight with a jaw like a horseshoe. Hollowood says, 'Give our young friend here a lesson, Bart.'

"The lesson lasted all of ten seconds. I popped him in the temple with a right hook, and the sonofabitch was out for fifteen minutes. I looked at the old man and asked, 'Who's next?' That was the last time I ever held a spit bucket. I was good, Duke, really good. I had a left jab that kept 'em honest, and a right hook that put 'em to sleep. I won three Ohio Valley Golden Gloves titles and two Ohio State Fair championships. In fact, I won every time I stepped into the ring as an amateur. I was a few tune-up fights away from going pro."

He halted the story, sipped his wine, and stared at Duke. "So, what happened?" Duke asked.

"Rather than go professional in boxing, I decided to go to the state penitentiary. I got hooked up with this heavyweight named Alexander Vojnovich, a Russian immigrant who lived in a little apartment over top of Whiteman's Drug Store. I'm up there one day, and in the corner of the room is a safe door mounted against a frame of two-by-eights. He was a safecracker, but not a very good one. I go over, kneel down, and start messing with it. Turns out, I was a better safecracker than boxer. I got it open in a couple of minutes. Vojnovich says to me in this thick Russian accent, 'You and me, Carmine, we could make a fortune.'

"Hell, I never had two nickels to rub together, so a fortune sounded pretty good to me. That night, we broke into the A&P and I cracked the safe. Opened it like that." He snapped his fingers. "We split four hundred dollars, and life was grand until the Russian got drunk and punched a cop a month later. He tells the cops that he'll cut 'em a deal—says he knows a kid who's been bragging that he did the A&P job, and he bets the kid's fingerprints were all over the safe. They were, of course. Vojnovich dodged the assault charge, and I went to prison for four years. I was still young, and I figured I would get out of the joint and go back to boxing. But, while I'm in prison, I try to defend a buddy of mine in a fight and get hit in the eye with a chair. Lost the peripheral vision in my right eye. Good-bye, boxing career."

"That's rough, Carmine."

"It's reality, my friend. I think I could have been a world champion. Instead . . ." He nodded toward the lounge. "We all made decisions, good and bad, and we have to live with them, but there's not a day that goes by that I don't think about the bad ones." He took a swallow of wine. "Anyway . . . after I got out of the joint, I got a job at the Fort Steuben Tobacco Shop, which was a front for a numbers-and-gambling operation for the Carlucci family in Youngstown. It was steady, and it beat working in the steel mill. I was going to work there a while, save some dough, and move to California—you know, get a fresh start. Donald Percy owned the cigar store and the lounge down the street here, which he was always bitchin' about. He's complaining about it one day, and I offer to buy it. I'd saved a couple grand, so he sells it to me. It was easy work. I collected bets and funneled them through the Carluccis, and I got 8 percent of the vig. It looked good on paper, but I was barely making enough to keep the place open. There were too many places in town taking bets.

"About that time, early '52, there was a turf war when the Antonellis started moving into the valley. It got bloody for a while, but the Carlucci family was no match for the Antonellis. They're vicious sons of bitches, and they muscled the Carluccis out. On June 3, 1952, I remember it like a heart attack, 'Quiet Al' Antonelli shows up at the lounge and he's holding the deed to the building. I figure he's going to push me out, but he offers me a deal. He'll sell me the building at a low interest rate, but it goes up two-tenths a year. He ups my part of the vig to 10 percent to start, but it drops two-tenths a year. He says he's going to cut down on the number of places taking bets, so I'll be able to cover the payments and make up the vig on volume. It seemed like a good deal at the time. I got a chance to buy the building, but they set their hooks into me, Duke, and I've been under the thumb of those bastards ever since. I still ain't paid off that building, and every year the percentage I pay the Antonellis increases. I can't keep it open much longer. Once I can't pay 'em, they'll take the lounge, and I'm out, and they'll get some other chump to take over. It's just a matter of time."

"That's not a smart business move for them to let you go under."

Carmine frowned. "Are you listenin' to me? These guys ain't Wall Street investment types. It's about control. They got me, and when they're done, they'll dispose of me. A few years back, Tony DeMarco thought I was shorting the Antonellis on their take. Frankly, he's perceptive as hell because that's exactly what I was doing. I thought I could squeeze a little off the top without being noticed, and I did for a while, but I got greedy. Tony sees the receipts are off and comes into the lounge with that devil dog of his and one of his goons, Emilio something-or-other, and accuses me of skimming. Of course, I lied my ass off. I said, 'The bets aren't coming in like they used to. Times are tough with so many guys being laid off at the mill.' He says, 'Carmine, mill rats always got money for booze, smokes, and gambling.' The next thing I know, Emilio something-or-other's got me by the back of the neck and I'm spread-eagle across the pool table—broke two ribs—and he's grinding my face into the felt. You understand what's going on here, Duke? This is *my* lounge. This is a place that I worked my ass off to keep, and now these two fucks are in there, knocking me around. Tony lets that Rott-weiler of his jump up on my pool table, and gives him just enough leash so that his face is about an inch from mine. He's barking, growling, blowing spit and snot all over my face, stinkin' to high heaven. Tony said the next time I cheated him, he'd let go of the leash. 'You're lucky I don't tell Mr. Antonelli,' he says, 'If this happens again, Carmine, I'll let The Great Zeus chew your ugly face off.' And he meant it. The bastard took every dime I made that day, and, before he left, he let that fuckin' dog jump back up on my pool table to take a shit. I never saw a dog shit on command, but I swear that bastard did."

He drained his glass of wine and refilled it. "That's my life, Duke. The Antonellis control it. I'm like a damn puppet. Don't get me wrong, I knew when I got into the gambling business I wasn't going to be dealing with the cream of society, but once those bastards get their fingers in your pockets, it never ends."

Duke blew out his air. "Man, I'm sorry, Carmine."

"You don't have to be sorry, you just got to be smart." He tapped his forehead twice with the tip of an index finger. "Don't let them get their hooks in you. You've got to fight that, no matter how hard DeMarco pushes. You know where I wanted to be by this time in my life? I wanted to be living in Florida in one of those little pink or aqua houses on the beach, someplace where I could walk out my back door and feel the sand squish between my toes. I'd have me one of those Adirondack chairs, and every morning I'd sit there and sip my coffee, smell the saltwater, and watch the sun come up over the ocean. Instead, I never see a sunrise because of the smoke and shit that belches out of that mill. Instead of breathin' in the ocean, I gotta go to work and smell stale cigars and stinkin' steelworkers." He looked at Duke and raised his brows. "No offense."

Duke laughed. "None taken."

Carmine groaned as he pushed himself off the stool, tossed back his wine, and set the empty tumbler on the two-by-ten before waddling toward the door. "Be smart, my friend."

CHAPTER SIX

The halls, Duke recalled, had seemed particularly bright that morning, as though the white paint was luminescent and emitting a stark light. He had just walked through the front door when he was greeted by an unfamiliar nurse who was young and pretty and had chestnut hair that hung in soft curls around her face. She smiled and said, "We have a surprise for you today, Mr. Ducheski."

She escorted Duke down the hall, though he had been there thousands of times. When she stopped in front of Timmy's room, she gestured toward the closed door with an open, upright palm, like a spokesmodel pointing out the features of a new Oldsmobile. When he walked into Timmy's room, the boy was sitting on the side of the bed, a happy nine-year-old in cuffed jeans, a white T-shirt, and black, high-top basketball shoes—Chuck Taylor All-Stars, the same kind his father had worn in the big game. Timmy's hair was combed and neat, his teeth polished and straight. When he smiled, the boy had a dimple in his left cheek, which Duke had never before noticed. "Hey, Dad, where have you been?" Timmy asked. "I've been waiting forever."

Forever, Duke thought. Yes, it had seemed like forever.

The boy snatched two baseball gloves and a ball off the bed and started toward the door. "Let's get out of here and go play a game of catch, okay, Dad?"

Duke grabbed hold of the doorjamb for support, his knees buckling at the sight of his only son walking across the room. "Timmy, you . . . you can talk."

Timmy beamed. "I know. It's great, isn't it? Can we go now?"

Duke didn't get a chance to answer his son. It was at that instant that he bolted upright in his bed, with tiny beads of sweat dotting his forehead, his heart thumping against his ribcage, and blood pounding in his ears. The dream had been so real, so vivid, that it took him a full minute to convince himself that it had been just that—a dream. Still, he jumped out of bed and began throwing on clothes.

The banging of dresser drawers awoke Nina. She turned on the lamp on her nightstand and asked, "What are you doing?"

"I've got to go see Timmy."

She squinted at the alarm clock on the nightstand. "It's three twenty in the morning."

"I think something's happened. I think Timmy's made some improvement, or something. I've got to go see."

"Why don't you wait until morning?"

He was already out the bedroom door and heading down the stairs, still running his belt through the loops of his jeans. It was a twenty-minute drive from their home on Frank Avenue in Mingo Junction to the Heinzmann Convalescent Center on John Scott Highway in Steubenville. He rapped on the locked door until one of the nurses let him in. "I've got to see Timmy," he said. He was no stranger to the nurse, and she opened the door. Duke ran down the hall until he got to Timmy's door. He took a breath and slowly pushed it open. A small mound of blankets pooled in the middle of the bed. Gently, he peeled them away from his only son.

Nothing had changed.

Timmy was curled in a fetal position, the skin taut and shiny over the bones of his face, a line of drool running from the corner of his mouth to the pillow.

He sat alone in the room and cried for an hour.

More than a decade after the dream, Duke could still hear his son's voice. It had been clear and happy and strong. "Hey, Dad, where have you been?" He was certain it had been Timmy talking to him. It was his voice; it was what he would have sounded like, if only he could talk. For years, Duke had vowed to get Timmy out of that place. That, like the dream, was just another fantasy. In his heart, he knew there was only one way Timmy Ducheski would ever leave the convalescent center.

Duke was still in his mill clothes when he went up to visit Timmy after work the day after Carmine DiBassio had made his late-night visit to Duke's Place.

They had cut the boy's hair that morning, leaving an army of black, quarter-inch bristles standing at attention around his head. It was done for sanitary reasons, but Duke hated it. It made the boy's appearance even more pathetic. Duke took a red bandana from his hip pocket and wiped at the line of drool that was running down the boy's chin and neck and soaking the collar of his gown. There was a folding chair in the corner, and Duke pulled it next to the bed. Timmy's eyes were focused on a time and place far removed from his surroundings, and they didn't move; there was no hint of recognition. He ran his hand back and forth over the bristles and said, "Hey, partner, I see they gave you your Marine buzz today, huh? Looks good. Looks sharp." His hand slid down the back of Timmy's head to a boney shoulder. "We're about ready to start putting the bar back together. It won't be long until we'll have Duke's Place open for business. Pretty cool, huh, Timbo? Wait 'til you see it; it's going to be something. Hey, look what I brought you—some carnations—red ones. They had them on sale at the florist." Duke snagged the dozen flowers from the foot of the bed and held them in front of Timmy's eyes, twisting them like a kaleidoscope. "Pretty, huh? They smell good, too." From the bottom of the nightstand he retrieved the vase he kept for Timmy's flowers. He tried to keep flowers in the room—reds and yellows and oranges. He told himself that, like his dad, Timmy liked bright colors. He filled the vase with water from the bathroom sink and placed it on the dresser in front of Timmy, in line where his lifeless eyes seemed to be locked.

He looked so tiny and pitiful in the hospital bed, his knees drawn up and crossed at the ankles; hands drawn up, limp and crossed at the wrists. The pupils looked upward as though fighting for daylight against the sagging lids. Soft, black facial hair covered his upper lip and crept down along his cheeks and under his chin. His flaccid muscle tissue was hardly noticeable under the translucent skin. His body was nourished by the bag of chalky fluid that ran directly into his stomach. His brain remained locked away in an unknown, unreachable expanse. It never got any easier. The visits were as painful now as they had been when Timmy was an infant and the wounds to Duke's psyche fresh.

Timmy should have graduated from high school by now and been enrolled in college, maybe playing basketball. Duke would have taught him his signature move—the jigger and the trigger. It should have been a time when Duke could still wrestle him into submission on the living room floor, but would feel it getting more difficult with each bout. His next birthday would be his twenty-second. There should be a woman in his life. They should be golfing and fishing and driving up to Pittsburgh to watch the Pirates on Sunday afternoons.

Instead, there were just quiet visits amid the odors, stains, sounds, and florescent lights of the institution. The nurses and staff gave Timmy wonderful care, but Duke hated that place. They were always cleaning, but it still reeked of urine and rotting flesh and disinfectant. A trip down the hall revealed room after room of those too infirm or old or mentally impaired to take care of themselves. It pained him greatly that his son was destined to spend his entire life in diapers, surrounded by the moans and wild screams of those who would welcome death.

Timothy Nicholas Ducheski was born at 9:22 a.m. on February 15, 1972. Nina went into labor late Valentine's Day afternoon, and Duke drove her to Steel Valley Medical Center in Steubenville. They were two children ready to have a baby. Duke never claimed to be an expert on birth defects, or their causes. All he could tell anyone was that Nina's pregnancy had been uneventful and all examinations normal. As she entered her third trimester, Timmy moved, jumped, and kicked in the womb, seemingly anxious to exit and begin his life. The doctor had given them every expectation of delivering a healthy baby.

Duke was pacing in the waiting room, where expectant fathers were relegated in the early seventies. Throughout the night, nurses stopped by the room to give him updates, assuring him that Nina and the baby were doing fine. According to Nina, at about 8:00 a.m. a nurse hooked her to a bag of intravenous solution. Nina said the nurse told her the drug would assist in the dilation of the cervix and increase the rate of contractions.

Thirty minutes later, a different nurse walked in and examined the label on the drug bag, and the blood drained from her face. She pulled the needle from Nina's arm and ran from the room. The once-feisty baby within had settled limp in her womb. Nina said there was no movement. In a moment, an army of nurses ran into the room and rushed Nina into surgery, where she delivered Timmy by Cesarean section. Duke knew nothing of this until the doctor came to the waiting room and said, "There's a problem."

He took Duke into the hall and said Timmy had been deprived of oxygen while in the womb.

"For how long?" Duke asked.

"I don't know. Too long."

Timmy wasn't stillborn, but he wasn't far off. He was dark blue when he arrived, and the doctor and nurses struggled to make him breathe.

Duke had long believed that it would have been infinitely more merciful to have allowed him to go peacefully from the womb to the grave. He also believed that things happened for a reason, though he struggled to understand why his son breathed but didn't know day from night or good from evil, and lived in a twilight from which there was no escape.

However, that was how things were to be—a life that was never a life. He didn't sue the hospital or the nurse or the doctor. He saw no margin in it. It was not intentional, and no amount of money would give Timmy his life back. The hospital's lawyer told them that Nina had been given a drug to induce labor, and she simply had a bad reaction. It was rare and tragic, but beyond their control. Was that true? Or did the nurse give her the wrong drug? Duke didn't know. He was nineteen, scared, and overwhelmed. The hospital agreed to cover Timmy's medical costs for life, and three months after he was born, he was moved from the hospital to the Heinzmann Convalescent Center, where he had breathed—Duke refused to say "lived"—within the same four walls for more than two decades.

Duke visited with Timmy for an hour that day. He told him about some of the things going on at the steel mill and the restaurant, but mostly they sat in silence. "I've got to get back down the river, partner," Duke said. He kissed his son's furry cheek, gave his calf a quick rub, and left.

CHAPTER SEVEN

When Moonie Collier's mother attended a parent-teacher conference when her son was struggling through the second grade, his teacher, Miss Conners, said, "Gladys, you're going to have trouble with this one. That boy doesn't know his alphabet from a submarine, and couldn't care less."

He grew up to be a big, raw-boned kid with hands so large they could almost hide a baseball, and a wide, round Moon Pie of a face, thus his nickname. As a teenager, Moonie had been the star pitcher for the Mingo High Indians and the American Legion team. Unfortunately, his IQ was about that of a baseball. Their high school coach once said, "That boy can throw a strawberry through a battleship, but he needs a map and Sacagawea to find his way to the mound every inning."

Education never became any more important to Moonie. In the early spring of his senior year, Moonie announced he was quitting school and taking a job on a river barge. "A river barge!" Duke said. "Three months before you graduate from high school and you're dropping out to take a job on a river barge?"

"I don't need a diploma to work on a barge. It's good money, and I'll get to see the country," Moonie said.

"All you'll get to see is that cesspool of a river. It's an open sewer for every factory along its banks. Goddammit, Moonie, use your brain."

But Moonie Collier hadn't used it up to that point in his life, so why break new ground? His maiden voyage was on the towboat *Allegheny Star*, which was pushing twenty-four barges of coiled steel to New Orleans. His mother was so upset that she refused to have anything to do with his decision, so Duke drove him to the locks in Stratton to meet the *Allegheny Star*. When they arrived, the first mate, a scrawny guy with an eye that listed off to the south, not much hair and fewer teeth, was standing on the gangplank with a cigarette dangling from his mouth, pissing in the river. Moonie said, "I'm Theodore Collier."

The first mate hocked and spit, further polluting the fetid water, then tucked his member back into his pants. "That's nice, numb nuts. Get on the fuckin' boat."

Moonie walked up the gangplank, a duffel bag slung over one shoulder, and said, "Thanks for the lift, Bo-Peep. I'll be in touch."

Early on a Saturday morning in February, just over five years later, Duke was awakened by a pounding on his front door. He was still half asleep as he pulled on his bathrobe. The pounding continued. He staggered down the stairs and opened the door to find Moonie on his front porch in an army uniform, all spit-shined and polished. He smiled, big and toothy, and said, "Hey, Dukie." It was the first time Duke had set eyes on him since the day Moonie walked up the gangplank of the *Allegheny Star*.

"Hey, yourself, Moonie. Where in the hell have you been?"

He shrugged like he wasn't too sure, himself. "Here and there, Guam, the Philippines, Saudi Arabia, wherever the army wanted to send me," he said, squeezing past Duke into the house. "They liked sending me places where it was hotter than blue hell. You were right about stayin' in high school. I shoulda done that. You got any RC Cola? You can't get an RC in Saudi Arabia to save your life."

Duke got dressed, and they went to Paddy's Diner in Georges Run. Moonie ordered coffee, tomato juice, and a double order of the breakfast hash. Duke had coffee and a sweet roll. Duke said, "Moonie, your last words to me were, 'I'll be in touch.' Generally, that doesn't mean five years later."

"Things happen; you know what I mean, Duke? By the time that damn barge docked in New Orleans, I was sick of it. We were supposed to unload and head back two days later. I collected my pay for the trip down, told 'em I'd be back, then booked. There was no way in hell I was getting back on that damn thing. You work on the boat, eat on the boat, sleep on the boat, play cards on the boat, shit on the boat. All guys. All drunk. I got into four fistfights on the way down. I had to whip one guy twice. It was nuts."

"What did you think, that they docked every night for shore leave?"

"To tell you the truth, I never gave it much thought. Big surprise there, huh? I disappeared into New Orleans. Man, that town jumps. I had a big wad of cash, and I wandered down to Bourbon Street—you ever heard of that?"

Duke smiled and nodded.

"If you can't buy it on Bourbon Street, then it ain't for sale."

"I'm not sure how that translates to you showing up at my door in a US Army uniform."

"Well, I had what you might call a small legal problem."

"I can't tell you how shocked I am to hear that. What happened?"

"This one night, I got drunk and went to a whorehouse . . ."

Duke started laughing.

"What?" Moonie asked.

"You were drunk in a New Orleans whorehouse. What were the odds that legal problems would soon follow?"

Moonie's brow furrowed, and his eyes became slits. "Do you want to hear this, or not?"

"Oh, by all means. Please, go on."

"I must have passed out, because when I woke up I caught this whore going through my wallet. I grabbed her and she screamed, and the next thing I know the biggest, blackest son of a bitch I'd ever seen in my life comes busting through the door, and I'll tell you, Duke, he wasn't in the mood to listen to anything I had to say. There was no reasoning with him, so I hit him right between the eyes, smacked that bastard with everything I had, and he just kind of shook his head like he was trying to get water out of his ears. I hit him again, and he still wouldn't go down. That's pretty much all I remember until the cops showed up. They had me down on the floor, this black buck and about eight whores sittin' on my naked ass, one of them bitches pinching my balls like she was testing pie dough. And that's how they hauled me out of there—handcuffed and naked. They cuffed me in the back, and

I couldn't even cover up my privates, not that that was a big concern to me at that point. I got to the holding cell, and there were two other naked guys in there, so it must be a regular problem. They charged me with assault and about twenty other things, all bullshit. I sat in jail for a couple of weeks, and they gave me a public defender who they must have hauled out of a garbage dump somewhere. He wasn't wearing any socks. I asked him what he thought of my chances, and he said, 'You're totally fucked.' So, the judge gave me a choice. I could do two years of hard labor in the state penitentiary at Angola, or I could enlist in the United States Army. Not much of a choice, really. A couple days later, I was on a bus heading for Biloxi, Mississippi, property of Uncle Sam."

They had just finished applying the first coat of stain to the mahogany bar, and the front room smelled heavily of mineral spirits. Moonie walked up and down the bar, working an old T-shirt into crevices where the stain had pooled. "We do damn good work together, don't we, boys?" he asked.

Duke snapped open a can of Iron City and toasted his friend. "That, we do, Moonie." Angel nodded in agreement.

Moonie took a hit off his tepid beer and wiped a sweaty forearm across an equally sweaty brow. Rivulets of perspiration streaked down his cheeks. "How long will it take us to finish it?" he asked.

"A week or so. We'll hit it with another coat of stain tomorrow, and it'll be ready for sealer by Friday."

"I can't wait to get it all set up." Moonie said.

Moonie was nearly as excited as Duke about the opening of Duke's Place. He was going to work evenings and weekends, tending bar. He had bought a book of mixed-drink recipes—a little paperback that he carried around in his hip pocket, studying it when he had free time. "You'd have graduated high school with honors if you'd studied your history the way you've studied that drink book," Angel said.

"I'm more interested in booze than anything those dead guys did," Moonie responded. "Test me. Ask me how to make a drink, any drink."

"How about a rum and Coke?" Duke asked.

"Come on, goddammit. Give me something with more than two ingredients."

"Okay, a Manhattan?"

"Good, a Manhattan. I know this one." He squeezed his eyes closed for a few seconds. "One shot of Canadian whiskey, preferably Crown Royal, a quarter ounce of sweet vermouth, and a dash of bitters. You stir it in a glass of ice and strain it into a tumbler, and add a cherry."

Duke tilted his head and smiled. "Damn, Moonie, not bad."

"Give me another one."

"How about a Maid Marion?" Angel asked.

Moonie's brows pinched in the middle. "Maid Marion?"

Angel nodded. "Yeah, a Maid Marion—how do you make it?"

"I never heard of a Maid Marion. Is that one of those foo-foo drinks you make in a blender and put a little umbrella in it?"

"Could be," Angel said.

"Well, we ain't servin' no damn drinks with umbrellas at my bar."

"Your bar?" Duke asked.

"That's right. When I'm behind the bar, I'm callin' the shots."

Duke put his hands on his hips. "Really? That's interesting. You know, Moonie, foo-foo drinks will help pay the bills, too."

Moonie waved at air and walked toward the front door. "Well, I ain't makin' no damn Maid Marion or none of them foo-foo drinks."

Moonie opened the front door and leaned against the unfinished drywall, letting a cool breeze blow over him. The rain had stayed trapped in the Ohio River Valley for twenty-four hours, the low clouds mixing with the exhaust of the mill. Across the street, two neon pinkish-orange signs in the windows of the Oasis glowed *EAT* and *DRINK*. A steady stream of steelworkers ran in and out of the Oasis, slipping out of the mill on their breaks for a quick shot and a beer, and to drop off their gambling spot sheets.

Through the rain and the dark, the pale lights of the business district spilled out onto the sidewalk. Cast against this hazy light, Moonie could see a solitary figure making his way up Commercial Street. An occasional lightning flash washed him in a white light, giving Moonie snapshot glimpses, like the flash of a camera in a dark room. The figure had stepped out of Carmine's Lounge and limped slowly up the street, carrying a battered, blue duffel bag in his left hand. His right hand remained buried in his jacket pocket where he was known to keep a .44 Magnum. His gait was slow and deliberate, his eyes forever on the lookout for trouble.

His name was Frankie "the Troll" Silvestri, a raffish, squatty, cockstrong courier for Joey Antonelli. He was a frightful sight. A birth deformity had left Frankie's right femur three inches shorter than his left, giving him a limp that caused him to flop forward on the shorter leg and drag the longer one. At best, he was five-foot-three. He carried a protruding jaw and a severe under bite on a massive head that was too large for his body. His appearance made children cry and caused adults to cross the street to avoid passing him on the sidewalk.

Frankie not only was hard on the eyes but also carried with him such a horrific body odor that he made the sulfurous coke plant smell sweet by comparison. Each time the Troll left the lounge, Carmine sprayed it with disinfectant to kill the odor. It was jokingly said that Antonelli's money was safe with the Troll, because not even the most desperate thief would get within ten feet of him.

Moonie watched as the Troll limped up Commercial Street and disappeared inside the Oasis. "That would be a good job, don't you think?" Moonie asked.

Angel and Duke were sitting on the floor, nursing their beers. "What job's that?" Duke asked.

"The Troll's."

"Oh, Christ almighty," Angel moaned.

"You think being a bagman for Joey Antonelli would be a good job?" Duke asked. "You're kidding, right?"

Moonie was immediately on the defensive. "No, I'm not kidding. I'd be out of the mill. The work would be easy, and, if you did your job right, I bet Antonelli would take care of you."

"Sweet Mother of Christ, Moonie. He'd take care of you, all right. If you screw up he kills you. Very much the same treatment they might give someone who, for example, owed them a lot of money for bad gambling debts."

Duke let the words hang in the air, hoping they somehow penetrated the thick cranium of his friend.

"I hear ya." He sipped at his beer. "I told you already. I'm not afraid of Tony DeMarco."

"And that's the worst thing you have going for you, Moonie," Angel said.

"I'd kick his sorry ass."

"Moonie," Duke said, "if Tony DeMarco came in here, alone, unarmed, you'd kick his ass. No doubt about it. But he doesn't play that way. He'd hit you with his car and break your legs, then have three of his goons hold you down while he took batting practice on your skull. That's how he plays. You've got to use your head."

Moonie jerked around and flashed Duke a hard glare. "I'll handle it."

"Okay, Moon, okay."

Moonie turned away from the door and slid down the wall. "You know, I've got a horse comin' in Saturday night, and I'll pay off those debts to Carmine."

"Yeah, you told me."

"You sure you don't want in?"

"Positive."

"How about you, Angel?"

"I'll pass."

Duke said, "And where are you going to get the money to put down on this horse? If you lose again, you're only in deeper."

"Quit worrying, Duke. Carmine isn't going to do anything. I'm too good a customer."

"Right. He comes up a couple thousand short to Joey Antonelli and decides to eat it rather than turn over the debt. You're playing with fire."

Moonie arched his brows and grinned. "Did I mention that I got a horse comin' in this Saturday?"

Duke crumpled his beer can and tossed it at the garbage can ten feet away. It hit the rim and skittered off.

CHAPTER EIGHT

Tomato sauce bubbled on the stove in a large, stainless-steel pot. Rolls and bread sticks browned on the oven's top rack. The lower rack held a spinach casserole. Veal cutlets fried and splattered in a skillet over a blue gas flame. The aromas of the kitchen filled the downstairs but could not totally overwhelm the stench of the cigar that Nina's dad puffed and chewed in the corner of his living room, where his feet rested on a leather ottoman as he stared blankly at a professional football game on the television. He sucked the pungent cigar and grunted when the grandchildren got too loud. Otherwise, you hardly knew he was alive.

A Frank Sinatra CD played on the stereo system that had been wired into the kitchen for Nina's mother. Her family loved Sinatra, and with the exception of an occasional Tony Bennett tune, that was all they played on the stereo. Duke was a Dean Martin fan. Martin—then known as Dino Crocetti—grew up a few miles away on Steubenville's south end. Duke once slipped a Dean Martin CD into the stereo, and it brought nothing but ugly glares. There was no love for the hometown boy. Nina's brother removed the CD and said, "We don't play that hack around here. Sinatra, and only Sinatra."

Each Sunday, Duke had dinner with Nina and her family. Like any unpleasant experience, after a while he had grown numb to the pain and had long before given up complaining about attending the dinners. Nina's mother insisted. Nina insisted. He went. They were early-afternoon affairs, beginning promptly at two, Italian feasts of pastas and meats and cheeses and wines. Nina's siblings and their families arrived after mass. The women went to the kitchen while the men smoked and drank wine from little juice glasses, sometimes joining Nina's father in front of the television, sometimes around the bocce court or horseshoe pit they had built in the backyard.

Nina had three sisters, all of whom lived around Mingo Junction. Then, there was the only son in the family, Nina's twin brother, Anthony Junior.

Anthony "Little Tony" DeMarco.

He was always the star of the Sunday dinners. About 1:30, he would enter the house like a Medal of Honor winner returning from war. He played the role of favored child to the hilt, always showing up with gifts—a bouquet of flowers, bottles of wine, fresh-baked desserts from an Italian bakery in Steubenville, or a box of Cuban cigars for his dad.

"Mama," he would call as he entered the kitchen.

"Oh, my Antoine," she would respond.

They all spoke in the Brooklyn-Italian, wiseguy accent that Tony had acquired after he began working for Salvatore Antonelli. His mother and father soon began using the same dialect, and Duke's wife followed. This was comical, as everyone in Mingo Junction remembered when the DeMarcos spoke with an Appalachian twang and were simply poor white trash living in Dago Flats. Their home was a sad, dirty frame where the gutters and steps sagged, and paint peeled in hunks, a combination of neglect and the scouring effects of the exhaust from Wheeling-Pitt. When Duke began dating Nina, her mother had a thick moustache and had been barred from every store in the area for shoplifting. The DeMarcos rediscovered their proud Italian heritage after their son found his calling as an Antonelli enforcer.

Each Sunday, Tony would stride into the kitchen smelling heavily of drugstore aftershave and hug his mother, throwing in three quick pats to the spine. She beamed at the attention and cupped his olive chin in her hands, leaving wispy streaks of flour on his stubble. He would then pull a brown envelope holding a half-inch stack of bills from an inside jacket pocket and press it into her hand. When he did, she looked positively orgasmic, and she would kiss him on the cheek before running off to the bedroom to stash the packet of cash. All this, under the watchful eye of

Jesus Christ, whose pewter form adorned a wooden cross in every room of the house. Mother DeMarco had a perverse acceptance of Tony and his ways. Her son was a vicious human being, a predator with the morals of a hungry alligator, and it was certainly no secret how he earned his money. But, he had moved them out of the ramshackle frame in Dago Flats and into a stone, three-bedroom Tudor on Mingo Junction's west side; he showed up every Sunday with a thick envelope of cash; and he paid for her electrolysis. Apparently, that enabled her to overlook a few personality flaws, such as a penchant for dropping seventy-year-old alcoholics over the side of railroad trestles.

Tony DeMarco had a reputation as an enforcer without conscience or peer, but this did little to quell his burning desire for respect. He had money and power, but the lack of respect—within the Antonelli family and on the streets of Mingo Junction—was a hot coal burning in his gut. At one time, he was a force with the Antonelli family. He went to meetings and dinners with Il Tigre and sat at the right hand of the old man. His opinion was not only solicited, but valued. But when Il Tigre died, Tony's future became as cold as the old man's corpse. From the moment Joey Antonelli whispered in his ear at the hospital, Tony simply took orders. He was in, but he was out. Although he ran operations in the Ohio River Valley with cool efficiency and made a lot of money for himself and the family, he was virtually ignored by the younger Antonelli, except when there was an opportunity to dress him down.

Duke was a particular thorn to Tony. He was a guy who made a lucky shot in a high school basketball game and was still milking the moment two decades later. It grated on Tony that Duke would walk down the streets of Mingo Junction in work boots and faded blue jeans, and people still went out of their way to speak to him. Tony wore expensive Italian loafers and custom-tailored suits, but the same people looked at him with the malevolence they would a streak of dog shit on the soles of their shoes. Unless they owed him money, most people in Mingo Junction saw Tony DeMarco for what he was—a thug who had wandered out of Dago Flats under the wing of a Mafia don. You could dress him up, but he was still the same wop who used to roll drunks for pocket change.

For years, Duke had been indifferent to Tony. He orbited Duke's world, but always on the outer reaches of the solar system; he would pass by at family functions, but he had no influence on Duke's daily life. Like everyone else in Mingo Junction, Duke knew what Tony did and for whom he did it, so he kept his distance. The closest Duke got to his brother-in-law was sitting across the table from him at Sunday dinners.

Things between them changed the Saturday after Duke informed Nina that he wanted a divorce and she hit him with the frying pan. It was early afternoon, and Duke was working in the garage at his fishing cabin, the radio blaring, and he didn't hear Tony walk up behind him. Tony grabbed Duke by the shoulder, spun him around, and jammed the barrel of a chrome-plated .22-caliber pistol into his mouth, splitting his upper lip before sliding it into the gap in his mouth where Nina and the frying pan had relieved him of his teeth. His left hand clutched Duke's hair on the back of his head, and he pushed the barrel of the revolver deeper into his mouth. His eyes were dark, dead, and depthless. It was, Duke assumed, like being neck-deep in the ocean and suddenly finding yourself nose-to-nose with a great white shark. Simply, he was at Tony's mercy. He saw Tony's thumb roll back and heard the hammer click into place, and he thought the life of Duke Ducheski had come to an end.

"I understand you want to divorce my sister," Tony said. Duke was afraid to move or try to answer. The gun barrel was gagging him. Tony waited a long moment before speaking again. "She doesn't want a divorce. I don't know why she wants to stay married to a dumb-ass Polack like you, but she does. So, let's make this easy. You forget about getting divorced, and we'll all get along, understand?" Duke nodded. "Good. My sister's bat-shit crazy and a pain in the ass. I got that. But you're the one who knocked her up, so you're going to keep her. You can keep pounding that little nurse on the side. I don't give a shit about that, but there's to be no divorce." He pulled the gun out of Duke's mouth and wiped it off on his T-shirt. "We have an understanding, right?" He pulled a clean handkerchief from his pants pocket and held it to Duke's lip until Duke raised a hand and applied pressure to the pulpy mess.

After a moment, Duke nodded his head and said, "I got it."

Tony slapped Duke twice on the open cheek. "Good boy."

Duke's indifference to Tony died that day. It was replaced with a combination of loathing and abject fear. Like any predator, Tony had seen the fear flash in Duke's eyes, and he knew the dynamics of their relationship had changed. Tony had inserted a gun into Duke's mouth and just as quickly inserted himself into Duke's psyche.

Tony relished this, and in the ensuing weeks at dinner he would drape a heavy arm around Duke's shoulder, pat him on the back, and call him "paisano." Duke smiled and pretended not to be offended. As dinner finished one Sunday afternoon and the women began cleaning up the kitchen, Tony grabbed two bottles of cabernet and two glasses, squeezed Duke's shoulder, and said, "Duke, my friend, my brother, let's go outside and enjoy this beautiful afternoon." Duke had planned to go visit Timmy. Instead, he obediently followed Tony to the side yard. Did he really want to be Duke's friend? Probably not. He was simply enjoying the control he now held.

It was a sunny afternoon and seventy degrees. They sat in two Adirondack chairs beneath a spreading maple that cast the entire side yard in shade. He poured a large glass of wine, tossed it back, and refilled his glass before offering Duke a drink. Duke took the bottle and poured himself a meager serving. Tony dusted the first bottle in short order. When he started on the second, his speech was slightly slurred.

There is a myth regarding the code of silence in the Mafia. Duke could only conclude that it was a myth because the only member of the Mafia he knew was his brother-in-law, and after a few drinks Tony couldn't keep his mouth shut.

"I can't drink too much," Duke said. "I go on two weeks of midnight starting tonight."

"Why do you do that?" Tony asked.

"Why do I go to work?"

"Why do you go to work in that dirty-ass mill, busting your balls for chump change?"

"Thanks for that."

Tony dug a hand into a front pocket and asked, "Do you know how much money I make?"

Duke shook his head. "No."

"A fuckin' lot, that's how much." He pulled his hand from the pocket and held an impressive wad of fifty-dollar bills in front of Duke's nose. "I made more money last week than you'll make in a year." He lifted his left foot off the grass. "These shoes cost more than your house." He pointed an index finger at Duke. "I could get you a sweet job with the Antonellis."

"Thanks for the offer, Tony, but I'm pretty content in the mill."

"You could wear a white shirt every day, and you wouldn't be cleaning dirt out from under your fingernails all the time." His eyelids drooped, and he gave Duke a smirk. "I read a book about Al Capone." (*Astonishing*, Duke thought, because he wasn't sure Tony could read.) "Did you know that when he went to baseball games, people treated him like royalty? He was like a fuckin' god to people in Chicago."

"That's your role model—Al Capone?"

"You wouldn't fuckin' understand." He finished off another glass of wine. "You're a good paisano." A bit of drool ran from the corner of his mouth, and he swiped it with a backhand, leaving a sheen of silvery spit on his black stubble. He sat in silence for a long minute, and Duke was ready to call it a day when Tony asked, "Do you know what I do, paisano?"

"Sure, you've told me a hundred times. You're an *associate* of the Antonellis."

Tony cinched up his eyes and shook his head, waving a hand in front of his face as though shooing a pesky fly. "No, that's who I *am*. Do you know what I *do*?"

"I've got a pretty fair idea."

"No, you don't. You think you do, but you don't. When Salvatore Antonelli had a problem . . ." Tony pointed a thumb to his chest. "He called me. *Me!* I was his number one man. Number one. You remember that science teacher from Steubenville who they found dead in the woods a few years back?"

Duke nodded. "Yeah, I remember. The one who committed suicide."

Tony laughed and took another hit of his wine. "In a manner of speaking, yes. If you owed the Antonellis thirty large and had no way to pay it back, it would be suicide." He roared at his own joke. "Kind of funny, he was this pillar of the community and won all them awards for teaching, but he was up to his queer ass in gambling debts."

"Whoa, Tony, maybe you . . ."

"We were waiting for him in his house—sitting in the dark. He turns on the light and right away starts cryin' and beggin' us not to hurt him. I fuckin' hate it when they cry. They should just take it like a man, ya know? I told him we just wanted to take a ride and talk, and the dumb-ass gets in the car. Personally, if I'm gonna get whacked, you're going to have to do it right there, because I ain't gettin' in no fuckin' car, I can tell you that, straight up. He's in the car, blubbering and really pissin' me off. He offered me a blow job not to kill him. Like I'd give up the chance to put one in his brain for a lousy blow job. I couldn't wait to get his sorry ass out of the car so I could kill him. I put one in his temple and dropped the piece beside him. It looked like a suicide."

"Holy Christ, Tony, I don't want to know all this."

He laughed. "We're paisanos, remember. More than that . . ." He poked Duke's shoulder twice with an index finger. ". . . We're family."

"You know who else I whacked?"

"Tony, I don't really want to hear about . . ."

"Sammy Stein, that lousy Jew bastard."

Duke's eyes widened at that bit of information. He was morbidly curious. "Sammy Stein? Really?"

Stein was a prominent businessman in the Upper Ohio Valley. He had a large produce company in Weirton, owned a chain of seven drive-through package stores, twenty car washes, a scrap yard, and the

Pier Restaurant in Follansbee. A few years earlier, he left for work on a Sunday morning and was never seen again. Rumors, speculation, and conspiracy theories filled the pages of the newspapers for months. It was one of the Ohio Valley's great mysteries.

"He only owed us a couple thousand bucks, but he was so fuckin' annoying, I had to kill him. You know what I mean, right, when someone is annoying you so bad that you want to kill them?"

"Not really, Tony."

He poured more wine, slopping as much outside the glass as went in. "I went to talk to him about his debt. Just talk, 'cause he was a good customer, but he was always a couple of bills in the red, and always fuckin' whining about something. Perpetuating the stereotype, you know what I mean?" He laughed, then took a drink of his wine. "So, anyway, I go to talk to him, and he starts giving me a rash of shit. Well, you know what I want when I come knockin' on your door? A little fuckin' respect. You understand?"

"I think so," Duke said, recalling the day when Tony had put a pistol in his mouth.

"I tracked him down at that fruit-and-vegetable warehouse he owned on the north side of Weirton. He holds out the money and, as I'm reaching for the dough, he drops it on the floor. Can you believe that shit? He drops it on the floor and says, 'There's your money, wop.' It was a Sunday morning, fuckin' Jew was the only one in the place. I thought, 'What the fuck?' I punched him in the face, and he hit the deck. Before he could get up, I took off my belt and looped it around his neck. I liked killing him that way because it gave the fat puke a little time to think about the gravity of his mistake. I wrapped him up in a plastic tarp and, here's the funny thing, I came down here for Sunday dinner. I was inside, eating spinach-and-cheese cannelloni, and Mr. Jew was cooking in the trunk of my car. I had a guy who worked at the blast furnace at Homestead Steel in Pittsburgh who owed me a favor, and that night, good-bye, Sammy. Let me tell you something, if you got access to a blast furnace, it makes for a very neat job."

Duke had been curious about Sammy Stein. However, once he

knew what happened, he wished he didn't. It was dangerous information to possess, the kind that could cause you to disappear like Sammy Stein. They sat in the Adirondacks for a few more minutes until the wine glass slipped from Tony's hand and he began lightly snoring. When Duke got home from his 12:00–8:00 a.m. shift, Tony was sitting in his car in front of Duke's house. As Duke made his way up the sidewalk, Tony stepped out of the car and stood between the open door and the frame and said, "About what I told you yesterday . . ."

Duke said, "I was pretty tired, Tony. I really don't recall our conversation."

"Good," he said, reaching over to pat Duke twice on the shoulder. "Very good. Sometimes it's good to have a faulty memory, huh?"

It was the fourth Sunday of September 1993. Following dinner, the men were in the screened-in back porch, playing pinochle; the women were sitting around the kitchen table, drinking white wine, gossiping, and laughing too loud. Duke slipped out the front door and took a seat on the glider on the porch. It was his favorite place to escape. He could rest his feet on the railing and overlook a slow bend in Cross Creek. It was a peaceful, quiet time. Smoke billowed out of the mill, caught a zephyr from the west, and dissipated beyond the West Virginia hills. In the distance, the muted roar of the open hearth vibrated through the valley.

Duke pushed slowly against the railing, enjoying the solitude. The sun was sinking over the hills to the west, casting long shadows over the yard. His eyelids were beginning to sag when he heard the door on the screened-in back porch slap shut. A moment later, Tony came around the side of the house, his cell phone in one ear, an index finger pushing against the other. In the gloaming, Duke could see the glow of red covering Tony's neck and ears. It was several minutes before he spoke.

"Yeah, I heard you the first eight times you told me. . . . I'm not being a wise ass, I just need to know what you want me to do about it . . . I don't fuckin' know. How would I know? . . . I haven't seen him . . . How should I know? A month, three weeks ago, I don't keep track . . . I will . . . I will . . . I said, 'I will,' goddammit . . . Huh? . . . Are you accusing me? . . . What? . . . You know . . . Uh-huh . . . Yeah, yeah, yeah . . . I'm going to hang up now before I say something I'll regret . . . I am . . . I will . . . I'm hanging up. Good-bye."

Tony snapped his phone shut, then bent over and rested both palms on his knees. He took a few cleansing breaths, then walked toward the house, trudging up the stairs to the front porch.

"Trouble in paradise?" Duke asked.

Tony jerked his head toward the voice, surprised to see his brother-in-law on the porch. "A little bit," Tony said. "I need a lift up to Steubenville."

"No, I . . ."

"Come on, goddammit. Give me a ride. I'm about out of gas and the station closed at five. I just need to run up to the newsstand and check on something. It'll take five minutes. Up and back."

A few minutes later, Duke was behind the wheel of the Jeep, with Tony in the passenger seat, heading toward Steubenville. Duke slipped a Dean Martin CD into the stereo just to screw with Tony. As they pulled onto Ohio Route 7, Tony's grinding teeth could be heard over the hum of the engine and "Ain't That a Kick in the Head?" They were barely out of town when Tony rolled his right fist into his left palm and said, "He disrespects me every chance he gets."

"Who?"

Tony reached over and turned off the CD player. "*Who*? Who do you fuckin' think? That little prick Joey Antonelli. Didn't you hear that conversation back there?"

"I heard you. I didn't know who you were talking to."

Tony twice punched the passenger door.

"Hey, easy."

The muscles in Tony's face strained and air whistled through his nostrils. "You know, the old man, Salvatore, he'd call me and we'd have a conversation that might last four seconds. He'd say, 'Tony, we got a problem with So-and-So. Deal with it. Let me know how it goes.' Click. He trusted me to handle it, but that whiny scrotum Joey, he treats me like I'm fuckin' retarded. I'm the most loyal guy he's got, and you know what I get in return? Smart-ass remarks and disrespect. I'm always taking it up the tailpipe from that son of a bitch. He expects me to do all his dirty work, all his heavy liftin', but he don't show me no respect. None. He wants to think I'm a joke, fine, I'm going to show him a joke."

He banged on the door three times.

"Tony, easy, this Jeep has to last me."

"You know what I've been doing?"

Again, Duke shook his head. "No idea."

"I've been tape-recording that dumb-ass. I got him giving orders to whack a couple of guys, shit on how he buys and sell drugs, him bragging about choking one of his whores to death, him talking about the gambling operation and how he's laundering money and hiding it from the IRS. It's dynamite shit."

"You what?" Duke asked, again, finding himself the recipient of information that he would rather not possess. "Have you lost your marbles? If he finds out, he'll kill you."

"He ain't gonna find out. I got cassette players by every phone in the house, and I record his phone calls." He reached into his shirt pocket, pulled out a cassette, and held it out where Duke could see it. "Joey's such a dipshit. He gets a couple drinks in him, and he can't keep his mouth shut." Duke looked over at Tony. Obviously, he didn't see the irony in the statement. "The old man, he never talked about anything unless it was one-on-one. Then, he always knew who he told. Joey, he talks all the time. He's got diarrhea of the mouth—always runnin'. He's going to try to run me out of the operation one of these days, or worse. When he does, I'm going to use the tapes to blackmail his ass."

"I don't need to know a lot about this, but don't they implicate you, too?"

"If I have to use them, the feds will give me immunity. I'm small potatoes compared to an Antonelli. He would be a real trophy. But, I won't have to. If you tried something like this with Il Tigre, he'd slit your throat. Joey, he's a puss. When I'm ready, I'll blackmail his ass to take control of my territory. I'll run the show and cut him out of the mix."

Duke pulled up in front of Herald Square News & Tobacco. "Tony, you wear me out," Duke said, nodding toward the front door. "Remember, you said five minutes."

He watched from the curb as Tony entered the store. There was a brief exchange between Tony and a thin, balding man with a cigarette tucked behind his ear. The man disappeared into a room in the back, then returned a few minutes later with a thick-shouldered guy who had a round head and slicked-back, salt-and-pepper hair. They spoke for a few minutes. The big man shrugged, and the side of his lip curled. Tony shook a finger at the man, who looked as though Tony had insulted his mother. The man jabbed at Tony with an index and middle finger, between which was the stub of a cigar, one end soaked in spit.

A few minutes later, Tony exited the store and climbed back into the Jeep, his face burning crimson. Duke put the Jeep in gear, pulled out onto Fourth Street, and turned east on Washington Street. As he drifted toward the traffic light at Ohio Route 7, Duke said, "I don't know what went on back there, Tony, but please don't feel compelled to share it with me."

CHAPTER NINE

On Monday morning, Duke made his way down St. Clair Avenue as the sun climbed above the craggy hills that rimmed the West Virginia side of the Ohio Valley. It was a clear day, cold and windless, and the smoke from the mill billowed into the sky in perfect columns. The first frost of the season had crept through the valley overnight, and a thin coat of sparkling crystals covered the grass and the steel handrail that wrapped around the sidewalk at the bottom of the hill. Duke crossed Commercial Street hunched at the shoulders, his hands buried in the pockets of a canvas jacket. He used two fingers to turn the knob and pushed open the door to Carmine's Lounge with a knee. His eyes teared when he entered the warmth of the lounge. He dabbed at his eyes with the cuff of his jacket and set his lunch pail and newspaper on the counter.

The lounge was quiet, the overhead lights dark. Only the faint, under-counter fluorescents burned. The perpetual gin-rummy game was absent, and Carmine's cigar was in the ashtray, cold, a dead ash protruding from its head, curling up like a fish hook. In the back, Carmine was standing with two thick-necked men who were sporting five-o'clock shadows at 7:28 in the morning. Through watery eyes, Duke saw both men turn away as he entered and walked toward the glass case holding the chewing gum. Carmine whispered to them and started his side-to-side gait toward the front of the lounge. He snagged two packs of spearmint from the case and slid them across the glass to Duke. "That's good," he said. "Keep your dimes. Go."

Duke looked at the goons. Their backs were to him, and they leaned in toward each other, whispering. One had his hands thrust into his pants pockets. The other's arms appeared crossed at the chest, straining the seams of his jacket; his head was as big as a basketball, and a roll of fat bulged above his collar. "Is everything all right, Carmine?"

"Yeah, fine, everything's fine." He swallowed hard, a look of panic consuming his face. "You go now."

"Who are those guys? Are you sure you're okay?"

"Yeah, Duke, everything's fine. Go on, get the hell out of here. It's just business, that's all."

"This doesn't involve Moonie, does it?"

"No. In fact, the numb nuts was in here first thing this morning and paid up. He's good."

"Really? He paid up? Everything?"

"Yeah, he's good, he's good. Now get out of here."

"So what's all this about? How come the lounge is all dark?"

"It's about my business, Duke, and it's none of yours." The old man's face looked more scared than angry. One of the goons turned around and gave Duke a hard look. It was Mr. Basketball Head. He had a tiny mouth and a thin, twisted nose. There are times in your life when you come into contact with people who live and operate in a totally different dimension, a place free of laws and conscience. The residents who populate this world could snap your neck like a piece of dry spaghetti. This man, Duke knew, was one of those people, and he got chills the instant their eyes met.

Carmine walked around the counter, put a flat hand between Duke's shoulder blades, and guided him toward the door. In a low voice he asked, "You remember our conversation from the other night, right?"

"Yes."

"Good, because if you forget, if you get weak and cave, these are the kind of mouth-breathers you'll have hanging around and telling you how to run your restaurant."

He pushed Duke out the door, slammed it closed, and rammed the deadbolt into place. A black sedan was parked in the gravel lot beside the lounge. A third man, a near-identical match of the two inside, was walking circles around the car, scanning the otherwise-vacant lot. Duke was relieved, at first assuming the goons were looking for Moonie. Apparently not. For a man of so little brains, Moonie sometimes lived a charmed life. His horse had apparently come in, and he dodged another bullet.

Duke continued up Commercial Street to the mill, clocked in, and went to the locker room, looking for his pal. Moonie's locker was closed and the shower empty. Four riggers were sitting on benches, playing euchre on the top of a plastic milk carton. "Anyone seen Moonie?" Duke asked the group.

None of their eyes left their cards. "Nope," the dealer finally said, turning under a nine of spades.

Duke walked across the yard to the administrative offices to see Angel, who worked in the mill's finance department. Angel was working on his second cup of coffee and a payroll audit when Duke walked into his office. Angel's nose was still his most prominent feature, though it no longer dominated his face as it had in his youth. His black hair was combed back off his face, and he sported an impressive moustache, which helped deflect attention from his nose. "Morning, Angel. Have you seen Moonie?"

"I have. He was in here a little while ago and reported off. You just missed him."

"Why'd he report off?"

"In all candor, I think he wanted to make a little show of his winnings. Apparently, he hit the trifecta at Mountaineer over the weekend. He's flush with cash, and it's burning a hole in his pocket. He said he was going to the Pittsburgh airport to get on the first plane for Vegas."

"Vegas?"

"His last words to me were, 'My luck has changed, Angel. I've got to keep the streak alive.'"

CHAPTER TEN

Frankie "the Troll" Silvestri was gone.

He and his black, 1990 Lincoln Town Car vanished late Saturday after picking up the day's gambling receipts at the Oasis. Rumors that Antonelli's trusted courier had skipped town with one of the year's biggest hauls hit the streets of Mingo Junction on Monday afternoon. The wagers covered that week's college and pro football games, and Friday's daily number. According to the most popular rumor, the Troll grabbed the bag of receipts from the Oasis, grinned mischievously at the manager, and quietly slipped out the front door, never to be seen again. It was said that he got away with more than sixty thousand dollars in cash. Joey Antonelli was apoplectic; Tony DeMarco was in a state of unbridled panic.

Duke heard the rumor while eating lunch at the mill. While he acted disinterested, he actually found it quite amusing.

"What did you hear, Duke?" Chinky Madrid asked.

"Why would you think I'd hear something?" Duke asked.

"Tony DeMarco's your brother-in-law, ain't he? Everyone knows that he's the one who controls the gambling for the Antonellis around here."

"He doesn't tell me anything about his business, and I don't ask. Frankly, I don't want to know."

However, Duke immediately thought of the ride he had given Tony to the Herald Square News & Tobacco the previous evening and the argument he had witnessed. Now, it all made sense.

By Tuesday afternoon, Tony had been on the phone with Joey Antonelli a dozen times. When he called at 5:00 in the afternoon and there was still no sign of the Troll, Antonelli screamed, "I need you to find a guy who looks like an iguana and walks with a limp. How fuckin' difficult can that be?"

"I've searched the entire valley," Tony said. "He ain't here, I'm tellin' ya. He's just disappeared."

"When you find that ugly little prick, I want you to put a bullet in every joint in his body. I want him to suffer before he dies."

"I understand."

Antonelli slammed down the receiver.

Tony turned off his tape recorder and smiled. "Keep talking, motherfucker, keep talking."

Eight days after the Troll had disappeared, Mama DeMarco walked to the front porch three times to tell her son that his dinner was getting cold. He ignored her. For more than an hour he had been pacing the front sidewalk, frowning and whispering into his cell phone. He had an index finger jammed into his open ear, which he removed periodically to slap himself on the forehead with an open palm. When he sat down at the table, the family took their cue from Tony, and dinner was unusually quiet. The din that normally accompanied the Sunday dinners at the DeMarcos' could drown out the roar of the blast furnaces. Not this one. Even the great Frank Sinatra had been silenced.

This suited Duke just fine, since it was likely that the family would eat quickly and leave the table. He joined the silence, wolfing down his pasta with pesto and sausage. Duke had things on his mind, too. Duke's Place was to open in about a month, and there was still a lot of work to finish. He hadn't been up to see Timmy in four days. After dinner, he planned to visit his son, get in a quick workout, then get back to work at the restaurant. When he passed on the coffee and the wafer-cookie dessert, it solicited a glare from his mother-in-law. "Sorry to dine and dash, but I need to go see Timmy and get back to work on the bar," Duke said, pushing away from the table. "Thanks for the dinner, Mama. It was terrific, as always." No one looked up from their desserts as he headed for the back door.

There was an afternoon fog hanging against the hillside, heavy and gray, a combination of mist and the roiling smoke from the mill being forced low by the heavy cover. Gray clouds put a dingy lid over the entire valley, as if God himself had tired of looking at the smoke and the filthy river and covered it from his view. Duke shoved his hands into his jacket pockets and walked into a light mist blowing down the hill from the west. He was nearly to the edge of the property and the safety of his Jeep when the squeaking hinges of the back door announced a visitor.

"Duke, hold up." It was Tony. He was smiling, having for the moment lost the scowl he had worn throughout the day. Suddenly, the happy paisano had returned. "Hey, I need to talk to you for a minute." He jumped down the two wooden steps from the back porch and made his way to where Duke was standing. He looked around and, for a moment, seemed distracted by the gloom. "Shitty day, huh?"

"Yep." Duke nodded his agreement. "What's up?"

Tony grinned. "My sister, she doesn't approve of you ownin' a beer joint, huh?"

"It's a restaurant and taproom, not a beer joint. No, she doesn't approve. But your sister doesn't approve of me breathing, either."

Tony leaned forward, his lower lip protruding. In his heavy, fake Brooklyn-Italian accent, he asked, "You want that I should talk to her about that? You know, tell her it's important to support her husband, something like that. I can make sure she understands."

"No, thanks, Tony. I'll handle it."

Tony nodded. He had a way of doing so that made him look extremely offended—brows furrowed, a slight shrug of the shoulders, a glance away, a quick release of breath. "Whatever. I was just trying to help. So, listen, once you're up and running, you're going to handle some spot sheets for me, right?"

"Gambling sheets?" Duke asked, knowing full well what he meant.

"We don't call 'em that. We prefer, 'spot sheets.'"

This was the conversation Duke knew was coming, the one Carmine had warned him about. "Tony, I don't want . . ."

"It's easy money, Duke. Simple stuff. All you got to do is keep the spot sheets and collect the wagers. They get picked up a couple times a week, and you get a cut. And, I guarantee there won't be any trouble with the cops."

"I'm just not interested. I want to run a nice, clean place."

"A clean place? A *clean* place? Are you insinuating my business is dirty, not good enough for your beer joint?"

Tony could turn around any conversation to make it an insult, putting you on the defensive. "That's not what I meant, and you know it. I don't want to take a chance on driving away business."

Tony laughed. "Drive away business! Duke, my friend, it brings in business. Every bar up and down the valley has spot sheets. They're harmless and very easy money."

"Let me ask you a question, Tony. If they're so harmless, how come I went into the lounge last week and there were guys in there with black overcoats and fingers the size of Coke cans telling Carmine how to run his business? He let Antonelli in years ago, and now he doesn't even have control of his own place. Louie Pitzaferato owned the Oasis for thirty years. Then, one day, Antonelli mysteriously owns it, and I'm guessing it wasn't the kind of real-estate transaction I'd read about in the newspaper."

"Carmine got careless," Tony said, his voice starting to climb. "He got himself in hock a while back. Fortunately, Mr. Antonelli was kind enough to bail him out in exchange for a portion of his business, that's all."

"Well, I want to make sure I'm never in a position for Mr. Antonelli to show me the same type of kindness. I'm not interested."

The finality to the comment made Tony's back stiffen. He was not accustomed to being told no. He composed himself, smiled, and brushed some imaginary dust off Duke's shoulder. "Give it some thought?"

"There's no reason to think about it, Tony. I'm not going to change my mind."

The considerable jaw of Tony DeMarco clenched tight, and a building, internal rage turned his olive skin crimson—a wave of red that erupted on his neck and cheeks and ears. "I see," he said, calmly. "Then, maybe you can do me a little favor, huh? Tell your buddy Collier that I want to talk to him."

"What do you want to talk to Moonie about?"

"What? You writing a fuckin' book, or somethin'? Just tell him I want to talk to him."

"He paid that money he owed Carmine."

Tony smirked. Evil shone in those eyes. He was a viper who could strike in an instant, driving for the weakness in a victim. "Let's just say I'm concerned. Moonie used to be such a loyal customer. But, for some odd reason, he hasn't been in Carmine's for a week. As a matter of fact, the last time he was in the lounge was just after the Troll disappeared. Hmm, isn't that interesting? The Troll disappears Saturday night, and Moonie shows up Monday morning and magically pays off his gambling debt. Do you suppose there's a connection?"

It was Duke's turn to fight the redness. A fire erupted in his belly and shot to his face. He fought unsuccessfully the urge to swallow a nervous gulp of saliva. "He hasn't been in Carmine's because he's been on vacation in Las Vegas."

"Vegas, huh? Damn. He must have come into some serious jack."

"He hit a trifecta at Mountaineer."

"Must have been a hell of a bet. You just tell your buddy I want to talk to him, and he had better be able to explain *exactly* how he got that money."

"You'll need a little more proof than your wild-ass speculation."

"Understand this, Ducheski, I ain't no fuckin' judge and jury. This ain't something I need to bring to a vote." He turned and started back toward the house. "Tell that dumb-ass to find me. He doesn't want me to come looking for him."

"If you're going after Moonie, you better take a couple of your goons, because one-on-one he'll kick your ass."

Tony smiled. "I'd never give him that chance."

CHAPTER ELEVEN

Sunday afternoons were peaceful times at the Heinzmann Convalescent Center. There was just a skeletal staff of three nurses, a nurse's aide, and an orderly, who spent most of his time smoking on the back patio. No doctors or custodial staff cluttered the halls. Even the patients seemed more at ease, and Duke often wondered if the doctors upped the weekend medication dosages for the benefit of the small staff. Most families who visited on Sundays did so right after church, so it was usually quiet late in the afternoon. On this Sunday, Duke spent a silent hour with Timmy. He hadn't opened his eyes, and he slept peacefully, without the occasional moans he so often emitted. Duke hoped his boy was dreaming of making shoestring catches in centerfield on a day when the sun was high overhead and sweat ran down his back.

By the time Duke walked back across the asphalt parking lot, the gray sky had started to break up, and spotty shafts of sunlight filtered down between the clouds. The west wind was shoving the clouds over the West Virginia hills, and the incoming air was crisp, free of the steel-mill pollutants that would again begin to fall when the wind died. He pulled out of the Heinzmann parking lot, turned left, and traveled down Lincoln Avenue before turning right on Wilson Avenue, a twisted, two-lane strip of asphalt that linked Steubenville and Mingo Junction away from the river. Those who used it regularly called the road, "the back door." At the southernmost edge of Steubenville was Antrim Park, a three-acre parcel that had been deeded to the city by the estate of Frederick Quincy Antrim. It was hardly big enough to create a park of any size, so the city had put in a small playground, some picnic tables, a shelter house, four tennis courts, and two basketball courts. Duke pulled into the gravel parking lot, laced up a pair of black Chuck Taylor All-Stars, strapped on a knee brace, and retrieved the basketball that had been rolling around on the floor of the passenger side of the Jeep.

Every winter and summer, Duke was approached to play on one of the local adult league teams. Some had even offered him under-the-table cash for his services. He always politely declined. He wanted to play. The competitive fire still burned, and Duke missed the game terribly. But reality was part of the equation. He knew he wasn't the player he had once been. He had undergone two surgeries after high school, and his right knee was a sad patchwork of metal, plastic, and scar tissue. The brace helped secure the joint, but his knee would never survive the pounding of actual games. If he couldn't compete at the level where he had once been, Duke Ducheski would rather not play.

Still, he loved stopping by Antrim on afternoons when the courts were empty and he could be alone with the ball and the hoop. Duke still had the eye, and he could burn hours draining shot after shot from all points on the court. There were few things he found as satisfying as the sound of the ball sailing cleanly through the rim and rippling the cords. The release was refreshing. For a few hours, he wasn't mired in a bad marriage or the caregiver of a mentally and physically handicapped son. Rather, he was simply a guy doing the thing he did best—draining the jumper.

Duke had been at the court for a half hour and was just working up a good sweat when he heard the sound of gravel crunching under tires. Moonie pulled into the parking lot in his 1983 Ford Fairmont—his beater car. He exited and slowly limped toward the courts.

"Hey, buddy," Duke said. "Welcome back. Where's your motorcycle? You ought to be taking advantage of the sunshine."

Moonie didn't answer. As Duke's old friend got closer, he could see that Moonie looked pale and tired. His cheeks were sunken, his pallor the color of cigarette ash, and the tendons between his neck and shoulders stretched like bridge cables.

"Jesus, Moonie, you look whipped. It must have been a hell of a week in Vegas."

"I didn't go to Vegas," he said. He broke eye contact and grabbed the end of a picnic table and eased himself onto the seat. Duke tucked the ball under an arm and walked toward him. "I gotta talk to you, Duke. I need your help." Moonie's voice cracked, as though he was on the verge of tears, and he began to shake—a nervous, uncontrollable quiver.

"What's wrong? Where've you been, Moonie?"

"I've been holed up at the Arlington Motel, that little place on Route 22, just outside of Tonidale."

A chill raced up Duke's spine and exploded into his shoulders and neck as he realized that Tony DeMarco's suspicions may have been right. "Why? Were you hiding?"

Moonie nodded. "I'm in trouble, Duke. Big-time trouble."

"Do you still have your room there?"

Moonie nodded.

"Can you make it back?"

"I think so."

"Okay, let's go. I'll follow you."

The Arlington Motel was a run-down, rent-by-the-hour shack just over the Pennsylvania line, east of the West Virginia panhandle, and not twenty-five minutes from the playground. In its day, the Arlington had been a nice motel with a pool in the middle of a horseshoe court of rooms. When the new four-lane road bypassed the Arlington, business dropped and the motel was sold several times, falling further into disrepair with each successive sale. The pool had been filled, and a weedy thicket of dandelions and foxtail grew inside a chain-link fence that was entwined with poison ivy. The frame building was sagging under its own weight; it was in desperate need of a major overhaul, or a bulldozer.

Duke followed Moonie into the room and winced at the pungent odor, a rancid combination of blood, decaying flesh, human tang, and greasy fast food. "Goddamn, Moonie, how can you stand it in here?"

"You'll get used to it after a couple of minutes."

"I hope not."

A heap of gauze and towels, fouled with the brackish crimson of dried blood, were heaped in the trash can in the corner. The bedsheets, too, were stained with blood. The flea market–grade furniture was littered with bandages and tape, salves and creams, scissors and cotton balls, and a week's worth of empty beer cans and fast-food bags. This was a highly unusual environment for Duke's usually fastidious friend.

"Christ almighty, Moonie, what the hell is going on?"

"I need help, Dukie." His strength seemed to be waning by the minute. He limped to the side of the bed and gingerly sat on its edge. He unhitched his pants and pulled them down to his knees. His right thigh was swollen, bruised, and covered with gauze and an elastic bandage. Body fluid and blood were dried on the beige elastic.

"Have you been to the doctor?"

"No."

Duke recalled his friend's unnatural fear of needles. During the construction of Fort Logan, Moonie stepped on a honey-locust thorn—as big as a sixteen-penny nail and needle sharp—and ran it through his foot. It exited the top of his PF Flyers, an inch behind his middle toe. Angel gagged and about fainted at the sight of the bloody protrusion, which came up through a shoelace. Moonie sat on the hillside, held his breath, and pulled the thorn free. He made us promise not to tell his mom, because even though he was the toughest kid in our class, he was terrified of needles and afraid she would make him get a tetanus shot. Instead, he tried to doctor it with some spit, gauze, and duct tape. Three days later, he had a roaring infection and ended up in the emergency room, loony with fever and a foot swollen three times its normal size. He was then the recipient of a battery of injections, one of which, of course, was for tetanus.

Slowly, Moonie unwrapped the bandage, revealing black and green and purple skin, in the middle of which was a badly infected wound.

Duke held his hands before his face in a prayer-like clasp. "Is that a bullet hole?"

Moonie nodded.

In a painful instant, Duke realized that Moonie's right leg was the least of his problems. Moonie lifted his shirt and peeled away a gauze strip that was held down with athletic tape. A partially healed cut extended across his chest, several inches below his nipples. The line was red and swollen and, Duke assumed, also infected.

"I thought I could doctor these up and get back to normal if I took a week off work and took care of it myself. They've just gotten worse, and I'm supposed to be back on the job in the morning. I don't know what to do."

"You've got a bad infection there, Moonie. If we don't get you to a doctor, you could lose that leg." Duke stepped to the edge of the bed and leaned down for a closer look. The rancid odor of rotting flesh was overwhelming. "Wait here."

Duke walked across the parking lot to the pay phone outside the motel office and made a collect call to Cara. "You never call collect," she said. "What's wrong? Are you okay?"

"I'm fine. It's Moonie. Look, Cara, I hate to ask you to do this, but I desperately need you to come to the Arlington Motel in Tonidale."

"Up by Pittsburgh?"

"Yes, and I need you to bring enough medical supplies to treat a couple of badly infected wounds."

"What kind of wounds?"

"Please don't ask me any questions on the phone. I'll explain when you get here. I'll be in room twelve."

She agreed, although reluctantly. It would take her an hour, since she had to run the kids over to her mother's. Duke was grateful, especially considering the fragile state of their relationship.

When Duke got back to the motel room, Moonie was still sitting on the side of the bed, rocking. "Cara's coming up, but you're probably going to end up in the hospital," Duke said.

"I hope not."

Duke grabbed a cooler—the green Coleman that Moonie took on his fishing trips—from the corner of the room, and took a seat five feet from Moonie. "Okay, partner, start at the beginning."

CHAPTER TWELVE

Eight days earlier, Moonie sat in a booth at the Oasis, slowly rolling an Iron City longneck between his palms. Between his elbows on a paper plate the size of a saucer were two pickled eggs that he had plucked from the jar on the bar. He was carrying a knot in his gut that was making it difficult to choke down his beer. Moonie's gaze traversed between the black-and-white broadcast of the eleven o'clock news in one corner of the bar and a beer sign in the other, where light scrolling behind a black screen gave the hypnotic illusion of exploding fireworks. He had seven dollars in his pocket and $14.59 in his checking account. Twenty-one dollars and fifty-nine cents, and it had to last him until Friday. He was, by his own painfully honest assessment, an imbecile. He told himself as much earlier that evening as he was leaving the horse track after his "sure thing" finished a strong eleventh. He sat in his car, thumped his head twice on the steering wheel, and said, "Moonie Collier, you are a flaming dumb-ass."

Now there was no way out of his debt to Carmine except to sell his most prized possession—the Indian motorcycle that he had painstakingly refurbished. Outside of his house, it was his only possession of any value. He owed Carmine two thousand dollars. Monday morning, first thing, he would go in and tell Carmine that he would have the money by week's end. There were several co-workers in the mill who would be interested in buying the Indian. He was in such desperate financial straits that he would have to take whatever they offered, which was certain to be far less than the bike was worth, but more than enough to cover his debt to Carmine.

In a lifetime of bad bets, none was as bad as the $1,250 he had plunked down on Muckraker's Pen. Moonie had pooled what he had left from his previous check, combined that with $812 he had in his savings account and the loose bills and change he had been stuffing into an old water jug at home. It was, after all, "a sure thing." Moonie had reacted in typical fashion to a tip he had received from a fellow electrician at the mill. The co-worker had told him about Muckraker's Pen, which was being handled by a new trainer, who was the friend of the co-worker's cousin. "The odds are gonna be high, and this bad boy is gonna smoke the field," he had told Moonie, who had been salivating over the potential winnings for a week leading up to the race.

Muckraker's Pen left the gate a seventeen-to-one long shot, and he didn't disappoint. He was running sixth into the first turn, eighth down the back stretch, and tenth heading into the final turn. He faded down the stretch and nosed out You Betcha for eleventh place.

This was the first time that his gambling habits had really gotten Moonie in trouble. He had gotten into hock with Carmine numerous times, but he had always been able to get himself back in the black, if only temporarily. He had no money left to gamble, and he knew he was out of time. Carmine had his limits, and Moonie knew he was pushing them.

It was just after 11:30 when the door to the Oasis opened and Frankie "the Troll" Silvestri limped in. The silhouette of a misshapen head on a too-small body was cast against a moonless night. For a moment, the Troll stood in the doorway, a dirty, tan raincoat hitched at the waist; the blue duffel bag at his side. Moonie lowered his head and watched the carbonation bubbles make their way up his beer bottle as the Troll passed— his horrid body odor lingering—and made his way to the office behind the kitchen, where a safe containing the wagers were kept. Moonie shifted sideways in his bench and watched highlights of college football games on the sports news. A few minutes later, the Troll emerged from the office, limped quickly through the bar, and left.

There are moments when a person's life is forever changed in that millisecond of time between when a misguided neuron flashes an electrochemical signal from the frontal lobe and the body takes action. This is the instant when fate and unintended consequences are set in motion. The snowflakes atop the mountain intertwine, catch a tiny gust of wind, roll, and manifest themselves into a thundering avalanche.

In the case of Theodore "Moonie" Collier, this defining moment occurred when his brain told him to set his beer on the table and follow the Troll out of the Oasis.

There was an awful roil in Moonie's belly—four beers, pickled eggs, a knot caused by a bad night at the track and the realization that it was going to cost him his beloved Indian motorcycle, and an acidic burn caused by misguided anger at Duke. *He always thinks he's so damn smart*, Moonie thought as he slipped out of the booth. Moonie could handle his own affairs. He didn't need Duke Ducheski telling him what he could and couldn't do. If he wanted to work for the Antonelli family, then, goddammit, he would go work for the Antonelli family. He was, after all, still the strongest son of a bitch at Wheeling-Pittsburgh Steel. He would work hard and keep his mouth shut. What other qualities did you need to be a bagman? So long as he didn't have to kill anyone, why shouldn't he work for the Antonellis? It would be a good job. And it might get him off the hook for the two bills he owed.

Those were the thoughts pulsing through Moonie's meager brain when the door of the Oasis closed behind him.

Moonie walked across Commercial Street and kept his eye on the Troll, who opened the trunk of the Lincoln and dropped the duffel bag inside. Out of habit, the Troll stood by the door of his car for a few seconds and surveyed the landscape, then slipped behind the wheel and drove south, out of town. Although a car got between them, Moonie could see the taillights of the Lincoln as it went through the S turn at the south end of the business district. He kept his Ford Fairmont several hundred yards back. He would wait until the Troll made his next stop so he could talk to him in private. He didn't want anyone—Duke, in particular—to see them talking. Maybe, Moonie reasoned, the Troll could get him access to Antonelli.

The Troll drove through Deandale and south on old Ohio Route 7, never going more than thirty miles an hour. As Moonie suspected, the Troll turned right on Georges Run Road and headed west on the winding road toward New Alexandria. Moonie lagged back. A light rain had started coming in from the west, providing him additional cover. Two miles beyond New Alexandria was the La Casa Grande—"the Grand," to the locals—a cement-block beer joint that sat near the entrance to the Adena Valley Mining Company's Mine No. 7. The Grand did a huge business from the coal miners, and it was the Troll's last stop of the night.

At the top of New Alexandria hill, just beyond the sprawling cemetery that covered the entire northern hillside, the Troll turned the Lincoln to the right, away from his usual route to La Casa Grande, and hit the gas, his taillights quickly disappearing over the hill towards Goulds Creek. Moonie did the same.

Despite the mist, the Lincoln kicked up enough dust on the gravel road that Moonie could follow his trail until the air cleared near the entrance to the old Tarr's Hill Mine, a deep-shaft operation that closed in the late fifties.

"Where in the hell is he going?" Moonie asked aloud. He stopped the car, turned down the radio, and rolled down his window, listening into darkness. He could hear nothing beyond the clattering of his own engine.

Making a move that someone with more brains and fewer beers might not have made, Moonie pointed his Fairmont up the old dirt road, which was barely more than a path worn through the woods by coal trucks, but now maintained by the traffic of young lovers seeking privacy. Dewy weeds drooped from both sides of the muddy roadway and slid along the sides of the car like so many paint brushes. The sides of the path were rutted and deep; the center was covered with high grass and weeds that appeared in the headlights, then rolled under the bumper. Honey locusts and maples and oaks sagged overhead, creating a dark tunnel of vegetation.

The road ended at a wooden bridge that spanned the Indian Hill & Iron Rail tracks, a short-line railroad that shuttled coal cars between the power plant in Brilliant and Broadway Station. The road split beyond the bridge, with one leg going hard north to the old mine and the lower leg snaking east, around the hill, to the abandoned sand quarry where Moonie had swum as a boy. As he came out of the clearing, Moonie could see the Troll's Lincoln on the quarry road just beyond the bridge.

Moonie pulled up on the bridge, edging forward until his rear tires rested on the wooden timbers. He hit the high beams and stared at the abandoned car through the light rain. After a few minutes, Moonie turned off the engine and lights, opened the driver's-side door, and stood, keeping one foot on the bridge and the other inside the car. There was no sign of the Troll.

It then occurred to Moonie that he had probably followed the Troll to a rendezvous spot. What had he been thinking? It was a very bad decision to follow the Troll, and Moonie decided to back out of the mud road and go home. He would sell the Indian motorcycle and be done with it. It was in that instant, just before he stepped back into the car, that the pungent odor of the Troll hit him, and Moonie felt the barrel of a revolver press into the base of his skull. He groaned, bracing for the moment when a bullet would enter his brain.

"Trying to rob me, motherfucker?"

Moonie didn't move. "No, sir."

"Don't lie to me. Why else would you be tailin' me?"

"I . . . I just wanted to talk to you. That's all. I wanted to ask you for a job."

The response surprised even the Troll, who snorted. "A job . . . what kind of bullshit story is that?"

"I'm serious. I want to work for Mr. Antonelli, and I thought you could help me out, you know, talk to him for me, put in a good word, or something."

"Yeah, I'm going to help you out." He pushed the revolver harder into Moonie's head. "You're that Moon Pie, ain't ya? I thought I saw you at the Oasis. I looked at Carmine's books tonight. You owe us a lot of money, fat boy. What were you going to do, rob me and pay Mr. Antonelli back with his own money?"

"No, really, listen, honest to God, I wasn't trying to rob you. I just wanted to get a job and . . ."

"Enough of the bullshit. Pull your keys out of the ignition and very slowly set them on the roof of your car." Moonie did as he was ordered. The Troll snatched the keys with his free hand and shoved them in his pants pocket. From the bottom of Tarr's Hill, Moonie could hear the howl of a train whistle as it echoed through the hollow. The bridge vibrated as the grind of the diesel strained against the grade. "Start walkin'. Get over there by my car."

"Really, Mr. Silvestri, I just wanted a job."

"If that's true, you're a moron."

Moonie took a frustrated breath and exhaled. "Yeah, so I've been told."

Moonie was smart enough to know the Troll intended to kill him. As they walked across the bridge toward the Lincoln, the Troll pressed the barrel of his gun into Moonie's spine. Moonie remembered from his self-defense training in the army that you should never hold a gun against a prisoner. This can enable a captive to make a move faster than you can squeeze the trigger. It was his only chance. Several feet from the car, as his left foot hit the ground just beyond the bridge, Moonie spun to his heel and jabbed with his right hand. The blow glanced off the Troll's ample forehead. The Troll fired. Flames shot from the barrel of the .44 Magnum, exploding like a cannon near Moonie's right ear and rupturing his eardrum. Moonie grabbed the gun with his left hand and twice pounded the Troll's nose with his right fist. It squished like eggs hitting a floor; the cartilage cracked, and blood spilled from the nostrils.

Another punch sent the Troll reeling backward. Off-balance, he fired again, this time hitting Moonie on the inside of his right leg. It just missed his balls and tore away a hunk of flesh on his inner thigh. Moonie again reached for the revolver with his left hand and dropped his right elbow between the Troll's eyes, and they tumbled in a heap onto the heavy wooden timbers of the bridge decking. He twice slammed the Troll's gun hand into the wood, and an errant shot was launched into the night. Moonie pinned the Troll against the deck and with both hands wrestled the gun from him.

As blood was running down his pants, Moonie jumped up and backed away, pointing the revolver at its owner.

"Goddammit, I told you, I wasn't trying to rob you," Moonie screamed.

He released the cylinder and emptied the chambers of the remaining shells into his hand. He threw them over one side of the bridge and the gun over the other. He took a breath and looked down at his leg. Blood was covering the crotch of his blue jeans.

An instant after he threw away the gun, Moonie realized the gravity of his mistake. Slowly, the Troll stood and smiled as he wiped at his bloody nose with the back of a hand.

"I still don't believe you," the Troll said.

He reached to his ankle and from a leather sheath produced a knife with a locking blade and holes in the handle, into which he slipped his fingers. When he unfolded the blade and it locked in place, it extended a glimmering eight inches. "You're dumber than you look for not killing me."

Moonie groaned at the sight of the huge blade. The weapon's design was dual in purpose. The holes in the handle enabled it to be used like brass knuckles in a fight. The other purpose was obvious. The Troll rolled the blade around and made a few slashing motions as raindrops hit the glinting steel.

"My God," Moonie said. "What are you, a walking aerosol?"

The Troll frowned. "Aerosol?"

"Yeah, one of those places where they keep guns and ammo and stuff."

"*Arsenal*, you fucking idiot. Christ, you're too stupid to live!" He started walking slowly toward Moonie. "Do you have any kids?"

"No."

The Troll slashed at Moonie, who easily evaded the blade. "Good. Mankind will thank me for killing you before you have a chance to bring more dumb-asses into the world." He slashed again, this time slicing Moonie's upper midsection with the tip of the knife.

Moonie ran, with his hand pressed to the bleeding wound, and limped to the other side of his car. The Troll couldn't run with his bad leg, so the only way he was going to catch Moonie was if he collapsed from lack of blood.

On the driver's side of the Fairmont stood the Troll, with blood still running out of his busted nose and onto his yellow teeth as he smiled. On the passenger side was his prey, scared, admittedly stupid, bleeding from his torso and thigh, his right ear throbbing from the gun blast.

While keeping an eye on the Troll, Moonie took a bandana from his hip pocket and tied it around his bleeding thigh, staunching the blood flow. "Listen, I know you don't believe me, but isn't there any way we can work this out?" Moonie asked.

The Troll nodded. "Sure there is."

"There is?"

"Sure. I can give you some choices, if that's what you like."

"Okay."

"I slit your throat."

Moonie shook his head. "I don't think I like that one."

"Okay," he said. "How about I give you your keys and you just drive on out of here?"

"I like that one a little better. What's the catch?"

"No catch. You just get in your car and leave. Of course, I'm going to tell Mr. Antonelli what you did tonight, and that will anger him greatly. You know what happened to the last guy who tried to rip off Mr. Antonelli? He got castrated with a pair of tin snips. It only took him a couple minutes to bleed out, but it's still not a good way to go. I'd be doing you a favor by slitting your throat."

Moonie took a breath. "Do I have any other choices?"

"Yeah. You can come out here and fight like a man. Maybe you'll get lucky and kill me and no one will find out. And, you get to keep the money."

"But I don't want to kill you."

"This whole concept of what's going on here is escaping you, isn't it, dumb-ass? Understand this: Only one of us is going to walk off the bridge."

"But, I . . ."

Fire flashed in the Troll's eyes and he jammed the knife into the front, driver's-side whitewall of the Fairmont. It hissed as an empty coal train passed beneath them.

"Hey, no, okay, okay, stop it, I'm coming."

The Troll backed up toward the middle of the bridge, grinning that constant, evil smile, blood smearing his teeth. Moonie stepped around the front of the car and into the open.

"This isn't very fair," Moonie said. "You've got a knife."

"You had a gun. You should have kept it." The Troll waved the fingers on his left hand at Moonie, beckoning him forward. "Say your prayers and step on out here."

The Troll stepped forward and slashed at air. He was much quicker than Moonie would have guessed. He used his good leg as a base, and lashed forward on the shorter leg. Moonie kept moving, watching, glancing to the ground in hopes of finding some kind of weapon.

The Troll charged forward again, the knife extended like he was making a saber charge. Moonie sidestepped the attack and grabbed the Troll's sinewy wrist with both hands. As they struggled, the Troll used his left hand to pound the side of Moonie's face. Moonie drove his shin into the Troll's balls. It was a clean and painful shot. The Troll winced but held tight to the knife, his fingers intertwined in the holes in the handle.

As empty coal cars of the train below rumbled on, Moonie brought his forehead down into the middle of the Troll's face, pounding the pulpy mass of a nose. The Troll pushed hard at Moonie's face, trying to dig a thumbnail into his eye. But Moonie forced his right forearm under the Troll's chin and ran forward two steps, pushing him backward and releasing his grip.

For years, the mining company had covered the bridge with creosote, an oil-based wood preservative. In the rain, the oil pooled in little slicks atop the water. When the Troll backpedaled, his deformed leg slid on the creosote. His momentum carried him back until his calves pressed hard against the short, wooden guardrail that lined the bridge. He couldn't catch himself. The inertia that would carry him over the side of the bridge could not be stopped.

In that moment, Frankie "the Troll" Silvestri knew he was going to die. The weight of his upper body began to slowly lose the battle against gravity. He struggled to stay upright, his arms parallel to the bridge railing and swinging in circular motions, the blade still glinting in his right hand. In the instant before he dropped, he instinctively stretched out his left hand, a silent and unrealistic plea for help. The hand was less than a foot from Moonie; he could have easily grabbed the Troll and pulled him back from the edge. But, at last, Moonie Collier understood. Only one of them would survive the night.

The Troll made a guttural grunt and started over backward. His deformed leg left the ground first, followed an instant later by the good one. He said, in a calm and accepting tone, "Shit."

Despite the darkness between the hills, Moonie could see the Troll fall, his arms flailing and his legs kicking. It was thirty feet to the roadbed. He dropped headfirst, striking the back of one passing coal car and then the front of the next. It was too dark for Moonie to see where the Troll had landed, but he assumed he had fallen into one of the empty coal cars that were now lumbering away. This was a problem, as Moonie's car keys were in the pants pocket of the recently deceased. There was another key on top of his refrigerator, but that was going to be a long walk, particularly with a hunk of flesh taken out of his leg.

From the edge of the bridge, he stood and watched, bleeding and waiting. As the last coal car passed, Moonie scanned the darkness, finally spotting a crumpled mass in the middle of the tracks. "Oh, thank you, Jesus," he said aloud, hobbling to the end of the bridge and moving sideways down the weedy embankment to the tracks.

The body of the Troll was chest-down in the middle of the tracks. He had landed diagonally, his neck and right arm pressed against one rail. The corpse was headless; the right hand, with its fingers still in the holes of the knife handle, was lying in the ballast outside the rails. Blood covered the rails, ties, and ballast.

"Oh, Mother of Christ," Moonie said, taking a step back from the body and gagging back a salty bile that filled his throat. He stared at the body parts for several minutes, afraid to look at the bottom of the ballast where the head must rest.

"I hope you died with your eyes closed, you ugly turd," Moonie said, wobbling and nauseated from the blood loss—both his and the Troll's. He took two deep breaths and looked down the side of the gravel ballast to where it scattered into a thicket of wild raspberries. What he saw scared him more than a headless Frankie Silvestri.

Nothing.

"This is not good," he muttered. The large, misshapen head that had scared children and adults alike was nowhere to be found. He walked to where the gravel met the thicket and peered into the bramble. Still, nothing.

Moonie walked slowly down the tracks, squinting into the raspberries. A raccoon ran out of the brush, causing him to jump backward and nearly fall. He limped twenty yards down the tracks, then back, pacing slowly between the rails. As he neared the body, he turned and scanned the other side of the tracks. Again, nothing.

"Crap," he yelled, twice kicking the corpse in the ribs. "This is all your fault, you freak." He kicked him once more, then sat down on the rail. "No, Moonie, it's your fault. What the hell were you thinkin'?"

The rain fell harder, soaking his jeans and causing the bloodstain to spread.

"I am so screwed. Could this get any worse?" He laughed and nodded. "Of course it could. You're Moonie Collier. You can always make it worse."

He was about to find out how right he was.

It began with an almost-indiscernible tingle in his loins. It lingered there for a minute, a somewhat-soothing feeling, before Moonie realized the tingling was the result of the vibrating rails. Another train was heading his way. As the westbound train of empty coal cars cleared Broadway Station three miles to the west, an eastbound coal train was idling on the siding. When the westbound train had cleared the siding, the eastbound train had been given the green light. The sharp light of the engine's head beam was peering from around the bend in the tracks, illuminating the trees and the carved rock ledge several hundred yards from Moonie.

"Shit, shit, shit!" he yelled, leaping to his feet. He grabbed the left ankle of the Troll with his right hand and reached for the severed hand with the other. For a moment, he hesitated and pulled his hand back. "No time to be squeamish, Moonie." He grabbed the blunt side of the blade that was still attached to the hand and started running backward, dragging the body by the ankle as it bounced on the ties. Moonie had only taken a few steps when his heel caught on the rail. As he fell backward, the hand and knife flew from his grasp, landing in the weeds. Moonie crashed on his tailbone and rolled down the ballast. The diesel was making the turn. He grabbed an ankle with both hands and ran up the embankment, the corpse flopping and trailing blood.

He struggled to get the body out of sight, dragging it under the bridge and hiding it behind a heavy growth of fountain grass and thistle. Moonie dropped to the ground behind the corpse as the head beam lit the bridge and the surrounding embankment. Lying on his back, head-to-toe next to the Troll, Moonie sucked in air. The loaded train groaned past, its axles squeaking under the weight.

When the engine had passed from sight, Moonie raised himself to his elbows. "You're not so damn tough now that you don't have a head, are you?" Moonie asked the Troll. "Yeah, you ugly turd, you thought you'd do mankind a favor, huh? Thought you'd kill me, huh? Guess not. You're dead; I'm not. What do you got to say about that? Nothin'. You know why? 'Cause you can't talk, 'cause you're dead and you got no head, which is an improvement over that God-ugly puss of yours. You know what else? You smell like a pile of horse shit." Moonie pushed himself to his feet. "Just lay there and keep your mouth shut. That shouldn't be a problem."

He stared at the stars, listening to the rhythmic clicking of the wheels over the track joints. His lip had gone numb, but the knife and bullet wounds burned like hell. His right ear throbbed. He used his fingers to probe the bullet hole in his thigh. It had ripped out a hunk of flesh the size of a silver dollar. He didn't move from behind the weeds until the train had been gone several minutes. Finally, he stood and looked down at the corpse.

"I'll be back in a minute. Don't go anywhere."

He limped back down the hill and into the weeds. The hand and knife had landed near a surface vein of coal, and Moonie found them in a few minutes. Once he located them, he stepped on the palm and wiggled the handle off the fingers. He folded the blade into the handle and slipped the knife into his back pocket. With his index finger and thumb, Moonie pinched the tip of the middle finger of the severed hand. He carried it halfway up the embankment and threw it up on the bridge.

"Thanks for waiting," he said. "Good news. I found your hand. I wish I could have found your ugly head." He grabbed the Troll's ankles and dragged the corpse to the rear of the Lincoln. There, he reached into the Troll's front pants pocket and fished around for two sets of car keys. "I'm going to borrow your ride, Trollman."

In the trunk of the Troll's car, Moonie found the familiar canvas bag that the Troll carried on his rounds. Moonie unzipped it and found more money than he had ever seen in his life. It was stuffed full of stacks of bills and receipts, each held together with rubber bands and paperclips.

"You don't need this, do you?" he asked the body lying by the back bumper. After a moment of silence: "I'll take that as a no." He limped back to his Fairmont and put the cash in his trunk.

Back at the Lincoln, he lifted the corpse into the trunk, then tossed in the severed hand. "I guess this is good-bye," he said, slamming the trunk closed.

Moonie drove the Lincoln toward the quarry and parked the idling car at the top of a small incline above a concrete abutment that once supported a large dredging line. It was twenty feet from the abutment to the water's surface. The water was at least eighty feet deep off the edge. Moonie made sure that the car was lined up, put his right foot on the brake, reached inside and pulled the gearshift into drive, and jumped back. The vehicle rolled down the grade, picking up speed as it went. After the front tires cleared the abutment, sparks flew when the bottom of the Lincoln scraped concrete before plunging nose-first into the water. Moonie walked to the abutment and watched as the car bobbed several times before the taillights disappeared into the depths.

A night of fighting for his life, being shot and cut, had left Moonie exhausted and weak. Fortunately, the bleeding had mostly stopped, though his entire leg was going numb from the makeshift tourniquet. Unfortunately, his work was not done. He returned to the Fairmont, moved it back into the brush, out of view of any train engineers, and was just finishing changing the punctured tire as the first rays of sun started to illuminate the hills. Another empty westbound train passed as he tightened the last lug nut. When the train had disappeared around the bend, Moonie struggled down the hillside and in the light of morning located the head of Frankie "the Troll" Silvestri in a patch of cattails in the marshy lowland near the ballast, about ten feet from the track. Much to Moonie's dismay, it was face up, the eyes open and still set in a hateful squint.

CHAPTER THIRTEEN

Duke stared at his old friend in what he knew was a look of slack-jawed disbelief. Even by Moonie's standards, this was an incredible story.

"By now you realize that asking for a job to work off a gambling debt is generally not an accepted business practice with the Mafia?" Duke asked.

Moonie nodded. "When I pitched his gun over the bridge and he still wouldn't listen to me, I knew I was in deep shit."

"Imagine that. So, after you found his head, what did you do?"

"Puked. I got about halfway home, and I had to pull over and heave. I couldn't get his stink out of my nostrils. Dealing with that body in the dark wasn't that bad, but looking at that gross head in the daylight was more than I could handle."

"What did you do with it?"

"I grabbed it by the hair and threw it in the trunk. I tried to wedge it in the corner with my tool box, but it got loose and I could hear it rolling around all over the place coming down New Alexandria Road."

Duke buried his face in his hands. "You put his head in the trunk of your car?"

"Where else was I going to put it? I didn't want that nasty thing rolling around in the front seat with me."

"Okay, but why did you keep it? Why didn't you just bury it or throw it in the quarry?"

"First of all, Duke, let's remember that I'd been *shot*. I'd lost a lot of blood, and I wasn't thinkin' too clear. Besides, I didn't have a shovel and I didn't have the time. The sun was coming up, and I looked like I'd been working in a slaughterhouse—my blood, his blood. I'll tell you, Duke, no matter how hard you try, you can't drag around a guy who's had his head and hand cut off without getting covered with blood."

"I'll take your word for it. Why didn't you just throw his head in the quarry?"

"Since you think you're so damned smart, let me ask you this: Does a human head float?"

"I don't know."

"Neither do I, and I didn't want to throw it in the quarry and then have it bobbing around like some kind of fishing lure."

"So, what did you end up doing with it?"

Moonie swallowed.

"The head, Moonie? What did you do with the Troll's head?"

Moonie looked at his old friend for several seconds, gnawing on his lower lip. "Nothin'."

"What do you mean, 'nothing'? Don't tell me that thing is still rotting in the back of your car."

Moonie swallowed. "No. Actually, you're sitting on it."

Slowly, Duke looked down at the triangular section of the green cooler between his crotch and thighs, then back at Moonie. "The head of Frankie Silvestri is in this cooler?"

Moonie nodded. "Yeah, but it's packed real good in ice. Real good. Frozen solid, pretty near. I put fresh ice in two, three times a day."

Slowly and with no small amount of dread, Duke stood and unlatched the lid of the cooler. Beneath several inches of cubes was a mass of black hair, below which protruded the mangled nub of a neck. "I turned him facedown," Moonie said. "It was creepin' me out, lookin' at his face every time I opened the lid."

Duke's gasp was audible, like a man who has been gut-punched, and he slammed the lid closed and took a deep breath. A headache was in its infancy behind his left eye; the roar in his ears sounded like jet turbines winding up for takeoff. "Jesus H. Christ, Moonie, were you planning to have it mounted?"

"No, goddammit. Every time I came up with an idea of how to

dump it, I came up with another reason not to. I was afraid of getting caught."

"So, the smart thing to do was to keep it preserved in a cooler in your hotel room?"

"I figured you could help me with this one. You've always got good ideas."

"In all the years you've known me, Moonie, how many bodies have I dumped?"

Duke paced the room, trying to come up with a solution to the myriad of problems Moonie was facing, not the least of which was Tony DeMarco. He looked at his watch. He regretted dragging Cara into the mess. Across the room he spotted a folding knife on the night stand. "That . . . isn't . . . ?"

"The Troll's knife? Yep."

"You kept it?"

"It's a nice knife. Besides, the little bastard laced open my chest and tried to kill me with it."

"So you thought you'd take a trophy?"

Moonie shrugged. "Spoils of war."

"I'm venturing into uncharted territory, here, Moonie, but I think one of the fundamental rules of killing someone and not getting caught requires you to get rid of all evidence linking you to the deceased."

"I thought about that, but, hell, I killed an Antonelli bagman and stole their money—how upset are they going to get over taking his knife?"

"Where's the money?"

"Under my bed."

"How much?"

"Fifty-eight thousand, three hundred and twelve dollars."

"No way."

"Trust me, Duke, I'm no math wizard, but I've had a lot of time on my hands and I've counted it a dozen times."

Duke pulled the cooler across the linoleum floor and slid it under a battered desk, then began picking up the trash strewn around the room and stuffing it into some empty fast-food bags. "When Cara gets here, you're not to mention anything about the Troll or . . ." He looked at his friend. "Or, anything. Let me do the talking. We clear?"

Moonie nodded. "She's going to want to know how it happened."

"I know. When she asks, I'll tell her . . ."

"Tell her what?"

"A lie. I'll tell her a big, fat, throbbing lie. Of course, she'll know it's a lie, but she's solid and won't ask a lot of questions." Duke continued to run around the room, cleaning and straightening. "How did this place get to be such a disaster? Don't you have housekeeping service?"

"At this place? The no-tell motel? I'm lucky to have running water."

Cara arrived an hour and fifteen minutes after Duke had called her. She carried an overnight suitcase, in which was the equivalent of a small pharmacy. Moonie was propped up in the bed, a sheet covering him from the waist down. He was exhausted and wan.

Duke had been watching for Cara and opened the door upon her approach. Her lips were tight, and the tiny lines that ran away from her eyes were stretched taut and white. She set the overnight case on the edge of the bed and looked at the slash wound on Moonie's chest. She gently touched the tender area around the gash and asked, "Do I want to know how this happened?"

Duke walked around to the other side of the bed and said, "Moonie has a girlfriend in Wellsburg. She's married. He went over to see her about a week ago and her husband came home. He had a gun and . . ."

Cara put up a palm and shook her head. "Duke, stop right there," she said. "That way, you won't have to continue to lie, and I won't have to be pissed at you for trying to shove a line of total bullshit down my throat."

"Fair enough. Show her your leg, Moonie."

Moonie pulled back the sheets and revealed his right thigh, swollen and bright red. There was no sign of shock or disbelief on her face. She spent several minutes inspecting the bullet wound. She pushed at a couple of places, and Moonie jumped both times. "When did this happen?"

"A week ago last night."

She looked around the room. "Do you have any towels that aren't covered with blood?"

"No," Moonie said.

"We need to clean that out. Let's do it in the shower." Cara helped Moonie into the bathroom.

Moonie straddled the edge of the tub, with his injured right leg inside. "I'm probably not going to like this, am I?" he asked.

"You're going to hate it," she said, taking a bottle of hydrogen peroxide from the bag. She poured it over the wound. It bubbled, and Moonie jumped. "Jesus, that hurts worse than getting shot."

She squinted. "I seriously doubt that."

When the bubbles disappeared, she poured again, repeating the procedure until the bottle was empty. The drain fizzed as the hydrogen peroxide percolated in the filthy pipes. She opened a second bottle and cleaned the chest wound. While it had healed much cleaner than the leg, it was still infected and would leave a deep scar.

"You should have gotten some stitches," Cara said.

"I couldn't."

"Why?"

"There were extemporary circumstances."

"*Extenuating* circumstances?" she asked.

"Yeah, whatever the circumstances were, I couldn't go to the doctor."

She walked him back to the bed, cleaned off some dead skin, and dressed and bandaged the wounds. "This has something to do with that guy of Antonelli's that disappeared, doesn't it?" Cara asked.

Moonie looked away and groaned.

"How'd you know about that?" Duke asked.

"One of the doctors who does shifts at Heinzmann said he was on call at the hospital last week when a couple of Antonelli's goons showed up at the hospital morgue. They heard there was a John Doe who died in the emergency room, and they said their cousin had disappeared and wanted to see if it was him."

"I'm assuming it wasn't their boy."

"The John Doe was about eighty and black—not your typical Italian mobster." She smiled and looked up from her work. "Rumor has it that this guy bolted with a bunch of gambling money?" She pulled a syringe from her bag and filled it with an amber fluid, an antibiotic to fight the infection. She rolled Moonie onto his side and buried the needle into his hip, but not with the same gentleness that was her trademark at the convalescent center, where she was known as the Velvet Needle.

Moonie jumped and yelped, "Goddamn, Cara."

She removed the syringe, capped it, and tossed it into the open case, then turned to Duke. "I'm betting that Mr. Collier had something to do with that guy's disappearance. Otherwise, why would he be holed up in this lovely place with bullet and knife wounds?" She shook her head. "Shot by a jealous husband? Is that the best you two could come up with?" Moonie and Duke avoided her glare like errant schoolboys standing before the principal. "I don't suppose I could convince you to go to the hospital and let a doctor look at that leg."

"No, I don't think that would be such a good idea," Moonie said.

She left him enough salve and bandages to change the dressing in the morning and promised to check in on him the following evening. "It's infected, but, surprisingly, you did a moderately good job at doctoring it yourself."

Moonie looked up at Duke and smiled.

"Call in sick for at least two more days." She looked at Duke. "Make sure he eats, and not just hamburgers and French fries. Try to find something with a little nutritional value, and buy him some vitamin C pills and multivitamins."

As Duke walked Cara across the parking lot to her car, she said, "I don't know what the hell is going on here, Duke, but I am not happy about it. I like Moonie and I know he's your friend, but he's a complete and utter idiot, and now he's got you involved." She threw her case in the trunk of the car and climbed behind the wheel. "I love you, Duke, but I'm not willing to put my kids in harm's way for you or anyone else. I don't want Tony DeMarco or any of his compatriots showing up at my house, looking for you."

"He won't. I promise. I would never get you involved."

"You already have." She dropped the car in reverse and started easing back along the gravel drive. "I would like it very much if you didn't get yourself killed."

And she was gone.

CHAPTER FOURTEEN

When Duke was a sophomore at Mingo High School, Ed "Kodiak" Kripinski, a burly, squat senior with a bad attitude and biceps like telephone poles, had taken a disliking to him. This was not good. Kodiak, who earned his ursine nickname for the thicket of hair that covered his chest, back, shoulders, and arms—and was always protruding from the collar of his shirt—was the defending district heavyweight wrestling champion, and not one you wanted on your bad side.

Kodiak had decided that Duke was in need of a severe ass-whipping. It wasn't for anything in particular; he just didn't like Duke Ducheski. Down in the Ohio Valley, that was enough to justify beating someone's ass. Duke was the starting quarterback on the football team and always got his name in the paper. Kripinski was an offensive guard and got mud shoved up his nose every Friday night for the privilege of blocking for Duke. This sat in his craw, because Kripinski thought Duke was a prima donna who didn't like to get his pants dirty. A good beating wouldn't change Duke's attitude, but it would make Kripinski feel better. He came over to Duke's lunch table midway through basketball season, sat down, and said, "I don't like you, Ducheski, and the next time I catch you out of school, I'm gonna kick your ass up between your shoulder blades." He winked. "Just thought you'd like to know."

The odds that Duke would come out on the better end of that matchup were astronomical. Mingo Junction was a small town, but Duke's plan was to make sure Kripinski didn't catch him alone until graduation, then hope he forgot about it.

A couple of weeks after the warning in the cafeteria, the basketball team returned from a game against Martins Ferry, and Duke walked behind the school where he could take the shortcut over the hill to his house. He did not see Kripinski's Pontiac in the parking lot until he heard the door latch open and saw an imposing shadow stretching across the asphalt parking lot. Duke got weak in the knees; this was not a bluff. "Take your jacket off, Ducheski," Kodiak said. "Me and you, we're gonna go."

Before Duke could make a plea for mercy or run back into the school, Moonie Collier walked out of the shadows of the fire escape. "What's the problem here, Dukie?"

Kripinski whipped his head around to see Moonie's silhouette looming large at the edge of the building. "This doesn't involve you, Collier," Kripinski said.

"The hell it don't," Moonie said, walking toward Kripinski. "Duke's my friend. I don't like people messing with my friends." Kripinski was still standing with his hands on his hips when Moonie sucker-punched him, lashing out with a fierce right hand that snapped the cartilage in the senior's nose and knocked him on his rear. Kripinski jumped up, blood running down over his lips and chin.

"Collier, you motherfu—"

Moonie snapped off another punch, this one landing square on Kripinski's mouth, causing him to reel back several steps before sprawling into the jagged barberry bushes that rimmed the parking lot. His upper lip was split below the left nostril, and blood poured from both wounds, covering his chin and dropping onto his varsity jacket. "If you get up, I'll drill you again," Moonie said.

It was the first time in his life that Kodiak Kripinski had been on the losing end of a fight. He wiped away the blood and fought back tears. "You can't protect him forever, Collier."

"The hell I can't. You touch him, ever, and I'll kill you. I swear to Jesus, I will."

Moonie put his hand on Duke's shoulder and led him out of the parking lot. "My car's around the corner. Come on, I'll give you a lift home."

Duke's knees were still wobbly. "What were you doing here?" he asked Moonie. "How'd you know he was waiting for me?"

"Angel told me what he said to you in the cafeteria. I've been keeping an eye on him. He told a couple of his buddies that he was going to jump you tonight after the game. I saw his car parked behind the school and figured he was up to no good."

It was at that moment that Duke truly realized what a tremendous friend he had in Moonie Collier. Moonie had made it his business to watch Kodiak Kripinski and be there when he made his move. That kind of friendship was rare. Moonie had been the most loyal friend Duke had ever known.

For that reason, Duke would never let him hang, even if it involved disposing of a mobster's frozen head.

After Cara left, Duke drove down the road to a diner and got both of them open-faced roast-beef sandwiches over mashed potatoes, along with green beans and milkshakes. As they were eating, Duke pointed at the cooler with a plastic fork and said, "I'm going to take care of that."

"No chance," Moonie said.

"Excuse me?"

"No way you're taking that thing out of here. I got myself into this; I'll get myself out. I appreciate you getting Cara up here to doctor me up, but you're now relieved of duty."

"You're in no condition to dictate terms to anyone, and you're in no condition to get rid of it. I'm doing it."

Moonie wolfed down his dinner like a starving dog. Duke handed him the rest of his meal, and Moonie took it without comment. He said, "If you take that thing out of here, it makes you complacent in the murder."

"*Complicit?*"

He blinked twice and said, "Whatever the right fuckin' word is, I don't want you involved. Look, you're Duke Ducheski, the Duke of Mingo Junction. Everyone loves you, and the restaurant is about ready to open. You don't need this aggravation. If you don't know what happens to it, you won't have to lie."

"But I already know what happened to the rest of him."

"Just let me take care of it, Bo-Peep."

"Can't do it, partner. I'll get rid of it, you get better, and we'll get this entire mess behind us."

"What are you going to do with it?"

Duke shrugged and held up both palms. "I don't know, Moonie. I'm venturing into uncharted territory."

Heading west on Route 22, cutting across the West Virginia panhandle, Duke found he could empathize with his old friend. The mind jumps around when you're driving down the road with a mobster's head sloshing around in your vehicle. Rational thought is replaced by skittish behavior, and ideas for disposal assault the brain with the rapidity of a pinball digit counter clicking off numbers. As he crossed the Fort Steuben Bridge, which spanned the Ohio River between Steubenville, Ohio, and Weirton, West Virginia, potential solutions came to Duke like streaks of tracer ammo shooting across his cerebellum, almost too quick to process. Unfortunately, for every solution he devised, he was able to manufacture a more compelling reason to ignore it.

He pondered sneaking the head into the mill and tossing it into the hopper car that carried iron ore into the blast furnace. The temperature in the belly of a blast furnace can reach 2,300 degrees. The head would dissolve like an ice cube on a hot skillet. However, this option required walking into Wheeling-Pittsburgh Steel with the cooler and somehow sneaking the head into a hopper car. It was far too risky.

The Ohio River offered a wide and deep repository, though he would have to get in a rowboat to get to the middle channel, where the water runs deep and fast. If he added some rocks to the cooler, poked some holes in it, and anchored the lid with some wood screws, it would sink. However, at this point, Tony DeMarco still had to consider the possibility that the Troll had skipped town. That wouldn't be the case if the cooler popped open and the head came bobbing to the surface.

There was an abandoned coal mine shaft, not far from where they had built Fort Logan, where it took a stone ten seconds to hit bottom. Again, Duke would have to park and lug the cooler up the hill. It was probably the most feasible of the plans, but he quickly convinced himself that he would get caught.

A safer option, he thought, would be to buy a twenty-gallon can of carburetor cleaner and let the head soak until it dissolved. The downside was having it inside the garage during the process. It was this last idea that finally slowed down his racing brain. "Carburetor cleaner!" he said aloud. "Jesus H. Christ, Ducheski, get a grip."

Only one point remained clear. Wherever he decided to dispose of the head, there had to be a compelling and logical reason for him to be there.

He turned south onto Ohio Route 7—Dean Martin Boulevard in Steubenville—and kept one eye on the speedometer, making sure he stayed just below the posted limit of thirty-five miles an hour. His palms were slippery on the steering wheel. His stomach roiled. The only logical answer was to bury the head, but where and when? The only answers he came up with were *deep* and *soon*.

He exited at Logan Avenue, one of the most precipitous roads in the valley, extending from Commercial Street to the west side of Mingo Junction. As he climbed the hillside toward the west, Duke assumed that ice water, brain matter, and other bodily fluids were slopping all over the back of the Jeep. It was only then that a plan formulated in his racing brain. He circled around the hilltop and drove down the alley behind his house, nosing the Jeep to the front of the garage. He went inside and rummaged through the rafters for a fishing pole and his dad's old tackle box. He had fishing gear at the cabin, but he didn't have a spade, which he would need in order to bury what was left of the Troll. As he was sliding the fishing gear and spade into the back of the Jeep, Nina walked out on the back porch, her left eye squinting. The interrogation was about to begin.

"What are you doing?" she asked, her arms folded over her chest.

"I'm going fishing."

"This late?"

"They bite at night, Nina."

"Where are you going?"

"To the cabin."

"Where have you been?"

"I went to see Timmy."

"All day?"

"Then I stopped at the park to shoot some hoops." Duke shut the hatch of the Jeep. "I'll be back later."

"Why are you taking a shovel?"

"To dig for night crawlers."

Her eyes turned to slits as thin as dimes. "You're not going *fishing*," she said, her arms still crossed over her ample breasts, and her mouth puckering up as though she was preparing to cough a vile mass from her throat. "You're going to see *her*, aren't you?"

Duke slowly shook his head. He wished he was going to see Cara instead of carrying out his obligation to Moonie. "Give it a rest, Nina. I'm not going to see anyone. I'm going to the cabin to go fishing."

"Don't you lie to me. You're meeting her at the cabin, aren't you?"

"I'm not meeting anyone, except a few unsuspecting bass, hopefully. I'm going fishing, that's all, and I'm going alone."

"You stay away from that filthy whore."

"I'll let you know if they're biting, Nina," he said, sliding into the Jeep. "I'll talk to you later."

She turned and went back into the house, slamming the door behind her so hard the entire jamb shook.

Tucked between the frame and the glass of Duke's dresser mirror was a black-and-white photograph, faintly yellowed and creased across one corner. The two men in the photo are in their early twenties and are standing in front of a massive black-walnut tree that had broken the soil long before the first white man ventured into Ohio. Both men have thick forearms crossed over broad and bare chests. They are pinching cigarettes between their fingers. The taller man, the one with the close-cropped hair, has an index finger down the opening of a Black Label longneck, and his face reflects the seriousness of his life, the sadness that tormented him after Duke's mother died. The face of the shorter one, Duke's Uncle Mel, is dominated by a lopsided grin and the whiskered outline of a heavy beard. A pair of fishing rods are propped against the tree trunk, the lines taut, hooks anchored in the cork handles. A tackle box—the very one that was in the back of Duke's Jeep—rests near their feet.

The photo was taken in the late fifties or early sixties at the family fishing cabin at the Jefferson County Rod & Reel Club near Bloomingdale. Duke's grandfather Ducheski was a charter member of the club and built the cabin in 1935. Uncle Mel died of leukemia two years after the photo was taken, and Duke inherited the cabin—pitiful as it was— after his father died. He had rehabbed it, and Nina and he had spent many happy weekends there early in their marriage. She had a garden out back where she grew tomatoes, green peppers, and cucumbers, the vines of which snaked along the hillside. It was a reminder to Duke that she had once been happy. The club had dissolved decades earlier, and most of the other cabins, like the black-walnut tree, had been reclaimed by the earth. The bass lake remained, though it was now rimmed by cattails and uncontrolled brush; a film of moss the color of limes floated in the shoals. A spillway, situated on the northeast rim of the lake, guided the overflow into Cross Creek through a hundred acres of marsh.

It was in this vernal pool that Duke planned to bury the head of Frankie "the Troll" Silvestri. He would bury it deep and hope that he was two millennia in his grave before some archaeologist uncovered the grotesque thing. He would park at the cabin, which would raise no suspicions, then head into the marsh with his fishing gear and the cooler.

To complete the deception, he swung past Paddy's Diner in Georges Run for bait. The truck stop sat in the shadows of the old Pennsylvania Railroad roundhouse, and except for an occasional slathering of white paint, the building and the menu had not changed in sixty years. Melba Mae Morgan was working her usual shift behind the counter. She cracked her gum as she set his check and two foam cups on the counter, one holding his coffee, the other his night crawlers. On his way out, he dropped a five-dollar bill on the glass candy case next to the cash register.

Duke drove north to Steubenville and caught Route 22, then headed west toward Bloomingdale. Even then, Duke realized he was overthinking his mission. Why did he think he needed night crawlers? On the remote possibility that he ran into someone, he could have said he was fishing the reeds with a crankbait. It would have been that easy. But his thought process was scrambled. A centrifugal force pushed out from inside his skull, and shafts of white light escaped through his eyes. The crackling in his ears sounded like frying bacon. His heart thumped on his rib cage. For a guy who never got rattled on a basketball court, Duke Ducheski certainly wasn't handling the pressure well. However, there was more at stake here than any high school basketball game. As he drove, he fumbled with the plastic lid on the coffee cup and took a sip, though the last thing he needed at that moment was a dose of caffeine to further fuel the internal fire.

He turned off Seminary Road and onto the gravel drive that encircled the lake. A few lights were on in cabins across the water. He pulled in behind his cabin, parked under the gnarled branches of an ancient Australian pine and cut the motor. He sat alone for several minutes, listening to the exhaust of his own breath and the droning of the distant traffic on Route 22. When he was convinced that his arrival had gone unnoticed by any of his neighbors, Duke exited the Jeep, fetched the cooler and the spade out of the back, and dashed several hundred yards to the marsh and the thicket of briar bushes, poison ivy, and prickly honey-locust trees. He could have run deeper into the thicket, but it was a swamp full of coyotes and snakes, which terrified him more than an angry Tony DeMarco. It was the ideal place to bury a head, if such a place actually existed. The marsh was illuminated by the light of an unfortunate full moon, and Duke felt as though he was performing on stage and under the lone spotlight.

After dropping the cooler and the spade, Duke returned to the Jeep, collected his fishing gear, then set the tackle box and pole on the bank of the lake, using a small, Y-shaped stick to prop up the rod. It would be his decoy if another fisherman happened upon the site. He ran back to where he had left the spade and cooler, and started digging between two sprawling briar bushes. He had sunk the spade twice when he heard the sound of a passing car. The crunching of gravel under the moving tires was amplified in the quiet night and within the tight confines of the hills that surrounded the lake. Duke stopped digging and listened, measuring each breath. He couldn't judge the direction, but he listened until the sound disappeared in the night. Most likely it was just someone circling the edge of the lake on the gravel road, heading toward a cabin on the far banks.

It had rained three times the previous week; the ground was soft and came up in thick chunks, and clods of dirt clung to the spade. The hole Duke made was two feet in diameter, wider than necessary for the head, but big enough to give him room to work, which he did at a furious pace. In ten minutes, he had gotten down nearly three feet. Sweat stains swelled under his arms, and his shirt matted to his back and chest. He was on the far side of four feet inside of twenty minutes. Fear and adrenaline kept him working at a torrid pace. Rivulets of sweat rolled down his face; droplets ran off the tip of his nose in rapid succession, disappearing into the hole.

It was going as smoothly as he could have hoped. Four and a half feet—deep enough that raccoons or feral hogs could not dig it up. He unlatched the cooler and turned his head as the soured mix of ice, mobster head, and rancid, death-stained water spilled into the hole. The water and ice fell first, followed by the splut of the Troll's head.

"Goddammit, Moonie," Duke said.

Duke couldn't not look. He shined his flashlight into the hole. The head had landed faceup. One eye was wide open, the other half closed. The eyeballs had receded deep into the sockets. His mouth was open, the lips had rolled back and were a grotesque, dark purple, his rotten teeth an extension of the black gums. Using the spade like a rake, Duke began scraping the dirt back into the hole, covering the head, then he threw in a layer of rocks to further deter any varmints.

As he started filling in the remainder of the hole, with the moon high overhead, Duke heard the sound of footfalls on the leaf-covered carpet of the woods between the makeshift grave and the cabin. It emanated from deep in the thicket, near the hunting path. He froze, each heartbeat reverberating in his ears. He suppressed an adrenaline rush that sent pinpricks of chills racing up his spine before fanning out over his shoulders and neck. *Tony DeMarco*, he thought. The bastard had tailed him.

Duke squeezed the spade and brought the metal end shoulder-high as though it were a battle axe. He crouched, motionless, peering through the moonlight that filtered through the pines and the arching maples, oaks, and cottonwoods that canopied the swamp. He tried to slow his breathing and gain his composure.

Behind the thicket, Duke thought he saw movement, a slow combination of sound and swaying brush making its way from the edge of the lake and crossing directly in front of him. At least, Duke *thought* he saw movement. Maybe it was a deer or a coyote, or maybe just the wind, but he could have sworn he saw a human form. He squinted and tried to blink the image into focus. Nothing moved. Was it the wind and his overworked imagination? Probably his imagination. Still, his thumping heart rattled his ribs, and he pushed a palm against his chest in a vain attempt to slow the beat.

Why, Duke reasoned in a moment of logical thought, *would Tony DeMarco be hiding in the brush?* He wouldn't. He would walk up to Duke and stick a gun in his mouth. This he knew for a fact.

Still, Duke squatted motionless behind the pile of dirt, watching and listening for movement. Minutes passed—five, then ten. The woods remained quiet except for the wind, the slap of the branches, and the rustle of the leaves. He eased back on his rear and pushed the remaining dirt into the hole with his feet. The falling earth barely made a noise, though in his mind each falling clump was a cymbal clash. Out of the corner of Duke's eye, he again believed he saw movement. His imagination was at full gallop, a mustang with steam pouring from its nostrils as it thundered across the plains. He furiously moved the rest of the dirt into the hole. Once it was full, he stomped on it for several minutes, working it nearly flat. He used the spade to rake some brush over the broken ground. Another car passed, this one quickly. He took a flat rock that he had dug up and slid it atop the grave with his foot. If for some reason he ever needed to find the location, which at the moment he couldn't fathom, the flat stone would serve as a marker.

He grabbed the spade and the empty cooler and ran back toward the cabin.

It was after midnight, and the full moon was high overhead when he grabbed several large stones from the bank of the lake, put them into the cooler, opened the valve, and heaved it into the water. He heard the splash but didn't stay to watch it sink. He picked up the fishing tackle and tossed it and the spade into the back of the Jeep. Before leaving, he dashed into the cabin and cleaned the mud off his shoes in the kitchen sink, washed his hands and arms, and mopped his sweaty hairline with paper towels. A tremendous pressure in his chest released as he slid the key into the ignition, fired the engine, and headed for home.

When he pulled the Jeep into the alley, Duke could see the television flickering in the living room. They rarely slept in the same bed anymore; Nina fell asleep on the couch in front of the television nearly every night. Duke unloaded the gear and put it back in the garage, then snagged the foam cup of night crawlers from the front seat and went in through the back door. Nina had been lying in wait, and she came into the kitchen as Duke was putting the night crawlers in the refrigerator. He had been anticipating another assault, but it didn't come.

"You're back already?" she asked in a calm voice.

"I could tell they weren't going to be biting, so I packed it in."

"What's that?" she asked, pointing at the cup.

"Night crawlers."

"Worms?"

"I bought them at Paddy's before I went to the cabin. The cup has a lid on it. They won't hurt anything."

She frowned, as though confused. "I thought you were going to dig for worms. Isn't that why you took the shovel?"

Duke swallowed hard. "I changed my mind. It was easier to buy them."

She stared at Duke for a long minute, nodded, and said, "I see," then turned and walked away.

CHAPTER FIFTEEN

Tony recruited Donald "Donnie Sweets" Staffilino to help him search for the Troll. Donnie was a muscular 6'3", had no discernible conscience, and knew how to keep his mouth shut. Tony and Donnie scoured the Upper Ohio Valley, wrinkling lapels and tossing around underpaid bartenders in every beer joint along the river, searching for some trace of their missing courier, and, more importantly, their missing cash. Their tactics were rarely gentle.

They traced the Troll's path and knew he had not been seen after he left the Oasis. There were no signs of the Lincoln, the money, or the enormous head of Frankie Silvestri. He had simply vanished. Antonelli had every cop that was in his pocket in the tristate area looking for the car, and they had the passenger lists checked for all flights leaving Pittsburgh, Cleveland, and Columbus within forty-eight hours of Saturday night. Nothing.

Antonelli was irate. One minute, he was screaming for Tony to find out who had killed the Troll and stolen the money. The next minute, he was convinced that the Troll had skipped town with the loot. But Tony DeMarco knew otherwise. The Troll would never have abandoned Antonelli. The Troll had an acute sense of self-importance that was tied directly to his job as a trusted bagman for the Antonellis. It was how he identified himself. It made him somebody. He had a modest lifestyle, and money was unimportant to him. The Troll's reputation as a member of the Antonelli crime family meant too much to him to jeopardize. Without that, he had nothing. Without that, he was just a misshapen freak.

Tony was convinced that someone had killed the Troll, but who?

Who would have the balls—or the lack of common sense—to mess with an Antonelli courier? The Carlucci family from Youngstown had been trying to worm their way back into the valley's gambling business for years. Even so, knocking off a deformed bagman seemed an unlikely approach. Tony still wondered how Moonie Collier had gotten the money to pay off his debt. He didn't seriously think the big dumb-ass was responsible for the Troll's disappearance. He wasn't that desperate. Or, maybe he was.

While Antonelli fumed and DeMarco pondered, Moonie returned to work at the steel mill on Wednesday, his leg heavily bandaged under his work denims. The leg was still tender, but he was able to walk without a noticeable limp. After work, Moonie sat in a chair at Duke's Place while Duke assembled the bar and drilled him on what he was to say when he was questioned by Tony DeMarco. *Yes, I was in the Oasis last Saturday. Yes, I saw the Troll come in and I saw him leave. No, I never saw the Troll after that.*

"What if he wants to know where you got the money to pay Carmine?" Duke asked.

"I'll tell him to go fuck himself."

"Moonie!"

"Fine. I'll tell him I hit the trifecta—I wheeled the eight horse for five bucks. He went off at 25-to-1, and a couple of long shots placed and showed."

"Is that true?"

"Yeah. It's the race I lost."

"If you had won, that would have given you enough to pay off your debt and still go to Vegas?"

"If I'd hit it, I'd still be in Vegas."

"Okay, and the answer to any other question is . . ."

"I don't know."

"Good boy."

Satisfied that his pupil was properly prepared, Duke sent Moonie to find and confront Tony DeMarco. Duke knew that Tony had been looking for Moonie, and the best defense was a frontal assault. Tony's car was at Carmine's, and Moonie was back in fifteen minutes.

"He asked me everything you said he'd ask me, including where I got the dough. I said, 'If it's any of your goddamn business, I hit the trifecta at Mountaineer.'"

"What'd Tony say?"

"He said, 'Get the fuck outta my face.' I blew him a kiss and left."

CHAPTER SIXTEEN

Duke was at the restaurant at 6:00 a.m. the day it was to open. He made a pot of coffee and toasted two pieces of wheat bread, which he ate dry, and sat at the table nearest the kitchen. It was quiet and dark, with the only light being cast from the hazy fluorescent tubes burning under the mahogany bar. Duke Ducheski took a few minutes to drink in the quiet and the solitude. The restaurant was filled with the scents of a spit-shined and renovated building—fresh paint, wood stain, varnish, and ammonia.

It was finally going to happen.

In just a few hours, he would unlock the front door, and Duke's Place would be in business. When he flipped the little toggle switch to turn on the sign in the front window, and twisted the brass knob that would allow the deadbolt to slide from its housing, his dream would become his reality.

He sipped his coffee. Crumbs of toast spread over the table as he ate. It was the day of a new birth, a new beginning. But in his solitude, his thoughts were of the fragility of life and his son. For as Duke prepared for a new life, he knew another was coming to a close.

Timmy was dying.

It had been six months, maybe eight, since he first saw the signs. They started creeping in from the sides of his consciousness, like the darkness that overtakes you just before sleep. At first, he tried to ignore them, a bit of self-denial, but in his heart he knew it was true. Timmy's spine had become more curved and was beginning to resemble a question mark. His shoulders hunched forward as his body curled further into the fetal position. As he did, his breathing became more labored, strained, and at times the boy struggled for a simple breath. The bones at his hips and shoulders looked as though they would push though his skin, which had become translucent and cold. He bruised at the touch. His eyes had always been distant, unknowing, but they were growing more dull and dry, and they were open less and less each day. Timmy's already-frail body was in rapid decline.

For reasons that he could not explain, Duke had never seen death as the Grim Reaper, the skeletal, black-robed, and hooded figure carrying a scythe that in myth accompanies the deceased to the other side. Rather, he had always seen death as a steam locomotive the color of dull coal, a black wreath encompassing its headlamp, black sashes draped along its side. The cab of the locomotive was always empty, and it pulled a train of passenger cars with darkened windows. A solitary figure, the conductor, perhaps, or Death itself, stood on a platform between two cars, rolling with the sway of the train, staring, saying nothing.

Somewhere on the distant horizon, far beyond the hills that encased Mingo Junction, Duke sensed the approach of that locomotive. He could not yet see it, but he felt its slow grind in his bones, and heard a whistle that ached in the darkness, its lonesome call traversing an expanse of unknown time and miles, until at last it reverberated within the hills of the Ohio Valley, a reminder to Duke that time was short. There would soon come a night when it would make its way over the foothills to the Heinzmann Convalescent Center. It would grind to a halt, a stream of steam escaping from valves near the coupling rods. The conductor would motion him on, and Timmy would step from this world into the next without once looking back.

Doc Kuhn had been in to visit Timmy the previous week. Duke was in the room and watched intently as Doc Kuhn, now in his mid-seventies, slowly moved the stethoscope up and down Timmy's narrow and arched back. Gently, he took the edges of the thin cotton gown and slid it over Timmy's spine, tucking it between the skin and the bedsheet. He took a breath and pulled the stethoscope from his ears, sliding it into the tattered, black bag resting at the foot of the bed. With the back of a right hand heavy with arthritis across the knuckles, Doc stroked Timmy's upper arm and said something that Duke strained to hear, but could not. After a moment, Doc looked over his shoulder and motioned Duke into the hall.

Doc Kuhn had always insisted on the protocol. "How do we know he can't hear and understand?" Doc had once said.

He got no argument from Duke. For years he had prayed that Timmy understood at least some of what went on around him. He followed Doc into the hallway and closed the door behind him. Doc Kuhn had delivered both Timmy and Duke. He was a dignified man with a neatly trimmed goatee and a full head of white hair. In one hand, he held a black, lacquered cane worn to the bare wood on the handle, and the tattered bag he clutched in the other.

"Nicholas, your suspicions are correct," Doc Kuhn said. "Timmy's body is in retreat. It's quickly failing him. His breathing is terribly labored. His blood pressure is low. I'm afraid there's not much good I can tell you."

Duke nodded, sadder for the pathetic life his son had lived than his impending death. "How long does he have?"

Doc Kuhn's smile was slight; his eyes narrowed, and he gave Duke a look of admonishment, a teacher to a pupil who should know better. "Nicholas, you know I can't answer that. It could be six days or six weeks or six months. I don't know. The taking of a simple breath is reaction, not thought. The tiny part of Timmy's brain that controls his breathing doesn't take much to keep functioning, a little oxygen and nourishment. Unfortunately, the rest of his body is shutting down. He's tired, Nicholas—tired and worn out." He shook his head. "I wish I could give you a better answer, but only God knows for sure."

Doc had delivered countless babies in Mingo Junction, and he was bedside when an equal number of its residents passed from this life. And, while Timmy had never enjoyed any quality of life, Duke sensed it troubled Doc Kuhn greatly to tell him that his only child was dying, even though Timmy's passing would be merciful.

"I never thought the boy would last this long," Doc said. "He has, to a very large extent, lived these many years because you've been here, nurturing him, Nicholas. In his own way, Timmy has responded to your love."

"Maybe I did him a disservice," Duke said. "It certainly hasn't been much of a life."

Doc Kuhn put his hand on Duke's shoulder and gave a squeeze. "Don't ever believe that. You have done all that was humanly possible. Be with him. God and Timmy will decide when it's time. If you think he's in pain, let me know."

Duke nodded, then remained outside the room for several minutes, fighting tears and listening as the slow plod of feet and cane echoed their way down the hall.

Duke went back into the room and pulled the chair close to the bottom of the bed. *Football stars*, he thought. Parents want sons who are football stars, and doctors, and lawyers, and astronauts. They want bold young men with broad shoulders and square jaws. In those rare moments of self-pity, he had the same desires. He had dreamed of Timmy soaring through the air in a scarlet-and-black Mingo Indians uniform, draining a fade-away jumper at the buzzer. Now, as he watched his son making a slow trip from this world, he wished only for one thing, one time—a simple recognition in Timmy's eyes. Just once, he wanted to know for certain that Timmy knew that someone in this world had known him and loved him and cared for him. Duke wanted the boy to know that his father was sorry for what had happened, and sorry that he hadn't been in the hospital room to prevent it. How terrible, to spend your life curled in a hospital bed, trapped in your own cocoon, deteriorating, unknowing of the world around you, or that someone desperately loved you. In these moments of self-pity, Duke believed that he was entitled to that simple request. Didn't God owe him that much?

Part of Duke wanted Timmy to go peacefully, to simply stop breathing. Another part of him hated the thought. He still had vivid memories of the dream and seeing Timmy dressed and standing at the side of the bed in his Chuck Taylor All-Stars, ready to go play. He wanted a chance to talk to that Timmy before he died. Over the years,

Duke had cried and apologized to Timmy countless times, but he wanted to do it just once when the boy could comprehend.

That, he knew, was never going to happen.

Duke stood at the front door and looked at his wristwatch. It was nine fifty-nine and twenty seconds. He watched as the second hand swept past the six and the nine. When it hit the twelve, precisely ten o'clock on the morning of Monday, November 8, 1993, he flipped the toggle switch, and the orange neon sign in the window facing Commercial Street flickered to life: *OPEN*.

He twisted the brass knob, unlocking the door, and Duke's Place was ready for business.

Everything was in order. The liquor license had been secured, the help hired, the kitchen's certificate of operation from the Jefferson County Health Department displayed above the service window between the bar and the kitchen, the cooler and bar stocked. Duke Ducheski could barely contain himself. It was not unlike the belly jitters he got before every game.

It was an overcast morning. The sky was low and gray, and spitting a light snow—a typical early-November day in the Ohio River Valley. The orange glow from the window seemed to brighten all of Commercial Street.

He had taken two weeks of vacation from the mill to launch the opening of Duke's Place. The first was a week of eighteen-hour days and frantic preparations to make sure everything was in order. Moonie, who was still gimping around on a tender leg, and Angel had been over every day after work to help with the rush of getting the bar reconstructed. It was a masterpiece in mahogany, and it dominated the back wall like the throne in a palace. The new wooden floor was down and buffed. The dining room, a separate enclosure away from the noise of the taproom, was rimmed with booths, and tables filled the center of the rectangle. In the taproom, a Wurlitzer jukebox was loaded with forty-fives—oldies and traditional rock 'n' roll—and a bootleg copy of the Miracle Minute. A television was placed at each end of the bar. There was a pool table—a quarter a game—and a disk bowling game.

The north wall was pine paneling, adorned with the photographs of the great teams and players from the valley, the centerpiece of which was an enlarged team photo of Mingo's state championship basketball team. It was a wonderful collage that would draw much attention.

Not thirty seconds after the neon light went bright orange, Stubby Wilhelm, a retired carpenter and teller of mendacious fishing tales, ran through the door. He had been sitting in his car at the light at Commercial and McLister when he saw the light flicker on. He pulled into a parking spot in front, pumped a nickel into the meter, and sprinted into Duke's Place as fast as his namesake legs could carry him. He looked around, puffing for breath, and grinned. "Am I the first?" he asked.

"Numero uno," Duke said.

"I'll have an Iron City draft," he bellowed, striding across the floor and reaching for his wallet. "Awful damn early for a beer, but this is worth celebrating," Stubby said. He fished for the most unblemished dollar bill in his wallet as he slid onto a vinyl stool at the bar. "You're gonna frame it, ain't ya, Duke? I'll give you a good one."

Duke opened the Iron City tap and poured the contents into a frosted mug. He set it on a paper napkin in front of Stubby, then held up his coffee mug for a toast. "To my first customer and my first dollar," Duke said, as glass and ceramic clicked. "I'll get a frame and a little brass plate that says, 'First Dollar, Stubby Wilhelm, November 8, 1993.' Whatta ya think?"

"You're the best, Duke," Stubby said, raising the mug to his lips and taking several hard swallows.

It wasn't another minute before Beanie Skidmore came running through the door, stiff-arming it open like a fullback, himself panting. It took a few seconds for his eyes to adjust to the light, and he could see his fishing nemesis Stubby at the bar, all smiles.

"Top of the morning to you, Beano," Stubby chortled, holding the frosted mug in the air in mock salute. No one was more ebullient in victory than Stubby Wilhelm. And no one was as sore a loser as Beanie Skidmore.

"Dammit, shit to hell," Beanie growled.

"Tough luck, Beano," Stubby taunted. "I bought the first beer at Duke's Place, and he's gonna put my dollar in a frame with a little brass plate. It's going to say, 'Stubby was first and Beanie Skidmore was second, just like every fishin' trip they've ever taken.'"

This made Beanie fume. "Rolling Rock," he muttered.

"Duke, you see that empty spot above the jukebox?" Stubby asked.

Duke nodded and grinned, preparing for Stubby's next salvo. "What about it?"

"Remember that bass I caught out at Tappan Lake a few years back?" Stubby spun his stool toward Beanie. "The eight-pounder. It sure would look good hanging on the wall over that jukebox."

Beanie moaned, "Oh, goddammit, Stubby. It wasn't no eight pounds."

"You're right. It was probably closer to nine, actually, and a hell of a lot bigger than anything you ever caught."

"Not bigger than my walleye."

"Well, you never had your walleye mounted. Too bad for you. How about it, Duke?"

"Why, Stubby, I think that wall is the perfect place for that bass. We'll put a little plaque up there with it and call it a nine-pounder."

Beanie about spit his beer across the bar. He said, "Well, goddammit, I got a picture of my walleye. Can I bring that in, Duke? It's a nice eight-by-ten."

"We'll put 'em up side-by-side—a little plaque for each."

Beanie smirked, and Stubby frowned, having lost a small portion of his glory by having to share wall space with his fishing foe.

Stubby and Beanie were the first of a steady flow of customers that started that morning and continued through the week. By Friday, the dining room was packed at lunch and the steel mill was sending for large carryout orders. When the afternoon shift let out Friday, the bar filled. Families and couples filled the dining room for the Friday fish fry. It couldn't have been a better first week.

The grand opening was Saturday night. Two hundred invitations had been sent. The place was decorated with streamers, and two troughs made of Wheeling-Pittsburgh steel were filled with ice and cans of beer at each end of the bar, where Liddy Sheares, one of the new waitresses, and Moonie would wear carpenter's aprons and pass out brews at fifty cents a pop. Against one wall of the taproom was a buffet table with trays of cold cuts and breads; shrimp; vegetables and dip; chips; pretzels; mini wieners in barbecue sauce; and little blocks of American, Swiss, and longhorn cheese skewered with colored toothpicks. On the bar and at every table were books of matches, shiny white, on the front of which was an orange basketball with "DUKE'S PLACE" in red, block letters trimmed in black arching across the ball.

A red carpet extended from the front door to the curb. Red, black, and white balloons were tied to the awning. At curbside, Carson Elliot and Angel were dressed in tuxedos and served as doormen. High school boys had been hired to serve as parking valets. For himself and the rest of the help, Duke had bought gray golf shirts with the basketball logo on the left breast.

By six o'clock Saturday evening, the first patrons arrived. By 7:00 the place was full, and by 8:00 it was standing room only. The jukebox blared and the beer trough was refilled three times. There was a thirty-minute wait for a table in the dining room.

Duke's Place was on its way.

Duke worked the bar, making drinks, dunking the overflow of bills in the office safe, and watching over the chaos. He moved his way down the bar and said to Moonie, "I can't believe how smoothly this is going."

"Don't say stuff like that," Moonie said. "You'll jinx it."

"It's going to work, Moonie. This place is going to make it."

They were four hours into the evening when Duke said, "I need a beer," violating his own no-alcohol-during-business policy. "Are you ready for one?"

"Always," Moonie said.

"Good. Come on in the back. I've got a proposition for you."

Duke's office was on one side of a short hallway opposite the restrooms. It was austere, but functional—a desk, a chair, an old couch, a safe, and a few mementos. Duke handed Moonie an Iron City that he had snatched from the nearly empty trough. He pulled the door shut and sat in the dilapidated office chair, blowing out his breath.

After Moonie had taken a seat on a folding chair and had thrown back two hard swallows of his beer, Duke asked, "Do you remember the night Kodiak Kripinski was going to kick my ass behind the school?"

"Sure. I remember," he said. "That guy was all bluster."

"He might have been bluster to you, but he would have throttled me."

Moonie shrugged. "That was twenty-some years ago. What's your point?"

"The point is, all my life you've been there to bail me out—when I was a mouthy kid on the ball field, or when Kodiak Kripinski was going to beat my ass. You were always there."

"Well, you've helped me out, too," Moonie said, raising his eyebrows. "Isn't that what friends do? I mean, I think what you did for me lately was pretty spectacular. Most guys would never do that for anyone."

"You would have done it for me," Duke said.

"Of course," Moonie said, hitting his Iron City and leaning his chair against the wall. "Hell, Duke, it's just that I'm good at watching your back and fighting. You're good with money and thinkin' and jump shots. It's a pretty good combination if you're going to be in the bar business."

Duke nodded. "Good point. That's what I want to talk to you about, Moonie. I know you wanted a piece of the restaurant, so if this gets off the ground, I'll sell you 15 percent. I've been giving it a lot of thought, and you put in a hell of a lot of work, and the only thing you've asked for is beer, so I think you're entitled. I'm going to crunch some numbers, but after the first couple of months, if things are looking good, you'll be part owner of Duke's Place."

A slab of white-hot Wheeling-Pittsburgh steel could not have put off more light than Moonie's face. "Duke, are you serious? That would be great, just great. I'll give you whatever you want for it."

"No money. It'll be sweat equity for everything you've done and everything you're going to do down the road. But, there's a hitch, Moon."

"Of course there is. What?"

"If you want to be part owner of Duke's Place, you've got to stop gambling."

The glow melted from his face. "What? Why? What's gambling got to do with anything?"

"I can't afford to have my partner in hock to Tony DeMarco and the Antonellis. I don't want them coming in here and busting the place to pieces because you owe them money. Or, worse, they take your 15 percent as payment. When that happens, I'm in the same hole as Carmine. He let 'em in the door years ago, and now they own him. I won't let that happen here. Not to mention that I don't want to be burying any more body parts. If I let you in, you've got to give me your word that you'll never put down another nickel. Not at the tracks, not at Vegas, not with Carmine."

Moonie winced. "Never? Goddamn, Duke. I stayed single just so I could gamble. What if I square everything up front? No more credit."

"No, Moonie. Nothing. No more gambling. You've got to give me your word."

Moonie looked away and exhaled.

Duke took a swallow of his beer, one brow arched high on his forehead. "Think about it, Moonie. I'm serious about this. If I cut you in and find out you're still gambling, you're out. Period. No questions asked. Not only is this the kind of thing that could ruin the business, but it also could ruin a friendship, and I don't want that to happen. If you don't want to quit gambling, I understand, but I need to know up front. Quite honestly, I think it's an attractive offer, considering all you've gone through in the past couple of months." Duke nodded toward his friend's leg. "So, give it some thought."

"I don't need to think about it, Duke. I'm in." He raised his right palm. "I'll never bet another dime—my right hand to Christ."

Moonie extended his thick hand, and they shook, sealing the deal.

CHAPTER SEVENTEEN

On the Monday after the grand opening, Duke worked at Duke's Place until after the dinner rush, then turned it over to Moonie. It was dusk when he got home, the sun already a dull glow beyond the hills, the shadows falling long across the backyard and quickly disappearing in the twilight. He entered through the back door, taking off his shoes in the tiny mudroom between the door and the kitchen. There were no aromas of warming food; the home was sterile and unwelcoming, dark but for the dancing glow of the television in the living room.

Nina was sunk into the cloth couch, curling in her favorite corner, feigning sleep with her hands tucked under her chin. She was wearing a faded yellow sweatshirt and a pair of black, polyester stretch pants that strained across her ample hips. In spite of the distance that had grown between them, it still pained Duke to think of the cute and happy girl she had once been.

Now, she was perpetually angry. Frown lines had grown prominent, running in deep creases at the corners of her mouth and across her forehead. Too many times he had wondered if he was the one who sent her spiraling down this path. But in his heart, he knew Nina DeMarco Ducheski had a closet full of demons that would exist with or without him. Angel once said, "She blames you for her problems, but only because you're convenient."

Of course, Angel was right. That's why Duke had to make the break. He no longer feared her outbursts or her brother's threats. He had to do this for his own sanity.

Certainly, it wouldn't come as a surprise. Three times before he had asked Nina for a divorce, and each time it met with the same theatrics—tears, promises to change, anger, and in one instance, a hot skillet across the side of the head. She would toss about the tenets of the Roman Catholic Church and the immorality of divorce. This attempt would be no different. Sadly, their relationship had devolved to that of a father and a rebellious teenage daughter.

He sat in the chair nearest her head, taking the remote from the coffee table to silence the volume on the television. Two spent cans of cola, a bowl with a puddle of chocolate ice cream in the bottom, and a *TV Guide* rested on the edge of the table nearest her. She took slow, steady breaths, but refused to acknowledge his presence. For a long minute he sat in silence, rolling the remote in his hand.

"Timmy's dying," Duke said. "I was there when Doc Kuhn stopped by last week. He doesn't know how much longer Timmy has, but he said the end is in sight. I thought you might want to go see him before he passes."

Nina ended her little game of possum, lifting her head so just her left eye was visible to Duke from behind the arm of the couch. She stared for a moment, then turned her view toward the television. "I've been meaning to go up and see him, but I just haven't had the time," she said.

"I understand perfectly. After all, your days are so jammed with watching soap operas that you can't drive five miles up the road to see your dying son." She ignored the jab. "Make time, Nina. He's your son, and he won't be here much longer. The very least you can do is visit with him."

"You say that like it's my fault that he's dying."

"It's no one's fault, Nina. But ignoring the unpleasantness won't make it go away."

Still, she was silent.

"How about sitting up for a minute? I want to talk to you."

"What about?"

"Us."

"What about us?" Nina lifted her eyes enough to see her husband, but was careful to avoid eye contact.

"Unfortunately, Nina, there's not much of an *us*, anymore. Mostly, it's you and it's me. And, since there's no chance of that changing, I don't see any reason to continue with this charade of a marriage." He paused a moment for another breath. "I want out, Nina. I want a divorce."

As the words left Duke's mouth, a wave of heat rolled over his body. It was the first time there had been true conviction behind the words. This time, he was ready to follow through.

"No! No, no, no," she said, sitting up straight, using the tips of her fingers to tuck her hair behind her ears. "We've been over this before. I can't. I won't. I will never give you a divorce. It's a sin against the church, and a sin against God."

"When's the last time you went to church, Nina, except to play bingo?"

"I won't. That's final."

"Let's work this out like adults, Nina. I'll give you the house. I'll do right by you until you can get a job and get on your feet . . ."

"The answer, Nicholas, is no. Under no circumstances will I give you a divorce, ever."

"In that case, Nina, things are likely to get real ugly, because I want out, and I'm getting out." He handed her an envelope. "These are the divorce papers from my lawyer. Read them. Everything is very fair."

"No," she yelled. "I won't have it." She threw the envelope at him. It hit his shoulder and slid to the crease between his leg and the side of the chair. Duke took the envelope and set it against the lamp on the end table at the edge of the couch.

"It's going to happen, Nina. Let's approach this like adults."

Perhaps it was the finality of his words that turned her anger to sadness. She swiped at tears with the back of her left hand. "Let's wait," she said, forcing a smile. "We can work this out. I'll lose some weight. Maybe we can have another baby; it's not too late. It'll be like it was when we were first married."

Duke slowly shook his head. "Nina, it can never be like it was when we first got married. Those days are too far gone. We were just kids. We're both different people, now. I've given it a lot of thought, and I want out. Read the papers and we can talk." He stood and headed toward the back door.

She followed him out of the living room and into the kitchen. "Don't go," she pleaded, tears now streaming down both cheeks. "Stay. Let's talk about it."

"We'll talk after you've read the divorce papers."

In an instant, her jaw began to quiver in anger, and sadness was replaced by rage that boiled her skin crimson. "I'm not reading those papers, and we are *not* getting a divorce."

"I'll talk to you later, Nina," he said, pulling the back door closed behind him.

After leaving the house, Duke drove to Cara's. When he knocked, she slid back the curtain on the front door, squinted into the dark, then opened it just a crack. "Nick, it's late," she said.

"Just give me a minute," he said.

She opened the door, and he slipped in.

Her ten-year-old son, K.J., was in his pajamas and sitting cross-legged on the floor in front of the television. He looked up and waved. "Hi, Mr. Ducheski. What are you doing here?" he asked.

"Oh, I just stopped in to see your mom for a few minutes. Is that okay?"

"It's okay with me."

Cara stepped away from the door and raked some wild hair out of her eyes. "What's going on?"

"I'm leaving Nina."

Her brows arched slightly, a sign of doubt. They'd had the conversation before. Duke had told Cara numerous times that he was going to get a divorce, but he had failed on each follow-through. He held out an envelope, which she opened to find a copy of the divorce papers.

"The night of the grand opening, after it was all over, I realized how empty it had been, because you weren't there," he said. "I decided that I didn't want another important event in my life to pass without you by my side."

CHAPTER EIGHTEEN

Although Duke's office was far from palatial, it provided a refuge from the mayhem that was Friday night at Duke's Place. When the men's urinal flushed, the rattling pipes shook the back wall of his office. It was a constant interruption on busy nights, but he rationalized that it was the equivalent of hearing the cash register ring as patrons made room for more beer. The walls of the office remained unfinished sheet rock; nailed, spackled, and taped, but still in need of sanding and paint. In the crush to finish Duke's Place in time for the grand opening, finishing the office walls had been one of the items he had tossed to the back burner.

From the bottom desk drawer he retrieved a pair of dime-store reading glasses and slid them onto the end of his nose. Out of sheer vanity, he kept the spectacles hidden. He couldn't help but smile as he stared down through the glass at the first three months' operating figures. They were astonishing. Never had he anticipated that Duke's Place would do this well. After salaries and expenses, he was more than $53,000 in the black. He was printing money. The Christmas and New Year's Eve parties had been as successful as the grand opening. It wasn't long before he had hired extra help to handle the lunch crowd and the Friday- and Saturday-night throngs.

While things were going smoothly at Duke's Place, Nina continued to be a problem. She was steadfastly vowing to oppose the divorce. To avoid confrontation, Duke spent most nights sleeping on the couch in his office. With each trip to the house, he moved a box of clothes or personal possessions out. After a few weeks, the only remaining object of his that had any value was the 1959 Buick Invicta in the garage. Beyond the Buick, he wanted nothing else, not the house, the furniture, or the memories. The apartment above Duke's Place had a working toilet, a shower, a blow-up mattress, and a small, black-and-white television. That was all he required. Once he had located a safe place for the Buick, he would drive it away, both a real and symbolic gesture of putting his previous life in the rearview mirror.

Moonie had been putting in a lot of hours at the bar. He loved working as the bartender, a job he took quite seriously. He had been good to his word and had stayed away from Carmine's, which was a relief to the little Italian, too. Duke feared, however, that he may have simply switched bookmakers. Moonie's newest friend, a thickset man who went by the nickname Rhino, had been hanging around the bar for several weeks. He stopped by at odd hours and always seemed to have a wad of cash. Duke also worried that he was a mole for Tony DeMarco, looking for an opportunity to force gambling into the bar. There was, of course, the possibility that this was his imagination once again running in high gear. Rhino was probably just some sad sack trying to sponge beers from Moonie. With the big guy having partial ownership in the restaurant, that wasn't likely to happen.

Duke was jotting down the last of the items on a checklist of "to dos" when Moonie poked his head in the door. "Ready for me, boss?"

He pointed toward the old couch with the eraser end of his pencil. "I liked it better when you were calling me 'Bo-Peep.' Sit down, and quit calling me 'boss.'"

Moonie grinned. It was his newest and favorite name for Duke. "Okay, you're the boss, boss." He laughed aloud.

"You're just your own best friend, aren't you, Moon?" Duke held out the checklist for him to grab. "Here's everything that needs to be done."

Duke was still grinding away at two jobs, working a steady daylight at Wheeling-Pitt, then at Duke's Place until closing. It was difficult, but he couldn't afford to leave the mill until he was absolutely sure his restaurant was going to succeed. He was struggling to find a balance, because he didn't want his jobs to damage his relationship with Cara, which had rekindled with his commitment to divorce Nina. Tonight, he was going to spend the evening with Cara. She had made arrangements for her parents to babysit the kids and had promised Duke a romantic dinner for two.

Moonie took a minute to read the list, mouthing each word. "No problemo, boss. I can handle this."

"You're sure?"

Moonie frowned. "You know, Duke, I don't want to belittle what you do here, but this isn't exactly rocket science." He reexamined the list. "Then again, I'm not exactly a rocket scientist. Let's see: turn off the lights, clear the bar, put the cash in the safe, mop the floor, restock the bar, fill the beer cooler, inspect the kitchen. I can handle it. Do you want me to lock the door when I leave?"

"Of course I want you to lock the door when you leave."

Moonie handed him the list. "Better put it on there."

Duke pulled the reading glasses from his nose and dropped them back into the drawer, fighting off a grin. "You're hilarious, Moon. Okay, buddy, you're in charge. While I've got you here, what's the story with this Rhino character?"

"What do you mean?"

"Who is he? He's been spending a lot of time around here. What do you know about him?"

"He's a good guy. He likes this place. Drops a lot of dime."

"What's he do?"

"Sales. He lives up the river, somewhere, but this is his sales territory. He sells key chains and pencils and stuff—'novelty items,' he calls them." Moonie pulled out a miniature flashlight emblazoned with the logo of a bank. "He gave me this. His company makes 'em. He said he would give us a good deal on all kinds of stuff like that. You interested?"

"Maybe sometime down the road. Are you sure he's legit? You don't think he's working for Tony DeMarco, do you?"

"God, Duke, how paranoid are you?"

"Very," he said. "Just keep an eye on him. I can't afford to have DeMarco or any of his flunkies in here."

"I thought you had a date," Moonie said.

"You're good with everything on the list, right?"

"I'm good." He sensed that Moonie was like a teenager whose parents were about to leave him alone for the first time. He was thrilled to be in charge and anxious for his boss to be gone.

Duke pushed away from the desk. "All right, my man. I'm outta here."

At 3:15 in the morning, Duke was awakened by Cara in the most provocative method she had at her disposal. After a few moments, he was at full staff; she straddled him and they made love for the third time. Cara's sexual appetite was insatiable, and in short order she had the first of three back-arching climaxes. Duke joined her on the third before melding into the sheets, spent. She allowed her full weight to slump on his body, sliding on the perspiration on his chest. Her cool hair fell down around his neck. They dozed for several minutes until he gave her three pats on the small of her back, his usual nonverbal signal that it was time to go.

"No," she whined. "Don't go tonight. Stay here." She pulled her head back and smiled. "Stay, and I'll make it worth your while."

"If you make it any more worth my while, I'll be a dead man."

She laughed and playfully bit his shoulder. "Why can't you stay?"

"I just don't want the kids to come by in the morning and find me . . ."

"The kids have seen you here before. The real reason is you want to go down to the restaurant and make sure Moonie got everything closed up to your satisfaction."

He smiled. "Thou dost know me too well, fair maiden."

"How about this? I'll let you go now if your naked butt is back up here tonight."

"Deal."

When Duke walked onto her porch, molten steel flowed from a ladle at Wheeling-Pitt, lighting up the dark sky. They stood on the porch for several minutes, embracing, relieved and ecstatic that soon they would be together.

"The divorce is going to be an ordeal," Duke whispered.

"You have broad shoulders. Besides, she won't fight it as hard as you think. Once it becomes public knowledge, I think she'll be too excited about playing the role of the martyr to fight it. She'll revel in being the victim." She reached up and kissed Duke softly on the lips. "That's what she does best."

Duke walked down the porch steps to the crumbling sidewalk that led to the pea-gravel driveway. He couldn't remember ever feeling this way about Nina, sad as that was. He had loved Nina, but he never felt like he needed her. He needed Cara and her love.

He eased the Jeep onto Sycamore Street and drove down McKinley Avenue. From Cara's, McKinley dead-ends into Hillside Drive, which sweeps to the left, past the Minute Market, for the long descent down Logan Avenue. He slowed and turned right onto Commercial toward the business district. It was a clear night, and the streetlights burned bright through the strip. Dim lights glowed inside the stores and offices, except for the bright, overhead lights that shone through the front windows of Duke's Place.

Duke groaned at the sight of the bright lights. "Dammit, Moonie." It was more than two hours past closing. The first item on the list he had given Moonie was, "Turn off the lights." He parked at one of the metered spots in front of the restaurant and got out. At least he had remembered to lock the door. Duke pulled the heavy ring of keys from his pocket and let himself in. It was a mess.

"What the hell," he said aloud.

The chairs had yet to be placed atop the tables, and the floor had not been swept or mopped. The kitchen lights burned bright. This wasn't like Moonie.

Duke walked toward the kitchen, which was separated from the taproom by two swinging, stainless-steel doors with windows shaped like half-moons. It was through one of the small windows that he saw the back door to the alley cracked open six inches, and his gut constricted.

"Moonie, are you here?" he called.

The bar was quiet. Duke walked into the kitchen, pulled the door closed, and turned the deadbolt, then walked back through the taproom and through the opening to the dining room. It had been mopped and cleaned. The clack of his heels against the hardwood floor echoed in the empty bar.

"Moonie!"

No response.

As he turned into the hall leading to his office, Duke saw blood, a thick river of maroon that reflected in the dull glow of the hall light. "Oh, Christ, Moonie," he said, dropping on his knees at his friend's side.

In the dim light, he strained to see the damage that was pulling the life out of his friend. There were bullet wounds in both knee caps. The front of his shirt and pants were sticky and red. Blood was everywhere. Moonie opened his eyes to slits, but there was no expression of recognition. There was just a slight rise and fall to his chest. Duke ran to his office and called 911.

"I need an ambulance at Duke's Place on Commercial Street, and you've got to hurry," he yelled. "My friend has been shot and it's very bad."

The 911 operator was asking more questions, but Duke dropped the phone. He unlocked the front door, then dashed back down the hall. "Moonie?" He put a hand on his carotid artery. The beat was faint. "Moonie? It's me, Duke. Can you hear me?"

Slowly, his eyes opened again. "Hey, Duke." He swallowed and grimaced. "Man, I'm so sorry about this . . ." He struggled to breathe; his words were barely audible. "It's a mess; I'm sorry."

"Moonie, for God's sake, don't worry about this. You're going to be all right, buddy. The emergency squad's on the way. Who did this to you?"

"You were right all along. That Rhino, he doesn't sell flashlights;

he's bad news. He said . . ." Moonie closed his eyes, swallowed hard, and winced. He licked at lips caked in dried blood. The lower lip was swollen and blue, a split in the skin was covered with darkened blood. "I don't think I'm going to make it, Duke." His eyes slid shut. The siren on the emergency vehicle echoed off the buildings along Commercial Street as it came out of the station house a block to the north.

"Moonie?"

Again, and as though with great effort, his eyes opened. They were dry and distant, dull marbles barely able to focus. They reminded Duke of the remote, unknowing look in Timmy's eyes. "Rhino must have . . . let him in the back door . . . after we closed."

"Who? Who'd he let in?"

"DeMarco. . . . You were right about him, too. He brought a gun, a big one with a silencer. He shot me in the knees first. . . . Kicked me in the face." He swallowed. "I couldn't do anything but take it. He kept asking what I'd done with the money, but I didn't tell him. . . . I told him I didn't have it, that I . . . I never had it." He winced and took several breaths, each getting shorter than the one before. "It's in our secret place—the safe where we kept the Cokes. Remember?"

"I remember."

"You keep it, Duke. Don't give it to that . . . rat bastard."

Tears began rolling down Duke's face as the life drained out of Moonie's. "No. You'll need it when you get out of the hospital. It'll be there for you."

"You keep it, Duke."

He closed his eyes as the front door banged open. Duke jumped out of the way as the first medic ran into the hall. He looked at Moonie, then briefly up at Duke, then he dropped down and ripped open the front of Moonie's shirt. "He's lost a lot of blood," the medic said. Another medic wrapped an oxygen mask around Moonie's face. As they lifted him to the stretcher and started carrying him out of the restaurant, Moonie looked up at his old friend. He seemed to smile, a little, or perhaps it was his face relaxing before his journey, and he closed his eyes a final time.

CHAPTER NINETEEN

I t was a good day to bury his best friend.

It was day as night in the valley, a time when the sun was screened from sight and streetlights burned at noon. The March sky was low and overcast, a malty mix of smoke and clouds, wisps of gray death that straggled in the wind and clung to the bare limbs. The mist was cold and constant, chilling to the bone those standing on a hillside of grass, deadened brown by the winter winds.

Yes, it was a good day to bury his best friend. Duke would have hated to see Moonie put in the ground on a clear and sunny day, a day that was good for living and one that Moonie would be sad to know he had missed. A day, perhaps, when he could have jumped on the Indian and driven for hours on the asphalt country roads that snaked west out of the valley. That would have seemed most unfair. Moonie had always enjoyed the little things—sunshine, drift fishing, iced beer on a sunny afternoon, the smell of Isaly's coffee. Duke had spoken of these small pleasures at the funeral. He kept his remarks brief, beginning them with: *"We had a fort—me and Moonie and Angel . . ."*

Duke didn't speak of the tragedy that felled his friend, but he talked instead of the wonderful friend he had lost.

"My dad used to say, as you go through life, if you have one friend, one true friend, you're lucky. He said a lot of people would claim to be your friend, but where were they when times were tough and the chips were down? I have been blessed in this life because for the first forty-one years, I've had two—Angelo Angelli and Moonie Collier. Now, of course, I have only one. I consider myself lucky to have had Moonie Collier as a friend.

When we were younger and my mouth got too bold for my body to back up, Moonie was my protector. Moonie's friendship was unconditional. What more could you ask of another human being? I'll never be able to replace him, and I will miss him terribly."

The American flag covering the casket was dampened by the mist by the time Duke and the other pallbearers carried Moonie from the gravel road to the green tent that covered the hole where he would spend eternity. The wind tore at their bare hands, and Duke was glad to set the casket on the canvas straps of the lowering crane. Just beyond the casket, a festoon of roses that Duke had purchased stood propped on a thin wire stand. A funeral-home employee stood behind the roses, keeping it upright against the wind, which had whipped the arrangement and torn it apart at the bottom. Ironically, it had taken on the shape of a horseshoe, and that made Duke smile.

Moonie's mother and her aged mother, who was suffering from Alzheimer's disease and was still unsure who was being buried, sat alone in the only chairs under the tent. Twice before the preacher could say the final prayer, the older woman loudly asked, "Who's in there? Who died?" Moonie's mother, looking wan and weak, didn't answer.

The cemetery at New Alexandria stretches across the side of the tallest hill in the area and is known simply as Cemetery Hill. (Coincidentally, it was just beyond the crest of the hill, maybe a quarter-mile, where the body of the Troll was spending eternity in the trunk of his Lincoln, submerged in the quarry.) On days when the wind was rolling in from the west, like this day, the gales snaked along the side of the ridge and unleashed over the hilltop. The squalls battered the tent, and its ornamental flaps cracked like whips, snapping in succession. Around the tent stood forty men, the black grit of the steel mill ground deep into their hardened hands and the creases of their faces. They hunched against the wind in ill-fitting suits that were worn at funerals and on Easter Sunday.

The wind all but drowned out the preacher, who again prayed for Moonie's soul and peace for his mother. The honor guard of Mingo American Legion Post 351 offered a twenty-one-gun salute, a local high school boy played "Taps," and a square-jawed man in dress blues presented the flag to Mrs. Collier. The preacher announced that those in attendance were invited to an open house at the Colliers', and it was over.

As Duke walked to his car, his eyes red and moist, he turned one last time to look at the bronze casket. Angel put his arm around his friend's shoulder and led him away.

The steelworkers and friends of Moonie Collier in attendance ended up at Duke's Place. Duke hadn't planned to reopen the restaurant until the following day, but it was the logical gathering place. He ordered three trays of Sicilian-style DiCarlo's Pizza from the parlor in downtown Steubenville, and opened the beer cooler and the cash drawer, trusting this brotherhood to the honor system. The steelworkers toasted Moonie and traded stories of his escapades, his incredible ability to throw a baseball, and the senselessness of his death.

"Why would you kill someone for a few hundred bucks?" one steelworker asked, commenting on the common assumption that Moonie had been killed in a robbery attempt.

"Because he was probably giving them the fight of their putrid lives," another said. "They probably had to shoot him before he tore them to pieces."

They talked about Moonie and asked Duke to retell a legendary story. It occurred when they were twelve and feuding with the South Side Commandos. After the Commandos made a nighttime raid and spray painted Fort Logan with, "Komanddos are Number 1," Moonie surveyed their handiwork and said, "I have a plan."

Inspired by a battle scene in the movie *Spartacus* with Kirk Douglas, Moonie stole an empty fifty-five-gallon oil drum from the Pennsylvania Railroad yard, and rolled it to the fort. He used a spool of No. 9 wire to wrap the barrel in newspapers, dried grass and weeds, and oil-soaked rags. On the day of the battle, he lugged a five-gallon can of gasoline to the fort, then sent Angel to challenge the Commandos to a frontal assault on Fort Logan This was nearly impossible because the fort sat atop a steep precipice. Militarily, only a fool would attack the position. Fortunately, the Commandos were led by just such a person—Stevie Bipp. Stevie was a pudgy kid who swore a lot and habitually spit streamers out the gap between his front incisors.

By the time he found the Commandos in their tree fort, Angel was a stuttering wreck. "H-h-hey, y-you g-guys are a b-bunch of p-p-pussies for attacking at n-night," Angel yelled. "Y-y-you d-don't have the g-g-guts to attack in the d-d-day."

Stevie Bipp laughed and mocked Angel. "F-f-fuck you, you s-s-skinny, little p-prick," he said. "I'll k-k-kick your ass the n-n-next time I c-c-catch you."

Frustrated by their lack of action and angered by the mocking, Angel went for the jugular. "H-h-hey, B-Bipp, this is y-y-your m-m-mom." Angel grabbed hold of an imaginary erection and began working it in and out of his mouth, pressing his tongue against the inside of his cheek for added effect.

"You're dead, Angelli," Bipp yelled as he climbed down the tree.

"I g-g-got to g-go. I g-got a d-d-date with your m-m-mom," Angel yelled as he sprinted back to the safety of Fort Logan.

Soon, Bipp and four Commandos were huddling behind the scrub brush at the bottom of the hill. They lobbed rocks at Fort Logan, but made no move at attack. Meanwhile, Moonie was dumping five gallons of gasoline on the rag-and paper-covered drum. "Insult his mother again," Moonie said.

Angel walked out the front opening of the fort and yelled, "H-h-hey B-Bipp, do you h-hear that?"

"I don't hear nothin', you stuttering moron."

"L-l-listen. D-don't you h-h-hear that wh-whistle? It's the t-t-train we're going to p-pull on your m-m-mom."

"Charge!" Bipp yelled, leading his Commandos up the hill. As they neared the halfway mark up the hill, Moonie climbed to the parapet of stone and dirt in front of the fort and yelled, "I am Spartacus!" He lit an entire pack of matches and dropped them on the gasoline-soaked drum. Flames erupted fifteen feet above the barrel and knocked Moonie back into the fort. He ran back to the parapet and kicked the barrel down the hill. It was a spinning, bouncing ball of fire that roared toward the scattering Commandos.

Moonie raised both hands high and yelled, "I am Spartacus. I am Spartacus."

Duke said, "Hey, Spartacus, you just set the hillside on fire."

There were twenty or so small fires directly in front of Fort Logan, and a grand blaze in a dead cedar bush. Gas-soaked rags and paper were flying off the barrel as it tumbled down the hill. It had been a dry summer, and the desiccated ground cover easily ignited. They watched, slack-jawed, as the barrel continued, burning its way through the undergrowth. As they ran down the hill and tried to stomp out the smaller fires, the soles of their tennis shoes melted and little pebbles melded into the soft rubber. A gust of wind pushed the blaze from the cedar bush into a grove of pines. The blanket of dried needles under two trees exploded in flames—*ba-whoosh, ba-whoosh*. Soon, the entire hillside was in flames. The billowing smoke lifted above the West Virginia hills and could be seen in Pennsylvania. It burned most of the hillside between Mingo Junction and Steubenville, and it took seven fire departments to put it out. Miraculously, Fort Logan was spared.

Like the warrior he was, Spartacus fell on his sword, took all the blame, and spent three days in the Jefferson County juvenile detention center. For years afterward, firemen in Mingo Junction called Moonie, "Spark-tacus."

Back at Duke's Place after they'd put Spartacus to rest, it was past midnight when all the boys finally cleared out. Leopold "Big Czech" Meisel was the last to leave. He was more than a little drunk, and Duke knew he shouldn't let Leo drive, but it wasn't worth the fight he would put up. Duke stood outside the restaurant until the taillights of Leo's car disappeared at the underpass. He lifted the black wreath from the door and went back inside, dead-bolting it behind him.

It was quiet in the restaurant except for the din of the steel mill, a muffled groan so constant that it was no more noticed by the people of Mingo Junction than was the brown water of the Ohio or the stone façade of the foothills. It was, simply, something that was always there, a sign that despite Moonie Collier's death, life continued in the Ohio River Valley.

Duke turned off the overhead lights, leaving the florescent tubes to burn under the rim of the bar, and grabbed a beer from the cooler. He eased onto a stool at the end of the bar and stared at his image in the mirror, slowly rolling the bottle between his palms. Duke's Place had long been his dream; now, he didn't know if he would ever again look at it the same way. How could he? Every time he walked to his office, he would step on the spot where Moonie took his last breaths. He couldn't pass it without seeing the real and the imagined—the very real blood-stains that had soaked into the wooden floor, and the ghostly image of Moonie Collier, more dead than alive, sprawled in the hallway. After the police had finished their investigation of the crime scene, Duke tried to remove the stains, but that section of floor had yet to be sealed, and the wood drank in the blood. Even in the darkness of the hallway, Duke could see the outline of the stain. In the darkness of his mind, he could see Moonie more clearly than the blood.

He longed to be with Cara. He would lock up the restaurant and go to her house, take her in his arms, bury his face in her neck, breathe in the scent of her hair, and never let go. No longer did he have any concern for Nina, her feelings, or her murderous brother. They could all go to hell. With two long gulps, he finished the beer, then scooped the haphaz-ardly stacked bills from the cash register and put them in the safe. As he reemerged from the darkened hall and cut behind the bar, Duke jumped when a figure emerged from the hazy light of the kitchen.

A charge of adrenaline boiled in his spine and exploded through his arms and legs like thousands of icy needles. His hands instinctively curled into fists that he drew chest-high. He hadn't taken a breath before he recognized the distinct silhouette of Tony DeMarco.

"Relax, Duke," he said, walking into the glow of the fluorescent bar lights. "I heard you were having a little impromptu wake for your pal Moonie. Me and the boys were just coming over to pay our respects." He looked around the empty bar. "But, uh, looks like the party's over."

Two men in dark sport coats over sweaters stepped out of the kitchen and stood in the shadows behind him. One Duke had never seen before—a fat-faced thug with oily hair and a soft gut that lapped over his belt. The other he recognized. It was the man Moonie had known as Rhino. "I'm assuming you know at least one of my associates?" Tony said.

"Yeah, but I'm not in the market for any key chains."

Tony pointed over his shoulder with his thumb. "Why don't you boys wait in the car? I'll only be a minute." They didn't like it; the fat one had his eye on some of the leftover pizza, but they did as they were told. After the two henchmen had disappeared into the kitchen, Tony stood at the far end of the bar and opened a gloved hand, revealing a brass key; he slid it down the bar top toward Duke. "You should be more careful with your keys, Duke. You leave these things lyin' around, anyone could get in here."

"Yeah, I guess you never know what kind of riffraff might wander in."

Tony grinned and began pulling off his gloves, one finger at a time. "I guess you know where I got that one."

It was Moonie's back-door key. Duke fought back the rage, the urge to go on the attack. It would be a fatal mistake that Tony was no doubt hoping he would make.

"What do you want, Tony?" he asked.

"What? A guy can't pay a social visit to his brother-in-law without wanting something?" He moved toward Duke and opened the box of DiCarlo's Pizza on the bar. He picked out a now-cold square with crust and took a bite. "Man, I love this stuff. This is the best pizza in the world."

"I'm sure they would appreciate your endorsement. 'Hi, I'm Tony DeMarco. And when I'm not killing innocent men or selling drugs to your children, I enjoy a good DiCarlo's Pizza.'"

He did not think Tony was capable of such speed. No sooner had the words left Duke's mouth than Tony's thick forearm was full across his neck, and he was pushed backward into the beer cooler. Duke's nostrils filled with the stale odor of liquor and tomato sauce. A pair of deadly serious brown eyes were inches from his.

"Go ahead, motherfucker, give me just one more reason to kill you. It's not like I don't have enough already."

"Is that what you're going to do, Tony? Kill me, too? Want to make it a clean sweep?"

Tony pushed forward with his forearm, shoving it hard against Duke's jaw and neck, forcing his head up and to the left, pushing so hard that Duke thought his spine would separate from the base of his skull. "You shut your mouth and listen to me, mister fuckin' washed-up basketball star. I am so fuckin' tired of your disrespect. Maybe once you're not family no more, I'll kill you just to watch you die." He was talking in the heavy Brooklyn accent.

"What do you want?" Duke eked out.

"What do I want? What the fuck do you think I want, you moron? I want to know what your idiot friend did with my money."

"What money?"

Tony yelled and pushed harder, this time nearly lifting Duke off the ground. "You're fuckin' trying my patience, junior. My money, where is it?"

"I told you before, Moonie didn't take your money."

Tony showed clenched teeth through a smile of frustration. "I know he took the money. You know he took the money. So let's make life easy for both of us, huh? Where . . . is . . . the . . . money?"

Duke slowly shook his head. "He never had your money. He never did. If he had it, don't you think he would have told you after you blew off the first kneecap?"

"He paid two grand to Carmine and blew town for a week, and I'm supposed to believe he didn't steal the money from the Troll?"

"He won that money at Mountaineer," Duke squeaked out. "He hit the trifecta."

"Really?" He relaxed his arm and pulled away. Duke cupped his jaw in his right hand and worked it back into place. This made Tony grin. "That's too bad, huh? That means I killed that poor bastard for nothin'." He paused a moment, waiting for a reaction that didn't come. "Let me tell you something, Ducheski. You're not dealing with an amateur. I know he didn't hit the trifecta. The most the trifecta paid that night was $1,200. I got connections at Mountaineer, and I checked it out. That dumb-shit friend of yours told me he hit for eight grand. He was a fuckin' liar. He looked me right in the eye and told me he hit the trifecta and had enough money to pay off his debt. No way. You don't lie to Tony DeMarco."

"So, you had to kill him? You don't know that was your money."

"You know, a stupid Polack like you wouldn't understand this, but I got a reputation to maintain. Word gets out that Moonie clipped Tony DeMarco for sixty large and I don't do nothin', people might start to think I'm getting a little soft, you know? I don't want that to happen. Sometimes you have to put a little blood on the floor, so to speak." Tony picked his gloves off the bar. "I'm going to leave now, Duke. But I want to tell you something, and for your sake I hope you're listening. If I find out that you know where he stashed the money, you're next, brother-in-law or not. I'll cut out your heart while it still beats."

He turned and started toward the kitchen, snagging the pizza box on the way out.

CHAPTER TWENTY

It was still an hour or more before dawn. Duke was stretched out on his back, eyes closed, with the soft sound of Cara's breath in his ear and the softness of her hair and breasts on his arm. Her left hand, open and relaxed, rested across his chest. He hadn't slept well—a few fitful hours at best. Even after they had made love, a time when Duke always dozed against her naked body, he fought sleep and twisted in the bed. His heart thumped and he pounded out short, staccato breaths, unable to get that full, cleansing breath, the relaxing sort that would help ease him into sleep. His brain would not shut down. It raced along. Moonie was lying in a pool of his own blood. Tony was smugly grinning as he shoveled a piece of pizza into his mouth. The images would not quit playing over and over in his brain. Three times that night, Cara had awakened and asked, "Are you okay?" Each time he nodded and stroked her hair until she drifted back to sleep.

"I've got to go," he said, rousing her. "I've got some business to take care of."

She grabbed his bicep with both hands and pulled him close. "No. Please, stay."

"I'll be back tonight. Promise. I've got to go." He kissed her on the cheek and quickly dressed. Under the cover of a moonless night, he slipped out the back door, pulling it gently tight, before walking into the woods behind her house.

The woods were dark and covered in an icy sheen. The dead weeds and grass sagged under the weight of the glaze, causing them to droop over the path and brush against his pant legs as he walked. These were the same paths he, Angel, and Moonie had traversed as boys, and they were still familiar to him despite the darkness. The trail was covered in crystals of ice and slick under his soles. Rabbits moved under the briars. The blackbirds of winter cried out their warnings that an intruder was near.

As he crested the hill behind Cara's and turned east, the faintest hint of morning was escaping from beyond the West Virginia hills. Duke picked up the pace, moving quickly to make the distance there and back before most of Mingo Junction awoke. Merely getting to the top of the hill had winded him, and he pulled hard for air. For a few minutes he stood at the crest, hands on hips, catching his breath. How many hours, he wondered, had a younger Duke Ducheski thoughtlessly and effortlessly run over those same paths? Now, simply making his way to the top of the hill had caused his hamstrings to tighten and his lungs to burn.

He ran the ridge of hills encircling Mingo Junction, and in another ten minutes, just as the first orange rays appeared over the blooming mill, Duke was standing amid the sad remains of Fort Logan. Time had taken its toll. A few honey-locust posts remained, but weeds and vines and dry rot had claimed much of the once-fine fort, and briars gnarled over ground that once had been beaten bare by their footfalls. Duke brushed the dirt from the corner of a car seat that was now little more than bare springs and a few scraps of cloth. He recalled that day long past when they had found the treasure in Andy Garfield's trash. "Can we have this?" Duke had asked Andy, who hated kids and had the disposition of a badger.

"I don't give a good goddamn what you do with it," he growled. "Just don't tromp over the flowers getting it out of here."

Then Andy stood and watched to make sure that not a single marigold was squashed. They hauled it to the fort. The three best friends spent many nights on the seat, rocking back and staring at the river and the reflection of glowing molten steel being poured from the giant ladles inside Wheeling-Pitt.

They had been pubescent teens when they had finally abandoned Fort Logan. Duke couldn't remember exactly when that had occurred. It had not been a conscious decision, like the formal closing of a military base, but rather a slow progression from childhood into an adolescence without forts and secret hideouts. One day, they left and never returned.

Until recently.

The car seat was wedged against a sandstone bluff. Beneath the seat was a two-foot square hole that the boys had dug and lined with plywood and No Parking signs they had taken from the junk heap behind the city street department garage. Inside the hole they had placed a safe that they'd rummaged from the dump. It no longer locked, but it was a wonderful addition to the fort—their secret compartment. They dropped it into the hole on its back so the door opened to the top. It was the ideal place to keep soda out of the heat and away from their predatory rivals, the South Side Commandos. When Fort Logan was still in active duty, the boys covered the opening with the sign, dirt, and the car seat. It was never disturbed or noticed. Over the years, the dirt had hardened atop the sign, and vines snaked across the ground so that no hint of a secret hiding place existed.

Duke nudged the seat forward. It was obvious that the ground beneath it had been disturbed recently. Working his fingers into the dirt, he found the edge of the No Parking sign and lifted. The dirt and stone slid off the metal. He pushed the sign to the side and found the safe remarkably clean, save for some rust around the edge of the door. After taking a steadying breath, he grabbed the handle and lifted.

Crammed inside the safe was the Troll's blue canvas bag. Duke worked it back and forth, prying it free. Unzipping the bag, he took a breath and said, "Christ, Moonie." The bag was stuffed full of bills, a patchwork of presidential green.

It was the first time he had cried since the night Moonie Collier died. Moonie's instincts had been to run back to their childhood fort and hide the money like they had hidden their sodas. It forced Duke to remember just how childlike Moonie could be. The sadness overwhelmed him. He dabbed at his tears with the shoulder of his jacket, returned the bag, and re-covered the hole with the sign and the dirt and the skeleton of the seat. The sun was now completely above the West

Virginia hills, burning the ice off the Ohio hillside as he began walking back to Cara's.

Duke Ducheski was consumed with renewed anger. As he walked, he plotted: How would he murder Tony DeMarco? It could be quite simple, actually. He played it out in his mind: He would simply renew his love for Nina and re-ingratiate himself with her family. He would dutifully attend the Sunday dinners, but this time he would laugh and smile when Tony laughed and smiled, and scowl when Tony scowled. He would act the part of the little lapdog, the role that Tony demanded from his friends. When the wine flowed, he would plead for a slightly drunken Tony to tell more stories. Oh, and what wonderful stories they would be. He would laugh and pat Tony on the back, and they would be great paisanos, confidants.

Then, one night several months later, Duke would be closing up the bar and Tony would stop by, and once again he would start badgering Duke about allowing gambling in the restaurant. Duke would wince and hesitate and say, "I don't know." Tony would drape a friendly arm around Duke's back and squeeze—not a friendly squeeze, but a strong, meaningful squeeze, a signal that he was tired of Duke dragging his feet. "I guess we can talk about it," Duke would say.

Tony, sensing that his brother-in-law was weakening, would say in his mock Brooklyn-Italian accent, "Sure, what the hell, it don't cost nothin' to talk, right?" He would laugh.

"Let's go back to my office," Duke would say.

And that's where it would happen. When the office door clicked shut and Tony turned to discuss business, Duke would have a pistol pointing right at his nose. Duke would let Tony get a good look at his eyes and understand the deadly seriousness of the moment. When that occurred, when Duke saw the terrified recognition on Tony's face, Duke would back him into the hallway, shoot him twice in the knees and twice in the chest, and let him die on Moonie's bloodstain.

CHAPTER TWENTY-ONE

Chief Hinton Jaynes was a caricature for every stereotypical, corrupt, small-town cop in America. He sipped cheap gin throughout the day from a pint bottle that he kept hidden in his bottom desk drawer, and he had been a two-way tackle for the Mingo High Indians in the days before facemasks. Those two separate but related facts had left his ample nose twisted and rutted, bright red, and lined with a road map of deep-blue veins. His jaw jutted out so far that his lower lip was always sucking in the upper and hiding it from view. The cigarettes he chain-smoked—nonfiltered Camels—stuck out from the lower lip like tiny erections, dancing when he spoke and coming dangerously close to igniting the tiny hairs that sprouted from his nostrils. The buttons of his always neatly pressed white shirts strained to constrain the belly, which had so devoured his gun belt that the handle of his revolver dug into his side each time he sat down. He was a monument to what excessive smoking, drinking, and a daily lunch of sausage gravy over biscuits at Paddy's Diner could do to a person.

Jaynes loved being the chief of police of Mingo Junction, Ohio. He particularly enjoyed leading the parades, getting out in front of the American Legion honor guard in his cruiser, red-and-blue lights flashing, waving and tossing bubble gum to the kids, all the while checking out their moms from behind his reflective sunglasses. He had coveted the job for as long as he could remember, although never for the right reasons. As a youth, he fantasized about using his authority to blow away the classmates who made cruel remarks about his weight or his pronounced under bite, which had earned him the nickname "Four-by," because it looked like someone had smashed him in the mouth with the end of a four-by-four.

The badge on his chest earned Jaynes a grudging respect in Mingo Junction. Or, at least that is how he saw it. What the chief interpreted as respect was actually abject fear. He had a long memory, a gun, authority, and a mean streak as wide as the Ohio River. It didn't matter to Chief Hinton Jaynes whether you respected him or simply feared him; he made no distinction between the two. The law in Mingo Junction was whatever he decided it would be. If you didn't like that, too bad for you.

Jaynes joined the police department after a hitch in the army. His climb through the ranks of the department had been less than meteoric, and the more he was passed over for promotions, the more disgruntled he became. He was once suspended after roughing up a sixteen-year-old during a routine traffic stop. He was twice accused of, though never charged with, offering women the opportunity to avoid speeding tickets in exchange for blow jobs. He was the only suspect when eight hundred dollars in cash and a gold wristwatch disappeared from the evidence safe. He languished as a patrolman for years before making sergeant, and he was passed over for the chief's job three times before council finally gave him the position in 1978. There were no external candidates, and he had more years of service than any of the other internal candidates. Perhaps, city council rationalized, Jaynes would rise to the challenge.

He didn't.

A week after his swearing in, Jaynes held a press conference to announce the formation of a special anti-vice unit that would focus on illegal drugs and gambling operations. "I'm putting the owners of these operations on notice. These elements are not welcome in Mingo Junction, Ohio," he was quoted in the Steubenville *Herald-Star*. "Anyone who thinks they're going to operate here is going to have to deal with me."

The message was crystalline.

The youthful fantasies of wanting to be the chief of police to exact revenge on his tormentors had long since been replaced by the financially advantageous realities of being a dishonest cop in the Ohio Valley.

The week after the article appeared in the newspaper, Tony DeMarco showed up unannounced at the chief's office.

Jaynes beamed at the sight of the young Italian, who was wearing a finely tailored suit and carrying a black attaché case. "Mr. DeMarco, how good to see you. Come in, come in," he said, rising from his seat to shake hands. Tony pulled the door closed behind him and was all smiles, though he keenly remembered how then patrolman Jaynes had called him a wop and jabbed him in the kidneys with a nightstick in the days when he was just a punk thug hanging around Isaly's. This, however, was not the time or place to relive those days.

"Congratulations on your new position, Chief Jaynes," Tony said. "It should have happened years ago."

"I appreciate your sentiments," Jaynes said.

Tony was playing him. They sat and exchanged pleasantries for a few minutes before Tony lifted the black attaché case off the floor.

"What's in there?" Jaynes asked.

"In here?" Tony asked. "Oh, just some of my business papers. You keep your business papers in file cabinets; I keep mine in my briefcase." He leaned toward the chief, one brow dipping low, and in a hushed tone asked, "Would you like to inspect my business papers, Chief Jaynes?"

The chief put his fingertips together, spread them, and then pressed his thumbs to his flat chin. "Well, as chief of police of Mingo Junction, I think it's only fitting that I be kept apprised of all the business dealings going on in my city. Sure, why don't you let me have a look?"

Tony stood before the chief and set the briefcase on the desk, clasps toward the lawman. He released the clasps one at a time, then slowly lifted the lid, revealing twenty neatly wrapped stacks of crisp, new, ten-dollar bills. The chief looked for a long moment, then fingered one of the stacks, flipping through it bill by bill. Tony had deliberately used tens to fill the attaché case.

"My associates asked me to deliver this as a token of their respect for you as an individual and an officer of the law," Tony said. He leaned across the desk and said in a hushed tone, "Ten thousand dollars, Chief, and it's all yours. Can I assume that you find this satisfactory?"

Still holding a stack of cash, almost in a trance, Jaynes jerked his head up and said, "Oh, yes. Yes, most assuredly. It's most satisfactory."

"Good." He gently lowered the lid on the attaché case and pushed the snaps closed. "Then, I can tell my superiors that you accept this small, what shall we call it, *gift*? A token of our appreciation?"

"You can tell them I accept their most generous gift, and with future considerations they can expect to continue doing business in Mingo Junction without interference from the police department."

"'Future considerations'?" Tony laughed. He whispered, "You mean hard cash, don't you, Chief?"

Jaynes smiled. "Correct. Hard cash. That's the language I understand."

Tony winked. "It's clearly understood, Chief Jaynes. Keep the attaché. The next time I or one of my associates visits, we'll be carrying an identical attaché. We'll walk in with your, what did you call them, 'future considerations,' in one attaché. We'll walk out of here with the empty. That way, no one suspects you're on the take."

Jaynes bristled at Tony's phrase, "on the take," but decided to let it pass. "Understood," he said.

Tony smiled. "Enjoy, Chief."

A month later, Tony was back in the chief's office with an identical attaché. The chief grinned as he opened it. The grin, however, faded quickly when inside he found only a small tape recorder. He looked at Tony, his lower lip stiff and engulfing the upper clear to his nose. Tony reached down and hit the play button.

"Good. Then I can tell my superiors that you accept this small, what shall we call it, gift? A token of our appreciation?"

"You can tell them I accept their most generous gift, and with future considerations they can expect to continue doing business in Mingo Junction without interference from the police department."

"'Future considerations'? You mean hard cash, don't you, Chief?"

"Correct. Hard cash. That's the language I understand."

Jaynes's face burned crimson. "You fuckin', double-crossing Dago bastard."

Tony shrugged, snorted a laugh, and held up both palms. "Of course I double-crossed you. That's what I do."

Jaynes opened the recorder, jerked out the cassette, and threw it on the ground, stomping it several times, an action that left the overweight chief sucking for air.

Tony didn't flinch, but he watched in mild amusement as he worked over a piece of chewing gum. "Chief . . . it's a copy. I wouldn't be dumb enough to blackmail you with the original."

Chief Hinton Jaynes sat, nearly in tears, his guts on fire.

"Don't feel so bad, Chief. Every cop in the valley falls for it. We've got every dirty cop up and down the river on tape." He took the chewing gum from his mouth and set the wad on the corner of the chief's desk, for the first time showing his true contempt for the fat man. "Here's the deal." From inside his suit coat he pulled a brown lunch bag, folded down and taped shut, and tossed it on the chief's desk. "The tape is an insurance policy, you know, in case you decide to find Jesus or you get a case of moral consciousness and try to drop the package on us, which I'm sure won't happen. But, just in case . . ." Tony let the words hang for several seconds while the face of Hinton Jaynes burned like the open hearth. "You'll get a regular package from me." He pointed to the one he had just dropped on the chief's desk. "In exchange, we—the Antonelli family—are to be the exclusive numbers game in Mingo Junction. We operate without restriction and we operate without competition. That's very important, Chief. This is now our turf, exclusively. We won't cause any problems, but you don't give us any, either. Understand?"

There was a roar in the chief's ears that could drown out the one from the blast furnace at Wheeling-Pitt. Every nerve ending in his body was on fire. How stupid could he have been?

"Chief!" Tony said, snapping Jaynes from his trance. "Do you understand?"

Jaynes nodded. "Yeah . . . I understand."

Duke was not hesitant to approach Chief Jaynes. Over the years, the chief had been a constant verbal target of Tony DeMarco at the Sunday dinners. Because of this, Duke incorrectly assumed that Tony was able to sell drugs and run a gambling operation only because the chief, like most people, feared him and the Antonellis. He had given no thought to the possibility of blackmail and payoffs. Why pay off someone, Duke reasoned, when you were powerful enough to operate without their consent? In his naiveté, Duke believed that the chief's desire to solve a homicide would outweigh his fear of Tony DeMarco.

When Duke showed up at the police department and asked to see him, Chief Jaynes lumbered up from his office and greeted him like a lost war buddy, pumping his right hand and slapping his shoulder. "Duke Ducheski, good to see you, son. Come on back and sit down. Can I get you a cup of coffee?"

"No thanks, Chief," he said.

"It's time for my refill," he said, pouring the remainder of the morning brew into a Lions Club mug badly in need of scrubbing. Duke waited, then tagged along into the office, taking a seat in the metal chair in front of the chief's desk.

The room was not so much an office as it was a shrine to Chief Jaynes. The walls were covered with photos of the chief and anyone of any note who had ever wandered through Mingo Junction. There was one of Jaynes shaking hands with Ohio State football coach Woody Hayes, who had gotten his first high school coaching job at Mingo High; Jaynes with his arm around the shoulders of actor Robert

De Niro when he was in town filming *The Deer Hunter*; Jaynes and Mingo Junction's Rob Parissi, lead singer for the disco group Wild Cherry, which had the mega hit, "Play That Funky Music." There were numerous letters of commendation and certificates of completion for law enforcement classes.

"I suppose you're wanting to know how the investigation into Moonie Collier's murder is coming," the chief said, maneuvering behind his desk and snagging a manila folder from the credenza in the process. The tab on the folder read, "Collier, Theodore," and it seemed woefully thin for the contents of a murder investigation.

"Yes, sir, that's exactly why I stopped by," Duke said.

The chief slipped a cigarette into the corner of his mouth, a conductor's wand that kept time as he spoke. "The first thing you should know is that I've personally taken control of the investigation."

"Yes, sir, that's what I heard. That's why I thought I'd stop by. I thought it was a little strange that I was the one who found Moonie shot in my restaurant, but no one has interviewed me yet."

The chief sat up a little straighter in his chair, his brow furrowed, and three distinct ridges stretched across his forehead. Duke's comment implied ineptitude, and that had riled him. After a calming breath, he leaned into the flame of his Zippo. "I've been meaning to get to you, Duke, but we've been so busy tracking down other leads that we just haven't had the chance to give you a call." He forced a smile. "I mean, after all, better to be tracking down real suspects, don't you think?"

"I guess so. Do you have any leads?" Duke asked.

"As of yet, nothing solid, but we're working on it. I can tell you this much, it looks like a robbery gone bad—probably done by professionals. They didn't leave any fingerprints—not a goddamn one. It was a tidy little job, I can tell you that."

"'Tidy'? Did you go into my restaurant after the murder? There was blood everywhere. Those bastards tortured Moonie before they killed him. Who shoots someone in the knees before robbing them? No way that was a robbery."

"They cleaned out your cash register. What else could it be?"

"That was just a cover."

Hinton Jaynes arched his brows. "Really? A cover, huh?" He leaned forward and put both elbows on the desk, his fat fingers interlocked, a gold wedding band strangling a ring finger. "A cover for what?"

Duke took a breath and exhaled slowly. "It was a professional hit."

The chief's frown slowly dissolved into a grin. "You're kidding me, right? Why in the devil would you think that? Who would want to kill a good ol' boy like Moonie Collier?"

"Joseph Antonelli and Tony DeMarco."

The chief shifted in his seat, a line of red creeping up around his shirt collar. He didn't want to hear the name Tony DeMarco spoken in his presence. The fact that Duke mentioned it in connection with a murder made it even worse. The chief took a nervous drag on his cigarette. "How do you know that? Well, how do you *think* you know that?"

"Tony thought Moonie had something to do with the disappearance of Frankie Silvestri and the stolen gambling receipts back in September."

"Frankie Silvestri? You mean that little crippled-up fella I used to see down around Carmine's Lounge? What do they call him, the Troll? That fella?"

Now Duke could feel the heat creeping up *his* neck. Jaynes was such a horrible liar. "Yeah, that little crippled-up fella, that's him."

"He disappeared? I didn't know that. When? And what are you talking about—gambling receipts?"

"You didn't know that the Troll disappeared with about sixty thousand dollars in gambling receipts in September?"

The chief shook his head and took a long hit off his Camel. "I don't know anything about it."

"How could you not know? You're the goddamn chief of police."

"Well, son, let me tell you a few things. First of all, I don't know where he would get gambling receipts in Mingo Junction. I don't tolerate gambling in my city. Secondly, no one's reported this Troll fella missing. Maybe he just went on a little vacation. And, lastly, if you call me the goddamn chief of police again, I'll wrap my nightstick around your skull."

The fire that exploded in Duke's belly was not an unfamiliar one. It was the same as getting kicked in the balls, an immediate ignition that burned every nerve from his testicles to his heart. Hinton Jaynes knew who killed Moonie; he just didn't care.

Duke stood and leaned over the chief's desk, teeth clenched beneath a curled upper lip. "I'll tell you what, Chief, how about giving me a nice, big, wet kiss on the lips? If you're going to fuck me, the least you can do is kiss me."

The gloves were off. The chief's eyes squeezed down to hateful slits. "You better watch your mouth, boy."

"Really? You think because your fat ass is parked behind that badge that I'm forced to show you respect?"

Anger flared in the eyes of Hinton Jaynes, his cheeks glowing to the color of boiled crab. Then, slowly, the eyelids relaxed, the cheeks cooled, and a conniving smile crossed his lips. "Maybe I should do a little more work on this. In fact, Mr. Ducheski, I think interviewing you would be a fine place to start. Moonie was killed in your restaurant, and where exactly were you that morning?"

"What's that got to do with anything?"

"This is an active murder case, Mr. Ducheski. No one has been eliminated as a suspect."

"That's total bullshit. You know I didn't kill Moonie."

"Maybe you staged it for insurance purposes? Sure would make a good newspaper story if you were under investigation, wouldn't it—former basketball hero being investigated for murder of lifelong friend? That would make for some nice headlines. Probably wouldn't do your business any good, would it?"

The message was clear, and, with the possible exception of the time Tony DeMarco had a pistol jammed in his mouth, Duke Ducheski had never felt so powerless. Without another word, he turned and left, the heat from his belly rolling clear up into his throat. He was angry at his own stupidity. Pissing off the chief was bad enough, but as he walked out of the police station, he realized he had just spoken into the ears of Tony DeMarco.

When Chief Hinton Jaynes suffered those rare pangs of consciousness about accepting the monthly bribes from Tony DeMarco, he found it easy to place blame. How could anyone expect him to survive on that piddly-ass salary the city paid him? Why, if the city had paid him what he was worth, he would have had no reason to start accepting the cash.

Besides, the people of Mingo Junction had no reason to complain. Their community was a safe place to live. He didn't tolerate loud car stereos or mufflers, or kids ramming their cars up and down the streets or squealing their tires. And if any of those peckerheads from Brilliant came up to raise a little hell, didn't he run their asses right out of town? Goddamn right, he did. Granted, he now had a messy, unsolved homicide on the books, but, truth be known, most people were more concerned about kids squealing tires than they were the death of Moonie Collier.

He was only giving them what they wanted. The mill rats loved to gamble. It was a part of their culture and their pathetic lives. He would have a riot on his hands if he tried to take away their football spot sheets. How else would they be able to fritter away their paychecks? Even without the payoffs from Antonelli, he would have made no attempt to kill the gambling. So, was it really a bribe?

Those were the thoughts running through his head earlier that afternoon when the DeMarco henchman they called Rhino stopped by the office. The receptionist had recognized Rhino, and she said only, "He's alone." Rhino walked into the office and tossed Jaynes the brown paper sack. "Enjoy your lunch," he said.

Jaynes held the money in his right hand and flipped the edges of the wad with his left thumb like a blackjack dealer with a fresh deck. The bag contained the regular thousand-dollar payoff, plus an additional five grand.

"There's a little bonus there for not getting too excited about Moonie Collier," Rhino said.

As he turned and headed out the door, Jaynes said, "Hold up a minute. I want to tell you about a conversation I had the other day."

CHAPTER TWENTY-TWO

The work schedule was wearing him down. Monday through Friday, Duke worked the daylight shift at Wheeling-Pitt, reporting to work at 8:00 in the morning and getting off at 4:00 in the afternoon. As soon as the whistle sounded, he ran across the street and showered in the apartment upstairs, then went right down to work behind the bar, his hair still sopping. Duke's Place closed at 1:00 a.m. Sunday through Wednesday nights. By the time he cleaned up and stocked for the next day, made beer orders, and dropped the cash in the night deposit, it was never any earlier than 2:30, and usually after 3:00. On Thursday, Friday, and Saturday nights, the bar was open until 2:00 a.m., so he was there even later.

Some nights after closing, he visited Cara. Most of the time he crashed on the couch in his office or the blow-up mattress in the apartment. He napped during his lunch break at the mill, and sometimes caught a little sleep in the early evenings before the heavy crowds arrived. Duke couldn't remember the last time he didn't feel like taking a nap.

On Sunday nights, he always closed the restaurant himself. Angel would stop by in the early evening, and they would pay bills and review the week's financials.

On the first warm Sunday of March 1994, a larger-than-usual crowd had gathered to toast the divorce of Pee-Wee Tomasi. Pee-Wee was falling-down drunk when Duke took his car keys and made his brother promise to take him home.

When Pee-Wee and his friends left, Duke made up the cash drawer for the next day and hurriedly mopped the floor. It was Cara's birthday, and he hadn't seen her all weekend. Saturday, he had gone to Steuben-ville and bought her a cake and an opal necklace for her present. He was anxious to give it to her. With the front of the restaurant locked tight, he backed out the kitchen door into the alley, cradling the cake he bought her in one hand and fumbling with his keys in the other. Duke had just inserted the key into the lock of the steel security door when out of the corner of his eye he saw the looming shadow of a man. By then, it was too late to react.

The thump to the back of his head sent the world into slow motion. He staggered and tried to stay upright, but the alley swirled, a burst of white light flashed across his eyes and frontal lobe, and his knees buckled. The cake slid within the box, like a deck chair in rough seas, and fell from his hands. Darkness closed in from the corners of his eyes, and he felt as though his torso was draped in a vest of lead. The bricks of the building and the gravel of the alley blurred, but only for an instant. He was unconscious before he hit the ground.

Consciousness returned before his vision. Men were talking, but the voices were garbled, and he could not dissect the words from the sentences. It was as though he was under light anesthetic—aware that there was a world beyond the haze, but not conscious enough to make sense of his environment. He was lying on a floor, that much he knew, and there was a fierce pounding in his head. It was that pain that had awakened Duke before he could open his eyes.

When finally he could lift his eyelids, light entered his pupils like hot blades. He could not regain his focus. The room was a swirl of sepia. A light burned overhead; it created a fuzzy, yellow glow that seemed to pulse with each beat of his heart; a misty outline of a figure loomed before him. Duke closed his eyes again, squeezing the lids in a vain attempt to ward off the pain. The voices in the room remained nonsensical, floating overhead like so much gibberish. Occasionally, he could discern the laughter. The pain in his head made him nauseated, and the pressure pushed up through his chest, leaving an acidic venom percolating in his throat. He wanted to vomit.

Duke was not sure how much time passed before his vision returned. It could have been minutes or hours. When the room started narrowing into focus, he saw the blurred figure before him in duplicate. Gradually, it melded into a single Tony DeMarco. It was only then that he remembered the shadowy figure in the alley and the thump to the back of his head. It stood to reason that Tony was involved.

"How's your head, Duke?" he asked. The words seemed to flow out of his mouth like sap from a maple.

Duke reached behind his head and ran his fingertips over a knot the size of half a tennis ball. The light from the room danced like smoke. He pinched his temples between his middle finger and thumb, and again fought back the bile that filled his throat.

Several minutes passed. Duke blinked his surroundings into focus. He recognized it as the rec room on the third floor of Tony's Victorian home. When the house had been owned by the Carothers family in the early days of the twentieth century, the room had been used for entertaining the executives of the steel mills. Tony had converted it to a party room with a big-screen television, a pool table, and a wet bar. One end was dedicated to fitness equipment. Duke sat up and then leaned against the cool stainless steel of Tony's universal gym. When he squinted across the room, he saw Tony standing behind the bar, grinning, and still waiting for an answer. It didn't come, so he posed his question again. "Your head, Ducheski? How's your head?"

"Hurts," Duke mumbled.

"Want some ice? That'll keep the swelling down," Tony said.

"Maybe not getting hit with a club would have helped keep the swelling down."

"See, that's what I like about you, Duke. You've always got something cute to say, no matter how bad the situation." Tony walked around and took a seat on one of the oak stools fronting the bar. Duke slowly turned toward the couch. Sitting there were two smiling thugs. "You've met Rhino," Tony said. "This other gentleman is a business associate of mine, Emilio." Neither man moved from the couch. Duke recalled Carmine telling him how Emilio something-or-other had roughed him up at the lounge.

Duke's vision returned fully. His head thumped with each pulse. There was swelling and a scrape over his left brow, where he dropped into the gravel of the alley. "What's this about?" Duke asked.

"We need to talk."

"You couldn't pick up the phone like a normal human being?"

"Telephones are so impersonal, don't you think? For important meetings, like this, there is a certain decorum that we like to follow in my circles, and that calls for providing transportation to the meeting."

Duke took several deep breaths, continuing to gather his bearings. He pushed himself to his feet, staggered for purchase, and held tight to the universal gym until the lightness ebbed from his head. "Okay, I'm here." Duke started across the room toward the bar with the stability of a newborn lamb. "What do you want?"

"My sister asked me to talk to you. This whole divorce thing has her quite upset." Tony crossed his arms and shook his head. "*Quite* upset. I told her that we'd have a conversation, you and me."

"You busted my head and dragged me up here to give me marriage counseling?"

"See, more cute comments. You crack me up. I'm not sure you appreciate how much pressure this puts on me, Duke. I would have thought after our last conversation about divorcing my sister that you would be makin' better decisions."

"I'm not sure you appreciate the deteriorated state of my marriage."

"You're missin' the point. I don't give a shit about the state of your marriage. It's when it starts interfering with my business that it becomes a problem. After the Troll disappeared, I had Joey Antonelli climbing a yard up my ass. If that wasn't bad enough, my sister starts calling, bawlin' and sayin' that she doesn't know what to do because you want a divorce and that you're out all the time screwin' that nurse, and on and on and on. I tell her, 'Nina, I ain't got time for this, right now.' You know, like all I got to do all day is listen to her cry about her marital problems. But, I gotta listen, 'cause she's my twin sister. Then my mom starts raggin' my ass about it. I've got an operation to run, and I'm spendin' all my time listenin' to two women whine about what a son of a bitch you are. Again, I tell Nina I ain't got the time. Then, a week ago, out of the clear blue fuckin' sky, she tells me that if I'll help keep her marriage together, she'll tell me where you guys hid the Troll's money."

Tony stopped talking and stared hard at Duke, waiting for a reaction. Duke rubbed the back of his neck. Tony was bluffing, he thought. Nina couldn't possibly know that.

Tony continued. "I ask her how she knows where you hid the money, and she says she just knows. She says she won't tell me unless I promise to help save her marriage. I tell her, 'Nina, this ain't the fuckin' time for you to be making demands of my time.' I'm out sixty large, and she wants me to fix her marriage. Anyway, I talked to her and, of course, she didn't know where the money was."

"Big surprise. Your sister didn't know what she was talking about."

"I know, right? But, I had to check it out, like I said, she ..." He stopped in midsentence, took Duke by the arm, and turned him around. "Jesus H. Christ, let me have a look at that knot. Emilio, for God's sake, I just wanted you to get his attention. I didn't want you to give him brain damage. Look at that lump."

"I know, boss, but I figured with that hard Polack head, I needed to give him a good thump."

They all laughed.

Tony reached into a drawer, and handed Duke a plastic sandwich bag. "Here, get some ice out of the freezer and put it on your lump."

Duke walked around the bar and opened the freezer door. As he reached for an ice cube tray, he yelled, "Oh, Mother of Christ," and he jumped away from the refrigerator, banging into the bar and knocking Tony's soda to the floor, where it shot foam across the carpet. Tony exploded in laughter, as did Rhino and Emilio.

"Ain't that the most gruesome fuckin' sight you've ever seen?" Tony roared, pointing at the decayed and frozen head of Frankie "the Troll"

Silvestri. The eye sockets were empty, and dirt was smeared on what gray flesh remained attached to the head. The mouth was agape and caked brown with dirt. Ice crystals were clinging to the scalp and brows.

"Poor Troll," Tony said. "He looks like a science experiment gone really bad."

"He didn't look much better when he was alive," Rhino said.

Again, they laughed.

Duke's urge to vomit was overwhelming. He assumed he was a dead man. Tony continued to laugh.

"Oh God, Duke, you should have seen the look on your face," Tony said, snorting. "That was classic. Classic. You looked like you'd seen a ghost." He held his chest and started to regain control.

"I gotta tell you something, Duke, and this is funny—if you think that ugly bastard smelled bad when he was alive, you should have gotten a whiff of him after he'd been buried a few months. We had him in the trunk of Emilio's car, and I was gagging all the way home. It was fuckin' terrible."

Tony walked behind the bar and flipped the freezer door closed.

"Better keep it cold in there. We don't want him thawin' out."

He opened the refrigerator and pulled out another Diet Coke, then stepped around the front of the bar and pointed at a chair next to the couch. "Sit down, Duke. We have a lot to discuss." He snapped open the can, took a drink, then smiled. "Let me tell you something, Ducheski, this is one of the best goddamn days of my life. You're probably wondering how in the hell the Troll crawled out of that hole, aren't you?"

"That question was crossing my mind." Duke eased into the chair and looked across the room at the front windows. He wondered, if he dove through the window, could he survive a three-story fall? Probably not.

"Nina and my mom rag my ass until I finally go over and talk to her. She tells me again that she knows where my money is. She tells me you came home one day and told her that you're going fishing. She thinks it's bullshit. She thinks you're going out to hook up with the nurse at the cabin, so she drives out to the cabin to try to catch you screwin' your brains out. She sees your car, but not the nurse's, and the cabin is all locked up and dark. She walks down the path a bit and hears you back in the woods. She gets a little closer and sees you digging a hole. She said there was a bright moon and she could see you plain as could be. She figures you're just digging for bait, so she beats it out of there before you catch her spying on you. You get home that night, and you're carrying a cup of night crawlers. She starts to wonder why you'd been digging for worms when you already had some, but she doesn't make the connection right away. It doesn't mean anything to her until I tell her I can't help her with her marriage because someone ripped me off for sixty thousand dollars, and that I think her hubby's pal Moon Pie was involved. Finally, she starts connecting the dots. She figures that was what you were up to—you were helping out your buddy by burying the cash. So she tells me about it. I go out with Rhino and Emilio; we don't find the money, but we got the next best thing. Do you know what that is?"

"Tell me."

"Proof that you've been a very bad boy, Duke. You've been lying to me."

Despite the throbbing in his head, that evening at the lake was as clear in his mind as that night had been. He had heard the car, but he had dismissed it as his imagination. The stirring in the brush hadn't been a deer. It had been Nina. "She saw me burying the Troll's head and thought it was the missing money?"

"Isn't that great? Ordinarily, I'd just kill you for this. But, this is better. See, if I'd found the money, you'd just be in the shit. But you buried the severed head of a human being who had been murdered. Do you know what that makes you, Duke?"

He nodded. "Complicit."

"Exactly," he said, laughing. "Isn't this great? Now, I've got to tell you this. Honest to God, this will just crack you up, too. Remember how I told you that I checked with a source at Mountaineer Park and that no one hit the trifecta the way Moonie said he did?"

"I remember."

"Total bullshit. I just made that up." He roared with laughter. "Joey Antonelli was worried that word would get out that people were knocking off his couriers, so he says he wants a head to roll for the missing cash—you know, set an example. I picked the most logical suspect—your pal Moonie. It was a guess, a total fuckin' guess. Can you believe it? I thought it might be him, but I had no proof—none, other than the fact that he was such a dumb-ass that he might think he could pull a stunt like that and get away with it. Can you believe my luck? I sent old Moon Pie to meet the devil on a roll of the dice. Then, presto, the Troll rears his ugly head again, and it's your dick in the wringer. I'm tellin' you, Duke, no shit, it's the greatest goddamn day of my life. How lucky can one guy get?" He grinned and kneeled down in front of Duke. "Duke," he said, all humor suddenly gone from his voice. "Where's the money?"

"I don't know."

Tony sipped at his Diet Coke and set it on the floor next to the chair in which Duke sat. "Okay, we're going to play a little game. It's called, 'Don't Bullshit Tony.' It's a very easy game; here's how it's played. I'm going to ask you questions and you will tell me the truth. In exchange for playing the game correctly, we won't play, 'Emilio, Go Get the Tin Snips and Start Cutting off Body Parts.' Understand?"

Duke nodded.

"Good. Let's try this one again. Where's the money?"

"I don't know."

"Eeeeeech," Tony said, mimicking a game-show buzzer. "Oh, I'm sorry. Wrong answer. Emilio, it's time to play your game."

"Tony, I'm telling you, I don't know. I told Moonie I didn't care what he did with it, but to keep me out of it."

"He rips me off for sixty large, and you—"

"It was fifty-eight thousand, three hundred and twelve dollars." Tony's brow arched. "I don't know what he did with the money. He and the Troll got into a fight because the Troll thought Moonie was going to double-cross him."

Tony frowned. "What's that mean?"

"The Troll and Moonie had been working together to rip you off for years."

"Bullshit," Tony said, twice poking Duke on the forehead with an index finger. "No one skims from Tony DeMarco and gets away with it."

"Moonie and the Troll had been working it for a long time. Moonie said that one time, a couple years back, he and the Troll got greedy and skimmed too much and you figured it out, but they caught a break because you thought Carmine was the one ripping you off. You took your dog down and threatened Carmine that if it ever happened again, you'd sic your dog on him, and then your dog shit on his pool table."

Tony's considerable jaw tightened, and his eyes turned to slits. "The Troll did that? He was the one skimming?"

Duke shrugged. "I'm just telling you what Moonie told me. He said he would go into Carmine's about every other week and fill out a gambling sheet and lose intentionally, usually on baseball or college football. On Saturday nights, after the games were over, he and the Troll would hook up somewhere on the other side of the cemetery in New Alexandria, near some quarry. He would fill out the same gambling sheet, but as a winner. The Troll would swap the sheets and take a thousand or so out of the bag for the winnings. Moonie got 50 percent."

"You're lying."

He was making it up as he went. Despite the blow to the head, Duke knew he might never walk out of the room if he didn't convince Tony of his innocence.

"Moonie was into Carmine for two thousand dollars, but the Troll told him he wouldn't cover the bets. The Troll said he was worried that you were onto him and the game was over. He told Moonie that he had to pay off the two thousand. Moonie got steamed and told the Troll that he needed some help, and things went south in a hurry. The Troll got skittish that Moonie might rat him out to you, and he didn't want to leave any witnesses. Apparently that's how things are done in your world."

Duke then related the story that Moonie had told him about the night he killed the Troll.

Tony said, "That fuckin' Troll." He turned and threw his soda can against the wall. "You're telling me that the Troll and that dumb-ass friend of yours were in cahoots together?"

"That's what Moonie told me. I didn't know anything about it until after the Troll disappeared."

"You're a fuckin' liar. I didn't like that smelly little prick, but if the Troll was anything, he was loyal to a fault. He would never rip off the Antonellis. Never."

"Is that why his head is in your freezer?"

Tony paced the room, his palm nervously rolling over his chin. It was several minutes before he was ready to continue. "So the Troll's dead, Moon Pie is dead, and my money is still missing. Well, let me correct myself: Joseph Antonelli's money is still missing. So, the more immediate question is, what are we going to do about you, Mr. Ducheski? The way I see it, we have a couple of problems, here. One, you lied to me. When I told you I thought Moonie was involved, you said he wasn't. You knew all along." He shook his head and clicked his tongue off the roof of his mouth. "Of course, I understand that. I mean, you were trying to save your own ass." Tony reached down and cupped Duke's chin in his thick right hand. "But, I hate to be lied to, and I'm very upset about that. Two, it appears to me by the evidence in that freezer that you are guilty of conspiracy to commit murder. Oh, the ugly, ugly headlines that could create. And last, but certainly not least, you went to Chief Jaynes and told him that I killed Moonie, didn't you?"

There was no reason to lie about this. The chief had no doubt gone to Tony after his visit. "You killed my best friend in the world, Tony. Yeah, I went to him. Hell of a lot of good it did."

"I'm a little disappointed in you, Duke. I run this town. Did you really think that the chief wasn't in my pocket?"

"Apparently, I should have."

"Yes, you should have. The next time you see the chief, you be sure to thank that fat fuck for your sorry life, because after I found the head and heard you had talked to him, I was ready to put a twenty-two shell in your brain. But, the chief talked me out of it. He said it would draw too much attention. You know, kill a dipstick like Moonie Collier, and who gives a rat's ass? But kill the great Duke Ducheski in Mingo Junction, that could cause some serious problems. I still want to kill you, but the chief came up with a better idea."

Tony opened the refrigerator and removed another soda. He snapped it open and allowed his words to hang in the air. He was thoroughly enjoying both the moment and his continued dominance over the former basketball star. When Tony offered no explanation of his plans, Duke raised his bleary eyes and asked, "What is it?"

"In exchange for your life, pitiful as it is, you're going to give us total access to Duke's Place," Tony said.

Duke's mouth dropped. "What? No way."

"It's not even up for discussion. Here's how it's going to work. First of all, from here on out, you're doing things my way. Period. No questions asked. Beginning tomorrow, you'll have spot sheets in the restaurant. In fact . . ." Tony picked a manila envelope off the bar and sent it sailing like a Frisbee toward Duke, who let it hit his shoulder and fall to the floor. "There's next week's sheets. I expect to see them on the bar when you open tomorrow. We'll give you a weekly list of anything else that we're making odds on—elections, the Academy Awards, whatever. It's all very simple. And, you *will* take the bets. And, for the privilege of handling my spot sheets, I'll take 15 percent of your gross income for the first year, adjusted by 2 percent each year following. I'll have a contract drawn up that spells that out, and you *will* sign it. Rhino and Emilio will drop in from time to time to make sure everything is going well. They drink on the house. Consider them your business and financial advisers."

Duke looked up, fighting both tears of rage and tears of desperation. "Maybe it would be better if you just shot me."

"I thought of that. And, I thought you might want to fight me on this. So, I'm taking some precautions." He reached down behind the bar and pulled up a bowling bag—red, with white diagonal stripes. "Recognize this?"

"Of course," Duke said.

"I found it in your basement. So, can you guess what we're going to put in this bag?"

Duke knew. It was to be the ossuary for the Troll's head.

"It'll be a perfect fit. Rhino and Emilio are going out to bury it somewhere within the city limits. If you renege on our little arrangement, I'll direct the chief to the Troll's grave. Of course, he'll find the head buried in your bowling bag. See," he said, pointing to the tag bearing Duke's name. "You were in such a tizzy when you buried the poor man's head, you forgot to remove the name tag. And, while you were knocked out, I plucked some of your hairs and put them in here, and there's a balled up handkerchief with your blood that I wiped off that cut over your eye. So, not only will they have your bowling bag, but they'll have some wonderful DNA evidence, too. All of a sudden, you'll be known for something other than one lucky jump shot."

Duke turned his head and stared into the hateful but gleaming eyes of Tony DeMarco.

"I win, motherfucker. Oh, and one more thing. No divorce. My sister wants to stay married, so your ass stays married. I want those divorce papers withdrawn this week, and stay away from that nurse. Now, pick up your spot sheets and get your Polack ass out of my house."

Duke had lost the opal necklace. He couldn't remember if it had been in his hand or pocket when he got whacked in the head, but it was gone. Soon, it would probably be adorning the neck of one of Rhino's lady friends. The first rays of sun were entering the valley when he got back to the restaurant. He called the mill and reported off work, then staggered back and crashed on the couch in his office. He was still there when the cook shook his shoulder and informed him that two men were waiting for him at the bar.

It was Rhino and Emilio. They walked him back to his office; Rhino sat in his chair at the desk. In his wide hands he concealed a cloth pouch, which he threw at Duke. "You staple the cash to the spot sheets. Very simple. No checks. Cash only. All bets must be clearly marked. Any discrepancies in the total on the sheets and the money collected comes out of your pocket." Rhino's tone was surprisingly civil and businesslike. "We'll pick up the daily number sheets every day. Winners are paid the following day. You have all week to collect the spot sheets. Put them in that bag. Understand?"

Duke nodded, fumbling with the cloth bag.

"Good," Rhino said, standing. "Just for the record, I didn't believe your bullshit story for one minute. And, if I was Tony, you'd be dead right now. I wouldn't give a shit what the chief said." And they left.

The gambling sheets were on the bar when the noon crowd came in. Men picked them up and said nothing. Nearly every bar and restaurant in the valley handled spot sheets; why would Duke's Place be any different?

Angel came in after getting off at the mill, saw the sheets, and immediately confronted Duke. "What the hell are you doing?" he asked. "Are you that desperate for money? How many times did Carmine warn you about this?"

He couldn't look his friend in the eye. "Angel, it's not something I can discuss."

CHAPTER TWENTY-THREE

It was no secret that the mob ran the vice up and down the Ohio River Valley. Steubenville had two illegal casinos and whorehouses that lined Water Street, which ran along the banks of the river. While vice was all around those who lived and worked in the valley, the mob remained a faceless entity that operated in the shadows and had no impact on their daily lives. The exception, of course, was the occasional mishap, like Pinky Carey. There were sixty thousand men working in the steel mills in the valley, and to the majority of them the name Tony DeMarco meant nothing.

But every man in Mingo Junction knew the name of Tony DeMarco. And the name elicited fear. They knew him as the tough guy from Dago Flats who had dropped out of high school, and yet, without visible means of support, had somehow bought and refurbished a spectacular Victorian brick home on Granite Hill. While they might not have completely understood the depth of his involvement in organized crime, they knew he was not one to be toyed with, and they gave him a wide berth. Tony DeMarco and his lieutenants were the type with whom you avoided eye contact.

Thus, as Tony, Rhino, and Emilio became more frequent visitors to Duke's Place, the locals started staying away. The dining room continued to do a brisk lunch business, and it was jammed for the Friday fish fries, but Duke could see the difference. He saw how the locals finished their beers and cleared the room when Tony or his goons walked in. Men playing pool would sometimes slide their sticks back in the wall racks and head for the door, leaving a table full of balls on the felt. The euchre players would fold their cards and leave.

Duke's Place had become Tony's favorite hangout, and the hub of his operation. He brazenly walked behind the bar and helped himself to beers out of the cooler, or got into the drawer under the cash register to examine the notebook in which the beer orders were kept. The first time Angel saw Tony inspecting the notebook, he said, "What do you think you're doing? You're not supposed to be in there."

It must have taken every ounce of courage the former ballerino could muster to confront Tony. Duke braced for the eruption, but it didn't come. Tony smiled and patted Angel twice on the cheek. "Not that it's any of your concern, little man, but me and your buddy are partners, now. I'm just checking on my investment." He slid the notebook back into the drawer. "I'm going to give you this one, but if you ever question me again, I'll splatter that giant schnoz of yours all over your face."

When Tony left the bar, Angel followed Duke into his office and said, "What the hell is he talking about? *Partner?*"

"As you might imagine, Angel, it wasn't my choice."

"What happened?"

Duke shook his head. "As much as I'd like to tell you, it's best you don't know. Right now, it's just something I have to live with."

Angel never brought it up again. Duke suspected he knew it had to do with Moonie's death, and Angel certainly saw that 15 percent of the gross was missing each month.

Duke had the old wooden door of his office replaced with one made of steel with new locks, at least guaranteeing some modicum of privacy. He felt like such a coward, silently doing as he was told—an obedient dog, a slave in his own house. The name of Duke Ducheski was on the wall, but his control was slipping away. Despite the long hours he worked, Duke had trouble falling asleep each night as his brain refused to shut down. Plotting revenge and fantasizing about Tony's death was exhausting. But, unlike the hazy dreams that filled his sleep, he knew there was no way out. Tony owned him. The payments on the gambling sheets were always ready when Rhino or Emilio came by to pick them up. The 15 percent monthly payment to Tony was slipped to him in a plain white envelope on the first of each month.

In the weeks after Tony had ordered Duke to stay clear of Cara, he saw her only a few times. She sobbed when he told her that he had withdrawn the divorce papers. At first, he tried to convince her—and himself—that the situation was temporary. She wanted to believe him, but they both knew it was over. The last time they were together was at a hotel at Station Square in Pittsburgh.

"You have to tell me what happened," she said. "The truth. This has something to do with Moonie, doesn't it? I want to know the truth."

"I can't. I don't want to put you or your kids in danger. I'm in a jam, a big one, and I don't know how to get out." He blew air from his lungs to keep from crying. "In fact, I might never get out."

She sadly accepted the end of the relationship. She said, "Nick, I'm sorrier than you'll ever know." She kissed him gently on the forehead and walked out of the hotel room and his life.

He had worked countless overtime hours in that filthy mill and scraped for a very long time to open Duke's Place. Moonie had died in a pool of his own blood there. Duke wanted to make it a success and point to it as proof that he had something to contribute to society besides a jump shot. And now, within months of its opening, he had lost control. He was going to end up like Carmine—withered and defeated. That's the way things worked with Tony DeMarco. He was like a stubborn mold. One day you see a spot on the basement wall. You bleach it, but it refuses to go away, and soon your house is condemned, eaten alive by the fungus.

If all that wasn't bad enough, Duke also knew that he was sitting on a time bomb. Somewhere, between the surface clay and the sandstone bedrock of Mingo Junction, the head of Frankie "the Troll" Silvestri was rotting in Duke's own bowling bag. Although he was faithfully adhering to Tony's orders, he knew that could change in a moment. Tony could wake up in a sour mood one morning and order Chief Hinton Jaynes to go dig up the head. In fact, Duke was sure it was only a matter of time until that occurred.

Duke Ducheski was unsure of his next move, but he knew he could no longer stand still.

It was a simple, two-and-a-half-car garage—cement block and windowless—pushed hard against both the edge of the house Nina and Duke again shared and the narrow alley that separated the backyard from the parking lot of the Russian Orthodox Church. There were two entrances—a steel double-wide garage door that opened onto the curved asphalt drive that dropped to the alley, and a windowless door on which Duke had installed two deadbolts. There was nothing fancy about it, but for years it had been his sanctuary, the place where he had sought solitude and refuge from Nina.

He had built an L-shaped workbench in one corner. The walls were adorned with pegboards, on which hung his tools in neat succession. An old refrigerator rattled at one end of the bench and held nothing but bottles of Rolling Rock, Iron City, and Miller High Life.

The centerpiece of the garage was his most prized possession, and the reason he had built it sans windows—a sparkling white, 1959 Buick Invicta.

It had been the only car that his dad had ever bought new, or nearly so. It had been used for six weeks by the Nazarene preacher who, in a moment blinded by the temptation of earthly possessions, bought it thinking that a man of his stature with God should be afforded the luxury of a fine automobile with fins. Unfortunately, the Nazarenes didn't tithe like the Baptists, and the good reverend quickly realized that the monthly payments were beyond his reach, so he was forced to put a For Sale sign in the rear side window.

Del Ducheski was not a man to be envious of others. But he coveted that Buick from the first time he saw the preacher driving it up Hill Street on his way home from the dealership. When he saw the For Sale sign, he went to the preacher's house with two thousand dollars cash, two hundred dollars less than the preacher needed to break even. The preacher moaned and groaned but finally took the offer.

Del took the keys, slid behind the wheel, and grinned as he drove down Commercial Street, watching the chrome-tipped white fins shine in his rearview mirror. It was the only time in his life that he bought anything on impulse, but he loved that car. It was a two-door hardtop, with a beige leather interior, a chrome, checkerboard grill, and slanted headlights that gave it the look of a stern, menacing face hiding a 445 Wildcat motor. Duke's father kept it buffed and treasured it. It was his Sunday go-for-a-ride car. No food, no drink. Keep your shoes off the seat.

There were only thirty-one thousand miles on the odometer when his father died six years after Duke graduated from high school. He left the steel mill forever on a late August day after the emphysema that sapped his strength and ravaged his lungs left him too weak to walk from the parking lot to his job at the hot strip mill. He sat down on a bench, crying, feeling like he was carrying a hundred-pound weight vest and breathing through a wet bath towel. He was barely fifty years old, but his lungs, hardened and scarred by cigarettes and the grit of the mill, were useless slabs of tissue with the texture of cardboard.

He struggled to the mill office, where Angel helped him fill out his retirement papers, then he drove back up the hill and went into the house to die.

It didn't take long.

Duke sometimes wondered if a person could simply will himself to die. From the day his wife had passed, Del Ducheski had never looked at life as a gift, but as something to be endured, each day existing to be marked off the calendar, one day closer to when he might see his lovely Rosabelle again, and they would be young and happy and without disease. That is how he spent his last days, sitting in the gloom, tethered to a green oxygen bottle by a clear plastic tube clipped to his columella, each breath sounding like a slipping transmission.

On a June evening, not one year after leaving the steel mill, Del Ducheski was sitting in his darkened living room—a bottle of beer in one hand, and a ham sandwich and a dill pickle on a paper plate on his lap—watching a rerun of *Gunsmoke*, when he suffered a hemorrhagic stroke that turned out the lights like a power surge fries a breaker box. He dropped his beer and slouched over; and that's how Duke found him the next day, the bottle lying on the threadbare carpet, a piece of sandwich still in his cheek.

The remainder of his estate was paltry—a falling-down house, a few sets of cufflinks, some knives, fishing gear, a gold pocket watch that had been passed down from his grandfather, and the Buick. The car was Duke's link to his father, a piece of Ducheski family history that tied him to the past. And thus it occupied the place of honor in the garage.

Duke was in the garage early on the first Saturday morning in May 1994, having slipped out of the house a few minutes before six. Nina was asleep on the couch and didn't stir, even when the back door stuttered on the linoleum. Once inside the garage, he dead-bolted both locks and opened the trunk of the Buick. It was stuffed with treasures of sentimental value—scrapbooks, trophies and awards, old family photographs, his mother's favorite quilt, her jewelry, the gold pocket watch, and pocket knives that his dad had carried in the mill, their handles worn smooth from use.

Shoving a hand into the bottom of a cardboard box that held the quilt, his varsity sweater, and a cigar box of Confederate paper money, Duke reached around until he found the tattered silk of his baby blanket. Sliding his hands between the folds, he wrapped his hand around the pistol's ivory grips.

It was a Colt .45 semi-automatic, M1911, known as the Commander. It had been Grandfather Ducheski's service revolver in World War I. His grandfather had boasted throughout his life that he had used the pistol when he fought in the Battle of the Argonne Forest with the 328th Infantry alongside the great Sergeant Alvin York, who had used an identical weapon. He had won the ivory grips in a poker game on the troop ship to England. The loser pleaded with Grandfather Ducheski, "But my wife bought me those grips right before we shipped out." Duke's grandfather shrugged and said, "Well, if you're fortunate enough to live through the war, she's going to be right upset when you get home."

As Duke pulled the weapon from the depths of his baby blanket, the ivory grips were cool in his palm. He rolled the pistol in his hand, examining the fit. Lifting the revolver at arm's length, Duke squinted his left eye and sighted down the gray barrel, setting the sights on a spot on the far wall. When the hammer snapped on the empty chamber, he flinched. Never in his life had he squeezed the trigger of an actual gun. Three more times he pulled the trigger. The snap of the hammer echoed in the quiet garage.

He closed the trunk and turned, resting his rear against the chromed fin on the driver's side. He removed the magazine and filled it with .45-caliber shells. When the magazine snapped into place, tentacles of ice gripped his bones and clutched his soul. He tucked the gun inside his waistband, covered the ivory grips with his shirt, and walked out of the garage.

He drove the Jeep through Brilliant and out New Alexandria Road, past the Quaker State station, and toward the township dump. Off to the left was a dirt road that led to a hollow carved from the hills by the Hudson Mining Company in the 1930s. The locals called it Cherry Canyon.

As a boy, he had roamed the canyon with his cousins, Mitch Malone and Johnny Earl, and he knew it well. He drove down the dirt road until the Jeep was hidden by the scrub and weeds. He left it parked in the middle of the road and made his way down a steep path lined with bull thistles and giant foxtail. At the bottom of the canyon, the path leveled out and followed the edge of a pond that filled the canyon's basin. The ground was littered with beer cans, blankets, and spent condoms.

The sun was cresting above the low hills to the east. The dew was heavy on the ground, and it soaked Duke's cuffs and work shoes. The achy sound of cicadas droned through the trees that stood guard along the rim of the canyon. Duke followed the path as it snaked around the base of the cliffs, working deep into the hills. The pond was long and narrow, full of boulders and bass. He could breathe easy in the solitude and, for the time being, the safety of being far from Tony DeMarco. The sky was wide and azure, with only a few wispy, scud clouds moving across the valley far to the north. It seemed as though he was in a small vale in Wyoming or Montana, and not just a few miles from the grind of the steel mill.

Duke walked a mile or more to the far side of the pond to an area called the Flats, a low spot between the sandstone walls where the air was filled with the stench of stagnant water. He found a half a dozen beer bottles and set them on a mound of dirt, then stepped off fifteen paces. With the toe of his shoe, Duke drew a line in the dirt, then smiled at his folly. He was preparing to defend his life, yet he felt compelled to draw a line in the dirt as though it was a free-throw contest.

He pulled the pistol from his waistband, took a cleansing breath, and raised his right arm. He aimed down the barrel, flinched, jerked, and fired.

Rock exploded on the high wall thirty feet above the beer bottles. The blast echoed down the canyon, and a cloud of rock dust floated toward the pond.

"Okay, Duke, this time, no flinch. Just squeeze the trigger."

He repeated the process, aimed, flinched, jerked, and fired.

Again, he burrowed a .45 shell high into the wall.

He smiled at his own ineptitude.

He had plenty of shells. He kept firing, and each shot moved its way down the wall, inching closer to the targets. The first explosion of amber glass occurred on his ninth shot. Duke Ducheski had never lacked for confidence and assumed he had gained control of the revolver. The next shot, however, kicked dirt three feet in front of the row of bottles, and the next clipped the limb of a honey locust.

When next he prayed, he would thank God for making Tony DeMarco broad across the chest and shoulders.

CHAPTER TWENTY-FOUR

It was just after three o'clock in the morning. The florescent haze of the lights under the bar threw only enough illumination to create reflections in the mirrors. Duke Ducheski was alone in his restaurant with only the rumblings of the steel mill to disturb the quiet. The night was a cacophony of sounds—vibrations, really—that caused the windows to hum as though the casings were home to a thousand angry bees. The blast furnace erupted, and the downtown shook—slow, but enough that you could see a ripple in your beer. Coal trains hummed behind the business district and caused ashtrays to crabwalk across the vinyl tables.

Duke sat at such a table, keeping a thumb on the plastic ashtray as a Norfolk and Western diesel streamed through town pulling a train of one hundred hoppers loaded with No. 2 bituminous coal from Powhatan Point, heading for a steel mill in Cleveland. Four amber sentinels disguised as Iron City longnecks stood guard over the table, only one containing fluid; sweat snaked down the bottle that was little more than half full. The ashtray was full of the dead and their ashes. The smoke from their still-live brother curled up around Duke's face. He only smoked when his nerves got the best of him, and he had been firing up one after another all day. An empty Marlboro hard pack was crumpled on the table next to his pistol. He was tired, full of beer, and twitchy with nerves, and he had a loaded .45 within arm's reach. Even in his current condition, Duke knew that this was not a healthy combination.

There was an eerie safety to the darkness. He recalled how he had feared the darkness as a boy, how the rumble of the night trains would

shake their house. He would cower beneath the covers of his bed, imag-
ining the locomotives and their cyclopean head beam as hulking mon-
sters seeking him out. Now, there was an odd security in the dark. It
gave him a few uninterrupted hours to think.

Tony DeMarco wasn't the least bit concerned about being con-
nected to Moonie's death. It would never happen. The chief had obviously been bought off, and in a few weeks the investigative file would be
relegated to a metal cabinet of officially still-open, but forgotten, cases.
Any physical evidence linking Tony to the murder, if it had existed, had
disappeared.

It was a cruel injustice.

If Tony DeMarco and Joey Antonelli were ever to be punished, it
would have to be by Duke.

And he had a plan.

It had started to formulate the night Moonie was killed. The plan
hummed in his head like the windows in Duke's Place hummed with
the sway of the passing coal trains. But unlike the vibration of the
windows, which rested when the trains passed, the droning in Duke's
brain refused to cease. It was there, morning and night, at the funeral
and at the cemetery; it was in his head at the wake and when he had
last made love to Cara; it was there as he wept at Fort Logan, and it
was there, at that minute, as he sat alone in the restaurant. At first, it
had been like a jigsaw puzzle that someone had emptied on the floor,
hundreds of scattered pieces, half upside down, none connecting. But
the more he thought, the more the hum continued, the more the plan
began to take shape. The outside edges were complete by the time he
left the cemetery; the wide blue sky of his puzzle filled in the days after
Tony had revealed the frozen head of the Troll. By the time Duke had
finished target practice that morning, the puzzle was largely complete.
Now, only a few scattered pieces remained.

He had thought it out, ruminated on it over and over, planned it
down to the most minute detail. Regardless of the outcome, there was
an incredible price to be paid. If he failed, he would pay with his life. If
it worked, at best, he would sacrifice his very being.

He loved being the "Duke of Mingo Junction." He could barely remember a time when it wasn't part of his persona. He loved it when people walked into Duke's Place, looked at the black-and-white photo of him throwing up what a few seconds later would be the winning basket in the biggest game in school history. He listened intently—and with no small degree of pride—as his customers retold their version of the story, then pumped money into the jukebox to listen to Red Kilpatrick deliver the Miracle Minute.

If he tried to bring down Tony DeMarco and Joey Antonelli, the "Duke" would cease to exist. Nicholas Ducheski might live on in some form, somewhere, but "the Duke of Mingo Junction" would disappear from the earth.

He hated to give that up.

But he also didn't see that he had many alternatives. A few months earlier, he had a wonderful life. Duke's Place was open and successful. Moonie was his business partner. He had a woman he loved more than he thought it possible to love another human being. Now, that was all in shambles. The restaurant was no longer his own, and Cara had been forced out of his life. His best friend was lying in a hillside plot at the New Alexandria Cemetery.

He owed it to Moonie.

Such a decision wasn't without its consequences. What about Timmy? If he left town, who would take care of him? Duke knew the answer. Nobody, and certainly not Nina. Timmy would be little more than the last tomato on a late-summer vine, alive by the simple fact that nutrients were being pumped into his body until it rotted and died.

That night, the life he had long known, the life of the Duke of Mingo Junction, began a slow walk toward a distant and unknown horizon as he committed to his plan.

CHAPTER TWENTY-FIVE

The lobby of the Pittsburgh office of the Federal Bureau of Investigation was cramped and full of vinyl furniture and tattered, outdated law-enforcement magazines. It looked more like the lobby of a hack doctor than that of the nation's premier law-enforcement organization. The bureau's shield was framed and hanging on the back wall. A woman with platinum hair and a mole on her cheek the size of a nickel sat behind a frosted-glass window, which she rattled to the side when Duke entered the lobby. "Can I help you?" she asked with a tone that indicated she really didn't want to.

"I'd like to speak to an FBI agent, please," Duke said.

She worked her chewing gum and stared at him for a moment. "Do you have an appointment?"

He shook his head. "No. I didn't know I needed one."

"What's this in reference to, sir?"

"I'd rather not say until I'm talking to an agent."

One brow arched, and she glared at him.

"What's your name, sir?"

"Ducheski. Nicholas Ducheski."

"Spell that, please."

"D-u-c-h-e-s-k-i."

"Thank you. Have a seat, Mr. Ducheski," she said, sliding the window closed with the perturbation of someone whose routine has just been disturbed.

Twenty minutes later, the door opened and an agent finally came into the lobby. His name was Michael Kinnicki. If there had been a thousand people in a room and Duke had been asked to pick out the cop, he would have put his finger on Kinnicki. He had a tired, chimp-like face with a beard so dark it had a purple hue over loose jowls. His hair was thin and smeared down with gel, and he had a wild spray of salt-and-pepper eyebrows meandering across his forehead. The tie was slightly askew over a white, short-sleeved shirt.

Duke stood and extended his hand. Kinnicki shook it without conviction. Duke sensed Kinnicki had been through this drill too many times. People would wander in off the street to share their stories of flying saucers and extraterrestrials, Kennedy-assassination conspiracy theories, their proof that the KGB had planted radio transmitters in their brains, or any number of other wild, delusional tales. As a young agent, Kinnicki had probably been amused by the walk-ins. Now, he just wanted them out of the office as quickly as possible.

He was, however, polite to a fault. "Mr. Du-kesky?"

"Ducheski. Nick Ducheski."

He nodded. "What can I do for you, sir?"

"I have some information I want to give someone."

"Okay. Shoot."

Duke looked around the empty room. "Do you want to talk out here?"

The agent winked. "It'll do for now." He pointed to an empty chair. "Have a seat. What's on your mind?"

"It's a complicated story."

"They always are," Kinnicki said, the slightest of smiles pursing his lips. "Give it a whirl."

"Well, a buddy of mine was murdered and—"

"Homicide investigations usually fall under the jurisdiction of the local authorities," Kinnicki interrupted, hoping to end the conversation in a hurry. "We don't really investigate many murders."

Duke could feel a wave of heat building under his collar as Kinnicki attempted to put him off. "Actually, I have a pretty good understanding of what the FBI does, Agent Kinnicki. A buddy of mine—my best friend in the world—was murdered by the mob. The local cops are covering it up, and I'm being blackmailed for a different murder. So, as you can see, I've got plenty of problems that the FBI can't help me with. But, I think I can help you with some of your problems, which would in turn help me with mine."

Kinnicki nodded. "How so?"

"The guy who committed the murder that I would like to see avenged is Tony DeMarco."

The agent frowned, as though searching the memory banks for the name. "Tony DeMarco?" he said. "I should know the name. Help me out. Who is he?"

"He controls the gambling and the drug traffic in the Ohio Valley between East Liverpool and Wheeling. He's an enforcer for Joey Antonelli."

"How do you know this?"

"First of all, it's common knowledge. But, I know more than most people because he's my brother-in-law."

Agent Michael Kinnicki's bushy brows looked like two cats had arched their backs on his forehead. "Why don't we go back to my office?" the agent said.

A second agent joined them in Kinnicki's office, which was a sparse nook whose only adornment was a framed black and white photo of Kinnicki and seven other agents gathered around a very constipated-looking J. Edgar Hoover. He had an institutional steel desk, in front of which were two chairs, government-issue, with soiled green cloth seats. It took Duke the better part of an hour to explain the sordid tale. Duke was truthful about everything except for the part about burying the Troll's head. He told them that Moonie had put the head in one of his old bowling bags and buried it somewhere.

"Where?" Kinnicki asked.

"I don't know," Duke said. "He didn't offer and I didn't ask. All I know is that it was somewhere around Mingo Junction."

The yarn left Kinnicki scratching his greasy scalp. The second agent, Forrest Gilman, who was the Pittsburgh office's organized-crime expert, thumbed through a manila file folder, occasionally lifting his head and scrawling a terse note on the inside of the folder.

"And you are married to Tony DeMarco's sister, right?" Gilman asked.

"Yes."

"That would be Nina?"

"It would." Duke swallowed. "How did you know that?"

"We have a pretty extensive dossier on Mr. DeMarco." He flipped back to the front page of the folder. "Anthony Dominic DeMarco. AKA: Little Tony, Tony the Tiger, Tough Tony, and . . ." The agent looked up from the folder and grinned. ". . . my personal favorite, Queer Tony."

"Queer Tony?" Duke asked.

"Didn't know that one, huh? Yeah, your brother-in-law likes guys. It's not something the Antonelli family likes to promote. But trust me on this one. It's true. He's not too happy with himself, either. When he's done, he likes to beat the living hell out of them, bust 'em up pretty bad. All that pent-up guilt. Must be tough on a good Catholic boy with all that Italian machismo."

Duke found the news slightly amusing and tried to choke back a grin.

Gilman tossed the file folder on Kinnicki's desk and leaned back in his chair, lifting the front two legs off the ground. "I've been tracking the Antonelli crime family for fifteen years, starting with Salvatore and now his kid. I've watched that prick DeMarco a thousand times. He's a nasty one. I've followed him and a half a dozen other Antonelli lieutenants all across the country—Florida, New York, Boston, Chicago, Los Angeles, and Jesus-knows-where-else. You know what I've got on them? Lots of file folders full of lots of rumors. Convictions? I got dick. They've been impossible to pin down."

Duke nodded. "Understood. So, maybe I can help you."

"Maybe you can," Gilman said. "Are you part of his inner circle?"

"No. Actually, I'm about as far on the outside as you can get."

"Can you work your way in?"

"I doubt it. If I wasn't his brother-in-law, I doubt I'd still be alive. But suppose I could produce irrefutable proof that DeMarco and

Antonelli are involved in organized crime—maybe not get them for my friend's murder, but what if I was able to prove some other things?"

Gilman leaned forward on his chair, settling it on all fours, and rested his elbows on his knees. "If you've got something on your brother-in-law that you'd like to share, we'd love to listen."

"And if I produce something, something good, then what? Who protects me?"

Gilman shrugged. "That depends. If your information is good enough, we'd protect you."

"Yeah, but for how long? The Antonellis have long memories."

"Forever. If you have information on Joey Antonelli that could help us put him away, we could get you in the federal witness-protection program—give you a new name, new job, new life. But the information would have to be exceptional. And you have to ask yourself, 'What's it worth?' I've got to level with you. It would be extremely difficult to move and take a new identity with your wife being Tony DeMarco's sister."

Duke shook his head. "It's not as much of a problem as you might think."

"Well, then, the ball's in your court," Gilman said. "How bad do you want to avenge your buddy's murder? Because it seems to me that this is your only option. The police chief is going to let this go cold, and we can't help you there. You give us some concrete information that will jam up Tony DeMarco and Joey Antonelli, and we'll take good care of you. Frankly, you probably don't have enough to put them away. It takes a hell of a lot more than hearsay—you know, the he-said, she-said stuff. You have to have tangible evidence. However, just so you know, the offer's on the table." Gilman pulled a business card out of his shirt pocket and handed it to Duke. "Just for the record, I'd love to see Mr. DeMarco and Mr. Antonelli as cellmates in a federal penitentiary somewhere, but I'm not sure you appreciate just how nasty these people can be. Think long and hard. You might be better off to find a new best friend and get on with your life."

CHAPTER TWENTY-SIX

Thursday was pinochle night at Carmine's Lounge, and it generally lasted until two o'clock Friday morning. The cast of regulars included Nate Shaw, the owner of Shaw Motors, who had thick and powerful hands, the lines and fine ridges of which were caked with decades of axle grease that he would take to his grave; the Honorable Judge of the Court of Common Pleas Hickman Jewell Pryce; ne'er-do-well Ugo Moretti, whose only job was as a part-timer on the Mingo Junction street crew and who lived in a scroungy flat above the VFW, but who always had cash for a card game; and Joe "Daddy Fats" DiCola, who owned the Rathskeller Restaurant in Steubenville and was a boyhood friend of Dean Martin. After he became famous, Martin would sometimes visit DiCola at the Rathskeller and treat the diners to a song or two. After this occurred a few times, DiCola would periodically tell a few well-placed blabber mouths, "Dino might be coming in Saturday, but keep it to yourself." It would soon be all over town, assuring Daddy Fats a full house on Saturday, even though Martin wasn't within three thousand miles of Steubenville, Ohio.

Carmine hated pinochle night. It lasted too late and invariably ended up in a shouting match, generally between Nate and Ugo. Nate owned the largest automobile dealership in the valley and had no tolerance for the indolent Ugo. However disreputable and lazy Ugo might have been, he was a tremendous pinochle player, and in reality this was what really angered Nate.

For hosting this weekly lovefest, Carmine received 10 percent of the pot. The Judge and Daddy Fats always spiffed him anywhere from fifty to a C-note each, depending on their luck. So, Carmine generally walked away with three or four hundred bucks, plus whatever he made from setting out a cooler of iced beer. Times being what they were, he couldn't afford not to host the pinochle game.

He also did it to keep the judge happy. Since he was operating a front business for the Antonellis, Carmine never knew when he might find himself standing in front of his honor. Judge Pryce was one of the few honest judges in the county, a devoutly religious man, a Methodist, who viewed gambling as a minor sin, a vice he was entitled to for dispensing a dose of the Lord with his justice. He frequently asked those convicted in his court if they had asked Jesus for forgiveness of their sins. Looking for an opening, the convicts would respond in the affirmative. "Yes, sir. I've seen the error of my ways, and I pray for forgiveness every night."

The judge would smile and nod, and say, "My son, you should know that the Lord Savior Jesus Christ forgives you of your sins. And, I forgive you of your sins. But the state of Ohio demands that you do six to twelve years in the penitentiary before forgiveness is granted."

The pinochle game ended at 1:30 on this Friday morning, and without incident. Daddy Fats and Nate lost a couple grand early and couldn't dig themselves out of the hole. They quit three thousand down. Daddy Fats grunted a good night and gave half a wave with a gnawed and soggy cigar butt. Ugo took his money and scooted. Nate said he didn't understand why Ugo couldn't spend some of his earnings on a box of breath mints. The judge simply pulled on his sport coat, tugged on his tweed cap, and nodded as he and Nate left together.

Carmine locked the door behind the judge, then quickly went to the back door and moved the deadbolt into the locked position. It gave him a chill each time he locked the back door, as though he was racing against time, a child trying to lock a door before a nameless monster burst inside. However, Carmine's monster had a name—Tony DeMarco.

Carmine had seen a subtle change in Tony over the past few weeks. He had been too friendly. Chummy, in fact. It was too much out of character not to raise suspicion. He continued to squeeze Carmine for every dime, but he was almost apologetic about it, blaming it on the pressure he was receiving from Joey Antonelli. Carmine knew better. Tony DeMarco never did anything without a reason. He had started asking questions about the business, always in a coy manner, as though he was simply making conversation and really wasn't interested in the answer. But Carmine knew he was listening to every word, absorbing every nugget of information. Tony wanted the lounge. That would give him a legitimate front business from which to run his operations, and, if it ever became an issue, it would keep the Internal Revenue Service off his back. Tony believed he could launder a lot of money through the lounge.

There would come a time, Carmine assumed, when Tony would lean on him to sell the lounge for a pittance. Tony would come into the lounge one day, drape one of his hairy, muscular arms around Carmine's shoulder, putting a clamp of a hand on the old man's trapezoid muscle, and say, "You're getting kind of old for this business, don't you think, Carmine?" As he spoke, he would tighten his grip on the muscle, reinforcing his message. "I think you should sell this place, Carm. Go south. Enjoy the rest of your life. You never know how long you've got left, you know what I mean?"

Carmine didn't know if he was strong enough to resist him. And if he refused such an offer, he always risked having what they referred to in Tony's world as "an unfortunate accident." Tony would then produce some bogus contract, and one of the corrupt judges in Antonelli's pocket would give him the lounge as payment due.

His fears were not without merit. Over and again, Tony DeMarco had proved himself to be unpredictable. It was sad, he thought, that a man couldn't feel safe in a place that was his own. At least it had been his before the Antonellis got involved. He hurriedly wiped down the table, scooped up the pile of twenties left for him, and turned off the single light inside the green, leaded glass shade hanging over the table.

Carmine checked up and down Commercial Street, then stepped out and locked the door behind him. His Chevy was parked just around the corner in the gravel lot, covered with a thin veil of fly ash from the mill. He looked around the lot, convinced he was being overly paranoid. Why, he reasoned, would Tony want to kill him? He wouldn't be able to run the lounge for much longer, anyway. The monthly debt to Antonelli consumed enough of his income that he was going to lose the place. He didn't know if he could keep the payments up for another year.

It was just before two o'clock in the morning when Carmine eased his Chevy over the lip of the gravel parking lot and onto Commercial Street. He drove through the empty streets to Logan Avenue and started up the hill, the orange glow of the mill lighting the sky behind him. He cut across on Kensington, near the Knights of Columbus Hall, and on to Bricker Avenue.

There were no streetlights at the end of Bricker, where the street dead-ended into the right-field fence of the ball diamond at Mt. Vernon Park. Carmine's house was the last one on the left. The house was dark except for a single light burning over the sink in the kitchen. Carmine hit the button on the garage-door opener, and the door started its slow ascent. He nosed to the entrance and started in before the door had completely cleared the header. As he pulled the car forward, Carmine never saw the solitary figure emerge from the thicket of rosebushes and slip just inside the garage.

The man was dressed in a dark sweatshirt and jeans, a cap pulled hard against his brow. He pressed himself against the inside wall, hidden in the shadows, and held his breath. The car door opened, and the dome light came on as the garage door began to drop. Carmine grunted and lifted himself out of the car. He never looked into the darkened corner. He slammed the car door shut and had taken only two steps toward the kitchen door when a hand came down on his shoulder. A bolt of adrenaline surged through Carmine's chest as he jumped and a pint of piss ran down his legs. He grasped for the .22-caliber revolver he kept tucked in his belt.

Duke knew he kept the gun in his belt, and he grabbed Carmine's wrist before he could get his fingers on the grip. "Carmine, it's me, Duke." Carmine continued to fight—his seventieth birthday was in his rearview mirror, but he worked out regularly with dumbbells and a speed bag and was surprisingly strong—and Duke struggled to shove him spread-eagle over the hood of the Chevy. "It's me. Relax."

Carmine quit twisting; Duke's weight pinned him to the car.

"Relax, Carmine, it's me, Duke. Duke Ducheski."

He slid Carmine off the hood, into a standing position. "It's me, Duke," he repeated.

The older man trembled like a cold puppy. His lungs ached from the shock, and tears welled in each eye. He sucked for air, dropping his palms to his knees.

"Carmine . . . Jesus, I'm sorry, I didn't mean to . . ." His words were cut short when the left hook of Carmine's youth lashed out and caught Duke flush on the cheek. The jolt sent Duke reeling back two steps and over the hood of the riding mower.

"You dumb sonofabitch, what the fuck are you doin', tryin' to get yourself killed? You scared me half to death," Carmine snarled. "Look at this. You made me piss my goddamn pants."

As Duke pulled a shovel out from under the small of his back and struggled to get up, he rolled his tongue around the inside of his mouth and spat a glob of fresh blood onto the garage floor. Already, his jaw was swelling under his right eye. "Damn, Carmine. I didn't know you had that much punch left in you."

"You still didn't answer my question."

"I wanted to talk to you, and I didn't want anyone to see me." Duke worked his jaw around and spat again. "I thought this was the best way to do it."

"Yeah, well, you were wrong about that." The old man leaned back against the car and took a few moments to catch his breath. "Come on inside, goddamn you."

The door at the back of the garage led into the kitchen, where Carmine dropped his cash bag on the Formica counter and opened the cabinet above the stove, removing a bottle of bourbon that was more empty than full. He poured a drink in a juice glass and tossed it down. He poured a second and walked down the back hallway and disappeared into his bedroom, returning several minutes later wearing clean pants and bedroom slippers, and carrying the empty glass.

"So, what's so damned important that you had to 'bout give me a heart attack?"

"I need a favor."

"I assumed that." He pointed to a kitchen chair. "Sit down." When Duke had taken a seat, Carmine said, "Okay, let's hear it."

"Carm, you did time in prison for safecracking, right?"

"That's ancient history. What of it?"

"Do you think you could still open a safe?"

Carmine flashed a look of disgust. "Of course I *could*. Why would I want to?"

"I need you to get into one for me."

"Uh-huh. And can I safely assume that it's not your safe?"

"That's correct."

"Then I'm not interested. I'm too old to go back to prison." He walked over to the table and sat down. "How much is the haul?"

Duke shook his head. "No money."

"Jewelry?"

"No."

"What is this, some kind of fuckin' riddle? You want me to crack a safe, but there's no reward?"

"Oh, there would be a reward, Carmine . . . a huge reward."

"You're talkin' nonsense. You sneak into my garage, scare the wits outta me, and now you're talkin' gibberish. Are you on drugs or something?"

"No, I just need your help."

Carmine looked hard at the younger man. It had been weeks since he had seen Duke, who had been too embarrassed to come into the lounge since DeMarco had set up shop at Duke's Place. "I told you not to let 'em in the door."

"I know. I didn't have a choice. Tony's blackmailing me for the murder of Frankie Silvestri."

"Really? You're the one who killed that ugly little shit?"

Duke shook his head. "No. Moonie did."

Carmine raised an index finger and slowly nodded his head. "I knew that dumb bastard would end up getting you in the trick box."

"I got myself in the trick box, Carmine. And I'm trying to get out. That's why I need your help."

"Well, I'm not particularly anxious to go back to the joint. I've been there. And, believe this, it's not a nice place."

"What if I could guarantee that under no circumstances, even if we got caught, dead to rights, would we never go to prison?"

"How could you guarantee that?"

"Because if we get caught, they'll find us floating in the Ohio River."

"Man, you're just making this more enticing with every passing minute. Get the fuck out of here."

"What if I guarantee that it could give you something better than money?"

"And what might that be?"

Duke waited a minute, knowing that he finally had the old man's attention. "The ultimate revenge on Tony DeMarco and Joey Antonelli."

Carmine stared across the table for a long minute, then two. He got up, poured himself another drink, then sat down. "So, what's the deal?"

CHAPTER TWENTY-SEVEN

Duke knew Tony had a safe. While most people would try to keep something like that a secret, Tony DeMarco liked to brag about the fact that he "needed" a safe. During a family Christmas party at Tony's—during a stretch when they had been "paisanos"—he had opened the basement door and escorted Duke to the dank bowels of the old house. Tony had again been hitting the wine hard, and with a slurred tongue said, "You get out of that steel mill and come work for me, you'll have so much money you'll need one of these, too."

Duke didn't take Tony up on the offer, but he did take note of the safe.

Duke and Carmine's first attempt was aborted and nearly fatal.

Duke had gotten on his belly and slipped backward through the old coal chute at the side of the house and was in the basement in seconds. Carmine, however, surveyed the chute and balked at climbing through. With his arthritic hips, gravity might take care of getting him in, but he was positive he could never get back out.

"Come on, Carmine, you can do it," Duke said. "I'll help you."

"I'll never make it. Go unlock the back door," Carmine whispered into the chute.

"The plan was to never go in the house, remember?"

"Plans change. You're the one who recruited an old man to help you, and I can't go down that chute."

Duke went quietly up the basement stairs and opened the door leading into Tony DeMarco's kitchen, where he came face-to-face with The Great Zeus, Tony's slobbering, vicious Rottweiler. As he had been trained to do, the dog had quietly listened as Duke climbed the stairs. When the door opened, the beast leapt from the floor in one furious movement, growling, an open maw with dozens of sharp teeth and slobber flying everywhere. Duke jumped back and tried to slam the door, but The Great Zeus had gotten his snout just inside the jamb. The growl turned to an uncharacteristic yip, and The Great Zeus jumped away long enough for Duke to slam the door. The entire doorframe shook as the dog snarled and clawed at the door. For several moments Duke stood frozen, holding the doorknob tight, fearing the enraged dog could somehow manipulate it open.

Through the keyhole he could see The Great Zeus, emanating a growl from deep in his guts and standing with his nose inches from the doorknob. It was another several minutes before Duke released the knob and ran back down the stairs. When he pushed the door to the coal chute open, he saw Carmine leaning down with his hands on his knees.

"What the hell's going on?" Carmine asked.

"I forgot about The Great Zeus."

"That dog?"

"Yeah."

"Where is he?"

"In the kitchen. I'm lucky to be alive. No way can I get past him."

"Shit."

Duke climbed out the chute and sprinted into the woods with Carmine hobbling along behind.

Two nights later, the second attempt was postponed because of rain. "It's got to be a neat operation," Carmine insisted.

The third attempt was planned for an overcast Saturday night when, from a conversation Carmine had overheard at the lounge, he knew Tony would be in Pittsburgh. As with the first attempt, Duke picked up Carmine and drove out Banyon Road, which ran between Goulds Creek and the Indian Hill & Iron Rail railroad branch that stretched between Mingo Junction and Broadway Station. Beyond the crest of Granite Hill, and just before the slag piles, a gravel road partially overgrown with bramble slipped off to the right. In the early part of the century, it had been the access road to the now-defunct Wednesday Creek Coal Company's No. 9 mine. Now, the road was used only by hunters and lovers, and on rare occasions, safecrackers.

It was at the end of this road that Duke parked the Jeep, and he and Carmine headed up over the steep backside of Granite Hill, a mile beyond which was the home of Tony DeMarco. As was the case during the previous trip, the walk on the soft, leaf-covered ground played havoc on Carmine's hips. By the time they arrived at the clearing behind DeMarco's house, Carmine was exhausted and eased himself down on a maple stump. "Let's get this done tonight," he said, puffing for air. "My hips can't take much more of this."

There was a single lamp burning in the living room, a light on in the upstairs, and a streetlight illuminating the front of the house. Duke slipped out of the woods and peeked into the window; no one was inside except for The Great Zeus, who was lying on his rug in front of the oven. With his grandfather's Colt pistol tucked in his belt and a flashlight in his hip pocket, Duke again opened the steel door of the coal chute and slid backward into the basement on his belly. As he did so, the cast-iron door closed over his face and then his arms. He went directly for the steps, making no effort to hide his presence. Why bother? The Great Zeus knew he was there before he entered the chute. Again, he peeked through the keyhole, and there the beast stood, mouth closed, shoulders tensed, leaning forward, listening. When Duke turned the doorknob slightly, The Great Zeus took one quick, silent step toward the door; the only noise was the faint scratch of his claws on the wood floor.

"Smart dog," Duke muttered.

He reached into his jacket pocket and pulled out a sandwich bag containing ground beef mixed with a powder that Carmine called, simply, "Sleep-tight medicine." Duke scooped the mixture out in his left hand, and jiggled the doorknob with his right. As The Great Zeus edged even closer, Duke pushed the door hard, catching the dog square on the snout. The impact knocked The Great Zeus back and sent him scrambling on the polished wood for a brief second, which was all the time Duke needed to throw the glob of beef on the floor and slam the door closed. The splat of the snack snagged The Great Zeus's attention, and Duke could hear him swallow the meat in three snorts.

It was 11:22.

Duke held on to the doorknob for several minutes, then peeked through the keyhole again. The Great Zeus was back at his station, shoulders tensed and ready for attack. Duke resealed the sandwich bag and slipped it into his back pocket, wiped his hands on his bandana, and waited.

At 11:35, he again peeked through the keyhole. The Great Zeus hadn't moved from his post at the basement door, but the medication was working its magic. The dog was staggering like a newborn calf, wavering, overcompensating, and struggling to remain upright. His eyes were glassy; his eyelids, starting to fall. With what remaining strength he possessed, The Great Zeus moved across the kitchen, one halted step at a time, toward his sleeping rug in front of the oven.

Duke opened the door six inches; The Great Zeus stopped and looked back. An inner instinct told him to attack. Slowly, he tried to turn, but he collapsed in a heap a foot from the rug. Duke waited a few moments longer until the dog's eyes closed and his breathing slowed to a steady rhythm. As Duke opened the back door, Carmine was already coming down from the woods.

"Lock the door," Carmine said, quickly brushing past. "And wipe up that grease spot on the floor."

"Good call, Carmine. I didn't even see it." Duke bent down and wiped it clean with his bandana. Carmine squinted at the sleeping dog. "I hate that mutt."

"That's your old buddy, isn't it?" Duke said.

"Why do people have dogs like that?" Carmine asked. "You might as well have a pet bear."

"It's a power thing. Tony fancies himself as the most powerful man in the valley, so he's got to have a dog that enhances the image."

Carmine shook his head and continued down the stairs. He set his tool bag on the floor in front of the safe, which was pressed against the back wall of the basement. Tony had encased the six-foot-tall safe in cement block. "What an idiot," Carmine said, running his hands over the front of the slick, black surface and sliding his fingers along the gap between the door and the edge of the safe. "Why did he bother to encase it in cement block? Did he think someone was going to throw it on their back and haul it out of here? Moron. He should have spent the money on a better safe."

"What do you mean?"

"It's cheap. There's a company in Chicago that cranks these things out like candy. They sell them to chain stores that slap their names on them, but they're all the same. It looks like a fortress, which attracts people who don't know any better..." He smiled. "...like Tony DeMarco, for example. It's a pretty simple mechanism. I'll have it open in ten minutes."

"Ten minutes?"

"If that. A safe like this—all it does is keep an honest man honest," he said, reaching into the tool bag and pulling out a stethoscope. "Ten minutes. Just stand there and try to be quiet."

"How old is this safe?"

Carmine frowned and shrugged. "Looks new—five, maybe ten years old."

"That's interesting. Let me ask you this, Carmine. How is it you know so much about this safe if you haven't busted one in fifty years?"

Carmine slipped the stethoscope ends into his ears, pulled a pair of glasses from his shirt pocket, and said, "How about you zip it up and let the doctor work?"

Carmine put a tiny notepad and the nub of a pencil on the floor, then shoved a penlight into the corner of his mouth, keeping the thin bead of light on the dial. He squinted as he slowly turned the dial, stopping every few minutes to move the stethoscope to another part of the safe door and to jot down a number on the notepad. Three times he restarted, following the road map he was creating on the paper.

It took twelve minutes.

"Here you go, junior." Carmine pulled down on the silver handle, and the door opened.

Duke pulled the flashlight from his hip pocket and shined it into the blackened shelves. As the beam of light brightened the inside of the safe, his eyes widened. "Jesus Christ, look at that! There must be . . ."

"Hundreds of thousands of dollars," Carmine said, completing the statement.

"At least." Some bills were wrapped and neatly stacked against the walls. Some were wound into rolls and bound with rubber bands. Some were stacked thick and loose against the sides of the safe. Twenties, fifties, hundreds. "I've never seen this much money in one place in my life," Duke said. "I never realized how lucrative being in the mob could be."

"Well, gather up whatever you're looking for, and let's get out of here," Carmine said.

Duke leaned in close and scanned the shelves, moving the wads of cash, watches and jewelry, a few loose gemstones, and gold and silver coins. He kneeled down and shined his light on the bottom shelf, where he found, neatly stacked atop one another, four audio-cassette holders. He opened the first and dropped the cassette into his hand. It was white and unmarked. In his pockets Duke carried identical tapes. He switched the first cassette, then repeated the process with the remaining three. "Okay, let's book."

Carmine looked at Duke in disbelief. "That's it? What the hell? You're not taking *any* of the money?"

"He'd notice that. Hopefully, it'll be a while before he notices these are gone. Besides, it's drug money. I don't want it."

Carmine blinked several times. "You're kidding me, right? So what? So it's drug money. It's his. Take it! What's with the tapes?"

Duke finally allowed himself a slight grin. "The ultimate revenge I was telling you about. How much did Tony take from you that night at the lounge?"

Carmine shrugged. "About three grand."

Duke reached in the back of the safe and grabbed a couple of haphazardly piled stacks of hundreds. "Here, will this cover it?"

"I had to get a new felt put on the pool table, too."

He reached to another shelf and snagged a stack of fifties, dropping them in Carmine's hand. "Good enough?"

"Yeah, I'd say that ought to cover it."

Carmine started to close the safe when Duke thrust his hand back in. "Wait a minute. Maybe I could find good use for a couple of those." He bent down and reached into the back of the safe, snatching three stacks of hundreds from a lower shelf. He jumbled the stacks around so it wasn't obvious that some had been taken. "Okay, close it up."

The door closed and Duke spun the dial, stopping it on the twelve, the same number where he had found it. He then took the bandana from his back pocket and wiped the dial, the handle, and the front of the safe clean. Duke followed the old man up the stairs and into the kitchen. The Great Zeus was sprawled on the floor, both eyes half open and glassy, the tip of his tongue protruding from the side of his mouth. Duke squinted and edged closer to the animal, putting a hand on its back. "Holy shit, Carmine," Duke said. "He's dead."

"Oh, now that's a goddamn shame, ain't it?" Carmine said.

"What did you put in that meat? You said it would just put him to sleep!"

"It did. He's going to sleep for a good, long time."

"You killed him? I can't believe it. Tony loves that dog. He's going to go crazy."

"Yeah, that breaks my heart, too."

"Christ, Carmine, it'll make him suspicious. He'll know someone killed him."

"What? He's going to think someone sneaked into the house to kill his dog? Relax. It's a good diversion. I don't know what you're up to, but, whatever it is, this will keep him occupied for a couple of days."

Duke pushed Carmine toward the door. "I'll see you in the woods." He dead-bolted the door behind Carmine, then backtracked down the basement steps, crawled out the coal chute, and disappeared into the dark.

CHAPTER TWENTY-EIGHT

For an entire day after breaking into Tony's house, Duke transcribed the tapes while holed up in a room with cement-block walls painted a dreary aqua at the Wee Bonnie Lass Motel in Bellaire.

The recordings turned Duke's stomach. As he listened and transcribed the tapes on a yellow legal pad, he realized there would be no shortage of people who would want him dead if they knew what he was learning. Tony had not lied. His plan was to get Joey Antonelli incriminating himself on tape, and he had been spectacularly successful.

Antonelli: I want that little fuck Andruluski dead.

Tony: Who are you going to have do it?

Antonelli: Alberto. I told him I don't care how he does it, but he better make it fuckin' painful. I told him to cut off his ears and bring 'em to me in a jar. I'll send them to his mother. Nobody fucks with Joey Antonelli. That little fuckin' Polack will wish to Jesus he hadn't tried to double-cross me.

Antonelli: Hey, Tony, guess what I'm holding in my hand?

DeMarco: I don't know, Mr. A, what?

Antonelli: A mayonnaise jar. Know what's in it?

DeMarco: Mayonnaise?

[Laughter]

Antonelli: Definitely not mayo.

DeMarco: I don't know. What?

Antonelli: Man, you got a short memory. That fuckin' Polack Andruluski's ears. That Alberto, he's a good man. He brought me his ears, just like I said.

DeMarco: Oh, Christ almighty, Mr. A. What are you going to do with 'em?

Antonelli: I told you. I'm sending them to his mother. Nobody crosses Joey Antonelli.

Antonelli: You were supposed to be my old man's number one guy, so how come I can't count on you to take care of this problem?

Tony: I don't even know what problem you're talking about.

Antonelli: Are you kidding me? Those niggers are the problem— J.D., Marcel or Marchel, or however the fuck you say his name, and that other gold-wearin' son of a bitch, what's his fuckin' name?

Tony: Andre.

Antonelli: Yeah, Andre, the mouthy one.

Tony: I don't get it. What's the problem? They buy a lot of flake from us.

Antonelli: And they're reselling it locally. The deal was they would move it back up to Detroit. Now, we're competing against our own shit.

Tony: I don't think that's . . .

Antonelli: I don't pay you to think, DeMarco. Jesus H. Christ. I gotta take care of this, too?

Tony: Let me talk to them.

Antonelli: I'm done fuckin' talkin'. I want them dead. You apparently aren't up for the task, so I'll get Alberto and Big Mike to take of it.

Tony: They're good customers.

Antonelli: Why can't you get this through that thick skull of yours? They're undercutting us with our own dope. I'm going to kill the sons of bitches.

Tony: The job is done?

Antonelli: Done. Alberto and Big Mike did nice work.

Tony: They were part of Deuce Johnson's gang. They'll come looking for them.

Antonelli: Yeah, well, good luck to them. Those dumb-asses agreed to meet us at the old hunting lodge. We buried them deep back by the old saw mill and torched them good before we covered them up. That purple Jap thing they were driving went into the compactor.

Tony: You sure you want to talk about this on the phone?

Antonelli: No one's fuckin' listening.

Tony: Okay, just asking. How much were they carrying?

Antonelli: Cash, about two hundred grand and change, and they were each wearing a couple grand in gold. I told Alberto and Big Mike not to shoot them in the gold. [Laughter] Those black bastards loved their gold.

Tony: Not a bad day's work.

Antonelli: Christ, it was beautiful. Too bad about the girl.

Tony: They shouldn't have brought her.

Antonelli: True that.

Antonelli: He's got to get with the program. No one is going to do business with the Carluccis in our backyard. He's disrespecting me. He would never pull this shit on my old man.

Tony: Want me to send Emilio over to talk to him?

Antonelli: No, I'm going to handle this one myself. Mr. Green needs to understand that we run the numbers in New Castle. Period. If he gives me any fuckin' static, any static whatsoever, I'll break his leg. If he doesn't understand after that, well . . . let's hope for Mr. Green's sake that he understands. If he takes one more dime for Carlucci, he's a dead man.

DeMarco: Mr. A, what happened to the guy in New Castle?

Antonelli: Our friend?

DeMarco: Yeah. [Long pause] You there?

Antonelli: Yeah. I don't want to talk about it on the phone.

DeMarco: Why? You think someone's recording us?

Antonelli: I don't care. They can record me if they want. I got nothin' to hide.

DeMarco: Absolutely not. You're a legitimate businessman.

Antonelli: Absolutely. In fact, Anthony, I'm a very reasonable businessman. But some guys, you know, no matter how many times you explain something to them, they just don't get it. You know what I mean?

DeMarco: [Laughs] I think so. Give me a hint.

Antonelli: Our friend, let's call him Mr. Red, [laughs] he thought that maybe he still wanted to deal with our friends in Youngstown. But I think he's seen the error of his ways. I understand he's out of surgery, and, after a few months of rehab, he should be almost as good as new. [Laugher]

The transcription of the tapes filled page after page of text, all full of incriminating conversations. When Tony had said that Joey Antonelli carelessly ran his mouth, he wasn't exaggerating. It took Duke until ten that night to complete the transcription, and it filled twenty-seven pages. He ate a late dinner of pretzels, a candy bar, and a Mountain Dew from the vending machine. From the pay phone outside the motel office, he called Angel at the restaurant.

"Things are fine," Angel said. "You need to put together a beer order for next week. Where are you, anyway?"

"If anyone asks, I went trout fishing somewhere in West Virginia." Angel probably assumed Duke was somewhere with Cara and didn't question him further. "Handle that beer order, will ya, Angel? I'd appreciate it."

He walked back to the room, flopped on the bed, and was asleep for the first time in forty hours. When he awoke at 8:00 the next morning, he showered and drove across the river into Wheeling, West Virginia, under a blanket of thick fog.

Duke pulled into a public parking lot off Jacob Street and checked his face in the rearview mirror. He looked like he felt—in need of more sleep and a shave. After paying the parking-lot attendant, he walked west along 14th Street to Chapline Street and the offices of the *Ohio*

Valley Morning Journal. It was just a few minutes after 9:00 when he entered the building and stopped at the security desk just inside the door. Despite his haggard appearance, the female guard smiled when he approached her desk. "May I help you?" she asked.

"I'd like to see Mr. Malone, please."

"He should be in any minute, sir." She pointed with the eraser end of her pencil to a row of battered chairs along a near wall and a table on which sat a coffee pot. "You're welcome to take a seat and wait. Help yourself to some coffee."

"I probably look like I could use a cup, don't I?"

She only smiled.

Duke poured coffee into a foam cup and took a seat, quietly waiting for his cousin to arrive.

Duke hadn't seen Mitch in three, maybe four years. His only contact with him during that time had been an annual Christmas card with a family photo and a photocopied letter that gave an update on the family and the various goings-on of his daughters. Duke remembered looking at the cards and thinking how drastically differently their lives had evolved. He had become a mill rat with a lunatic wife and Timmy. Mitch had gone to college, written a book, and become the editor of the *Ohio Valley Morning Journal.* The Christmas-card photo of the idyllic family—beautiful wife and two daughters dressed in matching navy dresses—had been like a dagger to his heart. He wasn't jealous of his cousin, just envious.

It was 9:15 when Mitch Malone walked into the lobby. His step was brisk and, except for some flecks of gray that were creeping in from the temples, he looked like the cousin Duke remembered from his youth—trim and with a quick stride. As he passed by the security desk, Duke said, "Good morning, Mr. Malone."

Mitchell turned his head, smiled, and said, "Good morning," then took two more steps before his brain began processing the image. He stopped, then turned back. "Duke!"

"Is this where I come to sign up for a subscription?"

Mitch gave Duke a hug and laughed. "Man, it's good to see you," he said. "What brings you down here?"

"I needed to talk to you for a few minutes," Duke said.

"I just happen to have a few minutes. Come on up to my office. Let's catch up. I've got an editorial board meeting at ten."

"It won't take very long," Duke said, following him into the elevator.

In his office, Mitch poured himself a cup of coffee and dropped in two packets of sugar. "That's a habit I wish I could break," he said. "I don't even want to think about how many pounds of sugar I've consumed in my coffee over the years."

"It doesn't look like it's hurt you much. You're looking pretty fit."

He patted his stomach. "Swimming. I joined the YMCA in Elm Grove and took up swimming. Great exercise. Easy on the joints." He stirred his coffee, shook the remnants of the brew from the spoon, and set it aside. "So, Duke, I haven't seen or heard from you in years, and then you suddenly show up unannounced at the office. I hate to sound cynical, but what do you need? I'm guessing you already have a subscription to the *Morning Journal*."

"Busted. Yeah, I already get the paper."

"So, what's up . . . really?"

"I need a little help."

"Shoot."

"I need you to take care of this for me." Duke slid the manila envelope he had been carrying across the table.

Mitch frowned as he opened the envelope and peeked inside. "Cassette tapes? What's on them?"

"Conversations that you would be better off not knowing about."

Mitch massaged his brow. "Okay. So, if I do this for you, Duke, could I end up going to jail?"

Duke smiled and shook his head, sipping at his coffee. "No, Mitch, there's no possible way you would go to jail."

"Could you go to jail?"

"No. If the guy I took those from ever finds out I've got 'em, jail would be a much-preferable option."

"Christ, Duke, what have you gotten yourself messed up with? Is your life in danger?"

"It's a long story, Mitch, and, frankly, I don't want to get you in the middle of it. I just need this one favor. No one knows I'm here. And nobody would ever think to come here looking for them. I just need you to hold those tapes until someone from the FBI comes asking for them. If you don't hear from me or someone from the FBI in two weeks, send them to this guy." He shoved a folded sheet of typing paper across the table. On it was the name of Michael Kinnicki and the address for the Pittsburgh office of the FBI.

Mitch rubbed his hands over his cheeks and slowly exhaled. "The FBI, huh? Duke, I love you like my brother. I'd do just about anything for you. But even for my brother, I wouldn't put my wife and kids in jeopardy. I need your word that someone other than the FBI isn't going to show up at my front door looking for these."

Duke shook his head. "I'd never let that happen, Mitch. Never. There are only two people in the entire world who know where the tapes are. You're one and I'm the other, and I'm not talking."

Mitch looked at the envelope for a long moment. "Is there any news value to those tapes?"

"Maybe not today, but with any luck there will be very soon."

CHAPTER TWENTY-NINE

After he left his cousin's office, Duke drove north on the West Virginia side of the river to Weirton, then over the Fort Steuben Bridge back into Ohio. He had lunch at the Big Boy on Sunset Boulevard, then drove out to the fishing cabin at the old sportsman's club. He sat alone in the dark, the dust heavy in his nostrils, thinking of his father, of Timmy, Cara, and his life, or what little might be left of it.

He had no way of knowing what, or who, was waiting for him at home. There was always a chance that Tony already knew the tapes had been stolen. No matter how careful he and Carmine had tried to be, they could have slipped up somewhere, leaving behind some minute evidence of their mission. Duke needed some time to get things in order, and, after that occurred, he hoped the bastard did find out.

It was late afternoon when he locked up the cabin and headed back to Mingo Junction. Duke nosed the Jeep into the alley and pulled it up alongside the house. He reached under the front seat and grabbed the pistol, slipped it under his belt, then untucked his shirt for cover.

There was an embankment from the alley to the walk leading to the back stoop. Duke had made the short climb thousands of times. On this day, however, it seemed like an insurmountable hurdle; his legs and lungs burned. He was tired, hungry, and scared.

He wanted desperately to be more angry than scared; he wanted to feel the way he had when he was coming back from Fort Logan after finding the cash Moonie had stashed. He wanted to feel the way he felt when he was returning from Moonie's funeral, his eyes tearing, his fingers squeezing the steering wheel as he fantasized that it was Tony DeMarco's neck. But it was hard to maintain that level of intensity. There were moments when he had second thoughts about his plan, doubts that he could pull it off. When that happened, Duke focused his thoughts on the image of Moonie bleeding to death on the floor of the restaurant, of Tony DeMarco leaning into his face, issuing an ultimatum in a breath of garlic and stale merlot. Normally, it enraged him. But as he climbed the stairs to the house, he was just too exhausted.

As usual, the shade to the back door mudroom was drawn—part of Nina's continuing effort to keep any trace of sunlight from entering the house. Sunlight wasn't her enemy as much as what it represented—life and the outside world. The back door was slightly warped, and he used his shoulder to push it forward.

Duke hadn't taken a full step into the mudroom when he froze, shocked by its unusual brightness and the solitary figure standing before the kitchen sink. It had been years since he had seen his wife look so beautiful. She was scrubbed and made-up, her hair washed, curled, and set with tiny ringlets framing her chubby face. She wore a floral skirt of red, purple, orange, and green, and a light-green top sculpted around the love handles at her waist. The scent of her perfume filled the kitchen. Even her fingernails had been buffed and polished.

She flashed him a look of disdain. "You look terrible," she said. "Where have you been?"

Duke leaned back against the wall and crossed his arms, astonished. "You, on the other hand, look terrific. Where are you going? Got a hot date?"

She rolled her eyes. "I'm going out to dinner. You don't expect me to sit around this house and rot while you go on with your life, do you?"

"I'm sorry, but who are you and what did you do with Nina?" She flashed another look of contempt, curling a corner of her upper lip. "Who are you going out to eat with?" he asked.

"My brother, if you must know. He's taking us all out to dinner to some steak house he likes up in Green Tree. You're welcome to come, if you like. He extended the invitation to all of us."

"What's the occasion?"

"He wants to be with his family. Zeus died."

Duke frowned, hoping to feign the look of bewilderment. "Zeus? The dog?"

"Of course, the dog. Do you know any people named Zeus?"

"I used to know a stripper named Athena."

She gave him a sarcastic smile. "Well, that certainly comes as no big surprise."

"So, essentially, he's having a wake for his dog."

"Tony loved Zeus. Some people are very fond of animals, unlike you."

"Well, that's just great. This is the best you've looked in years, and it's for a doggie funeral. How'd it die?"

"He doesn't know. Heart attack, he suspects. He came home and found the poor thing dead on the kitchen floor."

"Yeah. The poor thing."

She pulled a compact from her purse and checked her lipstick. "Are you coming?"

"No, but pass along my condolences to the bereaved."

Duke started toward the living room and the stairs, at the top of which awaited his bed. "You didn't answer my question," she said. "Where have you been for the last two days?"

"Fishing."

"Liar."

He didn't break stride. "Enjoy your dinner, Nina."

She muttered the word *bastard* as the door skidded open, and the glass inside the loose pane rattled as it slammed shut.

From the bedroom window he watched Nina until she had gotten into the car, made a U-turn in front of their house, and started up the hill toward her brother's manse. Duke walked down the hall to the bathroom and drained his bladder. Back in the bedroom, he locked the door and braced it with the chair from the desk. He took the revolver out of his waist and set it on the nightstand, just inches from his head. He needed a few hours of sleep before going down to visit Angel at the restaurant.

It was eleven o'clock when he awoke. The streetlight outside the bedroom window shone down like a beacon on Nina's car. For a long moment, Duke was disoriented after six hard hours of sleep. He sat on the side of the bed to get his bearings. The revolver was still on the nightstand, the chair still propped against the door. Grabbing the gun, Duke crept to the door and slid the chair to one side, then slowly pulled the door open. The house was quiet except for the droning of the television. Nina had returned, then, following her normal routine, had gone to sleep on the couch.

The steamy shower felt good, but Duke couldn't enjoy it for more than a few minutes. He dressed in the bedroom, stuffing an army duffel bag with some clothes before he left. Nothing remained in the room that he valued. He left the top of his dresser and his toiletries in the bathroom cabinet untouched. There were no outward signs that he was leaving. When he walked out the door in a few minutes, the room would look as though he were stepping away for a day, instead of a lifetime. He crept past the sleeping Nina, gently opened the back door, and quietly left.

As he eased his father's Buick Invicta out of the garage, he saluted the Jeep and hoped that he would never again lay his eyes upon it. He pointed the Buick east and drove down St. Clair Avenue, the familiar path he had walked daily to the mill, over Route 7, past his beloved Mingo High School, and on to Commercial Street. A few overhead lights burned at Carmine's as the poker games were just hitting their zenith. Headlights pierced a mixture of fog and gritty fly ash along Commercial Street. The damp air was acrid with the smell of sulfur.

The under-the-counter lights were on at Isaly's; the VFW was doing a brisk business. The lights burned bright inside Duke's Place.

Duke passed the Hungarian-American club and pulled into the alley behind Dr. D'Amico's office, backing into the cubbyhole space between the office and the garbage dumpster of the IGA. He went to the pay phone on the far end of the IGA, turning his head to the wall after dialing the number.

"Duke's Place."

"Angel, it's me."

"Glad to see you're not dead."

"Yeah, well, the night is young."

"What's that mean?"

"Nothing. Is anyone listening to you talk to me?"

"No. I'm in the kitchen."

"Good. Has Tony DeMarco been in tonight?"

"No. I haven't seen him in a couple of days. Why? Are you in some kind of hot water?"

"No, nothing like that. Look, I'm coming down. Unlock the back door for me."

He left the car parked behind the doctor's office and walked down the alley and into the kitchen. The grill cook was gone for the night. He cut through the back of the kitchen, through a door that led to the back hallway, and into his office, unnoticed. Angel came back five minutes later after seeing the faint light escaping from under the office door.

As he entered, Duke was just hanging up the phone.

"What the hell's going on?" Angel asked. "What did you do? And don't say nothing."

"Sit down," Duke said, moving an old Mingo High Indians gym bag from the couch. He took a deep breath and said, "It's best if you don't know. I'd like to tell you, Angel; you've been a friend for a long time, but if I don't tell you, then you won't have to lie."

"Lie to who?"

"To anybody who wants to know."

Angel slowly nodded. "Of course, you realize you're not making a nickel's worth of sense."

"I know."

"Why's Tony after you?"

"I don't know that he is."

"But, you asked . . ."

Duke held up his right palm. "Angel, I promise you that you'll find out what's going on very soon. You've got to trust me on that, and trust me that things are going to work out. Am I involved in something I shouldn't be? Maybe. But that's all I'm going to tell you. Have you been making the deposits?"

"Sure. I've filled the beer orders, but I need you to sign some checks for the bills."

"How much is in the checking account?"

Angel shrugged. "About twenty-six grand."

"Okay." Duke looked off for a minute. "What was the special today?"

Angel frowned. "Meatloaf. Why?"

"How about going to the kitchen and wrapping some up in foil for me—enough for three or four people. Throw some mashed potatoes and rolls in, too."

Angel shook his head as he left the office. He did as he was asked and returned inside of five minutes with two foil packages inside a paper bag.

"Great. Thanks. Appreciate it. I've got to run an errand."

Angel glanced at his wristwatch. "It's midnight. You're going to run an errand at midnight?"

"Yeah, well, it's hard to get everything done in an eight-hour day." He winked at his old friend. "I'll see you later."

Angel's brown eyes bore into him. "Will you?"

"What's that supposed to mean?"

"Well, I notice that your MVP trophy and your state championship medal are gone. Dean Martin's photo and your All-Ohio certificate have left the wall, and I assume they're all in the gym bag.

If you were coming back, they'd still be on display. Duke, tell me, please, what the hell is going on? I promise I won't say a word to anyone."

Duke stood and grabbed hold of the gym bag. "I'll be in touch."

CHAPTER THIRTY

After sex, Ricky always wanted to nuzzle up to the carpet of black hair that stretched across Tony DeMarco's stomach and chest. As long as Tony continued to enjoy the effects of a cocaine high, it didn't bother him to have his lover so close in the afterglow of sex. But when he came down, Tony would reel in disgust of himself and Ricky. The slightly built and naked man, barely twenty-two, served as a tangible reminder of what Tony really was and not what he pretended to be.

About the time Angel and Duke were having their conversation in the office at Duke's Place, Tony awakened in the bed, chilled from the down-shifting of passion and his cocaine high. Ricky was asleep, his arm draped over Tony's waist, his moppish hair a tangled mass on his shoulder. Tony looked over to the nightstand at the vial of cocaine that was left. He had enough blow left for another high, and a good one; Tony decided that he would snort the coke, then mount the little bitch while he slept, which would require no intimacy for Ricky, but satisfaction for Tony.

First, he'd piss and get himself an orange juice. Sex always made him crave orange juice. He pushed away Ricky's hand and walked naked to the bathroom, relieved himself, then pulled on his blue, satiny robe as he made his way down the stairs.

The light from the refrigerator exploded into the dark room, forcing Tony to squint as he fumbled for the half-gallon carton of juice. He swirled the container and flipped on the can lights over the sink and oven. He opened the cupboard for a glass, then dismissed the idea, choosing instead to drink from the paper carton. A thin rivulet of juice ran from the corner of his mouth as he took three hard swallows. He wiped at his mouth with a backhand as he slipped into a chair at the end of the table, his feet splayed in front of him. A nearly full moon bathed the kitchen in soft light; it was eerily quiet. This was when The Great Zeus would be lying at his side, head wedged between his paws, patiently waiting to be rubbed between the ears and receive a handful of treats that Tony kept in the crockery bean pot on the counter. The bean pot caught his eye, and he thought of how much he missed The Great Zeus. A dog so loyal would be hard to replace, but Tony would do it, and soon. Maybe he would get a Doberman this time. Whatever his choice, it would be a dog of strength and power and one he could train as an ally.

He enjoyed the silence, broken only by the distant sounds of the mill and the orange juice slapping the inside of the carton. The time was about right, he thought. He was tiring of playing up to Joey Antonelli. For years now, he had purposely pandered to him, calling him "boss" and "Mr. A," and grudgingly giving him undue respect. It made him smile to think his plan was working. Antonelli no longer viewed Tony as a challenger to the throne, but simply a loyal and beaten subject who had finally accepted his role as a mere contributor, not a leader. He had taken Tony into his complete confidence. It would be a fatal mistake. Soon, the wolf would be standing at the door of Joseph Antonelli, an evil grin on his face. He would assemble his men; Rhino and Emilio were already in the fold. He had several others in mind. When that was complete, he would reveal the tapes. When Joey Antonelli stopped crying and puking, Tony would produce a map and draw a line at the spot where the panhandle of West Virginia met Pennsylvania and Ohio. All of West Virginia and everything in Ohio south of the point would be under the command of Anthony DeMarco. All the drug and gambling profits would go directly to Tony. He would no longer answer to Antonelli or anyone else. It was to be his domain. *Sorry for your luck, Joey. I'm in; you're out. Fuck with me, and the tapes are going to the FBI. Kill me, and someone else will send them to the FBI. You can have control of Western Pennsylvania, Joey, but don't let me hear about you poaching on my territory.*

He would change his name, too. He would henceforth be known as Anthony "Big Tony" DeMarco, and he would be the head of the new DeMarco crime family. He liked the sound of that—the DeMarco crime family. He would be the don. And like his mentor, Il Tigre, his power would be absolute. Anyone who questioned his authority would be dealt with harshly. For appearances, he would marry and father a son or two. Someday, they would take over and run the business with the ruthlessness of their father. They would write books and make movies about his life—the penniless son of a beyond-the-tracks railroader who rose to power in the world of organized crime. His name would be uttered in the same breath as Capone and Dillinger and Gotti. Strength and intimidation were the only way to get ahead in this life, and he had proved that to be true.

He felt a little jump in the loins, a sign that it was time to go back upstairs and finish his evening. He closed the carton and started to rise when he noticed the moonlight reflecting off a shiny spot on the floor under the table. He bent down and ran an index finger through the spot; it was greasy and had a faint, rancid odor. Near the grease spot, on the outside of the nearest table leg, was a clump of ground meat that had grazed the varnish and gone unnoticed by The Great Zeus. Tony reached under the dried, brown clump and raised his hand upward, breaking it cleanly from the wooden leg. Embedded in the beef and clearly visible, like a gem in a gold setting, was the chip of a white pill. Tony scraped the pill with his fingernail, flaking off pieces of the powder.

"Son of a . . . ," his words trailed off. Immediately, his eyes lifted to the basement door. He made a frenetic dash down the basement steps. He was flustered and it took him three tries to successfully open the safe. His chest heaved, but he exhaled in relief at first glance. It didn't appear to have been opened. Piles of money still filled the safe. Perhaps some cash was missing.

"No, it's all there, Tony," he said aloud. "Relax. You're letting your mind play tricks on you." Why, he reasoned, would anyone take only a few stacks of money if they had access to hundreds of thousands?

And then the reason came to him.

They hadn't been after the money.

A fire that began in his balls soared to his heart and on to his face. He put a hand on each side of the safe and stood for a moment, his insides aching as he tried to catch his breath. He prayed that it wasn't true. Tony DeMarco, with the blood of a dozen men on his hands, was standing half-naked with cocaine dust on his lips when he began asking Jesus Christ for a favor. He dropped slowly to his knees and looked through the dim light for the cassette holders.

They were there, and so were the cassettes.

The tightness rushed from his chest as he exhaled. "Thank you, Jesus. Thank you."

He pulled out the first cassette. It was probably his imagination, but he still sensed something was wrong. The pain in his chest began to creep back. The cassette was white and unmarked, but it didn't look like his tape. Certainly it was just his imagination in overdrive. He grabbed the other tapes, ran up the steps, and slipped the first cassette into his stereo. Instead of his recordings with Antonelli, the mellow voice of Duke Ducheski's favorite singer filled the room—"You're Nobody 'Til Somebody Loves You."

"Dean fuckin' Martin," he growled.

He put in the second tape. More of the same—"Ain't That a Kick in the Head?"

And the third, though it was simply more punishment for Tony. "That's Amore . . ."

He pulled the tape player off of the shelf and smashed it against the far wall. "Son of a fuckin' bitch," he screamed.

Ricky appeared on the stairs. "Tony, what's wrong?"

"Get the fuck outta here, you little cocksucker." He grabbed an empty cassette case and threw it at Ricky, who was already running for the bedroom. "Get out!"

Tony slumped to the floor and laughed. "You are so fuckin' dead, Ducheski. Goddamn, I can't wait to kill you. I can't fuckin' wait. I'll give you credit, though, that took more balls than I thought you had." His bathrobe was open, his limp member lying across his thigh.

Sweat—a sour, fearful sweat—matted the thicket of hair to his chest and stomach. "So, you think you're going to blackmail the blackmailer, huh? Well, we'll see."

In five minutes he was dressed and heading out the door.

Tony DeMarco's face was a façade of calm when he entered Duke's Place. It was 12:45 in the morning. A few mill rats were trying to postpone the inevitable fight with their wives and nursing their last-call beers, watching the clock. "The fight can't start 'til you get home," they liked to say.

The barmaid had been sent home, and the kitchen was dark. Angel was filling the cooler beneath the bar, the last chore before locking the door and counting the money. He was not surprised to see Tony walk through the door, though he tried his best to act that way. He continued to stock the cooler until Tony got to the bar. "Beer?" Angel asked.

"Where's Duke?"

Angel shrugged. "He's not here."

Tony rolled his lower lip between his teeth. "Come here," Tony said, moving toward the hallway that led to the office and the restrooms. Angel tentatively followed. In a whispered tone, Tony said, "I didn't ask you if he was fuckin' here. I asked you where he was. So, just so we're clear, I'll ask you again, 'Where's Duke?'"

"I don't know."

Tony took a breath. "Listen to me, you weaselly little fuck, you better start talkin' or . . ."

"I don't know where he is, Tony," Angel interrupted, scared by the deadened look in Tony's eyes. "He was here earlier. He did some work in his office and left. I didn't ask where he was going, and he didn't say. I assumed he was going home to bed."

"Where'd—"

"I swear to God, I don't know. He didn't tell me. All he said was he'd be in touch, then he left. That's all I know."

Tony slowly reached out with his right hand and brushed some imaginary lint off Angel's shirt. "If I find out you're lying to me, you know what's going to happen, right?"

Angel's eyes drifted downward to the bloodstain on the hall floor. "Yeah, I got a pretty good idea what happens when someone pisses you off."

CHAPTER THIRTY-ONE

Cara had already unlocked her back door, waiting for Duke to appear in the moonlight that spread across her yard. She sat in the darkened kitchen and opened the door when she saw the familiar figure running up the grade from the creek.

There was an immediate and uncommon tension between them. She walked down the hall, her yellow terrycloth bathrobe cinched up at the waist and flapping against her heels as she walked. There was a time in the not-too-distant past when Duke would have peeled it away before they were out of the kitchen. She took a seat on the couch, tucking her feet beneath her. Duke grabbed a chair from across the room and set it right in front of her. Tears were streaming down both her cheeks.

"It's not too late," he said.

"Don't," she said, raking hair out of her eyes with her fingernails. "Don't say things that you know aren't true. It is too late."

"Maybe after I get settled, I could send for you."

"I don't want you to send for me, Nick. This has to be over. It is over. I love you dearly, and I always will. But I can't, won't, go with you. Not now, not ever. I know you think you're doing the right thing, but you're giving up an awful lot. You're not only giving up your identity, you're giving up a woman who loves you, and two kids who idolize you."

"You could have come with me. I wanted you to come with me."

"And then what? Leave my parents and my brother and sisters here? Huh? Hide in fear for the rest of my life? You want me to put my children in a home with a man who will have a price on his head by the Mafia? Really? Frankly, I'm not willing to take the chance that the people you're messing with are discriminate killers." She pulled an eyeglass case from her bathrobe pocket and handed it to him. He unsnapped the case and eyed its contents. "Do you know what you're doing?" she asked.

He nodded. "Thanks."

"I want you to go."

He nodded and stood. "I brought this for you," he said, handing her a brown lunch sack. "It's for the kids. It'll help pay for their education. Hide it, in case there's any trouble."

She took the sack but didn't look inside. Still, she could feel the bulk of the three thick stacks of cash that Duke had swiped from Tony's safe. She turned her head and refused to look at him again. He leaned across and kissed her wet cheek. "I'll always love you, too, Cara."

And in a moment, he walked out of her life forever.

She remained on the couch, tears dripping off her face and soaking her robe. She would still be sitting on the couch an hour later, when the front door was busted off its hinges.

CHAPTER THIRTY-TWO

I n the few seconds before the door was kicked open, Cara heard the hard footfalls across her porch. It sounded like a hammer beating on loose boards, as though the person inside the shoes intended to announce his anger in advance. She knew Tony DeMarco would be paying her a visit, and she really hadn't expected him to knock. Consequently, she wasn't totally shocked when he kicked the door and it fell into her living room. Still, she flinched, and a splintered piece of doorjamb flew by her head; the brass catch into which the deadbolt had rested blew into the kitchen like a missile. Tony DeMarco stumbled inside and into the small table next to the staircase, knocking a vase of silk flowers and a framed snapshot of the kids to the floor. The picture frame survived the fall; the vase did not.

She sat on the corner of the couch, half reclined, her toes tucked between the cushion behind her. She calmly looked at the damage, then at Tony, then said, "Some people find the doorbell effective."

He was in no mood. In two steps he was over her. "Where is he?"

"Where is—"

Before she could complete the sentence, Tony had two handfuls of her terrycloth bathrobe and jerked her to eye level. "Do not say, 'Where is who?'"

She had remained limp, causing him to struggle with her weight.

"I will snap your neck if you don't tell me where he is."

She remained calm and limp, a marionette in his thick hands. "He was here earlier. He left. He didn't tell me where he was going."

"You're lying."

"I'm not lying. He knew you'd be looking for him. He said he wasn't going to tell me anything that you could beat out of me."

He glared into her eyes for several silent seconds, then dropped her back to the couch. He turned away and ran his hand through his hair, then reached into his belt and pulled out his pistol. "Get dressed."

"Why?"

"Because I said so. Get your ass upstairs and get dressed. Your kids, too. We'll just see which he finds more valuable: you and your kids, or those tapes."

"Tapes?" she asked. "I don't know what you're talking about."

He stared down at her and wished he could kill her now, just to inflict as much pain on Duke Ducheski as possible. He would wait. Maybe, he thought, he would kill her in front of Duke. That would be even better.

Cara found herself surprisingly calm and unafraid, and she didn't move from the couch. "I'm not going anywhere with you. But I can tell you this: Duke has already determined what's important to him, and it's not me."

"What the hell are you talking about?"

It dawned on her that Tony didn't know. He hadn't figured it out. "You don't know, do you?" she asked.

"I don't have time for your games, bitch. Know what?"

A broad grin spread across her face. She was going to take delight in telling him. "He's never coming back, Tony. Duke said he was leaving Mingo Junction forever."

"Bullshit."

"Whatever it is you're looking for, tapes or whatever he took from you, he turned them over to the police, or the sheriff, or someone. He doesn't have them anymore."

"You're as big a liar as your boyfriend."

"He's no longer my boyfriend. Why can't you get that through your thick skull?"

The backhand sent her head flying back against the couch; in the next instant, his hand was around her neck, pressing hard under her jaw.

"Don't think for one minute that I won't kill you. I've killed women before, and I wouldn't hesitate to kill another, especially you."

She struggled to breathe under the pressure of his hand; his thumb was pressing up under her chin, closing off her air.

"Open your mouth again, and you'll find yourself at the bottom of the same blast furnace as your boyfriend."

He released his grip, and she slumped into the corner of the couch, holding her terrycloth robe closed with one hand, grasping her neck with the other, as a solitary tear rolled down her cheek.

"I'm going to find your boyfriend, and when I do, I'm going to kill him. You better watch your step, or you'll be next." He walked out the opening where the front door had been.

CHAPTER THIRTY-THREE

Duke arrived at the Heinzmann Convalescent Center at 1:30 that morning. That was not unusual. Over the years, he had frequently gone to the nursing home after working the four-to-midnight shift in the mill, and more recently after he closed the restaurant. The duty nurses had gotten to know him and did not mind the late-night visits. And Duke usually brought them leftovers from the restaurant. Tonight, he had the foil-wrapped meatloaf, mashed potatoes, and homemade rolls.

After delivering the food to the duty desk, Duke spent a few minutes chatting with the nurses, then walked back to Timmy's room. He pulled the folding chair away from the desk and sat alone with his son. It was dark except for the nightlight above the bed; silent, except for the sound of his own breath. Duke put his hand on his son's nearest knee, bony, bent, and cold, and gently massaged it in a circular motion.

"I told you about Moonie getting killed, remember?" he said in a tone just above a whisper. "It's been one big mess ever since. I'm so sorry about this, Timmy. I'm so damn sorry for all of it." Tears welled in each eye. "I'm sorry that you had such a short and miserable life. I hope it's better for you on the other side. I've got to believe it will be; I just have to believe that. I've got to go—leave Mingo Junction—and I can't take you with me. I'm sorry about that, too. I don't know what else to say except I'm so goddamned sorry."

Duke stood and ran some water in the sink and splashed it on his face to mask the tears, then walked back down to the duty desk and asked one of the nurses to come down and take a look at Timmy. Something, he said, just didn't seem right. Edna followed him back to the room. She was fiftyish, black, heavy, with a lovely disposition and Duke's personal favorite for the wonderful care she gave Timmy. "He's not breathing right, Edna," he said. "He's making a funny noise when he breathes." Duke demonstrated a wheezing noise.

Edna put the ear tips of her stethoscope in place and listened to his heart and took his pulse. "Everything seems normal, Mr. D. He's a little on the slow side, maybe, but nothing to be alarmed about."

"Are you sure?" he asked.

"I'm sure. Enjoy your visit." She smiled and left.

Duke sat back in the chair. "I've never told you about my dream, have I? A few years back, I dreamed that you got out of this bed and wanted to have a game of catch. I heard your voice, clear as could be. I don't know how, but I know that was you talking to me, wasn't it? That dream is very real to me, Timmy. I can hear your voice; I know what you would sound like if you could really talk to me. I always figured that was your way of telling me that things were going to be all right."

Timmy's eyes were slightly open, his mouth agape and dry. There was a slight gurgle to his breathing. Over the years, he had always spoken to Timmy as though the boy understood perfectly. He had long hoped that some of the words had gotten through.

Ten minutes passed, and he went back to the duty desk, where Edna was working on charts. "I hate to bug you again, Edna, but he seems to be laboring, and I really think something is wrong."

Edna looked up, a faint hint of aggravation in her usually pleasant eyes, and pushed herself away from the desk. She repeated the earlier procedure by checking Timmy's heart and taking his pulse. "This train's runnin' right on schedule, Mr. D."

"But he keeps gasping and wheezing, like he's in trouble."

"I'll make a note of it on his chart and tell Dr. Kuhn when he comes in."

"Okay, Edna, sorry to have bothered you."

She was gone without another word.

He walked over to the side of the bed closest to Timmy's curled frame. For several moments, Duke stroked his son's hair and rubbed his cold shoulders and arms, but said nothing. Gently, he pressed a kiss to his son's cheek and whispered in his ear, "Tell Moonie I said hi when you see him." Duke took a long breath, fought off tears, and allowed his hands to slip off Timmy's arms. He walked around the bed and peeked outside the door. Edna and her two co-workers were getting ready to delve into the meatloaf, making sandwiches with the rolls.

Duke pulled the eyeglass case from his pocket and opened it, revealing a syringe loaded with clear fluid—potassium chloride. He worked quickly and methodically. As he walked across the room, he removed the plastic cover from the needle. With the same calmness that served him so well on the basketball floor, he shoved the needle into the entry hole in Timmy's intravenous tube and injected the liquid. There was no hesitation. He had committed to the act.

Then, he sat on the edge of the bed, with tears running in rapid fashion down each cheek and leaping onto the sheets, and waited for his son to die. It happened in mere seconds. He rested a hand on Timmy's puny calf and watched as the pulse in his neck slowed, then disappeared. An overdose of the chemical sent his weakened body into an electrical malfunction, stopping the heart almost instantly. Timmy's barely palpable breathing slowed and stopped. His body slumped only a tiny amount. There was little difference between Timmy's living body and the shell that lay before Duke.

Where he had expected great sorrow, there was unexpected relief. The boy's suffering was over. He was at peace, and with any luck, Moonie had already draped a thick arm around Timmy's shoulder. Duke waited ten minutes, sitting in silence with Timmy. When he was sure that no amount of emergency heroics could save Timmy, he walked to the bathroom and flushed the syringe down the toilet. He then took the cheap pair of reading glasses from his shirt pocket, slipped them into the eyeglass case, and returned the case to his pants pocket. He didn't make eye contact with the nurses as he walked past the duty desk to the men's restroom and relieved himself. On his way back to the room, however, he stopped for a moment and made small talk with the women.

"How's the meatloaf?"

"Delicious," Edna said through a mouthful of sandwich.

"We've got the best food in the valley. You should come down and eat sometime. I'll treat."

The eyes of the three women widened. "You can count on that, Mr. D," Edna said.

"Enjoy," he said, making his way back to Timmy's room. He stood inside the door for twenty seconds, then bolted back into the hall and sprinted to the duty desk. The tears were real. "Something's wrong. I think he's gone."

This time, Edna's eyes didn't roll. She got up and ran; the other nurses followed. Edna had worked at the home for years, and death was no stranger to her. She took one look at Timmy and knew the boy was dead.

"Oh, sweet baby," she said, placing her fingers on a cold wrist that she knew bore no pulse. She placed her hand on his forehead and slowly moved it down his face, closing his eyes. "I'm so sorry. He's gone, Mr. D," Edna said, tears welling in her eyes. The tears weren't for Timmy; they were for Duke. "Oh, Mr. D, it's my fault. You said something was wrong, and I didn't see it."

The last thing Duke wanted was for Edna to think she was responsible for Timmy's death. "No, no, Edna. It's not your fault. You couldn't have known." He hugged the crying woman. "It was simply his time. It's a blessing."

Duke needed to sit. He went back to the folding chair and rested his head on his hands on the edge of the bed. For several minutes, he cried quietly into the sheets—tears of sorrow, tears of pain, tears of relief. When he looked up after several minutes, Edna was taking the intravenous tubes from Timmy's arm, straightening his body and brushing his hair. She placed a hand on Duke's shoulder as she walked past the bed.

"I'll leave you alone to be with your son, Mr. D."

In spite of his sorrow, Duke knew he couldn't waste time. He said his final good-bye to Timmy, left the room, and walked to the duty desk. "Will you call Dr. Kuhn, please? He said when the time came, he would sign the death certificate."

The next thirty minutes seemed to drag for hours. Dr. Kuhn agreed to sign the death certificate; there was certainly no need for an autopsy. He asked to speak to Duke, and Edna handed him the phone. "Son, we've known this was coming for a long time, and we know it's for the best. I know that doesn't make it any easier. You were a better father to Timmy than most men are to boys who are blessed with healthy bodies. I'm sorry for the joys that you were never able to experience."

"I'm sorry for that, too, Doc," he said.

The body was released to Millard Funeral Home. Duke waited in the hall while they loaded Timmy onto the gurney. His body was slid into the back of the station wagon, and Duke followed the vehicle through the empty streets of Steubenville, parking the Buick in the alley behind the funeral home. The employee backed the station wagon into the garage and was perplexed to see Duke standing beside the front fender of the vehicle.

"Did you want to stay with the body until things open up?" he asked, knowing that some people did not want to leave their loved ones alone.

"No, I want the body cremated."

"Yes, sir, I realize that, but we won't do that until later, when Mr. Millard comes to work around eight or eight thirty."

Duke shook his head. "No, I would like to have it done immediately."

"I'll have to call Mr. Millard and make sure that's okay. He usually oversees the cremations."

Duke reached into his pocket and peeled ten hundred-dollar bills off a wad of money and handed it to the employee, whose name was Dewey. "How about you just take care of it yourself? I'm sure Mr. Millard won't mind. If there's a problem, you can tell him I insisted."

"It doesn't cost this much."

"Whatever's left is yours."

Dewey slipped the money into his pants pocket. "I'm sure Mr. Millard won't have any problems with me taking care of this."

Duke helped Dewey get Timmy's body out of the back of the station wagon and roll the gurney into an inner hall. Dewey went into a back room and returned pushing a stainless-steel table, on which rested a cardboard cremation chamber. Together, the two men lifted Timmy into the box.

There was a moment of uneasy silence as the employee looked between Duke and the frail, sheet-covered earthly vessel of Timothy Nicholas Ducheski. "Did you want a minute alone to say good-bye?" he asked.

"Just a quick minute," Duke said.

Dewey nodded and walked into the back room. Duke pulled two credit cards from his wallet, and reached into the cremation chamber, slipping them under the back of his deceased son. "Take these with you, okay, pal?" he whispered.

He walked to the back room and met Dewey at the door. "How long will this take?"

"Depends on the body size. He's a pretty little guy. I don't think it'll take much more than an hour and a half, if that."

Duke nodded, slowly turned away, and walked into the waiting room. It was small, maybe ten-feet square, with a single window, a couch, and an end table on which was an instant coffee maker; a stack of brochures with the names and phone numbers of all the ministers, priests, and rabbis in Steubenville; several old magazines, their covers torn from the staples; and two fans, the kind you find stuffed in the hymnal racks on the back of church pews, with "Millard Funeral Home" printed on the handle. Duke made a cup of coffee and watched the first rays of morning light creep over the crest of the West Virginia hills.

CHAPTER THIRTY-FOUR

T he phone awakened Nina Ducheski from a hard sleep.

"Hello?"

"Mrs. Ducheski?"

Nina sat up on the couch and cleared her throat, still more asleep than awake. "Yes, who's this?"

"This is Edna Jackson from the Heinzmann Convalescent Center. I'm sorry to call at such a difficult time, but Mr. Ducheski left, and he forgot Timmy's bag of personal possessions—mostly the things that were on his dresser, the decorations and such. I'm sure he just got distracted, but I just wanted to let you know they were here; we'll keep them until he has time to pick them up."

Nina said, "I'm sorry. Who is this again?"

It was at that instant that Edna realized that Nina did not yet know her son had died. "It's Edna Jackson. I'm the night nursing supervisor at Heinzmann Convalescent Center. Mrs. Ducheski, have you talked to your husband tonight?"

"No. No, I haven't. What's this all about?"

Edna drew a breath. "Mrs. Ducheski, I am so sorry, but I thought your husband would have called you by now. Timmy passed away tonight."

It took a moment for the words to sink in. "Timmy's dead?" Nina shrieked into the phone. "Oh my God, how could this happen?" She began sobbing and wailing in a manner that made Edna clench her jaw tight. *You didn't know Timmy was dying, because you never came to visit,* Edna thought.

"Mrs. Ducheski, this has been coming on for quite some time. Timmy's been a very ill young man. Maybe you better get in touch with Mr. Ducheski. Would you please tell him that Timmy's bag is up here, and we'll keep it safe for him?"

Nina hung up without responding, pounding out the number to her mother and father's home. The phone rang ten times before Nina's mother answered. "Oh, Mama, Timmy's dead. He's dead. The home just called. Nick was up there, but he didn't even have the decency to call and tell me. What am I going to do? Timmy's dead." She cried and sobbed.

"Your father and I will be right over," her mother said.

Nina turned off the tears as she pecked out Tony's phone number. He was up and alert, awaiting reports from Rhino and Emilio, who were scouring Mingo Junction for Duke. "Tony," she said, crying again. "Timmy's dead."

"Timmy? Timmy who?"

"Timmy, my son, goddammit. He's dead. That bastard Nick, he knew and didn't even bother to call me. I am so upset. Can you come over, please?"

"What do you mean, Nick knew?"

"He was there. He was at the nursing home when Timmy died, I guess, I don't know for sure because he hasn't even bothered to call me. What kind of man does that? I was that boy's mother, goddammit."

What an unbelievable break, Tony thought. "How do you know he was at the home?"

"Some nurse called me. I had to find out that my son died from some nurse. She called because Nick left a bag of Timmy's belongings at the convalescent center. Can you believe how he disrespects me?"

"Where's Nick now?"

"I don't know. I don't care. That rat bastard. I hope he dies. Are you coming over?"

"In a little while, Sis. I'll tell you what I'll do, I'll run up to the convalescent center and get the bag for you and see what else I can find out."

"Oh, Tony, that would be so nice. Thank you. I want—"

The line went dead; Tony DeMarco was on a dead sprint for his car. Route 7 between Mingo Junction and Steubenville was clear, and he raced past Wheeling-Pittsburgh Steel's Steubenville plant and pulled off at Lincoln Avenue. He ran a red light at Harrington Road and arrived at the front door of the nursing home in just over fifteen minutes. The chameleon that he was, Tony put on a concerned face as he rapped gently on the front door. Edna was nearby, and she walked to the door but, not recognizing Tony, didn't open it. She pushed a button on the intercom and asked, "Can I help you?"

"Hello, yes, ma'am, I'm Timmy Ducheski's Uncle Anthony."

"Oh, please, come in," she said, pushing the door open.

"My sister just called, quite upset, and asked me to come up and pick up a suitcase, or something that contained Timmy's belongings?"

"Yes, I have them up here," she said, walking toward the duty desk. "Mr. Ducheski forgot it this morning when he left."

"Well, I'm sure he had a lot on his mind. My sister was quite upset, and I couldn't get many details from her. What happened?"

Edna shrugged. "It's hard to say. Timmy had been very ill for a very long time, the poor child. It could have been just about anything. Frankly, I think his little body just gave out, and Jesus called him home."

"Such a tragedy," Tony said. "Is Nicholas still here?"

"Mr. Ducheski? No, he left with the body for the funeral home."

Tony lowered his head and nodded. "Oh, I wish he would have called. I hate for him to be alone at a time like this." She handed him the bag. "Thank you. Thank you, very much. Did my brother . . ." He smiled. "Well, my brother-in-law, he's like a brother to me, did he say which funeral home would be doing the embalming?"

"Millard Funeral Home, the one on North Fourth Street. I asked Mr. Ducheski about services, but he said he didn't know. I think he was planning to have the body cremated."

"I see. And, you say that he did accompany Timmy's body to the funeral home?"

She nodded. "Uh-huh. I watched him pull out of the driveway, following the station wagon."

"I so wish he hadn't shouldered all this by himself." He took her right hand and patted the backside three times. "Thank you, so much. We all appreciate the care you gave Timmy."

She smiled and said, "You're welcome. We're all sorry for your loss."

As Tony disappeared out the front door and jogged to his car, Edna turned to her co-workers and said, "What a nice man."

The youngest nurse nodded and said, "Cute, too. I wonder if he's married."

In the narrow, gravel channel that separated Millard Funeral Home from the three-story brick apartment building just to its south, Tony DeMarco could see the white and chrome fins of the 1959 Buick Invicta protruding from behind the garage. "Duke, Duke, Duke," Tony said aloud in a chuckling, sing-song tone. "Good plan, my man, but you are such an amateur." Tony drove around the block and parked on a side street where he had a clear view of the car. He turned off the engine and slouched back in his seat, his eyes set on the Buick. He could not believe his good fortune. Duke was inside the funeral home, his heart probably racing, hoping that he could get out of town without being discovered. And there was Tony, the red-tailed hawk, biding his time on the tree limb, waiting for the bunny to stick his head outside the hole.

He had to piss, the natural reaction to the several cans of Diet Coke he had consumed since returning from Cara's and summoning his lieutenants. There wasn't much traffic, but he didn't want to be standing outside the car with his tool in his hand when the police cruised by or Duke returned to his car.

Uncomfortable as he was, Tony had no choice but to settle in and wait. Despite the bladder pressure, he remained delighted that he nearly had Duke in his sights. "I'm going to enjoy the shit out of killing you," he said aloud. He slouched and pressed his thighs together. "Goddamn, I have to piss."

The crematory at the Millard Funeral Home was behind a solid-steel door at the rear of the building, hard against the alley. The crematory could be accessed only through the steel door in the alley, keeping it well separated from the viewing parlors. The cremation chamber carrying the body was slid onto the concrete platform just above floor level. Gas jets on both sides of the body expelled flames that reached eighteen hundred degrees Fahrenheit. When the process was completed just over an hour later, all that remained of Timothy Ducheski was about four pounds of ash, and a few small pieces of bone and tooth. When the ashes had cooled, Dewey removed the remains with a hoe-like tool and placed them into a pan. He then ran the remains through a small grinder in an adjacent room that reduced the remaining bone and enamel bits to the size of coarse sand.

It was nearly six o'clock when the employee returned to the waiting room with a simple metal urn bearing the ashes of Timothy Ducheski. Dewey said, "I'll need you to sign some release papers, and that's pretty much it. I'm assuming you want to take the ashes with you?"

"I do."

The papers were typed and neatly arranged on a desk. Duke signed them and left.

At the same time that Duke was signing the documents, Tony DeMarco's bladder was preparing to explode. From the cup holder on the dash he snagged an empty Diet Coke can, unholstered his tool, and pressed the end of his member to the small opening and let go, alternating his line of vision between his business and the Buick. At first, he moaned in delight, but he had badly underestimated the volume of his bladder, and there was no stopping the flow. The can overflowed like a miniature geyser, and Tony lurched forward in his seat, trying to contain the urine as it ran over his hand and splattered on his seat, pants, and floor mat. "Goddamn you, Ducheski," he yelled, trying in vain to pinch off the flow. "I'll make you fuckin' lick this up before I kill you." The last half pint went splattering on the black floor mat.

He dropped the can outside the car and was reaching for his handkerchief when he saw the fins of Duke's Buick disappear behind the garage. "Oh, motherfucker," he yelled, reaching for the ignition key, piss dripping from his fingers. He pulled onto Fourth Street with his dick still dripping and hanging out of his pants.

Tony caught sight of the Buick's slanted taillights as they turned south on Ohio Route 7, heading back toward Mingo Junction. By this time, he had fished his handkerchief from his back pocket and wiped his hands. The inside of his car smelled like a roadside rest outhouse. He stayed back a safe distance and stuffed his member back in his damp pants as he swung onto Route 7.

Traffic was light, and Tony lagged back, staying out of Duke's rearview mirror. When he saw the turn signal on the Buick come on just before Logan Avenue, Tony started laughing. As the Buick turned right and started climbing the hill, Tony thought, *Ducheski, you are like reading a book.*

Duke placed the urn on the seat next to him and drove to where County Road 38 dipped behind Logan Hill. He pulled the car into the gravel turnaround, got out, and walked up the hunting trail on the backside of the hill. The sun was rising into a rare, clear sky. He stood for a moment at the overgrown parapet to Fort Logan. Spread out before him, the river made a slow bend to the north and straightened out for the stretch run past Mingo Junction. A barge laden with coal was moving slowly up the river; a coal train was crossing the river on the trestle just north of town. God, how he loved his valley. He would miss it.

He squatted in the dewy grass with the urn on the ground between his knees. "This is Fort Logan, Timmy. It's not much to look at now, but it was really something when I was a kid. I sure wish you could have seen it. I thought this would be a good place for you to be." He looked down on the river for a long minute. "I've got to go now, buddy. You take good care of Moonie for me 'til I get there, okay?"

He pulled the lid, turned the urn on its side, and began shaking it lightly, letting the ashes drift into the wind.

"That was so fucking touching, I can't stand it," came a mawkish and familiar voice from the dense brush.

The chills in Duke's ribs were like getting stabbed with a thousand frozen needles. From behind the growth emerged Tony DeMarco, smiling, his Beretta hanging in his hand at his side.

"Duke, you are the most predictable bastard I have ever known."

Duke looked at his brother-in-law, his head rolled back, and air escaped from his lungs. In a voice of resignation, he said, "Goddammit."

Tony said, "Do you remember when I played basketball against you in junior high? Remember, you were the big star and I was the scrub who never got off the bench? But I was the only one who could guard you in practice. Remember that?" He started walking slowly toward Duke, the gun now pointed at his chest. "I could stay with you like ugly on a baboon. You know why? Because you were too predictable. You only had two moves. You would either head fake left, drive right, or head fake right and pull up for the jumper. Every goddamn time. You could never go with your left hand—ever. You're predictable. That's why when I saw you get off at the exit, I knew this is where you were coming." Tony pointed at the weeds with the Beretta. "You know, the Knights of Columbus parking lot is just over the hill—it's a lot shorter than schlepping up the back of this mountain. But, I don't suppose you wanted anyone to see you, did you? . . . Yeah, I saw you pull off and said, 'He's going to take the boy's ashes and spread them up at his little fort.' Ain't that touching. And, what a coincidence that little Timmy died on the very night that you were going to boogie out of town. I'm sure you helped him along. I'm guessing that your nurse friend gave you a little something—potassium chloride, possibly—and you injected him. It stopped his heart, but no one suspected a thing, did they? After all, who would ever question the great Duke Ducheski?"

Tony walked closer, keeping the gun pointed at Duke's heart. The smile started to disappear.

"You must take me for a total fucking moron, Duke. You actually thought you could pull this off? Breaking into my house and stealing the tapes was bad enough, but what really pisses me off is that you thought you were so much smarter than me. Oh, by the way, I figured out that Carmine was probably the one who cracked my safe. Not smart on your part. He's the only safe-buster in a hundred miles of Mingo Junction. So, after I'm done with you, I'm going to kill him, too. See this?" he asked, holding up Timmy's bag.

Duke nodded.

"This was your downfall. You got careless. That nigger nurse up at death's doorway nursing home called Nina and said you forgot it. I volunteered to go pick it up, and they were kind enough to tell me where you'd gone."

"It must have really excited you," Duke said. "I see you pissed yourself."

"You can't even imagine how much pleasure I am going to get from killing you," Tony said.

Duke stared into the business end of the Beretta. His brain raced for an escape plan, but it seemed so hopeless.

"What's the matter, mister funny man, no cute little smart-ass remarks? Huh? The thought of your own death doesn't strike you as funny? I've got to tell you, I think it's fuckin' hilarious. We can do this one of two ways. I'll let you pick. One, you give me the tapes, and I'll be merciful and put a bullet in your brain. It's over in a hurry. No pain. Or, two, I start unloading clips in you—knees, elbows, shoulders, until you give me the tapes—and you will give me the tapes, because I know how to inflict a lot of pain while keeping you alive. Then, eventually, I will put a bullet in your brain. Your choice."

"Those sound a lot like the options the Troll gave Moonie."

"Is that a fact?"

"Yeah, right before Moonie killed the little shit and stole your money."

Tony jabbed Duke twice in the ribs with the barrel of the gun. "You got about ten seconds to make your decision. One, two, three . . ."

"I don't have 'em."

"Too bad for you, then. Four, five, six . . ."

"I gave 'em to the FBI."

"You're stalling, and you're lying. Seven, eight, nine . . . Oh, by the way, Duke, after I kill you and Carmine, I'm going to kill that miserable cunt of a girlfriend of yours, too."

"I can't believe that even you would sink that low."

"Oh, believe it, Duke, and I'll never lose a minute's sleep over it."

Duke forced a laugh and shook his head. "Yeah, well, I guess if your life's ambition is to be Joey Antonelli's bitch, congratulations, you've made it."

If there was anyone on that hillside that morning who was predictable, it was Tony DeMarco. Duke knew it would happen; he knew his words would cut Tony deep. His famous temper would flare and burn white-hot for an instant. When that occurred, Duke guessed that Tony would rake the Beretta across his face.

He was right. The instant Tony raised the Beretta, just before he brought it forth like a hammer, Duke flung what was left of the earthly remains of Timothy Nicholas Ducheski into Tony's open eyes and mouth. In the same motion, he ducked and rolled to his right. Tony fired twice. The Beretta sounded like a cannon going off in the narrow hills; the burrowing shells kicked dust a foot high. The Colt had been tucked into Duke's waistband, but the jarring fall caused it to slide inside his jeans, and he couldn't reach it. Things were happening at light speed.

Before Tony could blink his eyes clear, Duke came off the ground holding a rock the size of a softball and lunged at Tony. The rock came down hard on the side of Tony's head. It was not a clean blow; Duke's index finger on his right hand was crushed between the rock and

Tony's skull; it snapped at the joint. As they fell into a heap, the pistol remained in Tony's grip.

Blood poured from the gash in the side of Tony's head. Before he could get his bearings and fire another shot, Duke crashed down with the rock a second time, this time smashing Tony's gun hand. The gun flew from his grip. Duke pushed his left hand into Tony's face and climbed over him, diving for the Beretta. He grabbed it and rolled, coming up with it in his throbbing right hand.

Tony groaned. He was lying in the dirt, woozy from the blow to the head, and clutching his crushed right hand in his left. Duke walked around Tony and sat on the rotting railroad tie that once served as a bulwark for Fort Logan. Tony struggled to get up on all fours, wobbling and unable to lift his face off the rocky ground.

Using his left hand, Duke struggled to reach down the waist of his pants and removed the Colt .45 Commander. His finger pounded and made his right hand virtually useless. He pushed the Beretta into his belt behind his back and kicked the remains of the old car seat off the safe. He fumbled with the No Parking sign, unwilling to take his eyes off Tony or switch the gun to his damaged right hand. Using his foot and two fingers on his throbbing right hand, Duke moved the sign to the side, exposing the safe.

Tony started laughing and struggled to his feet, a stream of thick blood matting his hair and running down his neck, mixing with dust, sweat, and Timmy's ashes. Duke kept his gun trained on Tony.

"Goddamn, Ducheski, you've got more balls than I gave you credit for."

Duke tightened his grip on the revolver as Tony reached for his hip pocket.

"Keep your hands where I can . . ."

Tony pulled a handkerchief from the pocket and wiped the gooey mixture of blood and ash from his eyes. The blood from the gash in his head continued to run down the side of his neck, soaking his collar. He pressed the handkerchief to the wound and winced. "So, now what? You gonna shoot me?"

"No, that would be too easy. I think I'll just let the FBI handle you. I want to see you on the witness stand, afraid every second for your pathetic life because you know Joey Antonelli will kill you the first chance he gets. I hear all this talk about the Mafia code of honor. Well, let's see what they do when they hear those tapes and find out you were going to blackmail them."

Tony shook his head. "You must think this is a movie or a television show. That's not how things work. I'd rather you kill me. But here's the rub, Ducheski: I'm still in control. You don't have the balls to pull the trigger. What are you going to do, desperado?"

Duke pointed to the beaten footpath with the barrel of his pistol. "Tony, either you walk down that path, or I swear to Christ I'll put a bullet right in your heart."

Tony licked his gray lips and spat. "No, you won't. I know you. You don't have it in you. Not the great Duke Ducheski, hero of all Mingo Junction. You couldn't do it, especially if you had to look someone in the eye. If you had it in you, you'd have already shot me."

"Walk away, Tony."

"What are you hiding, anyway?" He strained his neck, trying to look beyond Duke. "You have my money hidden up here, don't you?" Tony smiled and tapped his forehead with the index finger of the hand holding the bloody handkerchief. "I'm a smart motherfucker, huh, Ducheski? You hid the money up here, and you need me to leave so you can get it."

"Go, Tony."

"No. That's not going to happen. I'm coming after you, and either you're going to run or I'm going to take that gun off you and kill you with it." He took a step; Duke aimed the Colt at his chest. "Don't test me, Tony."

Tony DeMarco grinned a hateful grin and took one more step.

It was his last.

In the instant that Tony lifted his leg, Duke recalled how Tony had talked about killing Sammy Stein, the Jewish produce distributor from Weirton. Tony said he enjoyed strangling Sammy because *it gave the fat puke a little time to think about the gravity of his mistake.* Stein had a moment of consciousness when he realized his life was about to end. Now, probably for the first time in his life, Tony DeMarco was the prey instead of the predator. It was his time to look into the eyes of a killer, and in that lightning streak of a moment, he realized the gravity of his mistake and how badly he had underestimated the will of Duke Ducheski. It was too late to stop the events that would kill him in another instant.

He didn't flinch. The muscles in Duke's left forearm tightened, and he squeezed the trigger. Tony heard the roar and felt the sledge-hammer-like impact to his chest as the bullet exploded through his sternum and pierced his heart. The impact blew him off the ground. He landed on his tailbone, arms and legs stretched out before him, and he tumbled twenty yards down the hill. The gun blast echoed through the hills and continued for several seconds after the body had stopped rolling.

Duke's arm fell limp to his side, the pistol loose in his fingers. "Can't go with my left, huh?" Duke tucked the revolver back into his belt and stepped sideways down the hill to where Tony DeMarco was sprawled on tufts of dead foxtail, faceup, his lifeless eyes staring into a cobalt-blue sky.

As kids, Moonie, Angel, and Duke would sometimes sneak into the Junction City Mine No. 2 and drop stones down the abandoned shaft and wait for what seemed like an eternity for them to hit bottom. It would serve as the perfect resting place for Tony DeMarco. He grabbed an ankle with his good hand and the cuff of Tony's pants with the thumb and three good fingers of his right hand, and started dragging the body the quarter mile over the north face of Logan Hill toward the abandoned mine shaft. Just walking the distance over the overgrown hillside was a daunting task; dragging a body without the full use of both hands made it an exhausting trek. Honey-locust trees, weeds, and thistles had grown high over the mine entrance; the wooden seal of heavy logs was solid, but the corner was still pulled from the side beams where they had moved it away years earlier. Duke crawled in on his belly, then dragged the body of his former nemesis through the opening. Light filtered through the splayed wood slats, golden beams in which swirled faint particles of coal dust that had kicked up when the body of Tony DeMarco slapped against the mine floor.

It was several minutes before Duke's eyes adjusted to the darkness of the mine. When he could begin to make out his surroundings, he sat down and with his feet started rolling Tony's body toward the shaft. His right hand throbbed and was almost useless in providing any stability. With each roll of Tony's body, blood mixed with the coal dust on the floor of the mine. It was an arduous task, but Duke took perverse pleasure in kicking the corpse of Tony DeMarco across the ground.

The elevator housing still stood guard over the shaft. Duke kicked aside one of the timbers that made a poor cover of the shaft, clearing just enough room for a corpse. Though he thought it a bit morbid, he fished Tony's gold money clip from his pants pocket, stripped it of a thick wad of hundred-dollar bills, and returned it. He took a cleansing breath and said, "Better than you deserve." He put his feet behind the corpse's thighs, and started to push. As he did, the legs folded and the bottoms of Tony DeMarco's expensive, custom-made Italian shoes were exposed to Duke. Each had a silver-dollar-sized hole in the sole. Duke Ducheski smiled at the thought of Tony DeMarco heading off to eternity without his wad of cash and with holes in his shoes.

And with that, he kicked hard and sent the corpse into the abyss.

He didn't remember hearing the body hit the bottom of the shaft. He was exhausted and sat for several minutes, catching his breath and his bearings. Pushing himself to one knee, Duke slowly stood, hunching at the shoulders in the low cave. He slipped the Beretta from his belt and tossed it down to its owner. This time, he listened. When the pistol clacked at the bottom of the shaft, the Duke of Mingo Junction turned and made his way back toward the light.

CHAPTER THIRTY-FIVE

By the time he walked back to Fort Logan, the pain in his right hand was sending showers of sparks up his arm. He retrieved the Troll's blue duffel bag from the safe and Timmy's urn from the weeds. A few minutes later, Duke wheeled the Buick back onto Route 38 and took the back road toward Steubenville. He was dirty, sweaty, and exhausted, but he felt oddly at ease about the morning's events. Within the space of a few hours, he had injected his son with a lethal dose of potassium chloride, and then put a bullet through the heart of his brother-in-law. And yet, he was eerily calm. Perhaps it was the fact that he was leaving the Ohio Valley forever that eased his nerves. More likely, he thought, it was because Timmy was in a better place and, hopefully, nowhere near the tortured soul of Tony DeMarco.

As he drove past the downtown exits to Steubenville, Duke eased the Buick into the left lane and, at the north end of town, turned up Stony Hollow Boulevard and drove to the bowling alley. His was the only car in the parking lot. He walked up to the pay phone mounted on the outside wall near the front door. The phone book had been stolen, and he had to call directory assistance for the first number he needed. The phone rang twice before it was answered.

"Yeah."

"Carmine, are you alone?"

"Who's this?"

"Duke."

There was a silence that lasted five seconds. "Yeah, I can talk."

"All right, don't say anything, just listen. Go up to Tony DeMarco's and help yourself to whatever's left in the safe. It's all yours. No one will be around for hours, and no one will ever come looking for you. Go now."

"Wait, wait, wait," Carmine said, violating Duke's only directive. "How long will it be safe?"

"Carmine, I don't have a lot of time. Trust me on this. Go now. Go get the money, the jewelry, whatever's in there that you want. No one will ever come looking for you, ever. You have my word."

There was another pause. "You're sure?"

"I've never been more sure of anything in my life."

Duke could hear Carmine start to giggle. He whispered, "Where's Tony?"

"We never had this conversation, Carmine. Buy yourself one of those little pastel houses on the beach and enjoy your life." He hung up.

The second number he knew by heart. Angelo Angelli awoke and groaned his greeting.

"H'lo."

"Jesus Christ, Angel, are you still in bed?"

"Duke?"

"Yeah, come on man, get out of the sack."

Angel bolted upright and summoned himself to alertness. "Duke! Man, I need to talk to you. Tony DeMarco came in late last night, looking for you, pissed as all hell about something, wanting to know where you were. I told him—"

"Angel, I know," he interrupted. "I know. Believe me, it's nothing you need to be concerned about."

"Oh, Duke, but he was pissed. I mean, pissed! I could see it in his eyes, you know that look he gets when—"

"Angel, be quiet for a minute and just listen. I want you to go down to the restaurant and get into the safe in my office. The combination is on the last page of the notebook in my desk drawer."

"Okay. What do you need?"

"I don't need anything. What's in there is yours."

There was an awkward moment of silence. "Are you ever going to tell me what this is all about?"

"Angel, you've been a great friend for as long as I can remember. Just read the letter that's in the safe. When you're done with it, burn it. Okay?"

"But, Duke—"

"I've got to go, Angel. Everything's in the safe. Don't worry about Tony getting in your face. Everything will be fine."

"But, Duke—"

"You take care, buddy."

Angel kept his ear to the humming dial tone for a few seconds, then hurriedly dressed and drove to Duke's Place. The cook was in the kitchen, preparing the specials for that day's lunch crowd. Angel walked straight to the office and found the notebook. Scrawled in pen was the combination: R-16, L-14, R-38, L-90.

Angel closed the office door and with a quivering hand began dialing the combination. On the floor of the safe he found a manila envelope. Inside were two legal-looking documents and a twice-folded sheet of paper. He unfolded the paper and found a handwritten note.

Angel:

Hopefully, I was the one who directed you to find this letter, otherwise, I'm probably dead.

I know this is going to be hard to understand, but it will become clearer in the months to come. First of all, I'm never coming back to Mingo Junction. I can't say why, but someday you'll understand. You're going to be asked a lot of questions about me. People will want to know where I am. You don't know anything, so you won't have to lie. Your only response should be, "I don't know."

In this envelope is the deed to the restaurant. Duke's Place is now all yours. Angel's Place, huh? The cost of the restaurant, building included, is $70,000. I'm financing the sale, and the terms of the agreement are that you pay me a dollar a month, interest-free, until the restaurant is paid off. (I'm not sure when you'll have it paid off, but it will be a while. You figure it out. You're good at math. Ha.) Also, I turned over the bank account to you. Take the document that's in the envelope to the Miners and Mechanics Bank and sign it. That will give you access to the money and the right to sign the checks. Whatever's in the account is yours. You've earned it.

It's all yours, buddy. You always wanted to run your own business, so here's your chance. I'd like it if you kept the picture of me making "the shot" up behind the bar and the championship record in the jukebox. That's your call, though, as it is your restaurant, now.

I know this is a lot to swallow and right now it doesn't make any sense. It will, over time. You've been a good pal, and I know you'll take care of the place.

I need you to do two things for me. One, burn this letter right after you've finished reading it, and, two, when they come asking what you know, please don't know anything.

Your friend,
Duke

Angel set the letter on the desk and looked at the deed and the document transferring ownership to him. The bank document required a signature and a notary seal, then the deal would be complete. He put the legal documents back in the safe and went into the men's room. Holding the letter over the toilet, he lit the bottom and held it until the flames licked at his fingers, then he dropped it in the bowl and flushed it away.

CHAPTER THIRTY-SIX

June 1995. If life could be any less fulfilling for the former Duke Ducheski, he couldn't imagine how.

It had been a year and eleven days, to be exact, since Duke had handed over the transcripts of the tapes to Agent Kinnicki. After a slight detour to a local emergency room, where his entire hand was set in a cast, he was flown to Fort Sam Houston in San Antonio, Texas, for safekeeping. It was a far cry from the mountaintop retreat he had first envisioned. He was living in a cottage on the grounds, and he had a civilian job as a file clerk in the basement of the medical center on the base. He didn't have to work, but it helped pass the time, and he got used to interacting with people under his new identity.

The prosecutors had admonished him not to make friends. That order had not been hard to follow, since he was the only file clerk working in the archives department, which was in a cavernous sub-basement that the employees called "the dungeon." There were a theater, a swimming pool, and a bowling alley on the base, but he had little interest in those, save for an occasional movie. He took his meals on the base and spent his evenings watching cable television, which was his only luxury. The cottage was small, was furnished with battered, government-issue furniture, and had a window air-conditioner that did little good when pitted against the insufferable Texas heat. To the accommodations, he had added only a clock-radio and two suitcases of clothes. The rest of his possessions, including the duffel bag full of cash, remained in the trunk of the Buick, which was in a secured, government-owned warehouse somewhere in Georgia.

He was now Ronald Edward Reynolds, born October 30, 1952, in

Chicago. At the FBI's suggestion, he had grown a moustache and sported a pair of wire-rim glasses. Fort Sam Houston was known to be a hiding place for protected witnesses, and there was speculation around the hospital that he was a witness in an international drug case. When his boss, Peggy, told him about the rumor, he asked, "Do you believe that?"

"You can be Pablo Escobar for all I care," Peggy said. "Just get those medical reports filed."

The occasional cigarette he once enjoyed with a beer had increased to a pack-and-a-half-a-day habit. And he had gained fifteen pounds that were showing up in a pair of love handles just over his belt. Once in a while, he walked to the base's outdoor courts to shoot baskets, but he couldn't motivate himself to work out on a regular basis. After work he would eat, then go home, drink beer, and fall asleep in front of the television, waking up at 3:00 a.m. to an infomercial, his skin stuck to the fake leather of the chair. The only piece of mail he received during that year came compliments of Kinnicki—a copy of the divorce decree, which granted Nina everything, including his Jeep.

He missed his freedom. He missed Mingo Junction more than he dreamed possible. He missed Timmy and Angel and Moonie and the cast of characters that had made Duke's Place a success. He missed Carmine. He missed being his own boss and making Duke's a success. His missed being the Duke of Mingo Junction. And, most of all, he missed Cara. Drinking alone, chain-smoking, and staring at the walls of the cottage were not helping.

Kinnicki called every week or two to update him on the case against Joseph Antonelli. The investigation was going incredibly well, Kinnicki said. They had found four bodies near a private hunting lodge near Youngstown, Ohio. Bullets recovered from what remained of the corpses matched guns recovered at Antonelli's house.

"This isn't like dealing with Il Tigre," Kinnicki said. "Turns out, these guys are amateurs and very sloppy."

Once they matched up the conversations on the tapes with other reports, they were able to link Antonelli with eight murders and a prostitution, drug, and illegal gambling operation that spread over three states. The Internal Revenue Service had been called in to investigate Antonelli's personal returns, as well as those of the car washes and coin laundries that he used to launder his money.

"Joey's organization is crumbling around him," Kinnicki said. "Some of his capos have offered their testimony in exchange for immunity. Others have just disappeared. Our boy Joey is going down hard."

"You still haven't found Tony DeMarco?" Ronald asked.

"Not a trace," Kinnicki said. "Either he took off and is lying low, or Antonelli got to him; that's the way I'm betting. He's probably at the bottom of the Ohio River."

"Or at the bottom of a mine shaft."

"Exactly."

Three months after that conversation, and two days before the trial was to begin, Ronald Reynolds was packed and ready to board a private military transport plane for Pittsburgh. He would be driven to the courthouse under heavy guard and wearing a flak jacket. He was nervous but relieved that the entire ordeal would soon be behind him. Then, the phone rang in his cottage.

"It's been delayed again," Kinnicki said, no longer bothering to identify himself. It was the third time the trial had been delayed.

"For how long?" Ronald asked.

"Could be a while—six months, maybe longer. Antonelli's lawyers know he's toast, so they're stalling. They say he's mentally unfit to stand trial, so they want to run a battery of psychological tests. The judge doesn't want to give them any ammo for filing an appeal, so he's giving the defense a wide berth."

Ronald said, calmly, "That's disappointing."

"I thought you'd be upset," Kinnicki said.

"No use getting upset over things I can't control."

The next day at lunch, Ronald walked to the base's credit union and withdrew his savings—nearly thirty-two thousand dollars, which included the money he had plucked from Tony DeMarco's money clip, three thousand dollars the FBI had given him when he was relocated, and everything he had saved while at the base. He then went back to the cottage and grabbed the two suitcases sitting just inside the front door.

Good-bye, Fort Sam Houston.

He wasn't staying captive another minute. He slipped the cash inside the smallest of the suitcases, left the key on the floor, and beneath a noonday sun walked past the guard shack toward downtown San Antonio. Less than a mile down the road, he stopped at Newton's Auto Sales, where he was greeted by a chubby salesman with mustard stains on the corners of his mouth. There was a 1984 Bronco on the lot that the salesman described as, "low mileage, very cherry, and a sweet deal for just sixty-six hundred."

After a brief inspection, Ronald said, "It's been wrecked. There are grip marks on the frame, the driver's side is full of body putty, and I'm reasonably certain the odometer has been rolled back. I'll give you forty-four hundred, green money."

After a visit to the registrar for his license plates and title, and a stop to fill the gas tank, Ronald Reynolds was westbound on Interstate 10 before 3:00 that afternoon. For the first time in months, he didn't feel a knot in the middle of his chest. It was a muggy, hot day in south Texas, but the hot air rushing through the open window was liberating. He didn't have a map and had no idea where he was going to end up. It didn't matter. He was behind the wheel of a Bronco, there was money in his pocket, and he had six months to explore the American West. He would drive until he saw something he wanted to investigate. If he stayed for an hour, fine. If he stayed for a week, that was fine, too.

It was on the backside of eight o'clock when he stopped in Balmorhea for gas, a cheeseburger, and a Dr. Pepper. His adrenaline was at full throttle. The former Duke Ducheski felt like he had busted out of prison, and he wanted to put as much distance as possible between himself and Fort Sam Houston. The headlights of the Bronco cut through the Texas night as he headed into El Paso and turned north on I-25. The night air was clean in his nostrils, and the sky was wide with stars. He napped at a truck stop south of Albuquerque, awoke at seven, ate breakfast, and kept moving.

Peggy was probably missing him for the first time. When he didn't show up, she'd start asking questions. Someone would check the cottage, finding his clothes gone and the key on the floor. Then, someone higher up the food chain would call the FBI in Washington, who would call Kinnicki, who would have to tell the agent in charge and the prosecutor, who would absolutely lose their collective minds. Ronald was sorry that his departure was going to cause Kinnicki heartache, but he couldn't stay put another minute.

He stopped at a discount store west of Albuquerque and bought a small tent, a sleeping bag, a backpack, camping supplies, a .45-caliber revolver, and a box of shells. When he hit Flagstaff, Arizona, he turned north toward the Grand Canyon, where he rented a campsite and spent five days exploring. He finished each day refreshingly exhausted. The love handles began to melt. He hadn't had a cigarette since leaving the fort. Dinner was fixed over a campfire, and he was asleep by eight o'clock. He awoke each morning sore and stiff, heated oatmeal over a fire, and headed out to the trails. When he awoke on the sixth day, he shaved off his moustache, neatly loaded his gear into the Bronco, and headed north. He stopped near Hatch, Utah, in the late morning and placed a collect call to Kinnicki.

He choked back a laugh when the operator said, "Collect call from Ronald Reynolds. Will you accept the charges?"

It took a few seconds for the alias to register with Kinnicki, who stammered for a second before blurting out, "Oh, Jesus, yes."

"Hey, my man, how are the Pirates doing?" Ronald asked.

"The Pirates! Don't talk to me about the Pirates. Where the hell are you? Jesus H. Christ."

"I'm alive and well and touring the great American West. You should go to the Grand Canyon, Kinnicki. You'd love it."

"I don't want to hear about the Grand Canyon. Get your ass back to Fort Sam Houston. Everyone around here is going crazy. We're in the middle of the bureau's biggest organized-crime investigation in decades, and you're gallivanting around the countryside. If you get killed, the entire investigation is in jeopardy."

"If I go back to the base, the investigation will definitely be in jeopardy, because I'll die of boredom. I couldn't stay there another day, Kinnicki. It was like being in a zoo. No one knows where I am or who I am. This is the best I've felt in months. I'm going to jump off the phone before you can trace the call. I'll check in every couple weeks. Tell the prosecutor I've taken up skydiving, too. That ought to put his boxers in a bunch."

He drove up into Montana and South Dakota and down into Nebraska. At Kearney, he rented a room at the Blue Moon Motel, a rundown little place that charged a two-dollar deposit for his towels. He didn't realize the Blue Moon backed up to the fairgrounds until the next morning, when the general clamor of the rodeo awakened him before the first bull was released from its pen. He had never seen a rodeo, and he had nothing but time.

Wearing sunglasses, cargo shorts, a floral-patterned shirt, and tennis shoes, Ronald Reynolds looked wondrously out of place next to several hundred men in cowboy hats and spurs, their cheeks stuffed with tobacco. He stopped by a concession stand being run by a 4-H Club. A woman in cowboy boots and tight jeans had her back to Ronald, shoveling coffee into a paper filter.

"Could I get a cup of that when it's ready?"

"You sure can," she replied. Ronald was inspecting a tray of donuts when she turned around. He glanced up, then whipped his head back for a second look. She was tall—almost 5'11"—in her midthirties, with deep-blue eyes and short, wavy tendrils of chestnut hair that danced around her temples and ears. The creases around her mouth deepened when she smiled, which she did when she caught him doing a double-take.

"Anything else?" she asked.

"Uh, yeah, one of those cake donuts, please."

As she handed him the donut in a piece of waxed paper, he instinctively checked for a wedding band; there was none. "That'll be fifty cents," she said.

He handed her a dollar and said, "That's good."

He took a seat in the bleachers to watch the juniors in a barrel-racing competition. He had watched for twenty minutes when a woman said, "You don't look much like a cowboy."

It was her.

"I don't?" he asked.

She shook her head. "Nothing about that floral shirt screams 'cowboy.'"

"What's it scream?"

"I'd have to go with 'surfer dude.'"

Ronald exhaled and looked away in feigned disgust. "I can't believe it. The guy at the tack shop said all the cowboys were wearing green-and-orange-and-teal floral shirts this summer."

She winced in mock sympathy. "I'm afraid he got you on that one, Tex."

He slowly shook his head. "Anything else?"

"No spurs."

"Oh, I've got spurs. They're in the car. I just didn't want to get them dirty before it was my turn to ride one of those cows."

She laughed aloud and extended her hand, "My name's Addie Mae."

"I'm Ron."

She smiled and held his hand a second longer than necessary. "Do you have someone in the rodeo, Ron?"

"No. I just stopped by to watch. How about you?"

Addie Mae pointed to a ten-year-old boy standing near the chute and looking very serious. "He's competing in the juniors." He had his mom's dark hair and long legs, and he was doing his best to look the part, his thumbs hitched in his belt, chewing on a foxtail stem.

"Good-lookin' boy," Ron said.

"Logan Matthew. He's my joy," she said. "One of them. The other's under that elm." She pointed to a girl of fourteen who sat cross-legged, pulling apart blades of grass and looking bored. "Brooklynn Renée—she doesn't know how to ride a horse and couldn't care less. She likes *basketball*, of all things."

Ronald straightened up. "What's wrong with basketball?" he asked.

Addie Mae sensed the jab and smiled. "Where are you from, Ron?"

"Here and there. Most recently, Texas."

"What brings you to Kearney?"

"The rodeo." He smiled; she didn't. "I was just passing through. I stayed over at the Blue Moon last night. Do you want to know what I've learned about rodeos?"

"What's that?"

"It's very difficult to sleep through one."

"I'm sure it is. Well, it was nice meeting you, Ron. I need to get back to the concession stand," she said, turning to leave.

"Wait a minute," he said, hopping down out of the bleachers. "Listen, uh, Addie Mae . . . would you like to go to dinner tonight?"

"Oh, I don't know. No, thanks. I don't really know you."

"I don't know you, either, but I'm willing to learn." She smiled. "It's just dinner. Meet me somewhere, you pick it, and if I turn out to be a jerk, you can always leave."

She looked at him for a long moment and said, "Okay. There's a steak house at Saint Paul and Winfield—Dom's. It's casual. I'll meet you there at seven."

A friendly, handsome stranger rolls in from out of town, lands at the Blue Moon Motel in Kearney, of all places, decides on a lark to take in a rodeo, comes to Addie Mae's concession stand, and she ends up on a dinner date. It was too bizarre. She drilled him with questions.

"Where're you from?"

"Texas."

"You still don't look like a cowboy."

"Not everyone in Texas is a cowboy."

"What'd you do in Texas?"

"Civil service. Worked for the government."

"Why'd you leave?"

"Ever work for the government?" She shook her head. "I was bored to tears. I had some money saved. It was time to find something new."

"Uh-oh, Tex, wrong answer. So, you just pick up and leave whenever something starts to bore you?"

"Generally not. This was a first."

"Uh-huh. Where'd you live before Texas."

"Near Pittsburgh, Pennsylvania."

"Wife?"

"Ex."

"Kids?"

"One. A boy. He died young."

"Oh, I'm sorry. What was his name?"

"Timothy. Timothy Ducheski."

"I thought your last name was Reynolds."

He stalled. "I'm sorry, what?"

"You said your last name is Reynolds."

"It is; so was his. Timothy Ducheski Reynolds. Ducheski was my mom's maiden name."

She nodded and seemed to accept the answer. "So, you quit your job, you had money in your pocket, and you decide to see the country and just happen to land in Kearney, Nebraska. That's your story?"

"That's it," he said. Her brows arched like two slinking caterpillars. "If the interrogation is over, maybe you could tell me a little about yourself."

Her name was Addie Mae Groat. She was raised on a farm outside of Netawaka, Kansas, and went to the University of Nebraska–Lincoln to study veterinary medicine. Her education was interrupted her junior year when she got pregnant to Jack Milnick, a middle-distance runner on the track team. They married and moved to Kearney, where he had gotten a job as a counselor with the juvenile court. Brooklynn was born the following December. Jack was not ready to be married. They struggled financially and argued continually. Shortly after her first meeting with a divorce lawyer, she learned she was again pregnant. Jack took a graduate-assistant position at the University of Missouri and never returned to Kearney. When the divorce was final shortly after Logan was born, she took back her maiden name. She was an office manager for a group of doctors and was five classes short of a business degree at the University of Nebraska at Kearney.

The evening passed quickly. At 10:30, she said, "The kids are home by themselves. I need to go."

Ronald asked, "So, Ms. Groat, did I pass the audition?"

She grinned and nodded. "You made the first cut."

This created a dilemma. He had been warned against developing friendships, and on the flight from Pittsburgh to San Antonio, Kinnicki said, "For the love of God, don't fall in love."

"Why would that be so terrible?"

"Because, when the dick gets hard, the brain gets soft. If you snuggle up to some woman, you better be dammed careful what you tell her. She tells one friend, who whispers it to her cousin, who tells her boss, who needs a favor from the union steward in St. Louis, who slips the information to a member of the mob. People start putting the pieces together, and pretty soon someone's whispering into Joey Antonelli's ear. And I assume you know what happens after that?"

"Nothing good," Ronald said.

"That's right, nothing good."

It was going to be a problem, because there was nothing about Addie Mae Groat that he didn't like.

Instead of driving out of Kearney as he had planned, he stayed on at the Blue Moon. After two more dates, he rented a furnished apartment near the university and took a job as a clerk in a local hardware store. He wore a red vest and a plastic name tag that said, "Ronnie." It gave him time to figure out how he would eventually tell her about his past. He wanted to tell her the truth, but Kinnicki's words always halted him.

He had been in Kearney three months when he left to meet Kinnicki and the federal prosecutor in Omaha for two days of trial prep. The evening he returned, he met Addie Mae at their favorite Italian restaurant. Their dinners were being placed on the table when he asked, "Am I ever going to meet your kids?"

"It depends," she said.

"On what?"

"On if and when you ever level with me and tell me why you really came to Kearney. I'm very protective of my kids, Ron. Most of the men I've seen since the divorce never got through my front door, because I didn't want to introduce my kids to a carousel of suitors. It must be obvious that I'm very attracted to you, but in my heart I know there's a lot you're not telling me. You work twenty hours a week in a hardware store, but you always have plenty of money. You're vague about your past and why you're here. Then, you disappear for two days and offer no explanation. Are you a drug dealer? Are you a Mafia hit man? Are you in the CIA? What? If this relationship is going to continue, I have to know."

"What if I can't tell you?" he asked.

"Can't, or won't?"

"Maybe both."

"In that case, this relationship is over."

She pulled her napkin off her lap, dropped it on the table next to an untouched plate of veal parmesan, and walked out. He caught up to her in the parking lot. As she reached for the door handle on her car, he jumped in front of her and blurted, "Wait, wait, wait, wait, please wait." He put both his palms up. "A hit man or a drug dealer? You're kidding me, right?" She crossed her arms and stared hard into his eyes, her lips squeezed into a tight ball. "Okay, you want the truth?" Her expression didn't change. "Fine. I'll give you the truth. Let's go to my apartment. I can't talk about it in a crowded restaurant."

"I'll go to your apartment, but I'm telling you something, Ron. The first time my bullshit meter goes off, I'm out of there."

She sat on the couch while he got two wine glasses and a bottle of merlot from the kitchen. "I don't want anything to drink," she said.

He set the glasses on the coffee table. "You will before the evening is over." He gave himself a full pour and sat back on the couch, turning slightly toward her.

"My name, the one I was born with, is not Ronald Reynolds. That's my real name now, but for most of my life my name was Nick Ducheski—D-U-C-H-E-S-K-I. Everyone called me Duke. I'm not from Texas. I only lived there because the federal government was hiding me and trying to keep me from getting killed. Before that, I had lived my entire life in a little town along the Ohio River in eastern Ohio—Mingo Junction.

"We had a fort—me and Moonie and Angel . . ."

CHAPTER THIRTY-SEVEN

Joey Antonelli and six of his capos were indicted on twenty-six counts of murder, racketeering, illegal narcotic sales, and a host of RICO statutes. There also were three indictments for corruption against Mingo Junction Police Chief Hinton Jaynes, who skipped bond and was later arrested while hiding out in a rented trailer in Lady Lakes, Florida. He died of a heart attack before he could be brought to trial. Two of Antonelli's capos were turning state's evidence, but the linchpin to the prosecution was the tapes—Joseph Antonelli at his boastful best, bragging about murders, ordering hits, and masterminding a huge drug, prostitution, and gambling operation.

Meanwhile, eleven hundred miles away, Addie Mae Groat was torn between her love of Ronald Reynolds and, like Cara before her, her concern for her children.

A week after his confession at his apartment, Ronald's phone rang early one morning. The only person who knew his phone number was Addie Mae.

He picked it up and said, "Hey, lover."

"Not on your best day, sunshine."

It was Kinnicki.

"How'd you get this number? It's unlisted."

"Uh-huh. Did you forget who I work for?"

"Apparently, I did."

"I was just calling to see where you want me to ship the Buick."

"The Buick? I thought you were keeping it until this ordeal was over."

"I did. You are hereby relieved of duty. Antonelli is taking a plea."

"You're kidding. Why would he do that?"

"Once he and his lawyer listened to all the tapes, Mr. Antonelli was suddenly very cooperative. He gets life in prison, but no death penalty, in exchange for his complete cooperation on any federal investigations into mob activities here, in New York, and in Chicago."

There was a moment of silence on the phone.

"So that's it?" Ronald asked.

"That's it. You're free to go live your life. Just so you know, Antonelli's lawyers are convinced it was either you or Tony DeMarco who gave us the tapes. They think we're hiding you both. For the record, you're the only one we've been hiding, and it would certainly be in your best interests to stay hidden."

CHAPTER THIRTY-EIGHT

On Saturday, September 21, 1996, Ronald Reynolds and Addie Mae Groat were married in a small church ceremony at the Netawaka United Methodist Church. Brooklynn Renée was the maid of honor; Logan Matthew was the best man. He adopted the kids and, as a gift to Addie Mae and her parents, took her last name. With the ill-gotten loot from the Troll, and his remaining savings from Fort Sam Houston, he and Addie Mae purchased a sporting goods and trophy store in Broken Arrow, Oklahoma—Groat's Sporting Goods.

Ron had a portion of their backyard blacktopped for a basketball court. Brooklynn developed into the best point guard in the area. Logan remained interested in his barrel racing and, to the amazement of his mother, also developed a passion for his father's favorite sport. He loved playing games of H-O-R-S-E and one-on-one with his new dad.

"We'll play one-on-one, but you have to pretend to be someone," Logan announced. "I'm Michael Jordan. Who are you?"

Ron Groat took the ball and wiped at the sweat on his upper lip. "I'll be Duke Ducheski."

Logan frowned. "Duke who?"

"Ducheski. Duke Ducheski. Don't tell me that you've never heard of the great Duke Ducheski?"

Logan shook his head. "No. Who does he play for?"

"Well, he's retired now. But he used to play for the Mingo Indians."

"I've never heard of them, either."

The Duke of Mingo Junction grinned and bounced the ball to his son.

EPILOGUE

There were two enduring theories surrounding the disappearance of Duke Ducheski.

Some believed he had been murdered by Tony DeMarco or the Antonelli family. The rationale ranged from Duke's infidelity to Nina to the possibility that he was stealing from the Antonelli gambling operation.

Others, the romantics, believed he vanished on his own accord or went into the witness-protection program to *avoid* being murdered by Tony DeMarco or the Antonellis.

Late in the afternoon after Duke dropped off the tapes in my office, two agents from the FBI field office in Pittsburgh showed up to claim them. They were a humorless duo, and their only question was, "Is this all of them?" It was, I assured them. They left without ever asking if I had listened to the tapes or made copies, which I had. Thus, I knew that Duke was in deep with the FBI's investigation of Pittsburgh's most powerful mob boss. Duke intimated to me that he might be killed. *If the guy I took those from ever finds out I've got 'em, jail would be a much-preferable option.* Thus, it was a very likely possibility that he was dead.

I had planned to cover the trial of Joseph Antonelli, hoping it might provide some clues to Duke's whereabouts. Unfortunately, Antonelli accepted the government's plea bargain and the evidence against him was secreted away. My Freedom of Information requests for investigative documentation were denied, as the information was deemed to be part of other, ongoing FBI investigations. This, I knew, was largely baloney, but it's a difficult point to challenge. I spoke to

Agent Kinnicki and the federal prosecutor, but neither would even admit to having ever heard the name Duke Ducheski.

After nearly two decades of fruitless searches, I was finally convinced that he was dead. Most likely, I thought, Joseph Antonelli had learned that Tony DeMarco had secretly recorded him and that Duke had stolen the tapes, and both men were fed into a meat grinder or a blast furnace.

Then, one day in early May 2014, I was reminded that sometimes, no matter how hard you work, there is no substitute for dumb luck.

Let me back up a step.

In the 1930s, my Grandmother Kaminski gave birth to triplets—all girls—Annabelle, Marabelle and Rosabelle. During a six-week stretch in the fall of 1952, each gave birth to first-born sons. Marabelle gave birth to me, Mitchell Malone, on October 7. Rosabelle gave birth to Nicholas Ducheski on October 30. Annabelle delivered Johnny Earl on November 21. Johnny was a phenomenal athlete who, after washing out of the minor leagues, decided to supplement his meager income by dealing cocaine. He was eventually caught and convicted and served a seven-year prison stint. After his release, Johnny recovered the nearly half-million dollars in illicit drug money he had stashed before being sentenced and moved to Texas to start his life over. He had cleaned up his act and was the owner of a successful excavation and construction business in the Fort Worth area.

It was late in the afternoon when my cell phone rang and Johnny's name and number appeared on my screen.

"What's up, cuz?" I asked.

"Mitch, I swear to Jesus, I just saw Duke," he said.

"What? Our cousin, Duke?"

"Well, how many goddamn Dukes do you know who would make me pick up the phone and call you? Yes, our cousin Duke."

"Where? Did you talk to him?"

"No, dammit, I couldn't. I was on a backhoe digging up Houston Street for a new sewer line in front of the Fort Worth Convention Center. He was on the other side of a chain-link fence walking into the convention center. I yelled at him, but it was too noisy for him to hear me."

"Maybe the guy heard you, but it wasn't Duke."

"It was him, goddammit. I know my own cousin when I see him. After I got the backhoe back on the trailer, I sat in front of the convention center for a couple of hours to see if I could catch him coming back out, but no luck. I'm telling you, Mitch, it was Duke, bigger than life."

I called the convention center and learned that the American Association of Independent Sporting Goods Dealers had been hosting its annual conference at the convention center. It ended that afternoon. The next day, I called the association's headquarters in Indianapolis and told the woman who answered the phone that I was the editor of the *Ohio Valley Morning Journal*—the truth—and that I was working on a series of stories on the challenges facing independent stores when competing against larger chains—a blatant lie—and I wanted to include the sporting goods industry. Would it be possible, I asked, to get the names of the association's members, so I could interview store owners from a cross-section of the country? She obliged.

She emailed me the list. It was broken down by state and contained the names of 1,207 members, the names of their stores, and some web addresses. That night, I started working through the list.

I didn't know what I was looking for. Obviously, I had hoped to find his name on the list, or a store called, "Duke's Sporting Goods." Neither appeared. I spent hours working my way through the list, looking up websites and bios, hoping to find some little nugget that would give me a hint of where he might be. The entire search was dependent upon the veracity of Johnny's supposed sighting, and that Duke was, indeed, a sporting goods dealer.

It was, at best, a long shot.

I had spent days hunched in front of my computer and had checked out more than eight hundred stores by the time I got to Oklahoma. I was almost resigned to the fact that I wasn't going to find him on the list and would have to attend the association's conference the following year in Anaheim for a firsthand look. Still, I soldiered on.

The first listing in Oklahoma was for Groat's Sporting Goods in Broken Arrow. As I did with all the websites, I looked for photos or bios of the owners, anything that might offer a clue. There was nothing on the Groat's Sporting Goods website that would make me believe it was owned by my cousin. Just before I went to the next name on the list, I clicked on a tab that said: "Sports Camps." Groat's sponsored a host of sports camps for baseball, basketball, football, softball, and volleyball.

My eye caught a line in the information on the basketball camps. It read: "While fundamentals are stressed at all ages, experienced players will learn more technical skills, such as cross-over moves, hesitation dribble, the wraparound, and how to jigger and trigger."

Jigger and trigger!

It was him.

The jigger and trigger was Duke's signature move from his days with the Mingo Indians.

Across the lane, three seconds, the jigger, behind his back, the trigger, from fifteen feet, the horn, the rim, it's up and, in! It's in!

My heart sounded like a bass drum beating in my chest. My fingers shook so badly that I could not type for several minutes. It was him. It was Duke Ducheski. He was alive.

Two days later, I left Pittsburgh International Airport on a flight to Tulsa, Oklahoma. I rented a car and drove to Groat's Sporting Goods, which was located in a two-story, brick building in Broken Arrow. It was early in the afternoon on Saturday, May 24, 2014—twenty years to the day that Duke Ducheski left Mingo Junction. A cowbell on the front door announced my arrival; my cousin was at the counter, writing up an order for a woman and her son. As I ducked into an aisle, he said, "I'll be with you in a minute, sir."

"Take your time," I said.

When the woman and her son left, he slipped a pencil behind an ear and started out from behind the counter. "What can I help you with?" he asked.

I turned to face him; he froze, frowned. Behind the perplexed eyes and the furrowed brow, he frantically searched for my face in his memory. It took just a few seconds.

"Son of a bitch," he said.

"I'm a newspaper man. I've been called much worse," I said.

"Mitch?" he asked, as though still not quite sure.

"Most people don't have this much trouble recognizing their cousin."

We hugged and laughed and both got teary-eyed.

I spent three days with my cousin, catching up on his life and learning the story you just read in this book. When I got back to Wheeling, I took a leave of absence to write it.

I fudged on a few things here. His name isn't Groat and he doesn't live in Broken Arrow, Oklahoma. I also changed the names of his wife and kids. He does own a retail store, and it may or may not be related to sporting goods. Joey Antonelli is in a supermax prison in Colorado, and I doubt he has the ability or the power to order a hit, but why take the chance?

Duke said he has no intention of ever revealing his new identity or returning to Mingo Junction. He's happy with his life and his family, which includes four grandchildren, and he doesn't want either disrupted. He said to say hello to everyone in Mingo Junction, and thanks for the memories.

When Mingo High School closed, the victim of consolidation, the trophy case was cleaned out and the school's hardware ended up in a storage closet at city hall. Angel Angelli was able to secure Duke's number 23 jersey, the state championship trophy, and the game ball. Behind the bar, next to a photo of Duke Ducheski launching his famous shot, Angel had a case built for the treasured items. The display is illuminated by three spotlights suspended from the ceiling.

And there, the legend lives on.

ACKNOWLEDGMENTS

This book is dedicated to Frances Kennedy, who recently left the Doe Coover Agency after many years as an administrative assistant. She is a lovely person with an equally lovely Irish lilt. Frances will always hold a special place in my heart. Years ago, when I was attempting to find an agent to help me make the switch from nonfiction to fiction, I sent a sample chapter of a novel to the Doe Coover Agency.

Frances plucked my chapter from the slush pile, read it, liked it, and passed it along to Colleen Mohyde, who has been my agent ever since. I will always be grateful to Frances for her discovery and to Colleen for her belief in my writing, her advocacy, and her sweat.

Thanks to my editor, Dan Mayer, who was phenomenal in combing through this manuscript and helping me work it into shape, and the rest of the team at Seventh Street Books, including my publicist, Jake Bonar; Vice President of Marketing Jill Maxick; and Senior Editor Jade Zora Scibilia, who has the most incredible eye for detail of any human being on the planet. It's an honor to be part of Seventh Street's talented stable of writers.

Special thanks to my wife, Melissa, whose support for the hours I spend in front of a keyboard is unwavering and unconditional.

ABOUT THE AUTHOR

Robin Yocum is the author of the critically acclaimed novels *A Welcome Murder*, *A Brilliant Death*, *Favorite Sons*, and *The Essay*. *Favorite Sons* was named the 2011 *USA Book News*'s Book of the Year for Mystery/Suspense. It was selected for the Choose to Read Ohio program for 2013–2014 and was a featured book of the 2012 Ohioana Book Festival. Yocum is also the author of *Dead Before Deadline... and Other Tales from the Police Beat* and *Insured for Murder* (with Catherine Candisky). He is the president of Yocum Communications, a public relations and marketing firm in Galena, Ohio. He is well known for his work as a crime and investigative reporter with the *Columbus Dispatch* from 1980 to 1991. He was the recipient of more than thirty local, state, and national journalism awards in categories ranging from investigative reporting to feature writing.